BLAZING PASSION

"You . . . don't understand," Jessica stammered, "This isn't right!"

Cole laughed, "Oh, but I do understand," he teased. "I want you."

Jessica looked up to see passion blazing from the man's eyes. There was something about him that frightened her, yet captivated her all in the same rush of twisted emotions.

Cole's hand entwined in Jessica's wild mass of coppery colored hair. He gently pulled her head backward. For a moment, his eyes locked with Jessica's. They were beautiful. They reminded him of the smoky haze which filtered up from an open fire. Then he took his forefinger and touched her mouth, sliding it along her moist lips, and he imagined how they would feel answering his passionate kisses. His mouth followed the path his finger had taken, blazing down on hers—engulfing her. . . .

BY JEAN HAUGHT

ZEBRA BOOKS
KENSINGTON PUBLISHING CORP.

ZEBRA BOOKS

are published by

KENSINGTON PUBLISHING CORP.
475 Park Avenue South
New York, NY 10016

First printing: March, 1984

Printed in the United States of America

To my mother—thank you dear one for everything. Also, to Jan Minter, my mentor, my friend.

Chapter One

The misty February sky shrouded the graveyard in a cloak of despair. Ice began to cling to the bare tree limbs and winter blew its frosty breath over the small windswept knoll. Never had Jessica felt so alone and desolate as she stared down at the two freshly turned graves. At least the fever had taken her beloved mother and sister quickly. They had not suffered as long as others had with the terrible disease.

She glanced sidewise, hoping to find some kind of comfort in her Aunt Agnes' thin, drawn face, but as usual, it was set in its perpetual frown.

"Come along, child," Agnes spoke, her words crisp and sharp, cutting like the wind. "There is no use in catching our death by standing out here in this horrible weather. We cannot help them now, except to say a prayer, and I believe that can be done in the warmth of the house or at the church."

"I was only telling them good-bye," Jessica sobbed, her words catching in her throat. Her eyes followed the minister and a few of their close friends as they hurried down the path, apparently anxious for some shelter against the fast approaching storm. The graveside service had seemed so cold and unfeeling, but with so many burials lately, perhaps everyone had been drained of emotion.

Agnes shivered and clutched her cloak tightly around her neck with her thin, bony hand. "I am going on to the carriage. I do not want you getting sick too, so you come along in a few minutes," she cautioned, "You hear?"

"Yes, Ma'am," Jessica muttered, thankful to be alone on the small rise of ground. Now she could say her farewells in private. The young woman stared silently at her mother's and sister's graves as the wind howled and whipped her skirt. She knelt down and tenderly patted the heaping mounds of earth. "Oh, Mama, Marsha, I will miss you so much!" she cried, her grief stricken voice disappearing into the wind. "Oh, God! If only father was here!" she cried. But he had left a month earlier to file a homestead on a small farm in Texas. He was going to send for his family as soon as he had found a suitable place and was settled. Now, Jessica could not help but think how heartbroken he would be when he heard about the death of his wife and one of his daughters.

When sleet began to pattern the ground, shivering, Jessica rose and started down the brick lined pathway. The wind caught the hood of her cloak, allowing her coppery colored hair to fly freely in the boisterous blast. It threw her off balance, causing her foot to slip off the rain slickened bricks. The thick black mud sucked greedily at her high topped shoe, when she pulled her foot free, the noise sounded loud and alien in the serenity of the cemetery.

"Come on, Jessica, you have been out in this weather far too long," Agnes scolded as she threw open the door of the coach and helped Jessica climb inside.

As her aunt tucked the furry lap robe around their legs, and settled down for the long ride back to Jessica's home, she stared at Agnes curiously. She could not understand her aunt. Agnes had arrived only that morning from New York City, for her sister's services, and had not been able to attend Marsha's which had been held two days previously. Not one flicker of grief or regret, not a tear or any sign of remorse had crossed the older woman's face. In fact, Jessica hardly knew the woman who had raised her mother after their parents had died many years ago. She knew Agnes was not much older than her mother, but could not have proved that fact by looking at them. Agnes was thin and wrinkled, and her face showed much bitterness, whereas, her mother, Margaret, had still retained the beauty of ageless youth. She recalled the only other time she remembered seeing her aunt. She was ten years old, and her father had been called away on business. Margaret had taken her two daughters to New York City for a visit in her husband's absence. Jessica could still recall how nervous and frightened her mother appeared to be when their carriage had pulled up in front of a tall two storied structure. She remembered the gloomy house as being drab and almost colorless, with dark brown shutters that were kept closed during the brightest part of the day to prevent the wallpaper from fading. She also remembered, all the time they were there, no one laughed. It was as though the very gloom of the house had crept inside their souls. Even Margaret's face had become pinched and severe during the visit. Time could not pass quickly enough for the girls. They wanted to be back in their tiny little home where laughter and sunshine filled the rooms.

Riding along the bumpy road, Jessica's thoughts drifted to her father. What would she do until she heard from him? She knew he had taken most of their money with him. He had wanted to leave more, but her mother had insisted he take as much as possible just in case expenses ran higher than anticipated. Margaret had claimed the food left from last year's garden would be plenty until the new garden started producing; that, along with their cow would provide enough, and if extra cash was needed, she could take in some sewing.

Jessica shut her eyes tightly, not knowing why she had had a moment of shame when her aunt had to pay for the burial expenses. Jessica shook her head, brushing away such thoughts as money and concern for herself. She should be thinking about her loss and how badly she would miss them.

"We have to talk, Jessica, we have to make plans," Agnes spoke abruptly. Her words broke into Jessica's private thoughts. "Naturally, you will return to New York with me."

Jessica glanced sharply at her aunt. She was obviously surprised at what Agnes had said. "But . . . I thought I would stay at home until father returned, or I heard from him."

"Nonsense! You are barely seventeen years old. Your mother would turn in her grave if she thought I would leave you alone and unprotected. Besides that," she added with a somber expression, "It would not be proper for you to live alone. I will not have it said that I shirked my duties during the family's time of need. You are young and need the guidance of an adult. It could be months before Jess returns or word is heard from him. You will simply have to come with me to New York for a while," she said firmly.

"But, Aunt Agnes," Jessica protested, "If I go to New York with you, what will father do when he sends for us? No one will be here to receive his message."

"We will leave word with one of the neighbors." Agnes frowned and cast a sidelong look at her niece, "There is something you should consider . . ." For once, Agnes seemed to be at a loss for words, but she faltered only a moment before continuing with her train of thought. "I realize what I am about to say will sound harsh, and possibly even cruel at this difficult time, but it must be said, and unfortunately it is left up to me to say it." She sighed heavily, "Do not set too much store in your father returning, or sending for you."

"What do you mean?" Jessica gasped. Tears welled up in the girl's eyes. There was a lump in her throat so big she thought it would choke her.

Agnes sighed again as she peered at Jessica over her wire-rimmed glasses. The wrinkles in her skin seemed to burrow deeper into her pallid flesh. "Jess Tate is a dreamer. He has never had any respect for other people's feelings. He certainly never had any for mine. He is always chasing some elusive pot of gold at the end of a distant rainbow, regardless of whom he hurts. For as long as I have known him, he has always wanted to see what was on the other side of the mountain or across the next river. I think it was fortunate that he settled down as much as he did in the past few years, but I knew it wouldn't last," she added smugly. "You should reconcile yourself to the fact that there is a possibility you will never see your father again. I understood that he went to that barbaric land in Texas. Do you realize that it is on the very edge of civilization?" Not actually expecting a reply, Agnes continued, "I am told that wild animals and savage heathens are plentiful. For all any of us know, Jess Tate has already met his maker." Either she did not realize or else she did not care, but Agnes' words were like a dagger plunging into Jessica's heart.

Not heeding the stricken expression which flashed across her niece's face, Agnes continued, her words rambling as though she was thinking out loud. "No, it is the only solution possible. Jessica must return with me. And how my health will hold up under the additional strain, I don't know. Heaven only knows how sick I really am. Then too," she pressed her fingers to a worried brow, "I cannot imagine how I will meet this extra financial obligation. I suppose I will have to let Norma go since paying her a salary will be next to impossible."

"Who is Norma, Aunt Agnes?" Jessica asked politely.

"Why, she is the girl who helps me. I have been reduced to opening my home to strangers! You see, I have had to convert it into a boarding house." She peered anxiously at Jessica and asked, "Your mother did do her duty and taught you how to clean, didn't see?"

"Yes, Ma'am!" Jessica answered defiantly. Of course her mother prepared her for the time when she would be a wife and mother in her own home! It was preposterous that her aunt should think anything different.

"Well, that is certainly one good thing. At least you will be able to assume Norma's chores!" Agnes said as she smacked her narrow lips.

Jessica wanted to scream as Agnes rambled on and on. Couldn't she see how badly she was hurting?

Couldn't she offer some form of comfort. Jessica's mother had just been buried, and all Agnes was concerned about was money! She was cruel and unfeeling, but Jessica could not say a word. She could only sit in a cloak of silence. She had always been taught not to show disrespect to her elders; to do so now would shame her mother's memory.

"I suppose I can rent Norma's room to another boarder and give Jessica the small room in the attic," Agnes mused aloud again.

"But, Aunt Agnes," Jessica protested, not being able to hold her tongue any longer. "If I am going to be such a burden on you, I can always stay here!"

"No, no, I cannot allow that. You have too much of your father's blood in you for you to be unchaperoned. You would probably come up with a fatherless brat in a matter of months," she spat cruelly. "After all, it is a fact that the spawn of the devil can only produce an evil seed!"

Jessica gasped and reeled as though she had been struck. "What do you mean by that?"

Agnes' brows raised smugly, "I am not surprised that your mother never told you. I suppose she had too much shame about your birth."

Jessica's gray eyes flashed angrily, "I demand that you tell me what you are talking about!"

Agnes gave Jessica a swift slap across her face. "Don't ever speak to me in that tone of voice, young lady!" she gritted angrily. Appraising Jessica quickly, Agnes knew this beautiful young creature was exactly like her father. Jessica's coppery colored curls had become wet during the services and now the curls had formed delicate patterns around the girl's pale, drawn face. Agnes caught her breath sharply. She hated to admit it, but the girl *was* beautiful, even though her features were drawn in her deepest hour of grief. Her skin was soft and satiny and not flawed by the usual smattering of freckles which so often accompanied flaming red hair. Her cheeks had been blistered by the cold winter wind, and they lent a delicate hue to her silken skin. Her classic nose lifted haughtily, and her lips were soft and inviting, with a lush tint of scarlet that men would find difficult to resist. But it was her eyes that captured one's attention. They were unusually wide and expressive beneath a pair of perfectly arched golden brows, but it was the sooty lashes that enhanced the forever changing gray mists of the girl's eyes. They looked as tempestous as the changing seasons, they could soften like a blanketing mist or swirl darkly with fiery anger as she had just proven. Or, the eyes could retreat into hidden shadows, such as they were struggling to do now.

Jessica had waited while feeling the scorching of her aunt's eyes raking over her. The pause gave her a moment to regain her composure from the sting of the slap across her face. "I'm . . . I'm sorry, Aunt Agnes, I should not have spoken so sharply." Jessica wanted to bite her tongue at apologizing but she felt she had no choice. "But, I simply have no idea what you are talking about." She had to add, "But, I love my father very much, I don't understand why you are speaking so badly about him!" her voice was beginning to sound shrill. She had taken about as much as she was able to stand.

Agnes gritted her teeth as she remembered many hatred-filled memories. "All right, I shall tell you," she said eagerly, almost too eagerly. "I used to be engaged to your father. We were two weeks away from being married when Margaret admitted that she was carrying Jess's child, which was *you!* Naturally, I made him do the decent thing by my poor innocent sister. And I have lived with the knowledge that it was I who sentenced her to a life of having to put up with your father's sadistic lustful demands. My only consolation was that she had to pay for her sins by having to submit to his desires! And that, my dear," she hissed viciously, "Is the truth to the matter as to why I cannot leave you alone. Evil is in your blood, and you are the living proof of your parents' sins! You would probably be a whore inside of a month and the mother of a fatherless bastard in less than a year." She shook her head and laughed ruefully, "Oh, no, I see your scheme now. You wanted to stay alone so you could run wild, but I have foiled your plans! You will come with me so I can see that you finally get some decent upbringing!"

Jessica sank into the hard cushion of the seat. She recoiled under Agnes' horrendous verbal assault. Agnes had to be lying! Her parents were not bad! They were not evil like she said! They were kind, and decent, and loving! Her existence was not the result of something sordid and ugly. Jessica looked at her aunt in horror. Her thin, wrinkled face was drawn into a maniacal rage; then slowly, Jessica realized why her aunt hated her family so badly. She realized why they had never kept in contact. If only she had known, she would have never sent for Agnes when her mother had died. And no wonder her father had turned to her mother. How he had ever seen anything kind in Agnes was beyond Jessica's comprehension. Now she was trapped. Doomed to live with a woman who hated her so much that it frightened Jessica. Her first impulse was to run away. But that would be impossible. She was underage, and with her father gone, Agnes, as next of kin, was her legal guardian. Besides, if she did run away, how would her father ever find her? She would not be able to let anyone know where she was if she was in hiding. Jessica took several deep gulps of air. No, at this time, she was powerless to disobey her aunt. She would have to go with her and wait patiently for her father to send for her. Patience would be her only means of escape!

The day they reached New York, the weather was as cold and frigid as the feelings that existed between the young woman and her spinster aunt. Jessica had only gone through the motions of breathing, eating and sleeping. She felt dead inside, and life would only return when she was free of her horrible aunt.

When the coach pulled up in front of Agnes' house, Jessica's heart plummeted even further into the pits of despair. It was exactly as she had remembered it. It was the same two-storied structure she had hated as a child. The dark brown shutters stood without color against the windows. Two high topped gables jutted at the roof. It reminded Jessica of a castle of old, harsh and weathered against the cold winter air.

Agnes showed Jessica to her room. It was only a tiny little cubicle, barely having enough space for a narrow bed and a badly scarred bureau. The room had one small window which a mere sliver of light shone through. Jessica had been instructed to come downstairs and help get the house in order as soon as she had finished putting away her things. Agnes complained that the house was in disgraceful shambles and been ill-kept while she had been away. Agnes had even refused to pay Norma her final week's wages.

Armed with mops, brooms, buckets of hot steaming hot water, dust cloths, and fresh beeswax, Jessica worked well into the night. Agnes had helped at first, but later started complaining about her back, so she retired as early as possible, leaving Jessica saddled with the remainder of the work. Jessica did not mind the hard work, even after the long tiring journey. It helped to numb her mind against the heartache she suffered.

The days passed slowly into weeks and the weeks eventually turned into months, and still nothing was heard from Jess Tate. It was as though the bowels of the earth had opened and completely consumed him.

The change from the quiet peacefulness of the New York countryside to the hustle and bustle of a thriving city, along with the loss of all she had loved, combined with living under Agnes' roof, caused as sudden transformation in Jessica. Her joyous laughter filled with the excitement of youth quickly disappeared. Her lithe, graceful spirit soon slipped into one that was burdened and unhappy. Gradually, she was able to tolerate her aunt's constant nagging and harping about how sinful she was, and how she would pay for her parent's indiscretion. Several times, Jessica came very close to running away. During the course of several months, a few of the male boarders had attempted to make advances toward Jessica. Agnes always found out, and each time, she would severely whip Jessica with a leather strap. Somehow, Jessica managed to stay. She knew if she left, she would never see her father again. It was as if all her emotions had eaten into the very core of her soul, hidden away, concealed beneath a stone exterior.

Whenever a boarder would slip Jessica a coin in payment for ironing an extra shirt, or mending a favorite dress, she would carefully hide it away in the back corner of her bureau drawer. It was always in her mind that she would hear from her father any day, and she would not have enough money to go to him. Deep within her heart, Jessica knew her aunt would have refused to give her the money. But nothing was ever heard of Jess Tate.

Jessica's only escape, and the only reason she was able to keep her sanity, was when she slipped from the house to a tiny little nook in the small park which lay close to the house.

During the spring and summer months, Jessica slipped away with every chance. Agnes demanded that she keep her hair pinned into a tight bun, but when she was going to her secret-hide-away, Jessica would release her hair from its restraints and let it stream behind her as she ran through the woods. She would lie on the grass and dream of far away places. She even let her thoughts drift to men. Who would she marry? Surely, he would be the most handsome man alive. He would be tall, and have broad shoulders. His hips would be narrow, and he would swagger whenever he walked, as he would be proud and sure of himself, but not arrogantly so. She knew he would treat her as though she were the most precious woman on the earth, just as her father had treated her mother. But whenever Jessica tried to visualize his face, it would remain cloaked in dark shadows. But he would be gallant and handsome, of this she was sure. Then, Jessica's face would blaze in shame as she imagined him taking her into his arms and smothering her mouth with kisses. Always, when Jessica's dreams reached this point, she would instantly recall Agnes' spiteful words, and wonder slightly if there was some truth to them since she had such wanton thoughts.

Summer passed into the fall of the year, then fall slipped into the throes of winter. The trees were without cover and the grass was dry and brittle. It became too cold for her to slip away. Jessica had been with her aunt for almost a year, and still no word from her father. And with that fact, no hope for a means of escape from the unhappy world in which she had been forced to exist.

One late afternoon, Jessica returned from the market. The weather had turned very cold, and Agnes had insisted they stock up on supplies. The girl entered the house quietly, hoping not to disturb her aunt. Agnes usually napped in the afternoon, and if she was able to slip in unnoticed, she would be able to sit down and enjoy a cup of hot tea before starting her round of afternoon chores. To Jessica's surprise, she heard excited voices coming from the parlor.

"Yes, Mr. Farley, I'm sure we will find this arrangement quite agreeable," Agnes' voice rang with an unusual cheerfulness.

Mr. Farley laughed, his words faded in and out as Jessica walked through the hallway, she was curious. "I realized there might . . . minor . . . involved. I will . . . my wife . . ."

Jessica strained very carefully, trying hard to catch each word their neighbor was saying. Could he actually be courting Aunt Agnes? A relieved smile broke across her face. Perhaps if she married, things would become different. But the next words she heard sent an icy chill into her heart.

"I am sure Jessica will be pleased with your courtship, Mr. Farley. She has reached an age where she should be thinking about marriage to a fine, upstanding gentleman, instead of having her head in the clouds, thinking her father will return for her any day. You know I have kept a constant vigil, keeping away any male suitors I did not think agreeable. You cannot know how relieved I was, when you approached me with your offer." Jessica could hear Agnes sigh, and she could imagine her aunt peering at old fat Mr. Farley over her glasses. "I am especially relieved now that the full responsibility of her keep has been placed upon my shoulders."

Jessica could not understand. She had been living with her aunt for nearly a year. She thought she had paid her way quite amply.

Agnes continued. "In the last letter I received from her father, he said he was going to try his hand in the gold fields in California. I made him see that a young girl such as Jessica had no business in that Godforsaken place. He agreed with me that she should stay here and make a marriage to a suitable man. Now, I am very pleased that that man will be you."

A loud roaring sound echoed through Jessica's ears. Her father had been in contact with them, and Agnes had not breathed a word about it. She had deliberately kept the truth hidden from her. Now she was trying to arrange a marriage between her and an old fat man. Flaming anger raged through her as she stormed into the parlor. "How could you, Aunt Agnes? How could you have kept father's return a secret from me? You know how much I have missed him! You know how I have been counting each day, hoping and praying that I would hear from him! How long has it been?" she demanded, her voice livid with rage.

"Now, Jessica!" Agnes gasped. "How dare you question me in such a manner! And in front of Mr. Farley! Shame on you!"

Jessica knew if the old man had not been sitting in the parlor, she would have received a stinging slap across the face, but she no longer cared. "I had the right to know that my father had returned!"

"But he did not return!" Agnes snipped cruelly. "Apparently he could not take the time. I merely received a letter from him, and when I informed him of your mother's untimely death, and suggested you would be better off here with me, he answered back in agreement." Agnes straightened her shoulders, "Since I am your legal guardian, I have decided to allow you a suitor. Mr. Farley, here, approached me. He wants to marry you, and I have told him you will, and I will not hear any arguments about it!" Agnes glanced nervously toward the man seated on her right, "Please forgive her, Mr. Farley, she isn't usually this sassy. I imagine it was a shock for her to find out her father does not have time for her anymore." She stared at Jessica, "I believe you owe me and our guest an apology for your rude outburst, young lady!"

Jessica looked dumbfoundedly between her aunt and the fat, bald headed man sitting beside her. How could she sit so calmly and demand an apology after completely destroying her life. For the first time since her mother's death, Jessica showed the grit and spirit she had been born with. "You mean old woman!" she muttered through tightly clenched teeth. "How dare you bargain with my life! How dare you treat me as if I had no rights. And how dare you keep the news from my father from me! As for *him*," she chortled strangely, casting a piercing glance at the man, "I don't understand you! You have constantly nagged about the evils of men and for me to be beware of them. You have even beat me because some of your precious boarders tried to take advantage of me, and it wasn't my fault! Now, you practically shove me into the arms of this filthy swine, and he was the worst of the lot!" she shouted, gesturing at Farley, who was turning a mottled shade of red by this time. "Do you know everytime I passed him on the street, he would try to pinch me if no one was watching?" she asked incredulously.

Farley leaped from the sofa and grabbed at his hat which had been carefully placed on a small elaborately carved table. "I don't have to stand here and be insulted!" his fat belly jiggled as he hurried across the room.

"Jessica!" Agnes gasped, horrified, "How can you speak in that manner? Mr. Farley, wait," she called after him, "I'm sure we can clear up this misunderstanding." It was clear that she did not believe Jessica's accusations.

"Good!" he growled. "I will return when we can all sit down and talk sensibly. But, my dear," he glowered at Jessica, "You will have to stop telling lies. That is one thing I will not tolerate in a woman, and you will have to learn to control that terrible temper of yours!" He planted his hat firmly on his head and marched with injured dignity out the door.

Jessica stared after him with an open mouth. She had never witnessed such audacity in her entire life. Every word she had spoken was the truth, plus so very much more. Mr. Farley had always looked at her as though he was undressing her with his eyes. And, any time an opportunity arose, he would find some kind of an excuse to place his fat pudgy hands on her. Once, he had even caught her at the clothes line and kissed her with his thick, wet lips. Just the thought of him doing it again sent shivers of disgust rippling through Jessica.

"Now, perhaps you can tell me the reason for such insolent behavior?" Agnes demanded.

Jessica's gray eyes narrowed, glinting like cold shards of ice. Her lips fell into a grim line, nothing like the childish pout that would have been there a year ago, but a new mask filled with hurt, frustration, and a feeling so foreign to her she could not comprehend what is was, because it was hatred. Jessica took a deep breath, knowing that her courage could not fail her now, "How dare you stand so calmly and question me about my behavior?" she spat. "You have betrayed me . . . I trusted you to tell me the truth!"

Agnes had the grace to lower her eyes. "I am sorry if you feel that way, Jessica," she finally replied. "But I was only protecting you from yourself. The responsibility of looking after you was unasked for." Agnes squared her shoulders determinedly, "But it was my duty to see you through. It was my duty to see that you did not throw your life away like Margaret did."

"My mother did not throw her life away! She was happy, and you were jealous of that happiness!"

Agnes pulled herself up to her tallest height. "I shall not stand here and be insulted." Agnes was trembling with rage. "Go to your room and when you have calmed down and can speak to me in a reasonable tone of voice, I will expect an apology!"

Jessica's eyes showed the contempt she felt. Without saying another word, she lifted her skirts and raced for the stairs, her small feet pounding hard on each step. she would show her aunt. She would not spend another night under the same roof with that mean selfish woman! She had no reason to remain. Her father was not coming for her. He would never return!

Yanking open the door to her room, Jessica rushed in and began tossing her belongings into a small bag. She was not neat and careful with her clothing, they were put into the bag without thought except to be able to leave as soon as possible. She carefully searched her secret hiding place for each coin she had hidden away, then she wrapped them in a handkerchief and pinned them to the inside of the chemise. Hastily glancing around the room, Jessica decided she had packed everything she would need. Then she walked determinedly down the stairs to face her aunt.

Agnes was busy clearing away the teapot and cups she and Mr. Farley had been using. Noting Jessica's bag, she demanded angrily, "Where do you think you are going?"

"I don't know and I don't care!" Jessica replied coldly. "I only know I cannot stay here a moment longer!"

Agnes looked into the girl's smoky eyes, and for a brief moment, saw a hopeless despair lurking behind her brazen facade. A smug grin touched her thin lips as she said, "You will be back. Begging me to take you in!" she spat, her lips curling into an ugly snarl.

"Never!" Jessica replied coldly. She whirled, her skirts flying to reveal several layers of petticoat, and strode into the entrance hall where she had dropped her cloak. She placed the woolen garment over her shoulders, then turned to say one last word. "I will never forgive you for what you have tried to do to me, Aunt Agnes!" She opened the door and slammed it soundly behind her as she stepped into the crisp coldness.

Agnes frantically opened the door; she was determined to have the last word. "You'll be back!" she shouted into the frosty air, "Crawling on your hands and knees!"

Jessica did not answer; she marched away, her shoulders set and determined, into the rapidly fading light of day.

Chapter Two

Jessica's thoughts wandered aimlessly as she roamed through the crowded streets of New York. For the first time in nearly a year, Jessica tasted the bittersweet morsels of freedom. But at what price? She had alienated herself from the only family she had left except for her father who by this time, must be in California. A shudder of loathsome hatred convulsed through Jessica. She would never consider Agnes as family again. That horrible woman had betrayed her, and she would hate her forever!

Jessica would have to push such thoughts from her mind for the present. She would have to examine this dilemma she was in, and figure on some way to get out of it.

She was alone and in a strange city. It *was* a strange city to her, even though she had lived in it for nearly a year. Agnes had allowed only short ventures away from the house to the shops and to markets which surrounded their immediate area. Now that she had left the familiar neighborhood, the shops and street vendors appeared to be bizarre and somehow foreign, almost frightening in appearance.

Her mind was in a jumble, filled with confusion. She could not understand why her aunt had treated her so badly. Why hadn't Agnes told her she had been in touch with her father? Why hadn't he insisted upon Jessica being sent to him immediately? She refused to believe he did not care. Agnes was mean to have tried to leave that impression. Now, he was lost in the throng of men who had crowded into California when gold had been discovered, although that event had happened several years earlier. It would be almost impossible to find him in that vast, large state. But the more Jessica thought about it as she walked, the more determined she became. Somehow, she would find a way to reach him, even if she had to travel across the continent to do so!

Staggering under the brisk force of the wind, Jessica turned the corner, and to her surprise, she nearly stumbled over a strange looking man. He had a large, swooping mustache, and wore a bright red coat. In his hand, he cranked on a small organ which rested on a stick. A weird little monkey danced and jumped to the music, then when the music stopped, the tiny little animal passed a tin cup in front of the people who had stopped to watch. Jessica laughed eagerly. The sound of her voice appeared to be as alien as her surroundings. When the man and his monkey moved further down the street, Jessica noticed a group of dirty men were watching her with wicked gleams in their eyes.

She suppressed a scream and started running. She knew they would be chasing her. Through the streets she raced, past shops and large looming houses, their features quickly disappearing into the darkness. She did not pay any attention to the people who had stopped and stared after her as she raced by. She was terrified that the horrible men were chasing her. Finally, not hearing any footsteps behind her, Jessica stopped and rested against a huge stone wall. She was exhausted. But now, she realized she must protect herself from the menaces of the city, whether they be real or imaginary. She had to find lodgings for herself before the darkness completely enveloped her.

Desperately clutching her bag, Jessica turned down a dimly lit cobblestone street. She saw an inviting three storied house with white painted doors and window shutters. It looked so friendly and amicable, she was relieved to see the sign, room for let, hanging in one of the spotless windows. Taking a coin from her handkerchief, Jessica approached the front door and knocked timidly. A matronly woman, large and buxom appeared and cautiously invited Jessica in.

"My goodness, child, what are you doing out on a night like this?" she asked.

"I'm looking for a room." Jessica nodded toward the window, "I saw the sign and thought I would apply."

"Well, yes, I do have a room for rent, but I do require references. Do you have any?" she asked curiously.

Jessica's face fell and tears threatened to spill from her eyes. "No," she answered in a small voice.

The woman quickly sized up her uninvited guest. Her blue eyes twinkled merrily as she asked in her quiet voice, "What is the matter? Tell me, have you run away from home?"

"No!" Jessica's reply came too quickly. When her gaze met with the woman's, she knew the lady had guessed the truth. "I suppose you could say that," she admitted, tears breaking her voice.

"There, there," the friendly woman comforted Jessica. "Come on in here and we will talk about it. My guess is that you would like to have a cup of hot tea."

"Oh, yes, thank you!" Jessica was starving and a cup of tea would certainly help.

The woman introduced herself as being Mrs. Bryce, and led Jessica into a room that was well lit, nothing like her Aunt Agnes' house. She took Jessica's cloak, and motioned for her to sit in the soft chair in front of the roaring fireplace. "Warm yourself for a moment while I bring us some tea. It is already made. I was just going to have some."

Mrs. Bryce disappeared through a door, and in a matter of minutes was back in the parlor carrying a tray that contained a teapot and two cups. After she had poured the steaming liquid, she handed a cup to Jessica then asked in her pleasant voice, "Now, suppose you tell me all about it. Why are you roaming the streets on a night like this?"

Jessica started slowly, then before she knew it, the words came like a dam bursting. It was not long before Mrs. Bryce knew all about her.

"You poor dear," Mrs. Bryce clucked sympathetically. "I usually have a firm rule, no references, no room, but in your case, I believe I will make an exception. Gather your things and I will show you the way."

"But . . . what about rent? I can pay," Jessica offered.

"No, that isn't necessary. We will talk about some definite arrangements tomorrow when you have had some rest."

She led Jessica up a steep flight of stairs around a winding, spiral staircase, opened the door to reveal a room much like the one Jessica had just left behind, only much prettier. "Here it is," she said with a sweep of her hand, "Such as it is. Actually it is a spare room I had fixed up just in case some of my boarders had out of town guests. Excuse the mess," she said, stacking a newspaper onto a chair. "I have not had a chance to clean it yet. A guest left late this afternoon. But don't worry," she was quick to add, "The sheets were changed this morning."

"Oh, it will be fine," Jessica assured her. "And thank you so much. You will never know how much I appreciate your kindness."

After telling Jessica where a few items were located, Mrs. Bryce left her alone. Seeing a pitcher of water and wash basin, Jessica hastily removed her blouse and began washing. Although the water was cold, it was very refreshing. She had just finished putting her blouse back on, when a knock came at the door. Opening it, Jessica was pleasantly surprised to see Mrs. Bryce standing there, holding a steaming bowl of soup.

"It is what we had left from supper. It isn't fancy, but it's hot and filling," she offered.

"How will I ever be able to repay you?" Jessica asked thankfully as she took the soup from the gracious woman.

"I am going to be very blunt with you, child." The older woman looked Jessica straight in the eye. "I will not mislead you, so the truth is in order. I happen to know Agnes Prince. She belongs to the same sewing circle as I do. She has spoken about you before, but I had no idea you were so lovely. It's odd that I never met you before, especially when we had our meetings at her house. I suppose you were being kept busy doing chores. I want you to get a good night's sleep and we will discuss your circumstances in the morning. Perhaps I can send for Agnes and see if we cannot come to a reasonable conclusion. You have my word that I will not send for your aunt during the night, though. Do you trust me?" she asked pointedly.

"Yes . . . Ma'am, I do," Jessica answered. Knowing she would be seeing her aunt in the morning disturbed Jessica. Her hands began to tremble. Mrs. Bryce said nothing about not sending her back to her aunt's house. Could she be forced to return since she was not yet of age? She could not take that chance! She would never return to that horrible place. Jessica looked around the cozy room, her haven against the storm was now only a stopping place in her journey.

"You go ahead and eat, child, and sleep well." Mrs. Bryce's face broke into a reassuring smile. "Everything will be all right, you'll see," she said as she bid her uninvited guest good night.

Jessica placed her soup on the bureau. She stared at it for a long time before starting to eat. Suddenly, she did not seem as hungry as she had been at first, but Jessica knew she would have to eat. It had been hours since she had had a meal. Suddenly, Jessica was ravenous. She devoured the food hurriedly. It was almost as if she was afraid it disappear. It was only after she finished did Jessica allow herself the luxury of tears.

Later, Jessica paced the floor restlessly. She would have to have a plan of action. First, she would have to secure a position somewhere in order to raise money for passage to California in order to search for her father. But what could she possibly do to raise the enormous sum she needed? She had heard people talk and had read articles about the rigors and hardships involved in an overland journey by wagontrain to California. The groups usually left from points such as St. Louis, Missouri, very early in the spring, just as soon as there was enough grass on the prairie to feed the livestock. But such a large amount of money was needed to outfit a wagon with supplies. She had also heard that a woman would not be allowed to travel alone. Her only other alternative was by ship around Cape Horn, but that passage fee would probably be as much as it was by going overland.

Jessica pondered the idea about returning to her old home and selling off the belongings that were left, but she realized most of the items only held a sentimental value, and if placed on the market, would bring very little money.

During her pacing, Jessica happened to notice a piece of paper tucked back beneath the bed. Getting down on her hands and knees, she discovered it was part of the New York newspaper. Jessica began to read with interest. She certainly hoped there would be some advertisements in it for employment opportunities. Turning the pages, Jessica's heart suddenly started pounded very rapidly. This was it! This was the answer to her prayer!

"Women! Seek your future on the golden coast of California! The *Sea Nymph,* located at dock thirty-three, pier nineteen, captained by the prestigious Captain A.E. Mahan, will be setting sail at dawn on the tenth day of January, 1857, for the mystic port of San Francisco. Two hundred passengers will be allowed on board. Women, this is your chance to escape the drudgery of sewing factories, and the opportunity to forever leave behind prison records. Start your life over, leave your past behind, and set sail with us. Only one child per woman will be allowed due to lack of space. The requirements are few: You must be twenty-five years of age or older, and be willing to marry your benefactor. But lest you forget, these men have been in the mining fields for years and many have made their fortunes. A legal contract will be signed as to this agreement when you sign up for passage."

Jessica read and reread the advertisement several times before laying down the paper. This seemed to be an answer to her needs. If only she was a little older. Jessica walked over to the bureau and stared at the reflection in the mirror. Perhaps, she could make herself look older than her years. She took her brush and stroked vigorously, brushing the coppery curls back into a severe bun. Maybe if she wore a scarf around her head, and kept her lips pulled into a frown, she could fool the captain. It was a chance she would have to take! Then, Jessica's eyes widened in horror. The advertisement said the ship would be leaving on the tenth, that was tomorrow! There would not be time to sign up! She would have to try and slip on board during the darkness of the night. A shiver of fear crept up her spine, to reach the ship tonight would mean she would have to face the dangers of the waterfront. She had heard many horrible things about them, what the sailors did to attractive young women who foolishly wandered too close. Could she face those dangers alone?

Slamming a fist into an outstretched palm, Jessica decided that was a chance she would have to take. She would stow away on the *Sea Nymph.* If only she could ward off being discovered for a day, surely they wouldn't put her adrift on the high seas.

For the first time in months, a satisfied smile flirted around Jessica's mouth. If only God was with her, by tomorrow night, she would be well on her way to California.

Chapter Three

The pre-dawn mists clung tenaciously to the old weather-beaten merchant ship, *The Sea Nymph*, as the rugged stalwart crew attempted to make ready the sails. The gangplank was lifted and the mooring lines were released from the pier, thus severing all bonds with the shore. The boatswain and first mate walked the deck belting orders in loud, booming voices. Curses rang throughout the ship as ropes were tautly stretched, blocks and sheaves groaned and creaked as the men strained, heaving the ropes through the pulleys. Their muscles rippled with strength as the sails made their slow tedious journey up the towering masts. The huge anchor was finally raised when the fleecy white sails gradually filled with billowing gusts of wind, swelling them until they appeared as puffy white clouds against the grey dawn of early morning.

The captain stood at the helm and skillfully steered the ship on a careful course through the crowded harbor. The deck was teeming with the women passengers and a few wide eyed children as they all stared solemnly at the disappearing shoreline.

Jessica awoke to the abrupt rolling motion of the ship. For a brief moment, she could not comprehend where she was, then the memories of the previous night came flooding back.

She recalled how she had attempted to disguise her appearance by carefully blending the smoky soot from a candle beneath her regal cheekbones, creating the illusion of having deeply etched wrinkles on her face, although a closer examination would have revealed the truth about her youth and beauty. She then had waited until the house was very quiet before cautiously gathering her belongings and creeping down the stairs and slipping unnoticed into the coldness of the brisk winter night.

She had walked for what seemed to be hours before finally finding a carriage to rent. It would have been foolhardy for her to have tried to find the waterfront on foot. At first, the driver had staunchly refused, claiming that the waterfront was too dangerous at night. It had only been after Jessica had offered him nearly all of her precious coins that he relented in his decision to follow the young woman's requests.

Jessica had hidden in the shadows among the many crates and boxes which lined the dock, and watched the activity aboard the ship with an avid interest. After being thoroughly satisfied that the comings and goings of the people were not questioned, she gained the courage to join a group of women who were boarding the ship in a hail of boisterous laughter and conversation.

Once on deck, Jessica had slipped away from the women and had slipped down a long flight of narrow stairs to a large room filled with barrels and crates.

Stumbling and moving more by feel than by sight, Jessica had been able to find a place between two barrels that was hidden from the sight of the stairway. Then finally, she had been able to fall into a light, fitful sleep.

Now, fully awake, Jessica blinked several times before her eyes could become adapted to the darkness of the hold. The door at the top of the stairs had been opened, and a faint glimmer of light filtered down, casting a pale glow on her hiding place, enabling her to barely see. After quietly looking around, she was satisfied that she was alone, but with all of the bustling activity coming from up above, she had no idea how long she would be alone. She struggled to stand, pulling muscles in her arms, legs, and back, muscles she did not know she had until spending part of the night on the hard wooden floor. She moaned at her discomfort, then a feeling of determination swept over her. At least this was better than her mere existence at her aunt's house. Just the thought of her aunt strengthened Jessica's irrevocable will to make her escape. She would never be beholden to anyone else again! Never!

Getting to her feet, Jessica placed the hood of her cloak over her blazing locks of hair. Creeping from her hiding place between the barrels, Jessica paused to gather her belongings. Glancing down, a horrified scream started to swell deep within her throat, for beside her hand, was a large rat scurrying slowly over the barrel top. Willing herself not to utter a sound, Jessica fled from the hold, climbing the stairs as rapidly possible. Her quick presence of mind told her that she would have to act like one of the many passengers, and to mingle with them, or the crew would become suspicious of her actions.

Clutching her small brown bag, Jessica walked slowly along the crowded deck. She was nervous and her knees trembled with fear. But soon, the skyline of New York started to fade in the distance, and with that came a slow relaxation, and a vast feeling of sheer relief.

A few children had lined timidly up against the railing after receiving strict orders from their mothers to stay clear of the crewmen and to keep out of their way. Jessica studied the other women. Some were tall, some short, some had brown hair, while others had hair black like the raven's wing, and still others and red and blonde colored hair. But what impressed Jessica the most, was the expressions of hope, awe, and the aura of anticipation that lay around them. Jessica couldn't help but wonder if her own face held the same expression. The tension and nervousness soon passed as Jessica's attention turned from the other women and focused on the huge breakers washing the sandy beaches which lined the Hudson River. The foul stench of the waterfront was left behind and the air was filled with a clean scent as the salty sea breeze gently touched her face. She was mesmerized, it was so peaceful.

"Isn't this wonderful?" a woman gushed breathlessly as she sidled up next to Jessica.

Jessica's eyes widened in fright as she gasped for breath. The woman's question had been so unexpected Jessica thought she had been caught. In her mind's eye, she had known her farce had been discovered. Immediately, she had seen accusing fingers being pointed at her, then even saw the portly captain barking orders for the lifeboat to be lowered and her taken off the ship bound in chains before being carted off to the infamous women's prison located just outside of the city.

Jessica exhaled a deep breath of air as she realized the woman simply wanted to chat. Turning her head, she quickly gave the woman a close, scrutinizing look. Her lively brown hair was being tugged capriciously by the gusting sea breeze. She had a pleasant face, but it was her eyes the impressed Jessica. They were a warm brown, and the faint creases around them and her full mouth could have only come from laughter, although it must have been a long time ago, because there was a certain sadness about her. She immediately sensed there was no danger surrounding this vivacious, friendly woman, in fact, she felt completely at ease in her company. "Yes, it is," Jessica finally replied.

"Aaron!" the woman shouted to her son who was pressed against the rail. "Lean back or you'll fall overboard!" she warned threateningly. Turning her attention back to Jessica, she said, "That child has so much energy, I can hardly keep up with him." Then the woman's eyes crinkled into a smile, "My name is Helen, Helen Graves," she said, extending her hand.

"And I am Jessica Tate, I am very pleased to meet you," she replied, grasping Helen's hand firmly. "I was beginning to wonder if anyone on this ship was friendly." Jessica was secretly glad that no one had approached her with conversation until now, but she felt so comfortable in the woman's presence, she had to say something.

"Jessica, I am going to come right to the point," Helen said bluntly. "I have been watching the other women all morning, and I want to talk to you."

"Yes? What about? Have I done something wrong?" concern edged into her voice. She could only pray she had done nothing to attract attention.

"Oh, no, nothing like that." Helen covered her mouth,

leaned closer to Jessica and lowered her voice, "Have you been down to our quarters yet?"

"No, I haven't," Jessica admitted nervously.

"Well, I have and they are awful! This old tub used to be a slaver!"

"A what?"

"A slave ship, one that they used to transport the poor creatures in from Africa. And believe me" she said with a lift to her brows, "There aren't any individual cabins except for a very few. I have been down there," her eyes grew wider as she described the horrors which lay below, "And, it is terrible." A shudder caused her to visibly shake. "There aren't even decent sleeping quarters. There are no beds, and really no bunks either. There are only planks of wood lining the sides of the ship, something like kitchen shelves in a pantry. They run from the very bottom, clear up to the top with only small ladders built every few feet. The shelves are made so one has to climb in feet first, and I would judge them to be only around three feet apart, and they only have thin cotton mattresses thrown on them." Noting Jessica's wide-eyed look of revulsion, Helen continued, "But if you think that is bad, I could see where the shelves used to be. The crew has apparently made the shelves roomier by dropping the shelves by a foot, and there are still signs of where the slaves were kept chained! It is horrible!" she added with a shake of her head. "And to think, we have to live down there for months!"

Dismay filled Jessica's small voice, "Oh, my, it does sound horrible! Just think about how those poor people must have suffered."

"Yeah, and are still suffering," Helen added. "But, listen, there is something else I want to speak to you about." Helen swallowed hard, her bravado was fading quickly. She said in a rush, "I want to ask you to share your immediate sleeping quarters with me and my son. You look clean, and I doubt if you are afflicted with lice or the itch. I know for a fact that many of these women came straight from the women's prison, and from the red-light district in the city. To be truthful, I don't want a diseased old whore sharing the bunk with me and Aaron."

"You mean some of these women actually have bugs crawling on them?" Jessica asked incredulously.

"I'm afraid so, but what is worse, most of them can't help it. They have had no chance to keep themselves clean, and some of them simply don't care anymore."

"How awful!" Jessica was shocked. She had always taken soap and water for granted. She had never been around anyone who was slovenly about their appearance. But after glancing casually around her, she could tell Helen was not exaggerating a bit. She stammered, "I . . . don't know who would be doing the most favor to the other. I would be happy to share your quarters with you!" She had no idea conditions would be this bad, and said as much.

"Yes, they are bad," Helen agreed. "But there is really nothing we can do about it now, except try and make the best of it."

"Are you from the city?" Jessica asked hesitantly. She didn't want to pry, but yet she did not want to appear unfriendly.

"Oh, heavens no. Aaron and I lived on a small farm upstate. My husband died a year ago." She sighed heavily, "Things became so difficult, when a friend offered to buy the farm, I sold it and moved to the city thinking I could find a job to support us. But I found out rather quickly I could not make it on what I was earning at the sewing factory. Imagine, they were only paying one dollar for a dozen shirts, and beef is running forty cents a pound! I simply could not make it on those wages. I saw the advertisements, applied and was accepted. This may sound callous, but I married for love the first time around, and I figure I can fall in love with a man who has money as well as one who is as poor as a church mouse. What about you, Jessica?" she asked abruptly. "Why in the world is an attractive young woman like you going to California? Don't you have any family?"

Jessica was afraid Helen would start asking questions. At first, she did not know how to answer. Her reluctance was apparent.

Helen rushed to say, "You don't have to tell me if you don't want to. I didn't mean to pry."

"You are not prying, Helen." Jessica took a deep breath, all the while staring straight into Helen's huge brown eyes. "I was simply deciding whether to tell you the truth or a lie."

Helen laughed. "At least you are honest about it!"

Jessica smiled timidly, "I will tell you the truth." She had made up her mind. She felt completely at ease with her newly found friend, and decided to trust her implicitly. "My father is in California. My mother and sister died nearly a year ago. I have been living with a maiden aunt. The situation there became unbearable so I decided to try and find my father. I guess there is something else you should know, I am not even eighteen yet, and . . . I didn't even pay for my passage, I simply walked on board like everyone else. Please don't tell on me?" she implored.

Helen grinned and shook her head. "Honey, believe me, I'm not gonna tell on you. But let me tell you something, I knew you wasn't twenty-five. There is no way you could look that old, and I even figured you for a stowaway." She lowered her voice, "Stick close to me and if one of the crew questions you, let me do the talking," she cautioned.

Jessica smiled her relief. It felt as if a ton of weight had been lifted from her shoulders. Feeling a developing bond starting to grow between them, Jessica and Helen fell into an easy silence as they watched the broad expanse of river slip into the open sea. The rolling swells of the ocean spread out before them; stark greens mixed with the sharp contrast of many shades of blue. But the serenity of the water did not fool either one of them. Like a lush, passionate temptress, raw and untamed, the sea formed soft, frothy waves beneath the now brilliant sun in the beautiful azure sky.

In a sense, Jessica felt as alone as she did the day her family was buried. She gazed out at the sea, stretching forever in all directions, feeling small in comparison—small and humble. It was as though her life was now as uncertain as the vast ocean. Seemingly, she had no control over her destiny and lay powerless in the hands of fate.

Standing, watching the false languidness of the water, Jessica felt a grief touch her heart. She suddenly felt as wise and old as the passage of time. She would never be able to turn back now, back to the innocence of youth, back to a simple time when all she had to worry about was what dress to wear, to finish her studies, if a special young man would ask her to the autumn dance, to complete her chores, or to walk over to her mother or father and place her arms around their necks. Even though her family had been gone for nearly a year, she finally realized the finality of her loss. At that precise moment, she knew a part of her life was gone forever, and the loss she felt was so deep and painful, it was hard to bear the burden of it. Jessica was alone—cast adrift to face the uncertain future, with only her wits standing between her and survival.

Chapter Four

The short, portly captain turned the helm over to his first mate. He turned around on the quarterdeck and stood in a powerful stance, his back was to the wheel, and his hands were placed on his hips as he let his eyes drift slowly over the women and children who crowded the deck. He cupped his hands around his mouth and shouted in a loud voice, "I want your attention! You women with children, keep them off the railing! I will not break the sails to pick up anyone who has fallen overboard." After waiting a moment for the anxious mothers to retrieve their children, the captain continued, "I want all of you to gather in the quarters below. I have a few things to say."

A loud clamor came from the deck as many of the women rushed to the doorway. Some started pushing and shoving. "Be orderly, ladies," the captain cautioned, "Be orderly, we have all the time in the world," his voice droned sarcastically.

Jessica and Helen each grasped Aaron's hand as they turned and waited in the line that quickly formed. As they walked down the narrow flight of stairs, Jessica's nose wrinkled in disgust before reaching the lower landing. The dark, damp room smelled of unwashed bodies, and reeked of the scent of dysentery. The women lined up against the bunks and waited for the captain to appear.

Captain Mahan soon followed, swaggering with each step he took as he walked up first one side then the other, not saying a word, but carefully appraising the women passengers.

"All right, ladies," he finally said. Grinning broadly and revealing badly stained yellow teeth, he sneered, "And I use that term rather loosely because I know most of you came from the streets of New York, where you have whored your bodies." Helen carefully placed her hands over Aaron's ears, not wanting him to hear that kind of language. The captain continued, "Those of you who did not come off the streets, came from the prison." He placed his arms akimbo and let his gaze travel slowly over the women. "So, we have a fine lot here; whores, liars, cheats, and thiefs!" He smacked a clenched fist into an open palm, causing several of the children to jump in surprise. "I want to make it plain right now that I will not tolerate a thief! If I hear of any stealing going on, I will personally put that person ashore when we reach the next port!"

As he approached Jessica, she trembled in fear. Not so much in fear of being discovered as a stowaway, but from the way he let his eyes travel over the more attractive women. His appearance was revolting. He had dirty red hair, and a full, unkempt beard. His huge belly hung below his belt, and tobacco stained the front of his shirt, and he smelled badly. From the glow of the flickering lamps, she could see his eyes; they were the most frightening of all. They were small and beady, and they looked cruel and hard, almost without feeling. To her horror, he stopped in front of her. She saw his eyes rake her face, then move lower, appraising the full curves of her young ripe body as a pirate might assess his bounty.

"Well, well, well, who do we have here?" he asked, smacking his thick, fat lips.

Jessica's eyes grew wide and her throat constricted in fear. She knew she had been caught!

"This is my younger sister, sir," Helen was quick to say. "At the last moment, I had to bring her along with me."

"I see," the captain said as his eyes swept Jessica's body once again before proceeding up the line. When he reached the bottom of the stairs, he stepped up on the second rung and turned to face all of the women. "There is something else that should be said, and I will warn you only once." He deliberately paused, knowing the lull would be more dramatic, "My crew are normal healthy men and I strongly suggest all of you keep your distance from them. I will not hold my men responsible if you act like . . . less than ladies." Captain Mahan stepped off the stairway and started walking back up the narrow aisle between the women. He ambled slowly with his hands folded behind his back. "Now that we have that out of the way, we will talk about water and food rations." He rolled his eyes upward and sneered, "I will remind you that we are on the Atlantic Ocean and not in New York City where water is readily available." He added, "Although, many of you apparently won't mind the shortage of bathing facilities. Sometimes we are lucky on these journeys and have enough rain so that water is not that much of a problem. If this proves to be the case this time, baths will be permitted as much as possible. I will warn you now, if water becomes scarce, I will ration you. And I will also mention, whenever water is kept in wooden kegs for long periods of time, it tends to become rank and stale. It is nothing to open a keg and find it alive with wiggletails."

"Why wasn't we told this before we left New York?" one woman asked.

"Would it have made a difference, Madam?" the captain answered. Looking at her coldly, he added, "No, I didn't think so."

Helen raised her hand, "I have a question, sir."

"Yes?"

"Will we be able to use the ocean water for laundry facilities?"

The captain snorted, "You can if you like, but it is likely the salt water will eat holes in your clothes, and it does tend to leave the material rather stiff." He walked over to Helen and traced his finger along her cheek. "I would hate to see such tender flesh chafed by stiff clothing."

She jerked away, "I was merely asking!"

"And I was merely answering, Madam!" he snapped in reply. Turning his attention from Helen, he said, "You women will be expected to take turns in the galley. If you don't work, you don't eat. And I would suggest you clean your quarters. It smells like a slop jar down here!" With that, he turned on his heel and walked quickly up the stairs.

When the captain left, low murmurs filled the quarters, murmurs of anger and of disbelief. Even to some of the street roughened women, the captain had sounded far too harsh. One of the women shouted openly, "Who does he think is is? Why couldn't he have had this stinking hole cleaned before we set sail?"

Jessica stared at the woman in bewilderment. A stale, stagnant odor drifted toward her nose. She wrinkled it in disgust. The captain was right, it did stink. Even though their quarters should have been cleaned before the ship left port, they would have to do something about it now. Jessica felt courage she did not know she possessed. She glanced at Helen, "I intend to do something about this horrible smell!"

She stepped up on a small crate and clapped her hands together in order to get the women's attention. All eyes turned toward her, some openly curious, and some hostile and questioning. She began hesitantly, but did not falter in her decision to speak to her fellow passengers. "The captain is right. Our quarters do smell badly."

"Yeah," one woman drawled, "But it isn't our fault."

"I agree, it is not our fault. The only thing is we all have to live down here now, so it is up to us to do something about it. I think we should all pitch in together and get this place cleaned up. Perhaps we could even form groups to do certain chores."

The same woman objected, "Who are you to tell us what to do?"

Jessica returned the woman's brazen stare. Their eyes were locked in open defiance. Her cheeks began to burn from anger. She couldn't understand why anyone would argue against making their quarters more livable. After a moment of frozen silence, Jessica replied, "I am simply a passenger who has to live and sleep down here for several months. I am not eager to live in this filth, and I am sure many of you feel as I do." She let her eyes trail questioningly over the crowd of women, hoping the majority would agree with her.

The woman who had been arguing with Jessica started walking toward her. She tossed her long dark hair insolently, her manner indicating she thought Jessica an unworthy adversary. She placed her hands on her hips, and her lips curled into an impertinent sneer. Stopping only inches from Jessica, she raised her hands and roughly shoved her from the crate. "Who are you to tell me what to do, *bitch*?"

While Jessica hurried to get back upon her feet, Helen spun the woman around. "Keep your hands off her!" she muttered threateningly. Not an ounce of fear sounded in her voice.

"Oh, yeah! What are you gonna do about it?" she asked as she sidled closer to Helen.

Jessica placed her hand on Helen's arm. "Don't, Helen. I can fight my own battles, besides," she glanced down at Aaron, "He's frightened."

The woman tossed her hair and glared at Jessica, "So . . . *now* you want to fight?"

"No, but I will if I have to!" Jessica answered, her voice sure and unafraid.

The woman saw Jessica was not afraid of her. Her eyes flickered several times and she took a couple of steps backward. But it was against her nature to avoid trouble. The way her large dark eyes glinted in the shadows proved she was delighting in the argument. "Well, I think you are afraid!"

"Wait just a minute, Rosie, you have gone far enough!" A tall buxomy woman stepped forward.

"Stay out of it, June!" the bullying woman shouted. "It isn't any of your business."

"I am making it my business, Rosie! All the girl was saying was that we needed to clean up this stinking hole. I don't believe I heard her order anyone around, in fact, she was simply making a point. And," she added further, "If the girl wants us to clean up this filth, I think we should all pitch in."

Jessica interrupted, "Thank you . . . June," addressing the woman by the name she had been called, "But she doesn't frighten me."

"I can tell that, kid, but I feel like we ought to show which side we are on. You weren't asking anything unreasonable."

Rosie sauntered closer to Jessica, "Look you," she muttered, "I don't care what June Smith says, and I don't care what you say! I don't like you! I don't like your looks, and I damn sure don't like your nicey nice ways! If you want this place cleaned up, then do it yourself!"

Before Jessica could say a word, June grabbed Rosie's shoulder and spun her around to face her, "See here, Rosie Rutledge," she pointed to Jessica, "*My friend* shouldn't have to clean up this entire hole. I'm willing to help, my other friend," she pointed to Helen who was staring ominously at Rosie, "Agrees with me and the kid."

Another woman who had been standing near June, spoke up, "My name is Linda Ballard, and I agree with them too!"

June's eyes glinted threateningly, "I have heard enough of your bitching. The kid asked for help and we're going to give it to her. And if you have any more objections, you can take it up with me!" she shouted, jabbing at her chest with her thumb.

Rosie looked at June then back to Jessica. She knew

she was outnumbered and had been backed into a corner. Spinning angrily on her heel, she marched back to where she had selected her bunk, all the while muttering under her breath.

June glanced at Jessica, raised her brows, pursed her lips, then lifted her nose high into the air as she said, "Now, what were you saying before we were so rudely interrupted?" she asked prim and properly.

Jessica ducked her head to keep from laughing out loud. She was so thankful she had received support from this woman. She hoped no one would notice how badly her hands were shaking as she climbed back up on the crate. Helen smiled at her reassuringly, in fact, most of the women looked at her with a bit of admiration shining from their eyes. Jessica knew she had earned their respect by standing up to that bully, Rosie Rutledge. Jessica realized it could have gone very differently if she had not received help from June. She definitely owed her a favor. One she would gratefully repay someday.

Jessica took a deep breath and began again, "Ladies, I noticed several buckets up on deck. I would imagine if we looked, we could find a mop or two. I'm not . . . trying to be bossy, but even though it is very cold, the sun is shining very brightly, we could gather these mattresses and take them topside to air while the floor is being scrubbed. Also," she wrinkled her nose, "If you look underneath the mattresses, you'll see where people . . . have . . . vomited, perhaps if those boards were scrubbed down too, it would smell fresher."

Jessica was met with a chorus of agreement. One woman offered some lye soap she had brought along with her, another offered some rags to clean with, while another volunteered to find the galley to see if they could use the stove to heat some water. It was quickly decided to use sea water so the captain could not complain about the use of fresh water.

When Jessica stepped off the crate, she headed for Helen, June, and Linda. "I want to thank you for stepping in and helping."

"That's all right, kid, we have to live down here too," June answered with a shrug to her shoulders.

"Please, call me Jessica."

June smiled, "All right." Then a frown quickly took its place. "You had better watch out for Rosie in the future. I know her and she's tough. Not only is she tough, but she also holds a grudge."

Helen stated calmly, "I'll help Jessica watch out for her. I think she did right by not letting that woman bluff her."

"That's right, but remember, don't let yourself be caught alone with her, or don't let her force you into doing anything foolish."

"Don't worry, I won't!" Jessica said as she pushed up the sleeves on her blouse. "I think I have wasted enough time standing here talking, now it's time to go to work!"

Soon, the hold was a mass of water and suds. The beds were quickly stripped and many of the women lined the walls scrubbing while others devoted their time scouring the rough floor. The sea water, mixed with the acrid odor of the lye soap, produced a pungent smell throughout the quarters. It was different, although not altogether fresh smelling, it was certainly an improvement over what it had been only a few hours earlier. By the end of the day, the thin mattresses had been brought back down, and everyone gratefully settled in for a good night's sleep. It was well earned, and many of the women felt gratified by the day's work.

At first, the days passed quickly as the women found many chores to occupy their time. But soon, time began to lay heavily on their hands. Even though petty arguments broke out, and senseless bickering erupted between the women, Jessica was amazed at the transformation which gradually came over the majority of the women. Most quit cursing, and started to keep their bodies much cleaner. Helen explained it was because the women had been given the gift of freedom. They had been rescued from their bondage from the slums and prisons, and from a life filled with misery and despair. Now, they had a future before them. Within a few months time, they would have a chance to marry decent men and start their life anew. With Helen's explanation, Jessica had mutely nodded her agreement. There was a future ahead for them, but what about her life? What would her destiny be? She was no longer the naive child who thought she could simply walk down a street in California and find her father. He would be one of thousands who had recently flocked to the vast new land. In her newly discovered maturity, she realized he might be lost to her forever, although, she vowed her search for him would never end.

Jessica's thoughts gradually turned into a different direction. She began thinking about the fact that she *was* on a marriage ship. What would she do if one of the miners wanted to marry her? Would she give up her dream of marrying a man she loved, or would circumstances force her to enter into a loveless life with a man she did not know? After being raised in a home filled with love and laughter, it would be hard to accept anything less, but it was still a fact she had to face.

When the *Sea Nymph* sailed through the area called the Devil's Triangle, the cool brisk weather turned into a severe storm. Gale force winds started to batter the ship. Sheets of water poured over the ship and oozed into the living quarters until every stitch of clothing became molded and mildewed. It was hard to tell day from night because of the ever present darkness. The old merchant ship clawed through every crest of each wave, then fell dangerously into the troughs. The vessel would list so badly at times, the passengers thought it was about to capsize and send them all into the briny deep. During the peak of the storm, no one was allowed on deck for fear they would be swept into the angry, raging sea.

During the week that the storm raged, Jessica spent most of the time in her bunk. She prayed fervently that God's hand would remain upon them, and that he would safely see them through this difficult time. During this terrible week, she realized what horrible atrocities the slaves suffered while being transported; shackled in chains, half starved, and even brutally beaten. She imagined the terror they must have felt when they encountered such storms. She swore then that she would never be a party to holding someone against their will.

After a week, the storm finally abated, enabling the *Sea Nymph* to continue onward toward its destination.

Later in the voyage, Jessica and many other of the women stood on the deck and stared in fascination as many exotic ports appeared as tiny dots on the horizon as they sailed by: Cuba, the Virgin Islands, and Puerto Rico. They even managed to catch a fleeting glimpse of the South American nation of Venezuela, before it too, disappeared over the horizon.

Captain Mahan might have been a cruel and crude man, but he was an expert seaman. He took full advantage of the winds, giving the ship her full sails, and the *Sea Nymph* gained back valuable time. Since the southern hemisphere is the direct opposite of the northern one, Captain Mahan wanted to beat the winter weather which would engulf the Horn by mid-May. He deliberately avoided the ports at Rio de Janerio, and the one at Montevideo, Uruguay. He claimed they would be wasting valuable time, and he promised they would take port in Valparaiso, Chile. He claimed the worst part of the voyage would be over and they could afford to take the time to stock up on fresh food and water. During this part of the voyage, the passengers were given one sour lemon a week to prevent scurvy. Helen flashed a brilliant smile each time she saw Jessica slip half of her fruit to little Aaron. Jessica felt the same as Helen; the child needed the fruit more than they did, because their diet was atrocious. By the time they had cleared the Horn, they were all reduced to eating shrivelled potatoes and salted pork which had to have the green mold scraped off before it could be cooked.

After they left the port of Valparaiso, the situation became much better. Fresh food was plentiful, and color soon returned into the cheeks of the passengers. Before long, the mood aboard the ship was the same as it was when they first left New York, joyous, and anticipating. Even though several month's journey still lay ahead, they were all confident the worst was over.

Jessica was careful to keep her distance from Rosie Rutledge. Although the woman never openly approached her, she let her presence be felt. Many times while up on deck, Jessica would began to feel strange and uncomfortable. She would then glance around her to see Rosie watching her carefully. It reminded Jessica of a she-cat playing with a mouse before devouring it. Jessica was careful whenever she happened to be near the railing. It would not have surprised her if Rosie had attempted to push her overboard. But the remainder of the voyage passed without incident.

It was a general topic of discussion about how well they were treated by the crew members. Many had expected to be accosted by the men, and a few were probably disappointed, but they were all treated like ladies, except for a few crude remarks made by the captain.

Six months after leaving New York, the *Sea Nymph* threaded its way past the rotting derelicts abandoned in San Francisco Bay. At one time, during the extreme height of the gold rush, more than nine hundred vessels had been anchored in the harbor, choking it until seaworthy ships could barely maneuver in it to bring in badly needed supplies. Only a small number of the abandoned ships remained above water, their broken masts jutting into the skyline like skeletons clawing at the blue sky. The bay still proved to be extremely hazardous to maneuver in because of the rotted sunken ships just below the water level.

The deck became a frenzied melee as the passengers prepared to disembark from the ship. Stacks and stacks of small trunks and bags were placed up on the deck. After being aboard for over six months, with only a brief stopover at Valparaiso, the women were all anxious to set foot on solid ground again.

The ship checked close to the wharf, and mooring lines were quickly secured when the ship maneuvered into its slip. Sails were lowered, and for extra stability against the waves, the anchor was lowered. At long last, they had finally arrived at San Francisco.

Chapter Five

Captain Mahan stood on the quarterdeck watching the women scurry back and forth. A wry grin touched his face. He was enjoying the passengers' excitement. "Ladies, I must have your attention," he finally shouted. He had to raise his voice several times before the women heard him. When the clamor had quieted down, he announced, "I really hate to disappoint all of you, but nobody can leave the ship right now." The smile tugging at his broad face revealed exactly how much he was actually enjoying their delay. "I cannot turn you ladies loose on the streets of San Francisco. I am fixin' to leave the ship in a few minutes to see if I can find someone to take you off my hands." He chuckled sardonically, "Not that finding someone will present a problem, but I believe it is my duty to see that the right people receive their merchandise." Taking a long breath, he continued, "I'm sure the miners didn't know exactly when to expect you, or they would have been here to meet the *Sea Nymph*." He made a sweeping motion with his hands, "Everyone just stay calm and I will go see if I can find someone willing to assume the responsibility of your care. There is one word of caution I want to leave with you though . . . it's quite possible the men's camp will be miles from the city. If that is the case, we could have a long wait on our hands if I have to send them word."

Stunned looks flashed from one woman to the other. They had never considered this aspect. It had always been assumed someone would be waiting for them. The idea that it could be days, possibly even weeks before they would be allowed to leave the ship was very disheartening.

Jessica, Helen, and June, sought a quiet corner to discuss this turn of events. Jessica's grey eyes flashed angrily, "I don't believe the captain."

Helen's brow wrinkled into a frown, "No," she said slowly, "Perhaps he is right. I can see how the men might be busy and not want to waste time waiting for us. Who knows, they may all live close to one another, or they could live miles apart. I really don't see that we have any other choice than to do as the captain requested. After all," she added with a shrug to her shoulders, "We don't have much choice. We're all practically penniless and in a strange city too. There is really nothing we can do besides wait."

June giggled, "Well, I agree, we may not have much money, but I would lay odds that we could have plenty by nightfall."

"How?" Jessica asked innocently.

June burst out in laughter and even Helen had to hide a smile. "Honey, I forget how young and innocent you are," June said when she had stopped laughing. "You are forgetting about the world's oldest profession, and that we are in a city with a lot of women-hungry men."

Jessica's eyes widened and her face blazed with embarrassment when she realized what June was talking about. Finally she sputtered, "Aww, June, you wouldn't do that."

"No, I wouldn't, not unless I was forced to." She raised her brows, her face showing years of wisdom, "You would be surprised what a person would do for survival. I know there have been many times I've sworn never to do something, then circumstances came up and I had to do what I said I wouldn't." She wrinkled her nose, "Does that make sense?"

"Sure, it does," Jessica said. "I know one thing though, I have been doing some very serious thinking and I don't know if I am going to stay around for the drawing."

"What do you mean?" Helen asked.

"Have either of you given any thought to how the men will select their brides?"

"No," Helen answered slowly.

"What if they place us on the block the same way they do the slaves back east?"

"You know, I have often wondered the same thing," June said.

Helen shook her head, "I don't think they would do that. I don't believe the women would stand for it."

"I know I wouldn't!" Jessica said adamantly. "But, I have been thinking about something else."

"What is that?" both Helen and June asked together.

"I have been thinking about slipping off this ship and asking around about my father."

"Jessica!" Helen gasped, "You couldn't do that! It wouldn't be safe for you on the streets."

"You may be right, but it is a chance I might take. I haven't decided if I will go with the rest of you or not. I know if there is any chance at all that I could find my father, I know I wouldn't."

"Why, Jessica?"

"Because I'm not fond of the idea of marrying a man I do not know."

June gave her a sidelong glance, "Perhaps, you're right, kid."

"June! Don't encourage her!" Helen snapped. "She'll get into trouble."

"Probably not—that is, if one of us went with her. She could ask a few questions, and then if she didn't get any good leads about where he is, we could sneak back aboard the ship and no one would be the wiser."

"That is a great idea!" Jessica exclaimed. "I believe it would be safe on the streets if there were two of us . . . that is, if one of you will go with me." Jessica saw Helen's eyes dart over to her son. She knew Helen would not be able to leave Aaron behind. Turning to June, she asked, "June, would you go with me?"

"Sure, kid. They left the gangplank in place, and in a little bit, the men will go to the galley to eat. We can make our break then."

It happened exactly as June had predicted. In a couple of hours time, most of the crewmen slipped down to the galley, leaving only a few on deck, and their attention was not on the women's activities, especially since one of them had slipped ashore and brought back several bottles of whiskey. Jessica and June, ambled slowly over to the gangplank, and when they were fairly certain no one was watching, they made a dash for the huge wooden crates stacked on the pier.

Helen stood on the deck and watched her friends disappear. She wished June had not persuaded Jessica to go ashore. There was an ominous feeling hanging over her—a feeling that nothing good would come of their escapade.

When Helen's attention was finally drawn back to Aaron, she turned and walked slowly over to him, took his hand and went down below deck to their quarters. When she had disappeared from sight, a shadowy figure came out from between two crates. It was Rosie Rutledge.

"So," she spoke aloud, a large smile beaming across her face, "You want to go ashore. Perhaps there is something I can do to help make your stay much more pleasant." Chuckling wickedly, Rosie looked around to see if anyone was watching, then quickly followed Jessica and June.

Chapter Six

The area surrounding the wharf was a filthy mass of crude shanties, deeply rutted streets, and debris lined walkways. People of all different nationalities were clustered on the streets; English, French, Spaniards, Mexicans, Italians, and many Chinese. Their voices raised a hubbub. Much to Jessica's and June's surprise, very little attention was shown them as they hurried from the waterfront. Both of the women were shocked. They had expected a thriving civilized city, but in actuality, they were in the midst of a huge shantytown, barely able to sustain human life.

Jessica stared at her surroundings in amazement. Having been protected and sheltered from the harsher elements for most of her life, she could not believe some of the sights she was seeing. Shacks had been erected from scraps of various materials, and they leaned precariously to one side. Tin cans had been scattered carelessly, and many were in heaping piles around the shacks. Slovenly and raucous looking men wandered aimlesly through the streets.

Jessica looked at June helplessly, "I . . . I don't know where to start," she admitted, as tears threatened to spill from her lovely eyes.

"It looks terrible, doesn't it!" June stated matter-of-factly. "Perhaps it won't be so bad once we leave the waterfront." June's voice trembled, sounding as if she was trying to convince herself more than her friend. Both women were wondering what they had let themselves in for, by even agreeing to come to San Francisco. What if all the men were like the dirty and uncaring ones they had encountered.

They walked hurriedly, passing many strange appearing people as they left the wharf. June had to tug at Jessica's arm several times when she stopped to stare openly at yellow-skinned men with pigtails hanging down their backs, and darker-skinned men wearing what she recognized as huge, rounded sombreros upon their heads.

"Hurry up, Jessica," June urged, "Let's get out of here! There's no telling what will happen to us if we linger."

Jessica mutely nodded her agreement, clutched at June's hand, and together they raced through the littered street. They had only run about a hundred yards when they turned the corner onto another street. Both of them stopped in open-mouthed astonishment as they realized they had simply been in the alley-way of a major street. The difference from the slum of the alley to that of the street was the difference of night and day. The wide street was still littered with trash and debris, and untidy men still walked the streets, but these buildings had been erected with thought and planning. They were made from sturdy brick and had neatly painted signs hanging on their storefronts.

Jessica breathed a sigh of relief. "This is much better. For a minute there, I thought . . ."

"I know, I did too!" June did not notice the shadowy figure which had been following them, ducking into a narrow opening between two buildings. "I would suggest we start asking questions if we hope to find out anything. How about that mercantile store over there?" she pointed at a sprawling brick building.

"It sounds good to me," Jessica stated, with an affirmative nod to her head.

They crossed the street, entered the store, and immediately, Jessica was transported back through time as she recalled the visits to the small general store serving the community where she had been raised. The pleasant scent of fresh leather, mixed with the heady aroma of freshly ground coffee. Two huge slabs of cheese rested on the counter, and beneath it was a barrel completely filled with pickles floating in briny water. Sawdust had been spread generously on the floor, and the walls were lined with rows and rows of shelves, filled with tins of food, bins of flour, sugar, and spices. Bolts of material had been heaped upon several tables in the center of the store, and leather harnesses hung haphazardly on nails. One side of the store's space had been completely devoted to picks, axes, shovels, and mining equipment. The entire store was very impressive.

Jessica approached the counter slowly. The man standing behind it looked very formidable as he frowned curiously at the two women. "Y'es? May I help you?" He was startled at these customers. It was an odd occurrence that two attractive women, other than saloon harlots came into his store.

"Yes, sir, I certainly hope so," Jessica spoke quietly.

She squared her shoulders deteminedly, "You will probably think this is a strange request, but I am looking for my father. His name is Jess Tate. Does it sound familiar to you?"

The man looked thoughtful for a moment before answering. "No, I really don't think the request is all that strange. Fathers looking for sons, brothers looking for brothers," he shrugged indifferently, "have come in here searching. I will say, so far, you are the first daughter asking about her father. The name doesn't sound familiar," he added abruptly. "Has he been here long?"

"I would say, anywhere from eight months to a year, I'm not sure."

"Did you just get off a ship?" the man wanted to know.

"Yes."

"Are you by any chance one of the gals who have been brought in here to marry some of the men?" he asked suddenly.

"Yes, sir, I suppose you could say that," Jessica answered, somewhat surprised.

"And you came along, hoping to find your daddy?"

"Yes . . . how did you know?" she asked, very astounded at the man's perception.

"It wasn't too hard to add two and two together," he shrugged off-handedly. "Cole Robertson was in here this morning, stocking up on supplies for you ladies."

"And, who is Cole Robertson?"

"Why, he is one of the bosses of that outfit that brought you here."

June, who had been silent, spoke up, "Sir, this is all very interesting, but we are anxious to know if you have seen or heard anything about the man by the name of Jess Tate?"

The storekeeper looked her squarely in the eye, "Ma'am, do you have any idea how many men pass through these doors on any given day? Do you have any idea how many men don't want their real name known? Do you have any . . ."

"But have you seen *him?"* she demanded.

The man sighed, "No, I haven't. But," he shoved a pad and pencil across the counter to Jessica, "If you will write down his description, later, when I have the time, I will transfer it to that slate over there," he said pointing to a huge black slate which was nailed close by the door.

Jessica gasped. On the slate were numerous descriptions of men. Her eyes quickly glistened with tears. It would be as bad as she had first thought. It would be a miracle if she could find him. Jessica reached for the pad and began writing. She had to cling to any chance, however small.

June asked curiously, "What about this company of men? You seem to know quite a bit about them? Are they far from here?"

The storekeeper sighed again, only this time he was beginning to show impatience. "Ma'am, I don't want to be rude. But, as nosy as you and her seem to be, I could stand here and answer questions all day long, and I simply don't have the time." He thumbed through an order book. "I have all these supply lists to fill, and I have wasted enough time on you. Time is worth a fortune out here, and I don't have the time, and I can't afford to lose the money I could make by standing here a-jawin' with you." He waved his arm, "If you want more information, go look for it somewhere else!"

While Jessica and June had been in the store, Rosie Rutledge had entered a large building just a few doors down the street. She was approached by a flashily dressed woman, sporting a long, thin cigar between her teeth.

"What ja know, girl? Are ya lookin' for work?" the bawdy woman asked.

Rosie shrugged, "Naw, not really, I got a letter from a woman by the name of Bernice Timbers, saying she had a place called The Golden Slipper. I noticed that's what the sign says out front. Is this the same one I'm lookin' for?"

"Where do you know Berny from?" the woman asked quickly, a new gleam in her eye.

"From New York. We used to work together." Rosie squinted one of her eyes, "She was . . . uh . . . let me put it delicately, asked to leave 'bout three years ago. Looks like she done all right by herself!" Admiration had crept into Rosie's voice as she glanced around the room, taking in the heavy red velvet drapes, the plush, over-stuffed couches, and the mahogany bar which ran the entire length of the room.

"What's your name?" the woman asked curiously, "And I'll see if Berny wants to see you?"

After Rosie told her, the woman disappeared through a heavy curtain separating the large room from the rest of the house. While the woman was gone, Rosie paid closer attention to the room she was in. Rich, thick carpeting lay on the floor, and a spiral staircase wound down from one of the upper floors. Paintings of naked women hung on the walls, and erotic sculptures had been placed on the tables at the end of the couches. Ol' Berny's done all right! Rosie thought as she looked around the elegant room admiringly. Rosie turned sharply around when she heard a voice.

"Well, well! Look here! If it isn't Rosie Rutledge herself!" Bernice Timbers stood with her arms placed akimbo, and a broad smile stretching across her thin face. She was a tiny little woman with short red hair, curled tightly around her face. She was dressed in a black satin dress, low in the front to reveal the slight swell of her breasts. Around her neck was a strand of magnificent pearls, and shiny earrings dangled down, almost touching her shoulders. Three short silver colored ostrich plumes, which had been tucked into a jeweled band, fanned the air over her head. "You're a sight for sore eyes!" she squealed as she ran to embrace her long time friend.

After the women had finished their lusty greeting, Rosie pulled back, "Bernice, I don't have much time. I need a favor and I need it in a hurry!"

"What's the matter? Are you running from the law?" Concern edged into Bernice's voice.

"No, it's nothing like that." Rosie hastened to say. "Like I said, I need a favor."

"You know I owe you so many favors, it would be hard to repay all of them." Bernice stated remembering her perilous escape from New York with the law right on her tail, and Rosie fending them off, all the way.

"I just got here, Berny. I came on the ship, the *Sea Nymph*."

Bernice laughed, "The marriage ship! My God, Rosie! Have you reformed?"

"Hell no!" Rosie swore. She gestured with her hands, "Listen to me, I don't have much time. I need to even a score and you are the only one I can turn to!" Rosie still could not believe her good fortune at finding Bernice so easily, and with Jessica right down the street. "While on the ship, me and another woman got in to it. Ha!" she snorted bitterly, "I said a woman, when in reality, she ain't nothing but a snotty nosed kid. But, she's a looker! She has a pretty face, and her hair will reach all the way to here," she pointed at the bottom of her buttocks. She's a little miss goody-good, and she crossed me once too often."

A sly grin broke across Bernice's face. "And what do you want me to do about it?"

"She and another woman are down the street asking questions about Jessica's father." A concerned frown dipped her brows, as she asked hurriedly, "You don't know a June Smith, do you?"

"From New York?"

"Yeah."

"I've heard about her, but don't recall ever meeting her."

"Good! Because she is the one with Jessica, and she might become suspicious. I'd like for you to go down there," Rosie continued with her devious plan, "and convince her that you knew her father. Tell her that you expect him almost any day, bring her back here, and we'll kill two birds with one stone."

"Oh? And how is that?" Bernice leaned forward eagerly, she was very interested.

"I get even, and you get a new girl for your place of business here."

"I don't . . . know." Bernice said doubtfully. "They don't take too kindly to shanghaing around here like they used to."

"Who will know? She's practically an orphan. If anyone misses her aboard ship, they will eventually come to the conclusion that she slipped off the ship, and fell into the clutches of a woman-starved man!" she batted her eyes innocently. "Besides that, you will make a fortune. I'll lay you odds, she is a virgin."

Bernice was definitely interested. "And how am I gonna convince her to stay here willingly?"

"Bring her back here and offer her something to drink," Rosie said simply. "Surely an old pro like you has something lying around to put into her drink?"

"What about this woman with her?" Bernice wanted to be sure it would work.

"So, you get two for the price of one! June is pretty good. She hasn't had a man in over six months. Keep her drugged for a few weeks, and I'll bet you won't have any trouble out of her." Rosie eyed Bernice desperately, "You've got to make up your mind and quick! Those two will be gone pretty soon. Please, Berny, do me this favor, will you?"

Bernice smiled easily. This was exactly what she had needed. She had just lost three of her best girls to the miners. They had suddenly decided to go straight, of course, because the miners had struck it rich, hurried their decision. Berny grabbed a lace shawl that had been draped over a chair. "All right, you convinced me, but for Pete's sake, go upstairs and take a bath, and stay out of sight!" she hissed. After asking a few hurried questions, Bernice quickly slammed out of the house, striding swiftly down the street to the mercantile store.

Chapter Seven

Jessica and June walked out of the mercantile store, downhearted and discouraged. Even though their quest had just begun both of them realized how futile the task was. June knew Jessica would not give up easily, so she prepared herself mentally for the search which was ahead.

"Do you have any suggestions where to go next?" Jessica asked hopefully.

"I'm not sure . . . unless we try some of the saloons. Men have a habit of turning up at them."

"But my father isn't a drinking man," Jessica protested.

"I'm sure he isn't, but when a man is away from his home and family, he is likely to do things out of character."

At that time, a tiny woman stumbled and fell toward Jessica. "Stupid steps!" the woman swore, kicking at the loose board she had stumbled across. "Thanks, honey, for catching me or I would have fallen down . . ." She looked up at Jessica and a startled expression flashed across her face. "Do I know you from somewhere?" she asked curiously.

"No . . . I don't think so," Jessica answered, confused. "I have just arrived here, and don't know anyone."

"Do you have a sister living here?" the woman persisted, she had to get an opening in which she could continue with the plan Rosie had devised.

"No . . . I don't. Perhaps you have me confused with someone else."

"Maybe I do, but you sure look familiar, though," the woman muttered as she started in the door of the mercantile. Waiting for Jessica and June to start walking off, it was difficult for Bernice to keep from laughing aloud. This was going to be easier than she had thought. "Wait a minute!" she shouted, before the two women had gone far.

Jessica and June turned back around to face the woman. "Yes, ma'am?"

"Don't run off yet," Bernice said as she started walking toward them. "I know you from somewhere, and so help me, I'm going to find out exactly where." Bernice stepped closer, and pretended to examine Jessica thoughtfully. "Perhaps I know your parents?"

Jessica gave June a sidelong look. An expression of hope shone clearly upon her face. "I don't know . . ." she began hesitantly, "I have reason to believe my father is living out here."

"What is his name?"

"Jess Tate."

Bernice squealed in delight. "Of course! I should have known you were Jessie's daughter! You really favor him!"

Jessica gasped, "You mean you actually know him? Have even seen him here?"

"Why, sure. In fact, I'm expecting him back almost any day now."

Tears clouded Jessica's vision as she looked up at June. She could not believe her good fortune. "You actually know my father?" she asked again.

Bernice laughed easily, "Yes, I know him. You must be his daughter, Jessica. He's told me quite a bit about you."

"But . . . how . . . how did you meet him?" she asked, for the first time taking in Bernice's scantily clad figure.

Bernice grinned, "Honey, I can see that you are shocked. Most girls don't want to believe their fathers visit women like me. Before you get the wrong idea . . ." she looked around her, obviously not liking her surroundings by the expression of displeasure showing on her face. "Why don't we go to my place and I'll tell you all about it."

Jessica and June followed Bernice eagerly. Neither could believe their search had already ended. They quickly reached the doorway of The Golden Slipper. Jessica's eyes were round with wonder as she trailed behind Bernice. Inside, Bernice bellowed out that she wanted coffee to be served in her private quarters. Jessica and June stood hesitantly as Bernice walked over to a door covered with heavy drapes. Sweeping back the curtain to reveal a long hallway, she said, "Come on back here with me, and I'll explain everything." She laughed, "Don't worry about being disturbed, my girls worked all morning and they are all asleep now, we don't usually get busy until around sundown."

Jessica gave one backward glance at the nude paintings and long mohogany bar as she followed through the curtains. Sitting down at a round table, Jessica and June waited anxiously for the woman to explain.

"I guess I should introduce myself, I'm Bernice Timbers, Berny, for short. I know you are Jessica, but who are you?" she asked her companion.

"My name is June Smith."

"Happy to meet the both of you." She decided to play her character to the hilt. "You all wouldn't by chance be looking for work, would you?"

"Oh, no!" Jessica gasped. She knew what kind of place this was, and did not want any part of it. "I only want to find my father. You said that you were expecting him?"

"Sure, in a few days or so. He makes it into town about once a month, and he's overdue as it is." She gave Jessica's hand a matronly squeeze. "I can see that you are upset over the idea of your father visiting such a place. Let me put you at ease. You see, right after your father arrived here, he was robbed." Seeing alarm spring into Jessica's eyes, she quickly reassured her, "He wasn't hurt, only his pride. My man found him out in the alley. He was bleeding from a cut on the forehead. Thomas brought him in here, we cleaned him up, and . . . I guess you could say we have been friends ever since. And," her eyebrows raised frankly, "Believe me, we only share a friendship, nothing else."

"Are you sure the man is *my* father?" Jessica asked, wanting to make certain her hopes had not been raised for nothing.

Bernice desperately struggled to remember the names Rosie had mentioned to her. One thing about Rosie, she was very good at eavesdropping. "Yes, I think so . . ." Bernice said hesitantly, "Was your mother's name Margaret? And, I believe . . . there was a sister . . . by the name of Marsha?"

Tears of relief flowed down Jessica's cheeks. This woman did know her father! She had actually seen and talked to him! She had to, since she knew her family's names. "Yes! Yes!" she said excitedly, "It is the same person! You have seen him! Oh! Thank you!"

"Have you been looking for him long?"

Before Jessica knew it, she had launched into all of the details about her mother's and sister's death, her Aunt Agnes, and the night she crept aboard the ship. She also told her about the journey around the Horn, and about her doubts and fears about finding her father. Jessica admitted her doubts whether she would have married one of the men if he had chosen her. "Now," she admitted laughingly, "I will not be faced with that decision," Then a shadow crossed her face. "You said . . . that he would be here any day now . . . June, what do you think will happen when we get back to the ship?" The expression of terror was in her eyes as she continued with her train of thought, "What will happen if the captain returns with the men?"

Bernice rushed to say, "There is no need in you returning to the ship. Why, both of you are more than welcome to stay here until Jessie comes." She pasted what she hoped was her most solemn expression onto her face, "You'll be perfectly safe here, no harm will come to you," she added when she saw unspoken thoughts flashing through June's mind.

"Oh!" Jessica squealed happily, "That would be wonderful! June, will you stay too?"

"I don't know, Jessica," she answered doubtfully. "My

name is on that contract, and I think I had better go back to the ship." She grinned, "I am sort of curious as to who I will meet. One thing is for certain, if I don't want to marry the man, I certainly don't have to! Besides, Helen will be wondering what happened to us."

After June had gone, Bernice and Jessica sat talking for a while. Jessica anxiously asked about her father, since she wondered what he had been doing during all the time they had been separated. Bernice craftily hedged on most answers. She did not want to say anything that would make this young beauty suspicious.

Bernice wrinkled her nose, "Jessica, I can imagine how everyday necessities on board a ship could suddenly appear as luxuries. If you would like, I could have you some bath water drawn, then after you bathe, I'm sure I could persuade the cook to set an extra plate."

Jessica's eyes grew wide with wonder. "A bath! Oh, that sounds heavenly. My clothes! I left my clothes aboard ship!" She was frantic at the thought of having nothing to wear.

"Relax, I'm sure I can find you something," Bernice said as she patted her hand. "I have girls here all shapes and sizes."

Jessica followed Bernice up the winding staircase to a small room that the women used for bathing. In the middle of the room rested a huge brass tub that Bernice boasted had cost her an arm and a leg, and a whole lot in between. However, Jessica did not really understand what she had been referring to, so she simply let the words pass by her.

Jessica took her bath at a leisurely pace as she relaxed in the hot, scented water. She delighted at filling the cloth full of water, then holding it above her, squeezing until tiny droplets of water beaded across her full breasts. Later, when the water had cooled, she climbed out of the tub and washed her long mane of hair. Knowing it would take several hours to dry since it was so thick and long, Jessica draped a towel around her and walked over to the door and opened it to a tiny crack.

"Bernice! Bernice!" she called. "I'm through. Do you have a robe I can wear?"

"Sure, honey," Bernice answered as she came out of a room carrying a flimsy dressing gown. "I had to dig down into the bottom of a trunk to find this. I think most of the girls' clothes would simply hang on you. Absolutely, I've never seen anyone with such a small waist," she said, all the while admiring Jessica's beautiful body. Rosie had been right. If she played her cards right, she could stand to make a mint off this young woman.

After Jessica had dressed, she looked around to see Bernice quietly laughing. Berny was laughing at the expression of shock on Jessica's face as she realized just how revealing the gown actually was.

"Are . . . you sure this is that you want me to wear?" Jessica asked modestly. The gown was a pale mint green in color. It had delicate satin ribbons instead of buttons, and the front swooped dangerously low. For a moment, Jessica was afraid to move for fear of her breasts tumbling through. Bernice had not thought to bring her any undergarments, and Jessica had never been dressed so seductively. Her face flamed a brilliant crimson over the way Bernice was openly admiring her. She had no way of knowing the madam was simply appraising her as being a worthy investment.

"Come on, honey," Bernice said with a wave of her hand. "I imagine you are probably half-starved." Knowing from experience what most people, fresh off the ships wanted most of all to eat, was bacon and eggs.

Soon Jessica was seated at the kitchen's dining table, and on her plate was the simple fare, but to Jessica's eyes and stomach, it was a delicious feast. Bernice had decided to let the girl eat before adding the drug to her coffee. After she had eaten, she pushed back her plate proclaiming she could not eat another bite. It was then that Bernice warmed her coffee, and slipped a small vial of liquid into it. A broad smile graced her face when she saw Jessica drain the last drop.

"Ooh, that was delicious! Thank you, very much."

"That's all right, honey, nothing is too good for Jessie's girl." She stood up, "I hate to bust up having enjoyable company, but I think it's time you went upstairs."

"Oh, must I leave so soon? I really enjoy visiting with you," disappointment was evident in Jessica's voice.

Bernice chuckled, "I really think you ought to go upstairs; we will be opening for business in a few minutes, and I don't think you ought to be downstairs, especially dressed the way you are. Why, one of my customers might mistake you for one of my girls."

"Oh!" Jessica said slowly. She shook her head, suddenly feeling very dizzy. Perhaps she had eaten too quickly.

At that time, the door to the kitchen flew open and a giant of a man stood in the doorway, but Jessica had become too groggy to see his features.

"Cole!" Bernice shouted angrily, "What in the hell are you doing here?"

"I came . . . for some . . . fun," he slurred drunkenly.

Seeing Jessica start to slump in her chair, he muttered, "Her! I'll take her!" He screwed up his face, "Don't recall ever making love to a red-headed woman."

"Now, Cole," Bernice scolded as she hurried over to his side. She motioned for one of the girls to help Jessica up to a room. "You don't want her," she whispered as she sidled up close to him. "She's a new girl, she hasn't been properly trained."

"Doesn't matter," he mumbled, "I still want her."

Even though Cole Robertson had a day's growth of beard on his face, and even if he was staggeringly drunk, he was still the most handsome man in all of San Francisco. He stood well over six feet, his skin was golden bronzed from the sun, and his hair was jet black. He reminded Bernice of the Greek gods she had read about. Not an ounce of unnecessary weight was on him, his shoulders were broad and wide enough to hold a woman and comfort her to the fullest of his ability. He was always a welcome sight at her place. He didn't mind spending money, and he always treated her girls gentlemanly, never leaving them bruised and battered the way some men did.

"Well? Do I get her, or do I go somewhere else?" he demanded as he staggered against the door. Damn women, anyway, he thought angrily. They would sell their souls for a tiny bit of security. He had learned that a long time ago.

Bernice was busy thinking. She hated to lose Cole's business for the night, having always made a good profit from his visits. But she knew if she turned a man loose on Jessica before the drug had time to take effect, she could possibly lose a valuable piece of property. "Let . . . let me check, Cole. I'll see what I can do." Bernice hurried up the stairs and raced into the room where she knew Jessica had been taken.

"Berny . . . I feel so strange," Jessica muttered hesitantly. It was odd. She really didn't know who was standing over her, but in her drug-fogged mind, she knew Bernice was there. Also, she couldn't figure out why she was feeling the way she was. Only a few minutes ago, or was it hours, she had been eating and laughing and talking. Now, she was barely aware of what was going on around her.

"What do you think, Kate?" Bernice asked. "Reckon it would be all right to send Cole in here?"

Kate knew what was up. They had acquired several women the same way as they had this one. Since she owned a small percentage of the house, she hated to lose Cole's business also. She knew he had threatened to leave. His voice had echoed all through the house when he had shouted at Bernice only a few moments earlier. "I would rather have Cole break her in than some of the trash that comes through those doors. You know for yourself, if the wrong man gets hold of an innocent girl, she can be ruined for life."

"I know, I know!" Bernice snapped. "What I meant, do you think she is under enough?"

"Yeah, I believe so. Cole's so drunk, I don't think it would do any good if she struggled or not." Kate shrugged her shoulders, "Try it, ya ain't got any money tied up in her. If you end up losing her," she added indifferently, "You ain't lost nothing."

Bernice leaned over Jessica, "Honey, do you hear me?"

"Mmmm," she moaned, "Yes . . ."

"Honey, I am going to send you some company up. I

want you to be really nice to him, do you hear?"

Jessica tried to focus her eyes but could only manage to see a shadowy figure standing over her. She could think coherently, or so she thought, but could not understand why everything was spinning and blurry. Sure she wanted some company. Didn't Bernice know she enjoyed talking with her?

Cole paused inside the doorway. He walked unsteadily over to a small table, set his new bottle of whiskey on it, then sagged onto the bed to remove his boots. It had been a long time since he had paid a visit to the Golden Slipper. It had been a long time since he had had a woman, almost too long. It didn't matter that she was a tramp. All women were tramps in one way or another. Each eager to sell their bodies for money, or for a home and children. Either way, they were all out for one thing, regardless whether they were considered ladies, or whether they were considered tramps. He cared nothing for them, except when he needed to slake his desires. A long time ago, a woman had taken his heart and used it for all it was worth. He vowed that that would never happen to him again.

Cole gave a casual glance to the woman lying on the bed. At least she was an attractive woman. He squinted through bloodshot eyes. For a moment there, it had appeared that the coppery mane of hair had ringed her head like a halo, but he had been mistaken. Angels did not live at the Golden Slipper. He stood, nearly losing his balance as he grabbed hold of the bedstead to steady himself. Then, he slowly began to remove his shirt.

Jessica managed to open her eyes enough to see a

large shadowy figure standing above her. It couldn't be Bernice, she wasn't that tall. Her mind gasped in recognition. No one was standing there! She was simply having a dream! And it was her favorite dream about the man she knew she would marry, the man who had visited her dreams, whether sleeping or awake, for many years now. She couldn't help but marvel at the way her subconscious was playing tricks on her, how *real* the dream appeared to be! Perhaps it was because she was so happy. Perhaps it was because, now that she had found her father, she wouldn't be forced into a loveless marriage. Even in her drug-induced mind, Jessica realistically reasoned to herself that she had not had a dream about her beloved ever since she had come to terms with the fact that she might have to marry a man she did not know. Jessica gave a squeal of delight when she felt her dream lover slip his arms around her waist. It had never been this vivid before. She might as well relax and enjoy it.

Cole slipped his massive hands around the woman's tiny waist. "What is your name, sweetheart?" he asked.

"You know my name, it's Jessica," the woman answered breathlessly.

"Mmmm, Jessica," he mouthed as he pressed his body closer to hers.

"Love? What is your name? All of these years have passed and I still do not know it."

Cole was aware enough to answer. It was true, he had been drinking heavily, but he had not had too much to drink to know how badly he suddenly wanted this woman. Her skin was so soft and satiny. It was creamy and easy to touch. Her breasts were so firm and rounded, they gave him extreme pleasure when he touched them, ever so lightly at first.

Jessica was very aware of the strength in her lover's hard, muscular arms. She felt his fingers trace delicate patterns across her breasts until the tips jutted upward, bringing her untold pleasure. A crazy, tingling sensation shot through her veins. She struggled to resist the fiery flow of passion her dream aroused in her. It was a feeling that was foreign and alien to her, yet one that sent chills of delight all over her. Why not enjoy her dream, it could not hurt anything.

Cole found her mouth with his, exploring the honeyed sweetness with his tongue, enjoying, savoring each primitive sensation she brought him. Cole kissed her lips, her lovely throat, and then her full, rounded breasts. His tongue found one jutting nipple and his long, sinewy fingers found the peak of her other breast.

Jessica's tiny fingers clutched at her lover's mat of hair on his hard, muscular chest. She had never known such pleasure in her life. A slow burning sensation started in the very pit of her stomach and reached all the way to the most secret place between her thighs. She wanted him with all of her might. Even though Jessica was innocent, she knew this was her destiny, her place in life, that being in the arms of the man she dearly loved. At that moment, she would have sold her soul for it not to be a dream. She desperately wanted the ache in her loins to be appeased.

Jessica's eyes widened momentarily when she felt her legs being pulled apart. She felt shameful for enjoying herself so immensely. If she had been awake, she knew she would have blanched with shame for having such graphic dreams. Jessica gasped in pain when she felt something long and hard enter deeply inside her. Pain!

Pain! There was not supposed to be pain! Jessica began to thrash wildly on the bed. She wanted it to stop hurting.

Cole was surprised at this unexpected response. Although most of the tramps he had known before had delighted at his lovemaking, a few had feigned an unnatural response, but he had never known such a frenzied answer to his passionate thrusts. And the feel of her was different. Her womanhood closed over his maleness with a firmness he didn't know possible. In Cole's drunken state, he had no way of knowing Jessica was writhing in pain.

Later, Cole moved off the woman and reached for his bottle of whiskey. Something was wrong, but he could not put his finger on what was bothering him. Shrugging his shoulders when he couldn't figure out what was bothering him, he turned the bottle up, drank a hefty portion of the amber liquid, then turned back to the woman. Seeing tears staining her lovely cheeks, remorse suddenly filled him. Had he hurt her? He had not meant to. Nothing was worse than for a man to hurt a woman, regardless if she was a tramp or not, a woman did not deserve pain in the act of making love.

"Sweetheart," he muttered tenderly, "What's the matter? I wasn't too rough with you, was I?"

"You hurt me!" she sobbed bitterly. In her fogged mind of reality, Jessica knew her dream lover wasn't supposed to bring her pain. She had imagined the love shared between a man and a woman was something pleasing as her dream had been when it first started. Not the burning, searing pain she had experienced when her lover had started making love to her. How could dreams hurt?

"Shhh, my sweet, don't cry. I didn't mean to hurt you," Cole muttered gently. "Next time, I'll show more restraint. I guess I was too hungry for a woman," he whispered as he pulled her back into his arms. At the feel of her in his arms once again, Cole suddenly felt another rush of desire for the lovely creature. He knew he was in for a night of extreme pleasure.

Jessica at first offered a small amount of resistance when her dream took her back into his arms. But when he wound his hands through her tangled mane of hair, she could feel the tension leave her, especially when his lips found her mouth again. If a man could be beautiful, Cole was. He was like a magnificent pagan god. His features were no longer in a shadow, but clear and precise as he pressed close to her. She could see his steel blue eyes as they scorched her body. She could feel his mustache tickle her lip as he kissed her, and could feel the burn of his unshaved face against her cheeks. Suddenly, the pain between her thighs disappeared as quickly as it had started and a warm feeling of wanting, longing took its place. Her lips met his with an apparent ease. She marveled at the taste of him, as he delighted in the taste of her. Her nails raked his back in pleasure when once again, his mouth found her breasts. She felt the taut muscles of his stomach grow rigid as her hands trailed downward, as she sought to feel his masculinity He have an involuntary gasp of surprise and he trembled with delight when her hand timidly found what it sought.

Cole gave a muffled groan. Not being able to stand it any longer, he tossed her onto her back and mounted her, plunging his maleness to the hilt of her womanhood. This time, she did not move with a frenzy. Instead, she too, gave a muffled groan of delight. Taking what was so freely offered, Cole moved with deliberate ease, savoring each pleasurable sensation as Jessica's legs locked around his thighs. He could feel her heels digging into his flesh as she moaned in sensual ecstasy. The tips of her breasts burned into the flesh of his chest like a branding iron burning her mark into him. It was only a matter of moments before Jessica started answering each penetrating thrust with passionate movements of her own.

Jessica did not attempt to understand what was happening to her. It was beautiful, yet something was wrong. Was she as her aunt had accused? Did she have the scarlet soul of a tramp? Was her blood tainted because of the sins of her parents? These fleeting thoughts raced through her mind momentarily before she pledged her being to the unrealities her mind had created. Her head began to spin once more, but it was not from the drug, but from the peak of passion as her dream lover sank his teeth gently into the soft part of her shoulder. She felt her loins start to churn tumultuously like a mass of boiling clouds, threatening to unleash its fury at any moment. Then, when it happened, a fire shot through the very essence of her soul, sending exploding shivers of rapture through her entire being.

Cole sensed her passion reaching its height of pleasure. His body knew how to match the moment of intensity, to strive for the towering plateau of exhilarating satisfaction.

Together, for one long moment lasting an eternity, they soared into the lofty heights of heaven, past the moon and the stars, and onward, into the black void of the universe.

Much later, after they had drifted back to the endless bounds of earth, Jessica snuggled contentedly in Cole's arms. This is everything I thought it would be she thought, before slipping into the fascinating land of appeasement and euphoria.

Little did either of them know or realize what stormy clouds lay in their future.

Chapter Eight

Somewhere outside in the distance, a rooster flapped his wings and crowed for daylight as the first muted rays of dawn crept into the darkened room. A gentle breeze tugged at the lace curtain hanging over the slightly opened window, and the faint but rapidly fading glow of moonlight enhanced the shadows which formed on Cole's handsome face.

A woman's passionate, throaty laughter mixed with the sounds of a man's heavy footsteps disappearing down the long narrow hallway which ran the entire length of the Golden Slipper.

The noise awakened him instantly. With the first stirrings of awareness, Cole realized he was not alone in the room. His hands instinctively reached for the holstered gun hanging on the bedpost. As quickly as his reflexes had reacted, Cole's tensed muscles relaxed when he felt the gentle softness of the young woman snuggled closely to his side. For a moment, a rush of tenderness swept over him as he gazed at her sleeping form. A strand of her long beautiful hair had fallen across her mouth and moved each time she breathed. He chuckled, the sound coming deep from his throat as he remembered the night he had spent with her. He had been drunk, but not drunk enough to forget how she had felt in his arms. A slight frown creased his brow. Something was not quite right about her, but it was nothing he could immediately put his finger on. He simply could not understand why such a beautiful woman had turned to a life filled with a steady procession of men. Sighing deeply, Cole shook his head and shrugged off his puzzlement.

Being careful not to disturb Jessica, Cole eased his weight from the bed. Placing his bare feet onto the floor, he stepped on a filmy gown where it had been carelessly tossed the night before.

Cole crossed the room to where his clothes lay in a crumpled heap. Fumbling with his shirt, he withdrew a match and a slender cheroot from one of the pockets. He then stepped over to the night table and poured the remainder of the whiskey into a glass. He sat down in a huge, overstuffed chair, raked a thumbnail over the match head, lit the cigar and let the smoke curl lazily upward, which caused one of his eyes to squint in protest. Deep in thought, he raised the glass to his lips and sipped the whiskey slowly. It helped to ease the sudden pounding throb in his head.

An abrupt, lonesome yearning swept over him. For a moment, the longing to return to his old home was almost overwhelming. At that precise minute, he would have gladly given ten years of his life to have been able to stand in the middle of a freshly plowed field and let the rich black earth sift through his fingers. He closed his eyes and recalled how peaceful the land was after a sudden shower; how the grass smelled, how the wildflowers sprouted overnight, and how the oaks, giant elms, and pecan trees swayed in the gentle breezes late in the afternoon.

In his mind's eye, he could see his mother wipe her hands on her apron, then push back a stray wisp of graying hair from her face. He could smell the delicate aroma of freshly baked bread just as it came from the oven. Then, he could see a patient smile slip across his father's face as he tried to show his son how to mend a broken harness.

Cole abruptly jerked his thoughts back to the present. He knew better than to dwell on the past. Every time he allowed himself the luxury of fond memories, Melissa had a way of creeping into his mind. Melissa! Just the sound of her name caused a churning rage in the pit of Cole's stomach. She had betrayed him! She was worse than any tramp or harlot he had ever chanced to meet, and he hoped to never meet the likes of her again. At least when he knowingly sought a release of his desires with a woman such as this, he knew exactly what he was getting.

Cole looked again at the woman sleeping so peacefully and innocently. He felt the familiar stirrings of passion forming in his loins. He looked at the woman more closely. Her long beautiful hair flowed all the way to her waist. Her face was so angelic, she reminded him of a pretty china doll. But Cole knew what fiery passion lurked beneath her fragile exterior. She was all woman, he had discovered that last night.

Cole quietly got to his feet and padded softly to the bed. He wanted her and he wanted her badly. Easing down beside her, he leaned over and pushed the fiery lock of hair away from her face. The sheet had slipped down to reveal a firm, breast peeking up at him. The nipple was a soft golden brown, and the tip was sensually rounded. He could feel his maleness grow rigid with desire. Swinging his long muscular legs over onto the bed, Cole bent his arm and propped his head upon his hand. He wanted to watch her for a moment.

With his free hand, Cole picked up a strand of her hair and rubbed it between his fingers. Shaking his head, he couldn't understand how some men didn't take the time to make love to a woman, they simply used her for sex. To kiss and fondle a woman only proved to heighten both their pleasures. Cole leaned forward and pressed his lips to her earlobe. First, he nibbled gently then his tongue flicked out and tasted the silken skin. His breath teased at her sleepiness, causing her to stir ever so slightly. A soft smile touched her lips as she stretched; a long, lazy, contented stretch. In her mystical land of pleasant awake-asleep, Jessica's hands reached out to caress the matted chest which pressed close to her.

With a muffled groan, Cole quickly nudged at her shoulder, turning her on her back and took her into his arms. Jessica's eyes opened instantly.

For an instant, her eyes blinked in confusion and uncomprehension. She felt stark terror at waking up in a man's arms.

"Wha . . . what, who?"

"Shhh," he hushed, "I want you, I want to make love to you."

Everything happened quickly. Thoughts ran rampant through Jessica's mind. What was happening? Who was this strange man? Why was she in his bed? Jessica struggled to understand what was going on. Then the faint, misty land of shadowed memory came rushing back. This man had actually made love to her last night! And he had made love to her repeatedly. Shame washed over her as she realized that she had responded to his demands.

"You . . . don't understand," she stammered, "This isn't right!"

Cole laughed, "Oh, but I do understand," he teased. "I want you."

Jessica looked up to see passion blazing from the man's eyes. There was something about him that frightened her, yet captivated her all in the same rush of twisted emotions. A cold prickly feeling swept over her. She knew he meant to have her!

"No!" she shouted in a harsh whisper. She tried to squirm away from his grasp, but his arms held her like strong bands of steel.

Cole stared at the woman in surprise. His hold on her momentarily loosened. He couldn't understand her sudden resistance. Then it dawned on him that she was playing games. He threw back his head and laughed. A memory of something happening a long time ago flashed through his mind. He had been with another woman during the same kind of circumstance. After answering his passionate demands, that woman had suddenly started fighting him. He remembered pulling away from the woman in confusion. He had never had the desire to take a woman by force, even one who willingly sold her body to strange men. He recalled how the woman had chided him when he had pulled from her embrace. She explained how she enjoyed offering resistance to her customers, and how it placed much more excitement into the act and how it drove the men into a passionate frenzy.

Cole grinned down at Jessica. Apparently she wanted to play the same sort of game. He would certainly oblige her. He knew her protests would soon turn into hollow, half-hearted objections, then she would turn into a wild, thrashing vixen. A knowing smile spread wide across Cole's face. He knew this was going to be the best yet.

Cole's hand entwined in Jessica's wild mass of coppery colored hair. He gently pulled her head backward in order to have a better approach to her red velvet lips. For a moment, his eyes locked with Jessica's. They were beautiful. They reminded him of the smoky haze which filtered up from an open fire. They flashed with a spark of anger as she tried to pull away from him.

"So, you want to play?" he chuckled, honestly believing the woman's spurt of resistance was part of her routine with customers. He pressed his weight against her, stilling her struggles for a moment. Then he took his forefinger and touched her mouth, sliding it along her moist lips, parting them. He could see her tongue, pink and wet, and imagined how it would feel answering his passionate kisses. His mouth followed the path his finger had taken, blazing down on hers, drawing, engulfing her, his tongue thrusting into her sweetness.

Jessica's protests were smothered by Cole's lips. She could feel the thick mat of hair on his chest bury into her breasts. She managed to free one of her arms. Pushing with all of her might, she shoved, but the big man would not budge. Instead, it seemed only to intensify his ultimate goal.

Cole's desire had already increased to its fullest height. His lips never left hers, and when his tongue plunged once again into the sweetness of her mouth, he yelped and pulled away just as he felt her teeth start to clamp down on his tongue.

"Don't bite, honey," he warned, "That's not part of the game. You play this part well, but we don't have any doubts as to who the winner will be, do we?" his eyes blazed a warning with their scorching probe.

Jessica pressed back against the pillow. She was scared. His thinly muttered threat was not to be taken lightly. She didn't know what he would do if she tried to bite him again.

She wrenched away from his grasp, but it only caused the man to hold her more tightly against him. His hands reached to clamp around her wrists as he slid them high above her head.

"Now, that's better," he said, accepting her sudden acquiescence with relief. His gaze drifted slowly down to the two mounds of firm flesh burning into his chest. His head lowered and his tongue plied first one nipple, then the other. He could feel his loins tremble with desire. His mouth opened to taste the entire area around each of her breasts, then it went back to her throat, nibbling, kissing and tasting.

Each place his lips touched, seemed to burn as if on fire. Jessica's eyes grew wide with each unexplained emotion that coursed through her. This man was raping her, and she was starting to enjoy it! Her body was betraying her. A fire was starting to glow between her thighs, and she couldn't explain it. Her body had turned against her, like a demon responding to its own devilish demands. Jessica could not understand what was happening to her, she only knew she was tingling with a newly budding sensation that was completely alien to her. No, not completely alien, for she knew she had felt the same feelings the night before. It was as though this man had unleashed a volcano which had been building deeply within her since she had become a woman.

A growling noise of satisfaction erupted from Cole, one that sounded as though he knew he had won the battle. He gave one last pull at her breast, the sound smacking of pleasure, before placing one knee between the woman's thighs. She was not quite yielding, but yet, her resistance was slight.

Jessica looked up at the man above her. Her lips were frozen, her mouth could not open to utter any protests. She realized this man was under the wrong impression of her. She sensed he was not the sort who would knowingly take a woman against her will. Her eyes made one last desperate plea for him to stop, but deep inside she was afraid he would hear her unspoken plea and not continue with his loving assault. Little did she know that nothing could have stopped Cole at that moment.

Cole placed his other knee between Jessica's thighs. His hardened shaft found her womanhood, and it plunged full length into the moist depths. He paused a moment before moving, savoring each tingling morsel of pleasure.

Jessica gasped deeply when Cole entered her. There was a brief moment of slight pain, but only from the size of him. Then she could feel her insides grasp at this masculinity as she accepted his invasion. She trembled with pleasure and moaned in ecstasy. Nothing was more important than the need to have him—all of him.

Jessica thrashed wildly against Cole as his mouth reclaimed hers, marking it with his searing brand. Her nails dug into his back as his mouth went to the now passion-gorged, pink tipped breasts. Her hands sought his tousled hair as she urged him onward. She wanted him as badly as he wanted her. Her hips thrust eagerly upward, and her legs locked around his buttocks. The pleasure was so supreme, she thought she would burst in two from the thrill of it.

Cole could feel the very essence of his soul being pulled from him by her churning loins. He had never known any greater pleasure. Each of his senses was affected. Then, when he finally felt the swelling release, he knew she was there with him. There was no need to delay the final act of pleasure.

A few minutes later, Cole slumped on the woman. She was now docile and mewing a contented sigh. He didn't want to leave her. Instead his movements were slow and deliberate, precise and sensual. When he realized what had happened, he blinked in surprise. His desire had not been sated. His desire was still as firm and hard as it had been in the beginning. His thrusts grew more forceful as the woman's smoky gray eyes flew open in surprise.

"Oh, no!" she moaned, "I can't, not again!"

"Hush, my sweet," Cole laughed. "I know if I am able, then you'll be able also."

"But . . . but . . ."

Cole's mouth closed over hers to end her protests. His hands explored each part of her body as he felt his maleness swell even larger with ardent desire. God! She was like a vixen who had crept into his blood and possessed him with her wily spell. His teeth found the softness of her breast, he nibbled at the tender flesh, but not painfully so, just enough to make her squirm with newly budding passion. Cole moved gently within her, soft strokes of passion, not the frenzied pace of just a few moments ago.

Jessica thought her loving torment would never end. This man whom she had dreamed of all of her life was plundering her body, using it as he may, and she was thoroughly enjoying every sensual, rapturous moment! Why was it that she was feeling no shame? She knew she had never felt such wild, delicious emotions. She desperately prayed for sanity never to return.

Much later, Cole lay beside the woman feeling a complete contentment he didn't know possible. The rapid pounding of his heart had eased considerably when he turned to the woman, "I'll say one thing, honey, you are certainly the best!"

Jessica's mind came crashing down from its plateau of lofty heights. "What . . . did you say?" she stammered.

"I said you were the best," he repeated.

"Oh, God!" she cried as her hands flew up to cover her head. "How did this happen?"

"What do you mean?" he asked, sudden concern filled his voice. Not that he was overly concerned for the woman, but he was puzzled. Then his brows dipped deeply into a frown when he saw a stain on the sheets. It was not a stain that he had ever seen before, but he had heard about it. Could this woman have been a virgin? Surely not! What would a virgin be doing at the Golden Slipper? But still, there was a certain question in his mind. It seemed as though he could remember a different feeling when he had first taken her last night.

Cole's thoughts were interrupted when a knock came at the door. It wasn't like Berny to disturb him when he was in a room with one of her girls. "What is it?" Cole shouted.

"Boss? It's me, Ed," a masculine voice called from outside the door. "Miss Timbers didn't want me to come up here, but I told her that it was really important."

"All right!" Cole sighed, "What is it?"

"Can I come in, or do you want me to stand out here and talk through this door?" Ed asked, sounding a little embarrassed and uncomfortable.

"Just a minute," Cole answered as he slipped on his pants and hurried to the door to let the man in.

Ed walked into the room and his eyes grew wide with wonder at the beauty of the woman who lay cowering under the sheet. He couldn't help but envy Cole for a brief moment. Then he tore his eyes away from the woman when he realized she had been crying.

"Well?" Cole demanded as he placed his hands on his narrow waist, "What is so important that I had to be disturbed?"

"We need you down at the ship." Ed swallowed hard then continued, "Captain Mahan's head count didn't tally with ours and he is refusing to let any of the women leave the ship until he gets more money. I counted the contracts and they are different from the head count."

"How many are they off?"

"Only one, but the captain claims there are two more women. He claims he brought a hundred and seventy-eight women, and he wasn't going to settle for passage for only a hundred and seventy-six. He just about threw a wall-eyed fit when I suggested that he go ahead and release the women to me and could settle the differences later. The fellow insists upon talking to you now!"

Cole swore under his breath. He knew something like this would happen. He had known all along that men could not bargain for wives like a piece of cheap merchandise. That was one of the reasons he had disapproved of this arrangement. "Damn it!" he swore aloud, "If any of us had any sense, we'd ship them all back to their homes in New York!"

Ed smiled thoughtfully, "Yeah, I guess so, but you know as well as I do, all those men would have your hide nailed to the highest tree before morning."

Jessica, who had pulled the sheet over her head to try and hide her shame, cringed at Ed's news. She realized she was one of the women they were talking about. What would she do? Dawning of realization had touched her mind and she concluded that Berny had lied to her. She must have drugged her in order to use her for immoral purposes. She would have to try and escape from that woman's evil clutches. But there was something that prevented her from being able to tell this man the truth. She wasn't sure she could face him and tell him what had really happened. True, he had been the one who had ravished her body. He had been the one who had taken her virginity. But after her wild abandon of response, would he believe she had been innocent?

Her attraction for him was so strong she couldn't bear for him to look at her with disgust. She couldn't bear to see any look other than love in his eyes. Even though he had taken her, used her for his own pleasures, she knew Cole was not to blame. She had been presented to him as a slut, and she had acted like one because of her responses to his lovemaking.

Jessica knew she had lost something precious. She would have proudly stood by the man's side for all of eternity, now that would never be. Her punishment would be fitting for the crime of her surrender. She had lost all that was dear to her. She realized in that brief moment of truth that no man would ever measure up to the one she had just encountered. For a moment, the knowledge of her loss was so great, she didn't think she could stand it. But then with a surge of determination, she knew she could not stay here. She could not bear to live the life of a tramp. She would have to escape Berny's house of ill-repute. As soon as Cole was gone, she would somehow find a way to escape.

Cole had hurried and dressed. As he walked toward the door, he stopped suddenly, took some coins from his pocket, and stepped back to the bed where the woman lay huddled beneath the sheet. He pulled the sheet back, kissed her on her cheek, and whispered, "I'll say it again, honey, you are best! If I can possibly make it, I'll be back!" He kissed her again then placed the money on her pillow. He stood, then in several easy strides, he crossed the room and closed the door quietly behind him.

Jessica lay trembling in fright and remorse. She waited until all sounds of his leaving had disappeared, then she quickly leaped from the bed and searched the room for something more substantial to wear than the filmy gown that was lying crumpled on the floor. Finding nothing else, she picked up the gown and slipped it over her head. Seeing the shining coins gleaming on the pillow, she picked them up, knowing she would have to have money to make good her escape. Clutching them tightly in her hands, she walked to the door and cautiously opened it.

The door was pushed open with a loud jolt. Berny was standing in the doorway, and behind her was a huge man with olive colored skin. Jessica's eyes flew first to Berny then to the man. A shudder of fear coursed through her. The man was leering at her, a greasy smile that revealed stained and yellowed teeth. Revulsion swept over her like wildfire. She was trapped!

"Going somewhere, honey?" Berny asked sweetly. Then her sly grin changed to a scowl as she backed Jessica into the room.

"Yes . . . I am. I am leaving. You . . . tricked me!" Jessica accused.

Berny swept saucily past Jessica and stared at the rumpled covers on the bed. "Maybe so, but from the looks of things, you really don't have any complaints coming." She whirled to face Jessica, "We can make a fortune!"

"Oh no! I have already said, I'm leaving and you're not going to stop me!" Jessica started for the door once again, but the huge man barred her way.

"Stop her, Manuel!" Berny ordered, but it was unnecessary, the Mexican had already grabbed Jessica by her wrists.

"Let me go! Let me go!"

"Shut your mouth!" Berny shouted as she rushed to close the door, hoping to prevent Jessica's screams from drifting through the house. "Manuel, keep her quiet," she muttered.

Manuel slapped a thick and dirty hand over Jessica's mouth and his other hand spun her around to hold her in a vice-like grip. She could feel his hot breath upon her neck. Her eyes grew wide with horror when she felt the huge man's hand close over her breast.

"Now, you keep your yap shut or I'll turn Manuel loose on you! Do you hear?" Berny grunted through clenched teeth.

Jessica didn't have to be warned twice. She could feel a hard bulge in the Mexican's trousers, as he pressed himself closer to her and made lewd motions with his hips. She twisted her head around and upward to look at him. He was grinning wickedly at her, and a few drops of saliva were in the corners of his mouth. A shudder went through her. This was the worst feeling she had ever experienced. She closed her eyes and prayed silently for God to let her die.

Berny sensed her dwindling rebellion. "You keep fighting and I'll let him have you!" she hissed. "Manuel, you stop that!" she ordered.

"Si, Senora," he said, disappointment washing over him.

Berny walked over to the chair and sat down. She crossed her legs, letting one foot swing easily. "Now, it's like this, I'm going to tell you one time and one time only how I run my operation. You be good to the customers and I'll be good to you. You can make more money here than you ever believed possible." Glancing at Manuel, she said, "Take your hand away from her mouth."

"But, I don't want to work here! How could you have done this to me? How could you? You tricked me! You never knew my father, it was simply a ruse to get me here! Why? Why?"

Berny shrugged her shoulders, "Young and pretty girls are hard to find. I needed another girl, and you were handy, besides that, I owed someone a favor."

"You owed someone a favor?" Jessica repeated.

"Yes, and I like to repay old debts."

"You mean someone set me up for this? But who? I have no enemies! Surely no one could hate me this much!" Jessica had forgotten about Rosie Rutledge.

Berny shrugged again, "Doesn't matter. You're here now, and I intend for you to stay here. I can't trust you not to try and escape, so I'll have to keep you confined to this room for a few days. But let me warn you now," she wagged a bony finger in Jessica's direction, "I don't have much patience, but I don't want your spirit entirely broken. You give me one ounce of trouble and I'll have men lined up in the hall for you."

"I'll kill myself first!" Jessica swore aloud, fully intending to carry out her threat.

Berny looked at her coldly. "Yes," she said finally, "I believe you would." She walked over to the bed, picked up a sheet and began tearing it into thin strips. "I'll fix it so you won't hurt yourself. I've found me a gold mine, honey, and I certainly don't intend to lose it before I strike paydirt." She motioned with her head and Manuel brought the now struggling young woman over to the bed and threw her on it. He held Jessica down while Berny bound her hands and feet to each bedpost. Then she stuffed a gag into her mouth. "Manuel, go downstairs and bring back that brown bottle and a spoon, I'll give her something to keep her calm." She figured to keep Jessica drugged for a few days and gradually break her in to the business. If she could only keep her sedated, she would have a chance at keeping the young woman captive.

Later, before the drug completely took effect, Jessica lay strapped to the bed, languishing in her misery. All hope for escape had vanished. Her life was over. She would never submit to the plans Berny had made. Her threat had not been idle. She would kill herself before allowing men to take her, to use her for their own pleasures. As the final wave of misty blackness washed over her, Jessica knew her only possible chance for escape rested on the shoulders of the handsome stranger.

Chapter Nine

Cole hurried through the lobby of the Golden Slipper with Ed following closely behind. The stiffness of Cole's back showed exactly how angry he was.

Right from the beginning, Cole had made it clear that he thought the men were making a big mistake by sending for city women. He claimed that they had lived by the streets and had been brought up in a completely different way of life. Many were criminals, many were street tarts, and only a few would be what they could consider decent women.

A wry smile touched Cole's lips when he thought about William Stockard, the captain of their mining company, how it was formed and why they had sent for so many mail order brides.

Cole Robertson and William Stockard went back a long way together. The older man had met Cole when he was just a kid, still wet behind the ears. He had taken the kid under his wing and taught him how to be a man. They rode for the Texas Rangers for a while, then drove a few head of cattle, then had headed out to California a few years after gold had been discovered.

They and over a hundred other men had camped along a creek bed high up in the mountains, panning for gold which showed a nice amount of color. But none of them had come close to the fortunes they were all seeking.

One night, William was sitting beside their campfire when suddenly, he stood, threw his plate into the fire, and shouted, "I'm tired of all of this! We're all damn fools for nearly starving to death!"

Several men sitting around different campfires chorused their agreement. William called them together, and the other men, curious as to what he had to say, gathered around.

"Men, we're all fools! There are over a hundred of us scattered up and down this creek bed within a couple of miles of each other. We're like a team of fine horses, but each of us are pulling in different directions. I'll bet none of you can recall the last time you had a decent meal, or a suit of clean clothes. We're all so dogged tired when we get back to our camps we can barely hold our heads up, much less attend to the chores that need doing around a camp."

"I agree," one of the men said, "But what can we do about it?"

"Plenty. That is, if you men are agreeable?"

The man glanced back at the other men in his group and they were nodding. "Go ahead," the man said, "Tell us what you've got in mind."

It was apparent that William had given the idea a lot of thought as he started telling the men his plans.

"All of us have been getting a lot of color lately," William started slowly. "One or some of us are bound to hit the mother lode before long. There's enough gold out there to make all of us rich men." He took a deep breath and continued, "How well do we want to live while we're doing all of this mining? There are some of us who really don't know that much about prospecting, and some don't know much about cooking, mending, or carpentering." He watched the men carefully to see their reaction. "I was thinking that we could form a mining company, and pool our resources. The better miners could work in the mines, men who are better cooks could stay at the camp and cook decent food, men who were carpenters before coming west could build some houses so we could have shelter for the winter. The men who have families could send for them."

"What about the money, though?" one man wanted to know.

"That's the simplest part yet, we just split it equally among us."

"But what if I'm one of the lucky ones who strike a big vein? Wouldn't that be sort of like cutting my own throat?"

William shrugged his shoulders, "Perhaps so, but on the other hand, what kind of guarantee do you have that *you* will be that fortunate? What if I hit it, or Cole, or maybe Ed Baker? What if your claim plays out? At least my way, we'd all stand a chance to make a decent living, and have a decent existence until someone does hit the mother lode."

By this time, many of the men had crowded around, listening to what William had to say. Most of them thought he was talking sense.

They talked among themselves for a few days then decided William Stockard had a good idea. They voted

William to be the captain of the camp, then voted a governing council. The former Texas Ranger was correct; the camp had to have some order, and everyone figured he was the man to do it.

Everything went well until a few of the men's wives started arriving from back east. Then the men who were without wives began showing their discontent. By this time, the camp's population had grown to over two hundred men, and nearly all of them were without women.

William placed advertisements in the New York newspapers and made arrangements with the *Sea Nymph* to transport the women to Cailfornia. His main concern had been that enough women would not sign up to come west. Everyone knew there would be trouble if some of the men ended up without a woman.

Cole could smell trouble as he and Ed made their way to the slip where the *Sea Nymph* was docked. They made their way over and around various crates of many sizes. Cole's furious mood made his footsteps quick and precise.

When they reached the *Sea Nymph,* Cole stood at the bottom of the gangplank and looked upward. The deck was teeming with a swarm of angry women. Apparently the captain's decision wasn't too popular with them.

"I would like permission to come aboard!" Cole shouted. Although he had never been to sea, he did know a few rules and procedures which had to be met before boarding.

The first mate had been watching for Cole. He shouted back that permission had been granted and that Cole and his man were welcome to aboard immediately.

Cole and Ed climbed the gangplank and when they reached the deck, they ignored the furious questions from the angry women as they were led to the captain's quarters.

Cole's eyes quickly took in the disorder of the room, and he could smell the odor of cheap rum. He wasted no time being polite. "I understand there is a problem about releasing the women!" Cole blurted angrily.

"You're damn right there is a problem!" the captain slurred. "Your man wasn't going to pay me enough money! I brought one hundred and seventy-eight women around the Horn. Our agreement was for their children, up to twenty-five, were to receive free passage. I brought fourteen young'uns with me, so there is no charge for them, but," he wagged a finger in Cole's face, "You are not going to rook me out of the passage for two women!"

Cole frowned. He was inclined to believe the captain. He felt if Mahan was trying to deliberately cheat them, he would have claimed more passengers than the two that were missing. "Are you sure you counted the contracts right?" he demanded.

"Mr. Robertson, I have been counting long before you were even born!" Captain Mahan said icily.

"Captain Mahan, I'm not doubting your word. You feel you are owed a certain amount, and I have to account to the men who sent me to collect the women. I'm sure you can understand my situation. If I spend passage money for a hundred and seventy eight women and only bring back a hundred and seventy-six, I'm in trouble. I'm sure if we discuss this problem sensibly, we can work it out to our satisfaction."

When he saw how reasonable Cole was acting, Captain Mahan calmed considerably. "I see I will be able to do business with you," he growled.

"You say you had a head count of one seventy-eight, do you have any idea what happened to the other two women?"

The captain shook his head, "I have been trying to think who is gone and for the life of me, I can't. I was waiting for you to get here before having the women line up. Perhaps if I can look at all of them, I can figure out who is missing."

Cole nodded in agreement to the captain's suggestion. "I believe that is the best solution. If you can find out who is missing, then maybe we'll be able to discover when they left the ship. I might add however, if they are the sort of women who would leave the ship, then perhaps we might not want them."

The captain's face turned red with anger. His jowls shook as he glowered at Cole. "Look, Robertson, I don't care what happens to the women once they leave my ship. I lived up to my part of the bargain when I brought them here. I tried to meet the requirements you set before I left New York. But if a few women slipped in that don't suit you, then that's too bad, because we were faced with a very difficult task!"

Cole's eyes turned to glassy shards, "Look, Captain Mahan, I wasn't suggesting that I was going to pick and chose the women, I was simply making a statement. However, since you appear to be touchy about the subject, I do intend upon checking the women closely to see just how much you've lived up to our agreement!" With those words, Cole spun on his heel and marched angrily out the door.

Captain Mahan sputtered his indignation a few

times, then thought it would be wise not to argue with the man. He had barely met their requirements with a few of the women, and it might be best to leave well enough alone.

Cole, Captain Mahan, Ed, and the captain's first mate, Thomas, walked the deck up and down the lines of women which had formed. At first the women had swarmed around the men asking questions about when they would be able to go ashore. The captain silenced them with a few words. He told them the sooner they quieted down, the sooner they would be able to leave.

The captain stepped up on the quarterdeck and spoke to the women in a loud, booming voice. "Ladies, this man is Cole Robertson. He is responsible for taking you to meet your new husbands. There has been a delay in your leaving the ship because a few of you are missing. Now, as soon as we have your cooperation and you decide to tell us who those persons are, the sooner you will all be able to leave." His voice droned on and on, "Now I will be the first to admit that the head count and the contracts don't tally." He counted off on his fingers, "I know I'm shy the one contract because of that little red-headed gal . . ." his words hung in mid air as his eyes quickly scanned the lines. The red-headed woman was missing!

He hurried down from the quarterdeck and rushed to where Helen was standing. "Where is that little red-headed gal you claimed was your sister?"

Helen's eyes widened and her face blanched with fear. She didn't know what to say or to do. Pulling Aaron closer into her grasp, she finally admitted in a small voice, "I'm not sure, sir."

Captain Mahan pointed a dirty finger at Helen. "You! You come with me!" He spun on his heel and motioned with his head for Cole to follow.

When the trio reached the cabin, the captain held the door open for the woman, then slammed the door behind her.

"Now, what do you mean, you're not sure where she is? She's your sister, isn't she?"

Helen stared at the floor. She could feel blood pound through her head, and a loud ringing sound blasted through her ears. She had never been this frightened. Her only hope was that Jessica had indeed found her father and was safely away.

"Perhaps you don't hear too well, dearie. I asked where the girl was!" the captain asked coldly.

Helen raised her eyes up to meet his hateful glare. "I can honestly say that I do not know."

The captain hit his desk with a doubled fist. He struck it so hard a glass fell over on its side and rolled, crashing to the floor. "I'm tired of this nonsense!" the captain shouted angrily. "That girl is no more your sister than I am. I deliberately let it slide when you told me the lie because I didn't think there would be any problems. But now, since she has jumped ship, I suggest you tell us what you know about her and tell us right now!" he demanded forcefully.

Helen's lips set into a thin white line. When she spoke, her voice was cool and precise. "I have nothing to say. I don't know where she is, and besides, I refuse to betray my friend."

Cole started to say something, but the captain hushed him. "I know how to handle matters like this better than you do." The captain looked back at Helen, he cleared his throat and began talking once again. "You have a little boy, don't you?"

Helen looked up at the captain in surprise. A glimmer of fear showed in her eyes. "Yes," she admitted slowly. It had startled her that the captain's memory was so good, especially when he had spent so much of his time swilling cheap liquor in his cabin during the voyage.

Captain Mahan strutted around his cabin, his hands were placed arrogantly on his hips. "I'm through messing with you. You can tell us what we need to know or be prepared to pay the price."

A clammy hand of fear gripped her heart. "And what price is that, sir?" she asked quickly.

Captain Mahan let a cold and deliberate smile touch his lips. "I'm tired of you women playing me for a fool. Since you have refused to answer my questions, you have cost me a handsome amount of money. Are you prepared to pay that red-headed gal's passage?" he asked suddenly, slamming his hand down on the desk.

"Why . . . I . . . don't have that much!" Helen stuttered.

"And I don't intend to lose the price of a woman's passage!" the captain thundered.

Again, Cole started to speak but Captain Mahan silenced him with a wave of his hands. "Mr. Robertson, I really don't think you should interfere. After all, it was by your orders that the contracts and head count be tallied correctly. I intend to get every cent that I have coming to me!" He turned back to the woman and shouted, "You will either tell me where this woman is, or else you will pay for her passage!"

Cole did not agree with the captain's threatening tactics, but by observing the expression on the woman's face, he knew Mahan was succeeding in his roughshod way of obtaining the information from her. He felt that the captain was making empty threats, but the woman did not realize this.

"I have already told you that I do not have the money to pay her passage!" the woman said fiercely.

"Then I have no other choice than to place a debtors bond on you. You will have to work for me until the debt is paid!"

"And how do you intend for me to do that?"

"I have a roomful of witnesses that would swear under oath how you claimed that woman was your sister. We may be in California, but they still have laws even in this barbaric place."

Helen's voice grew wild with frantic hysteria, "Please answer me, how do you intend to make me pay the passage?"

"That is the easiest part of all!" the captain smirked. "You will have to stay aboard my ship and work for me. I'm sure the cook could use some help, then . . . there is always plenty of laundry to do. I figure," the captain squinted his eyes and added thoughtfully, "that three or four trips around the Horn will be sufficient."

"You mean you would force me to stay aboard!" Helen gasped. All sorts of thoughts flashed through her mind. Terrible things could happen to her. She and her son would be entirely at the mercy of Captain Mahan and his crew.

The captain shrugged helplessly, "You leave me no other choice."

Helen knew she had been beaten. As much as she cherished Jessica's friendship, she could not disregard the health and safety of her son. Just the thought of his pale and colorless face brought sudden tears to her eyes. She would have to tell all she knew about Jessica's mysterious disappearance.

She began in a quiet voice, "All right, I'll tell you what I know, but it isn't much!" she added.

"How about letting us be the judge of that," the captain hastened to say. The smile which suddenly appeared on his face showed his immense joy at having won.

"First of all, Jessica isn't my sister . . ."

At the mention of the name, Jessica, a cold, prickly feeling went over Cole.

"I didn't know her before we met on board ship. She and I began talking when we first left New York, and we struck up a friendship almost instantly." Helen stared at the floor, "To my knowledge, she was running away from a maiden aunt. She claimed her father is out here in California somewhere." Helen buried her head into her hands. Ragged sobs tore at her breath. "You're making me betray her!"

Cole stepped forward and patted the woman's shoulder. He had never been able to stand to see a woman cry. "There, there, it's all right," he soothed. "If she's out there alone in this city, then perhaps you will be doing her an act of kindness." Cole had no way of knowing how true his words actually were.

Helen turned her tearful eyes up at Cole. "I don't know where she is! You have to believe me! She and a mutual friend left the ship to see if they could find some word of her father . . ."

"See there! See there!" the captain exclaimed happily. "I told you there were two women missing, and she's proved it!"

"No, you have it wrong. June came back, but she was alone. She claimed that Jessica had found her father, or at least had word about him."

"And who is this other woman?" the captain demanded.

"No, I won't tell you!" Helen crossed her arms stubbornly. "You'll try to punish her the same way you've done me."

"I haven't done anything to you yet!" the captain glowered at Helen.

"Look, Ma'am," Cole interrupted. This entire scene had gone far enough. "No one is going to hurt you or your friends. I think I should introduce myself properly." He thrust out his hand and clasped Helen's in a handshake. "My name is Cole Robertson. I was sent to collect you brides for the men at the camp. You see, Ma'am," he continued, "Those men work very hard for their money, and they have shown how much they trust me to bring all of you back for them. I have their money. I will have to answer to them for each dollar I spend to get you all back to camp. If I come back with a few of you women missing, then I am going to have some tall explaining to do." He rubbed his hand over the stubble on his face, then smiled, showing a row of even, white teeth. His smile was brilliant and dazzling. Cole Robertson definitely knew how to turn on his masculine charm. "I promise you again, no harm will come to you or to your friends." His eyes meet hers, and then Cole knew she would do as he had requested.

"I . . . believe you, Mr. Robertson."

"Please, call me Cole."

"All right, Cole."

"Will you tell us the name of this other woman?"

"Her name is . . . June Smith."

Cole nodded his thanks. He walked over to the door

and opened it. "Ed?" he asked. "Will you please ask a Miss June Smith to come to the captain's quarters?"

"Sure, boss," Ed was quick to say.

In a few moments, June walked into the small quarters. She looked first at Helen, taking in her tearstained face, then her eyes flew to the captain, then to Cole. "What's going on in here? Don't you men have anything better to do than to bully a defenseless woman?" She hurried to where Helen was standing.

"Now, see here . . ." the captain began angrily.

Cole threw his hands up into the air. "Just a minute, Captain Mahan! Let me handle this. You've done nothing but antagonize these women. Miss Smith, could you tell me where you left a woman by the name of Jessica . . .?" he looked questioningly at Helen.

"Tate," she finished the name for him. "Why do you want to know?" June asked haughtily.

Cole quickly told June the reason why all the women had to be accounted for. He told her about the captain's threats to Helen and why they needed to know Jessica's whereabouts. He finished by adding that the young woman might not be safe alone in the city.

June frowned, took a deep breath, then said hesitantly, "You know, I have been worrying about her."

"Tell me, did she find her father?" Cole wanted to know. If the woman was safely with her family, there was no need to force her to abide by a contract she had never signed.

"Well . . . that's what is strange and it also bothers me. Somehow, it was just too convenient . . . too pat."

"Please explain, Miss Smith." Cole had the strangest feeling she was going to tell him something he didn't want to hear.

A doubtful, worried expression crossed June's face as she began, "Well, Jessica and I left the ship yesterday, stopped and inquired at a few places without any results. Then, when we were coming out of a mercantile store, suddenly out of nowhere, a strange woman appeared claiming Jessica looked familiar to her. We started talking and before we knew it, this woman said she knew Jessica's father. We went to this woman's place," June ducked her eyes nervously and added, "It was a place where . . . where ladies shouldn't go."

"Exactly where?" Cole interrupted.

"It was a . . . bawdy house."

"No, I knew what you meant, what was the name of the place?" Cole was very eager to hear her answer. He hoped desperately that it wasn't the Slipper.

"I'm. . .not sure, Golden something."

A sinking feeling settled over Cole. He had known what her answer would be.

"To go on with my story," June continued, "The woman convinced Jessica that her father would be there within a few days or a few weeks. Jessica decided to stay and wait for him. I was invited to stay too, but I really didn't feel right. And I really didn't feel right about leaving Jessica there, but I don't think I could have changed her mind." June stared down at the floor then she suddenly blurted, "Do you think she's in some kind of trouble?"

"I don't know, Miss Smith." Cole answered honestly. He toed the floor with his boot. He had answered her question truthfully. Jessica was not in trouble if she had stayed willingly. But if she had been tricked into staying at the Golden Slipper, she could be in dire straits indeed.

The stained sheet, the half hearted protests and reluctance came flooding back. If the woman had been duped into staying there, why had she responded so freely to his lovemaking? Cole knew he ought to question these women further about this Jessica Tate's character.

"Miss Smith, I want to ask you something and I want you to be very honest with me."

"I *have* been honest with you, sir!"

"I know you have," Cole soothed the woman's injured feelings. "What I meant . . . well, listen to my question and you'll know what I meant. Would Jessica be the type of woman who . . . would willingly go to work at a bawdy house?"

Helen exploded in anger, "Never! Jessica is a very innocent young woman! She's only eighteen years old. She has lived a very sheltered life, first with her parents then with a maiden aunt after her mother died." Helen's face had blanched with fear. "Mr. Robertson, do you believe Jessica is being held at this place against her will?"

"I don't know."

June eyed him suspiciously, "You seem to have a lot of questions. Why did you ask them?"

Cole looked to first one woman and then the other. He admitted truthfully, "I believe I have seen her."

Helen's hands clutched at the corner of the captain's desk. "Mr. Robertson, I ask you again, do you think Jessica is being held there against her will?"

Cole shrugged his shoulders, "As I said, I don't know."

Helen grabbed at Cole's shoulders. "Jessica is not the type of person to be there! You have to save her! You have to get her out of that place!"

Cole's mind raced over the events of the previous night. There was a good chance these woman were right. He knew Berny Timbers very well. There wasn't anything she wouldn't stoop to if she thought there was a profit in it. He recalled how soft and tender Jessica had felt when she had snuggled closely to him. He remembered thinking how differently she had felt when he made love to her for the first time, how she had thrashed wildly against him. Had it been a response caused by pain or by passion? Cole wished he had not been so drunk. Then he certainly would have known. Another thought flashed through Cole, one that caused a sick feeling in the pit of his stomach. It was a feeling he could not understand or explain. Jessica was at the Golden Slipper. It was a place where women sold their bodies to men. A sordid picture formed in Cole's mind—a picture of Jessica in another man's arms! He had only had a brief but sensuous encounter with this woman, but he knew at that moment he could not bear the thought of her in another man's arms. The memory of Jessica's silken body pressed close to him in a passionate embrace was more than Cole could bear.

"Captain Mahan," Cole said abruptly, "Release these women."

"You mean, these two?"

"No, all of them."

"But what about . . ."

"I'll pay the passage fee you ask."

"But . . . what . . . about . . ."

"Never mind that!" Cole snapped with an impatient wave of his hand. "I said I would pay what you have asked." Cole went to the door and called to Ed. When the man came into the cabin, Cole requested that he remove the money belt strapped to his waist. While they were counting the money out to the captain, Cole told Helen and June to go tell the other women to get ready to leave the ship, that they would be ready within the hour.

Later, as the women were filing off the ship, Helen and June approached Cole. They wanted to know what he intended to do about Jessica.

"We have set up camp on the outskirts of town. I plan to get you women settled there, then, later this afternoon, I will go the Golden Slipper and see what I can find out. If this woman is being held prisoner there, I'll wait until dark, then rescue her." With those words, Cole whirled around and stalked off, leaving Helen and June staring after him in open mouthed wonder.

The vivid picture of Jessica stood boldly in Cole's mind; her crimson red lips, her smoky gray eyes, her tousled coppery hair, and the feel of her silken embrace as she pressed closely to him in the moment of passion. He hurried across the deck and down the gangplank, urging the women to hasten their steps. He had to rescue Jessica. He had to get her out of that place before it was too late.

Chapter Ten

The long procession of women walking through the streets brought many different reactions from the men lining the storefronts. Everyone had been aware that a ship of brides had been expected, but no one was prepared for the sight of so much femininity as the women walked proudly through the streets. Some of the women stared back with open grins playing at their lips, but most of the women had put aside the previous bravado they had shown aboard the *Sea Nymph*. Most were frightened, and even the more blusterous acting women were a little awed and yes, even proud of the respect that was suddenly shown them.

Many of the men were curious, but all who did not have a wife or a woman were envious. They had been in the wilds for many years, living the life of celibacy, living their lives without the soft durable strength of a woman's comfort. It was not the thought or idea of a sexual partner; instead, it was the memory of being a small boy and feeling the soothing touch of a mother's hand against a feverish brow. The memory of the delicious smell of fresh bread coming from the oven, the memory of a helpmate, and also the memory of a togetherness, a bonding relationship that had been prevalent since the beginning of time.

A few rowdies gave cat-calls and hoots of delight as they shouted indelicate obscenities, but they were soon silenced under the baleful stares of the other men.

The men were delighted with the sight of the children. In many instances, it had been years since they had seen the innocent scamperings of children. It was an almost reverent feeling of expectation which settled over the men as the line of women passed.

Cole had bought five wagons to carry supplies back to their thriving little town. It would take at least two weeks of constant travel to reach their final destination. The terrain was rough and difficult to cross, it would be hard on the women and children, but something worthwhile never seemed to be easy.

After the women were settled in at their small camp, Cole mounted his horse and made his way back into town, toward the Golden Slipper. Time was of the essence to him. His first impulse had been to barge into the saloon and take her. But common sense told him that would be inviting disaster.

Cole stood across the street from the Golden Slipper, studying it while pondering his next move. He had frequented the place enough to know Berny had several henchmen guarding it, to discourage men who had caused trouble in the past, and to discourage trouble from happening in the future. He decided against entering the building from the front. He walked up the street and slipped into a narrow alley, then he circled around to the back. When he entered the kitchen, a pang of guilt stabbed at his conscience when he recalled a beautiful red headed woman sitting at the table the previous day.

A fat Mexican woman was standing over a stove stirring food in a huge black pot. She turned around and smiled at him when he entered. "Senor Cole! Back so soon?"

"Hello, Maria," Cole answered in fluent Spanish. Pulling a coin from his pocket, he asked her to go to the front and buy him a bottle of whiskey, which she eagerly complied.

After she returned with the bottle, Cole opened it and took a long pull. He needed all of his awareness about him, but for the plan he had in mind, it was necessary that he smell of whiskey. Flashing a brilliant smile of thanks, Cole then asked where Berny was.

"She is in her room, Senor. She had a very busy night last night. She also left strict orders not to be disturbed."

"Aww . . . she won't mind if I go up. You know that," he said casually.

Maria frowned slightly, then nodded. This hombre was different from other men. She knew he had spoken the truth; Miss Timbers would not mind at all.

Cole took the steps two at a time until he had reached the top of the stairs, then he stopped and peered around the corner to see if anyone was in the hall. His eyes widened when he saw Manuel sitting in a chair outside the room which he had shared with Jessica the previous night. Manuel had a rifle lying across his lap.

Cole jerked backward, avoiding Manuel's sudden upward glance. Kneeling down, Cole poured part of the liquor out of the bottle, then splashed a little on his clothes before stepping out onto the floor.

Lurching down the hall, staggering and stumbling, Cole began humming a bawdy tune in his off key voice. When he reached Manuel, he swayed slightly and asked in a slurred voice, "Where is Jessica? I wanna see her again!"

A look of disgust flashed across Manuel's face. "She can't see you now, gringo. There are plenty of other whores, go to one of them."

Cole fawned at Manuel's shoulder, patting it drunkenly. "But I wanna see her! I liked her!"

Manuel shrugged his indifference., "I say she is busy, go on, gringo."

Cole thrust the bottle forward, "Wanna drink?"

Manuel swung his arms around, bringing the rifle level to Cole's stomach. "I said, move on gringo!" he spat. "There are other whores for you to visit. Senorita Timbers is saving this one for special men!"

Rage boiled in Cole, but he simply raised his brows and backed away. This man had been the first to pull a gun on him without suffering the consequences. "All right!" he said, mustering as much indignation he figured a drunk ought to show. "Why didn't cha just say so." He turned around and staggered off, muttering under his breath, hoping Manuel believed his act of drunkenness.

Staggering back down the hallway, Cole stumbled through the door he knew belonged to Berny. She was asleep on the bed, but when the door opened, she awakened instantly.

"Cole! What on earth are you doing here?"

Cole lurched sideways and waved his near empty bottle high above his head. "I wanna have a party. I wanna go see that little gal I was with last night, but

Manuel wouldn't let me."

Berny gave a sigh of exasperation, "Oh Cole! You mean you woke me up out of a sound sleep to complain?"

"Nope," he grinned stupidly, "I just wanted to visit that little gal again."

Berny looked at him for a moment, her eyes cool and calculating, but when she spoke, her voice was light and cheerful, "She has a headache; I guess you were too much for her Cole."

Cole giggled again. He decided to play his part to the hilt. "Pshaw! Her head shouldn't be the part that's hurting." Staggering closer to Berny, he said, "I want Jessica, where is she?"

"Honey, why do you want that hussy for? I'm here and just as available."

Cole curled his lip. This was too good a shot to pass up. "Afraid you won't do, Berny . . . not after her. And you had better be careful of her, she'll have all of your customers."

Berny laughed but it was strained. "Now, Cole, that isn't nice."

Cole squinted one of his eyes. " How long has she been here? How come I haven't seen her before?"

"Jessica is new, honey," Berny said as she took his arm and started walking him toward the door. "You have to go now, Cole. Go somewhere and sleep it off."

"But . . . but, I wanna stay and see Jessica."

"Do I have to call one of my men?" she threatened.

"No," he answered sheepishly.

"Then go!"

Cole staggered toward the door. "All right." He weaved as he opened the door. "I can tell when I am not wanted." He placed a wet kiss on Berny's cheek, "Bye, pretty lady." Then he turned and staggered back through the door, picking up the bawdy song where he had left off.

When he reached the bottom stairs, he passed by Maria without uttering a word. Haste was of the utmost importance. He now knew that Jessica was being held against her will. He had known Jessica was still there because Manuel stood guard outside her door. Even that in itself wasn't too unusual. Many of those kind of women received threats at one time or another, but that combined with the fact that Berny turned down a chance to make a handsome sum of money left no doubt in Cole's mind that something shady was going on.

Waiting until he was out of view of the building, Cole stopped to examine the upper story. Being careful not to be seen, Cole strode back toward the house and quickly scaled a gutterpipe which ran down from the roof. He cautiously made his way around the sloping roof, ducking underneath each window until he came to the room he figured Jessica was in. Peering inside, Cole felt a rush of anger surge through him. Although the light was quickly fading, he could make out a form on the bed. It was Jessica, and she was tied to the bedposts!

Sliding the window up, and climbing inside, Cole was careful to be very quiet. He walked over to the bed and stared down at the woman. Her cheeks were tearstained and her eyes appeared to be swollen. A quick glance told him that her bonds had cut deeply into her wrists. Cole angrily pulled a knife from its sheath and cut the strips of cloth which kept her prisoner. He was cutting the bonds that were holding her feet secure when he heard her moan.

Jessica had been slipping in and out of unconsciousness for an hour now. The drug had slowly started to wear off. She sensed a presence in the room before she ever felt the release of her bonds. Sheer terror raced through her veins. She was scared that Manuel and Berny had come for her. Jessica tried to open her eyes but they would not obey her command. A scream welled deep in her throat, but the gag in her mouth prevented her from uttering a word except a slight moan. Then she heard a gentle voice, a soothing voice, as someone leaned over her to remove the gag.

"Hush, don't make a sound," the soothing voice cautioned. "Manuel is standing guard outside the door."

It was Cole! She had been saved! Her only hope had been that he would return and he did. Jessica could feel the tears of relief slide down her cheeks.

"Oh, Cole," she whispered groggily. "I prayed that you would return for me."

"Shhh, don't talk, he will hear you. I had to wait until dark before I could attempt to rescue you." Cole leaned close to her ear so she would be able to hear him better without whispering too loudly. "I don't know how badly you've been hurt, but please, don't utter a sound." Cole wasn't afraid for himself, but if Manuel heard them, he might enter the room and start shooting. He had been taking care of himself for a long time now, he wasn't afraid of a gunfight, but Jessica could get hit by a stray bullet. "I'm going to have to lift you over my shoulder in order to climb down the roof. I'm not going to hurt you," he reassured her.

Jessica nodded and bit her lip. She was aware of enough of the situation to know she must do as Cole had asked.

Cole easily scooped her into his arms. Her weight was so slight, it wasn't difficult. He carried her to the window and climbed out onto the ledge, then he hefted her over his shoulder. He knew this part would be difficult. He had to balance her perfectly in order to climb down the drainpipe. For the first time, Cole cursed his Texas boots with their heels. He wished for the moccasins that many of the mountain men wore.

Edging along the roof, Cole slipped once, but quickly regained his balance. When he reached the drainpipe, he cautioned Jessica to hold tightly. They slide down the pipe fairly easily. The pipe strained under their weight, but surprisingly, it held them.

When Cole touched the ground, he shifted Jessica back into his arms and started running. He reached his horse, climbed on, then hurried out of town toward their camp.

Jessica's arms had curled tightly around Cole's neck. For the first time in what seemed an eternity, she felt safe and secure. The night air did wonders at clearing her drugged mind. Her emotions were in turmoil. Her life had changed so drastically in the short time she had been in San Francisco. No, that wasn't exactly true. Her life had been changed when her mother had died. It seemed as though her fate had been placed on a pre-destined course and nothing could stop the direction in which it was headed.

How much would this man affect her future? She knew she had been drugged or she would have never responded to his embraces the way she had done. But still, she knew she would have never responded if he had been someone else. The man who taken her virginity, the man who then rescued her from a life of horror, was indeed the same man who had filled her dreams since she had become a woman. How could she be in love with a dream? It was a question she could not answer. It was a certain feeling, call it intuition, call it fate, call it wishful, but it was a fact, a fact she could not ignore. She felt drawn to this man. She knew if given a chance, she would love him with all of her heart and soul. Surely he had some feelings about her or he wouldn't have risked his life to rescue her. Why hadn't he spoken to her. Not one word had been said since they had left that horrible place. She had felt his arms tighten around her periodically, but other than that, no personal contact had been made.

What did this man think of her? Did he think she was a tramp because of where he found her? Why had he rescued her? Could it have been he was so enamored over her charms? Surely not! But something was behind his actions and she was going to find out what they were.

"Stop, please stop!" she cried.

Cole quickly reined his mount to a halt. "What's the matter? Are you sick?"

Jessica lifted her gaze to meet his. "How did you know?" she asked, their faces almost touching.

"How did I know what?" Cole growled. He suddenly felt very uncomfortable.

"How did you know that I needed to be rescued?"

Cole sighed. He realized Jessica was confused. It would be better if he explained what he knew about the situation now than to wait until they reached the camp. "Do you think you can stand?"

"Yes, I think so," Jessica answered, suddenly shivering in the cool night air.

Cole released his hold on her, thus allowing her to

slide from his grasp. He threw one of his long legs over the back of the saddle then swung down to stand on the ground beside Jessica. Seeing she was shivering in the flimsy gown, he removed the blanket from his bedroll, wrapped it around her shoulders, then led her to a huge flat rock and urged her to sit down.

Jessica's eyes were wide with bewilderment. Her gaze never left Cole's face as she said, "I feel as though I have been caught in some terrible nightmare. I still don't know if I have waked up yet or not. Can you tell me why you came after me?"

Cole squatted on his haunches in front of her. She was a pitiful sight. Her long hair was tangled and tousled, her cheeks had tearstains on them, her eyes were red-rimmed and swollen, and her face was full of many unasked questions. He sighed deeply, "I can certainly understand why you are so confused. You see, my full name is Cole Robertson. I have been in San Francisco for several weeks waiting for you."

"Waiting for me?"

"Waiting for the *Sea Nymph*. I was sent to bring the brides back to Utopia."

"Utopia?" Jessica mouthed again. This was becoming more confusing,

Cole sighed deeply, "Yes, Utopia. The place where you women are supposed to go, the place where your husbands are waiting for you."

"Oh!" Jessica said quietly.

Cole fished in his shirt pocket for a cheroot, but never slowed his explanation as he lit it. "This morning when I left . . . er . . . was called away from your room . . ."

"I can explain that."

"Never mind!" Cole snapped with an impatient wave

of his hand. "You asked for an explanation, and if you will quit interrupting, I will try to finish."

"I'm sorry."

Cole seemed not to pay attention to her apology as he continued, "I was needed at the ship. It seems that the head count didn't tally with the contracts and the captain was wanting more passage money that he had women. We discussed the problem and apparently you made quite an impression on him, because he recognized the fact that you were one of the women who were missing." Cole didn't mention the fact that in his opinion she would have left a lasting impression on anyone. "We questioned two women . . ."

"June and Helen?" Jessica interrupted again.

"Yes, and the longer they talked, the more certain I was that *you* were the woman in question." He glanced up sharply at Jessica. "To be honest, I was hesitant at first. I really didn't know if you were at the Golden Slipper by choice or not. They kept telling me how innocent you were, but I kept recalling how eagerly you came into my arms."

Jessica's face blazed as she too, remembered their lovemaking. "I can explain that," she stammered.

"You don't owe me any explanations, lady!" Cole hissed, condemnation filling his voice. Anyone could claim innocence, but he knew better.

"But . . . but . . . I do. I was tricked!"

Angrily, Cole grabbed Jessica by her shoulders. "Look, *you* asked for an explanation, not me! If you will keep your mouth shut, I'll try to finish!" Cole could not explain his anger at her. He only knew he felt the burning need to lash out at her, to hurt her as badly as he had been hurt. When that thought crossed Cole's mind, he blinked in surprise. Why was he hurt? Was he mixin his hatred between Melissa and Jessica? Was his pas love overshadowing his future? He would have to shov her she meant absolutely nothing to him, that she was woman who had accidently entered into his life. "T continue," Cole said abruptly, "Helen and June man aged to convince me that you could possibly be i trouble. When I investigated, I discovered they ha been right. So . . . here we are." he added indifferently.

"You . . . mean . . . I . . . thought you rescued m because you cared," Jessica said sheepishly.

"Humph! That's right I do care!"

Jessica's eyes flew to Cole's, but the elated feelin lasted only a brief second when she saw how cold his eye were.

"The men at Utopia put a lot of trust in me. I wasn' about to disappoint them. So what if one of them gets soiled dove? I warned them right from the very begin ning that they would be getting the wrong class o women, but no one would listen to me. So if one of th men gets tarnished goods, I suppose deep down inside that's what he knew he would be getting."

"So you only rescued me because one of the mer would have had to go without a bride?" Jessica's questio was more or less a statement of fact.

"Yes."

Anger raged through Jessica over Cole's pious atti tude. He was not going to listen to reason. He though she was a tramp because she had responded to him. I would do no good to tell him that she had been drugged. He was too set in his opinion of her. At that momen though, she felt a searing loss. She knew Cole was the man for her, and her life would be incomplete withou him by her side. After his anger had subsided, perhaps then he would listen to reason, but to argue further would only serve to heighten his animosity.

Jessica stared at Cole for a long moment. Even though the darkness prevented her from seeing his eyes, she knew they were icy shards, blazing with cold and calculating anger. She could feel them piercing into her soul. Clutching the blanket tightly around her shoulders and mustering as much dignity as possible, she said, "I am sorry you feel that you have to play God and cast your judgment on me. You have tried and convicted me without so much as a word in my defense." She raised her head arrogantly, "I believe you said you were taking me to the camp. I would like to go there now, I'm sure Helen and June will be worried about me."

Cole stared at her for a moment longer, then he whirled around and strode over to his horse. He mounted it, then wordlessly extended a hand to Jessica.

Chapter Eleven

Several fires dotted the area around the camp. Some of the more industrious women had raked leaves and spread their blankets upon them for more comfortable sleeping arrangements, while others had merely spread their blankets on the bare ground.

Freshly washed laundry hung on wires that had been tautly stretched between trees, and the aroma of a hearty stew wafted deliciously through the night air. Women were sitting around the fires, some were staring silently into the smoking brightness, but all appeared to be listening to Ed and the other wagon drivers as they talked about their life in Utopia.

When Cole and Jessica came riding into camp, Ed leaped to his feet. He was holding Helen's little boy, Aaron in his arms, and the child had fallen asleep. He was careful not to awaken to boy as he gently handed him to his mother.

"Boss! Glad to see you made it back all right!" He reached a hand upward to help the woman from the front of the saddle. His brows shot up in surprise when he saw she was the same woman he had seen Cole with at the Slipper. His mouth formed a silent exclamation of surprise as he looked first at Cole then Jessica.

Everything happened quickly. Helen gave Aaron to a lady to hold, and she and June rushed forward to Jessica. Each noticed her scanty gown, but neither of them said a word about it. They began to bombard her with seemingly hundreds of questions.

Ed watched silently as Cole led his horse over to a place which had been cordoned off for the animals. His bushy Irish brows shot up with interest. He realized his friend was angry by the stiff way he carried himself. He also knew the red-headed gal had something to do with it.

"Boss, you all right?"

"Sure," Cole replied with a forced cheerfulness. "Just taking care of my horse." He glanced back at Ed and noticed a slight frown between his eyes. "I said that I'm all right!" he said, pronouncing each word distinctly so Ed would not misunderstand him.

Ed ignored Cole's pointed words. "Do you want me to unsaddle him for you?"

"No, I just want to give him some grain. I plan on going back into town a little while."

Ed didn't hedge any longer. "Cole, isn't that the same woman . . ." He stopped when he saw the fiery expression on his friend's face.

"I don't want to talk about it, Ed." he snapped, as he turned and strode back toward the camp. When he came into view of the women, he was swamped with questions. Finally, he waved them away and stood up on a wooden keg. "All right, ladies, if you will all calm down, I'll answer your questions."

"How come our husbands didn't come to meet us?"

"Where is Utopia?"

"Is there any danger of being attacked by Indians?"

"Wait a minute!" Cole threw his hands up in the air. "I will *not* answer any questions, but I will tell you something about your new home." Cole smiled ruefully at the women and their silliness, but after giving it a moment's thought, he came to the conclusion that if the position was reversed, he might be just as inquisitive. He smiled again, "Ladies, if I answered each one of your questions, we'd be here forever." He raised a finger to make a point, "But no, there is no danger of an Indian attack." This remark brought a titter of laughter from the women. "You want to know about Utopia, all right, I'll tell you." Cole took a deep breath. Utopia California, is a culmination of a man's dream. That man being Captain William J. Stockard. It was he, and he alone who had faith that a town could be built and civilization established when civil men were barely present." Cole explained to the women how the mining company was formed, and how Utopia was born. The respect, admiration, and even the love Cole felt for William Stockard was evident in his voice.

Cole accepted a cup of steaming hot coffee that was thrust into his hand. He continued after taking a sip of the scalding liquid, "Many of you are wondering about your future husbands. William said to tell you that there would not be an automatic pairing off. He said that you should all be given time for nature to take its course, that love would find its right path." Cole finished his coffee, placed the cup on the tailgate of a wagon. He was careful not to let his eyes drift in Jessica's direction. "I know that most of you are curious as to where we are heading. Utopia is located in a small valley, in the foothills of the Sierra Nevada Mountains, near the Stanislaus River. It's a magnificent country. Trees, flowers, and wildlife are abundant. But don't let the beauty deceive you, it's also a dangerous country. You do have to be on the look out for grizzlies and other wild game. The soil is rich," he explained, "Rich enough for us to plant fields and fields of food for the coming winter." Cole's voice had grown almost reverent while he described the beauty. "But, like any paradise, there can also be devils. During the winter, a man can almost go mad from loneliness."

Even though the women had been told Cole would not answer questions, a woman hesitantly spoke, "Mr. Robertson? I know you don't have time to answer all of our questions, but I think I have one that needs to be asked."

"Yes, Ma'am, go ahead."

"We have all heard of the loneliness that sets in when a person is confined during the perils of winter. We've even heard how some people have suffered starvation, and how some have even reverted to cannibalism. If this country is so harsh in the winter, then why don't you move into the lower valleys until spring?"

Cole looked at the woman, a smile playing at his lips. "The answer is quite simple, Ma'am. It is something called *gold fever.* It will do strange things to a man. It can drive an honest man to be a thief, or the reverse can apply too. Basically, if the mining claim was abandoned through the winter, there would be some hearty soul who would brazen the frigid temperature and file on our claims. As you can imagine, that would lead to very serious consequences." Looking around him, Cole added, "I believe we are all tired and need some rest. I think it's about time we turned in and try to get some sleep. We will be leaving by first light of morning." He stepped off the keg and made his way back to where the horses were cordoned.

Many curious glances were cast in Jessica's direction, but no one approached her with any questions. They seemed to sense she did not want to answer them.

Later, when the camp was quiet, Jessica, Helen, and June sat in front of the now dying fire and talked quietly. She told them how she had been drugged and of Berny's apparent intentions of keeping her prisoner and forcing her to work in that horrible place. She did not mention the interlude with Cole; instead she simply left the impression that Cole had merely seen her there and pieced two and two together when it was discovered she was the woman who was missing from the ship.

"You know, I have been thinking," June said thoughtfully, "I figured it was a little too pat that Berny would approach you with the story of her knowing your father. It really makes one wonder . . ."

"I have been thinking about the same thing too," Helen added. "Of course, I wasn't there, but June and I have been talking. There was a problem about Captain Mahan releasing us from the ship until all were accounted for. He couldn't get the head count to tally. He kept coming up two women short. Now we know who one of the women was, and June and I have been trying to figure out who the other one is, and I think I have a very good idea."

"Who?" Jessica asked.

"Rosie Rutledge." Helen said smugly. She was

pleased with herself for having figured out the mystery. "Just think about it; she had a grudge against you, then when she disappeared from the ship, you were mysteriously shanghaied into a bawdy house. From what June related of Berny's conversation, she *had* to either get her information from your father, or from someone who knew you. I seriously doubt that woman knew your father, so that only leaves Rosie. What do you think?"

Jessica's smoky gray eyes took on a dangerous cast to them as she listened to what Helen had to say. Her friend was right! Rosie had to be the one who betrayed her! She was the one who had momentarily cast her into the fiery pits of hell! Rage choked Jessica's voice as she tried to reply to Helen's suspicions. "You must be correct, Helen," she finally sputtered. "So help me, if I ever get the chance I'll, I'll. . ."

"And I'll be right behind you!" June muttered indignantly.

"Right along with me!" Helen added forcefully.

The three women looked at each other, then burst into muffled giggles. Jessica knew she didn't have a thing to laugh about, but it helped to ease the tension.

"At least we have one consolation," June stated, trying to hold back her laughter. "Nothing serious happened. It's not everyone who will be able to tell their grandchildren that they were actually shanghaied into a bawdy house!"

Jessica forced another laugh. She seriously doubted she would ever tell anyone about her episode at the Golden Slipper. That was a brief part of her life she wanted to forget ever happened. Everyone thought she was decent, everyone except Cole. He knew what she was. Jessica knew she would have never allowed Cole to make love to her if she had been fully aware of what was happening. But he had made love to her, and she had responded with a wanton abandon. What did that make her? Was she a tramp? A slut? A woman whom he would avoid socially? Jessica couldn't help but recall the hateful words her aunt had spoken to her. She had said that tainted blood ran through Jessica's veins. Could it be true? It was also humiliating the way Cole had rebuffed her pleas for him to understand. It galled her to think she had actually pleaded with him.

Jessica's silence was mistaken for weariness. Helen and June stood, and announced they were going to bed, and urged Jessica to follow.

It was very late that night when Cole rode away from the camp. He had first led the horse away from the immediate area before mounting him. Secrecy was of the utmost importance. He had a task to perform, a task that was eagerly looked forward to. He had a score to settle with Manuel. Berny was a woman, regardless of what she had tried to do, Cole could not fight her, but Manuel was different. He had pulled a gun on him. True, the man was doing the job he had been hired to do. But Cole had seen the wicked gleam in the man's eyes. Manuel had actually wanted Cole to resist him. He had wanted to pull the trigger on the rifle.

Cole had no intention of killing Manuel. That was not his purpose. His purpose was to make Manuel think twice before holding another woman against her will; he would also think twice before aiming a gun at a man without using it.

Later, upon returning to the camp, Cole gingerly touched the large bruise on his cheek and cautiously wiggled a jaw tooth. From past experiences,

Cole knew the tooth would tighten up within a few days. Even with his bruises, he felt an elated sense of satisfaction. He had shown Manuel what a real man could do.

Chapter Twelve

The following morning started with a flurry of activity although stars were still scattered across the heavens, appearing like a lacy blanket of light in the sky. A cool breeze rustled the grass and trees, and the tangy sea air was still prevalent, hanging heavily across the hills surrounding San Francisco.

The delicious scent of pan bread and sizzling bacon filled the camp. Enough food was also cooked for a light, mid-day snack. It was explained that they would not be stopping unless it was absolutely necessary until they reached Coyote Creek.

Ed had not mentioned the colorful bruise on Cole's face, other than the fact that he sure hated to see what the other fellow looked like. The man sensed it was all somehow tied in with Jessica, but did not press the issue. Cole was his friend. He would confide in Ed when the time was right.

They were off! Traveling the final leg of their long, tedious journey. Cole led the way with Ed following in the lead wagon, while the other wagons trailed behind them. The women walked, some three to four abreast beside the covered caravan. Two men had come along to help guard the supplies and to drive the small herd of cattle that had been purchased in San Francisco. Chickens had been hobbled and placed in wire cages, these were tied to the outside of the wagons. And the wagons were huge! They were the heavy, durable Conestogas that had been bought very cheaply when their previous owners had reached their destination. Only a few years earlier, it would have been impossible to buy a wagon such as these noble giants. Shelter was so difficult to come by during the height of the gold rush, anything habitable was used. Now since the rush had leveled off goods were easier to buy.

Jessica had avoided the piercing stares Cole had cast in her direction. She knew she didn't have much, but she did have her pride left. She couldn't bear the thought of him seeing her watch him. As she walked along with June, Helen, and a little short lady named Brenda, Jessica could feel a lifting of her spirits. She had to have faith that everything would work out for the best. Apparently the mining camp was now a thriving little town. Perhaps she could work and make her own way without having to take a husband. She placed a lot of hope in Cole's speech last night. He sounded as though Captain William Stockard was an honorable and civilized man. Surely he wouldn't force her into marrying a man she did not know.

Jessica gave a rueful laugh. Here she had been worrying about having to marry a man she did not know, when she had already given her body to a stranger. And the horrifing thing about it was, if given half a chance she would gladly give him her heart.

The small rolling hills were lush with vegetation. The landscape was anything but monotonous. Trees and multi-colored plants dotted the area. The air was noticeably different after they traveled away from the tangy, sea air which surrounded San Francisco. It now smelled fresh and clean, and washed by the brilliant sun.

The older children volunteered to help with the cattle. They learned quickly. It wasn't long before they picked up long sticks to chase the strays back into the herd.

Cole pushed aside all of his nagging doubts and concentrated on the trail. It felt good to be back in the saddle, leading wagons and driving cattle. It was something that came naturally to him. It brought to mind the years he and William rode together in Texas. Those were good times. No worries, no obligations. And their life out here had been good until the men all voted to send for wives. It wasn't that Cole didn't like women—he did. But the frontier was too harsh on a woman. A woman needed soft and frilly things. She needed bright lights, dances, and a whirl of social activity. Cole knew there would soon be trouble when the women reached Utopia. The men would soon start arguing among themselves, they would start getting greedy and selfish, wanting more for them and their wives. Perhaps it wouldn't be so bad if the women were frontier women, but they were far from it. The streets of New York were ill equipped to prepare the women for the rigors of life here in California. Cole finally shrugged off his ominous thoughts. He had told them, now only time would prove if he was right.

It was late in the afternoon before the small caravan reached Coyote Creek. They had not made as good time as Cole had hoped. The months of inactivity on board the ship was telling on the women, but surprisingly, only two had complained. Fires were soon built and tripods stretched over them and food was prepared. The wagon drivers set about making supper. They knew the women were really too tired to cook. After the meal, the women washed the dishes and put dried beans on to cook slowly over the campfire for the next night's meal.

After the evening chores were finished, a bit of daylight was still present. The women all went down to the creek, took off their shoes and waded in the water. There were simply too many of them for proper baths.

Jessica, finding herself practically alone at the camp, looked into the supply box and removed a bar of castile soap, and a soft turkish towel. She had to wash her hair. It was full of dust, and when she had been held captive at the Golden Slipper, she had perspired so heavily, her hair now fell limply down her back.

Picking her way carefully over fallen branches and curling vines, Jessica walked a good distance from the wagons before turning toward the creek. She wanted a moment's privacy to reflect on her ordeal and to make plans for her future. When she reached the creek bank, a grim feeling of disappointment swept over her. The bank was far too shallow for her to bend over and lather her hair properly. Then an impish grin flitted over her mouth. It had been years since she had gone skinny-dipping. Looking cautiously around her and seeing no one else, Jessica quickly decided to take a bath and wash her hair. Swiftly pulling her dress over her head, Jessica then removed her petticoat, and stepped out of her bloomers and shoes. Testing the water gingerly with her toe, she flinched from the cold. She realized it must be a stream coming from the upper mountains and fed by melting snow. Taking a deep breath, she waded out into the stream, then when the water was up to her waist, she dove in head first. Hot blood pounded through her veins as the water struck her full force. The icy water was so tingling, Jessica came up sputtering. Gasping for breath, she swung her head sideways, flinging her hair wildly about her face. Tiny droplets of water dripped from her chin and nose as she stood for moment to regain her breath.

The water was stimulating, but she knew she would not be able to withstand the cold very long. She splashed back to the shore to get the soap, unaware of the tall dark figure watching her from the brush.

Returning to the center of the creek, Jessica quickly lathered first her body then her hair. Gooseflesh popped up on her skin. It was a feeling combined with torture and extreme pleasure, almost erotically so. The water lashed at her body in a mania of voluptuous frenzy. Jessica dove into the water once more, this time to rinse off the soap. Instead of breaking through the water at her normal place, Jessica came up a few feet further out in the stream. She lost her footing and stepped off into a deep hole. Her head broke the water again. She flailed her arms, and struggled for breath and secure footing. Panic filled her. She was in trouble! The water was so cold, she could not command her arms and legs to move into swimming strokes, only in floundering motions.

A scream tore at her throat as she felt herself being pulled down into the swirling stream. Water filled her mouth. She knew she was drowning! She could feel her body relaxing as it submitted to the ominous fingers of oblivion.

Suddenly, Jessica could feel strong arms wrapping

around her. Salvation! She desperately clutched at the bands of steel, which in turn, pulled both her, and her rescuer under the churning water. A silent scream welled deeply from within. Her lungs burned as she struggled for air, but there was none. Finally, after what seemed like an eternity, they broke the surface of the water. A sharp blow to the head accompanied by a gutteral command quieted her struggles. She quickly became docile in the arms of her rescuer as he regained his foothold then carried her from the now placid shallows of the mountain creek.

Cole carried Jessica to the bank, and laid her on the ground. Her skin was blue-tinged, and her chest did not rise and fall with the steady breath of life. He rolled her over onto her stomach and placed her arms high above her head, then rhythmically started pressing on her back. He didn't know how much water she had swallowed.

"Come on, damn-it, breathe!" he shouted, never breaking the tempo of his resuscitation attempt. This was not just a human life hanging in the balance, it was Jessica! He had to save her, he simply had to! After pumping the water from her chest, Cole quickly rolled her over, tilted her head back, pinched her nostrils together and began breathing into her opened mouth.

Jessica could not ever remember hurting so badly. Her chest was one huge ache. The nerve endings screamed in agony. She coughed painfully and grimaced, then her eyes fluttered. Why was Cole leaning over her with such a worried look in his eyes? Her teeth began chattering and violent shudders enveloped her body. Not only was she suffering from the cold, but from the trauma and the shock of almost drowning.

Cole hurriedly looked for something to cover her with. Spying the towel and her clothes neatly folded into a small heap, he raced over, grabbed them, then ran back to Jessica. Unfolding the huge towel, he wrapped it around her. He knew he had to get her warm. Cole quickly gathered her in his arms to carry her back to camp.

Jessica came fully awake. "No . . . please . . . don't carry me back . . . like this." she stuttered.

"I've got to get you warm."

She struggled in his arms. "But you can't carry me back like this!"

Cole stopped. He looked down at her, his eyes taking in her naked loveliness. He could imagine the shame she would suffer if he did carry her back to the camp without any clothes on. He knew she had already been the object of a lot of gossip. It suddenly bothered him that anyone would think badly about this young woman. Then he shook his head stubbornly, "But I have to do something, you're freezing."

"Can you build a fire?" she asked through chattering teeth. Her eyes pleaded with him to do as she asked.

Cole set her on the ground. Unthinkingly, he felt in his shirt pocket for a match. Realizing they were wet, he forced a grin, "I'll be right back." He took off running toward the camp.

While he was gone, Jessica staggered over to where her clothes were lying in a rumpled heap upon the ground. She slipped her petticoat over her head, all the while, her hands were trembling so badly, they could barely obey her commands. Then an uncanny feeling swept over her. Cole had saved her life. She thought she had been alone, but he must have been there all along.

Why had he been watching her? He had made it plain the night before how he felt about her. She had seen the look of contempt in his eyes. A hot, heavy flash of anger stung her pride. After all of the fear and degradation she had been forced to suffer, then after his refusing to listen to her explanation, why was he now skulking around spying on her? He had made her feel so dirty by his uncaring remarks, why did he suddenly risk his life to save hers?

Cole came crashing back through the bushes. His quick appraising glance took in the fact that she had started dressing. While he gathered some tinder and firewood, he shot questioning looks in her direction, but not a word was spoken until he had a blazing fire roaring. Then as Jessica huddled close to the fire, Cole propped his hand on the butt of his gun and with his icy, dark blue eyes, gave her a wry smile and shook his head. Making a clicking sound with his tongue, he said, "Can't you stay out of trouble?"

"What?"

"Every time I run into you, you are in some kind of trouble," he gloated with an arrogant toss of his head.

Jessica could only stare at him in open-mouthed wonder for a moment. Why, he acted as if she nearly drowned on purpose. "Of all the nerve!" she sputtered. "I didn't ask for any help. I . . . I . . . could have managed just fine, even if you hadn't come along!"

Cole laughed. "Sure you could have," he agreed mockingly. Then his grin finally touched his eyes. "Do you know you look like a drowned rat?" Actually, a drowned rat was the last thing he had on his mind. He kept seeing her as she had waded into the water. He remembered the stirring she had caused to spring in his loins. There was something about this woman that bothered him. Several times during the day, his thoughts had drifted toward her and the memory of the night spent in her arms. Although it was something he did not want to face, it was a fact; he craved her as a thirsting man craved water.

Jessica shivered under his cold, piercing eyes. She could feel his eyes raking her body, taking in the way her breasts molded against the soft, filmy material of her petticoat. She suddenly wished she had had time to put on her dress while he had been gone to get the matches. She raised her head defiantly before whirling around and picking up her dress, then she quickly drew it over her shoulders, but still, there was discomfort betwen them. Mustering as much dignity as possible, she retorted, "I'm not an expert like you, Mr. Robertson, so I have no idea what a drowned rat looks like!"

Cole glared at her hard for a moment, then his tense facial muscles relaxed. "This is a dangerous land, Jessica. You always have to be on your guard. These creeks around here are very deceiving, but I guess you found that out." Not allowing her time to say anything, Cole added, "Why did you come way off down here? Why didn't you stay with the other women?"

"Because I wanted to be alone. I . . . I had a lot to think about, and some of those other women . . . look at me strangely. It's as if . . . they somehow know what happened between us."

"And it bothers you?" Cole asked. His brows furrowed into a frown. Why should she care what the other women thought about her. Women were all alike.

"Of course it bothers me," she answered, willing her eyes to stay locked with his. A flicker of hope touched her heart. Perhaps he would now give her a chance to explain. "I don't know why you are so positive in your belief that I am a loose woman. If you would admit it, you would know that I was innocent when we . . . when you . . . the night we made love." she stammered. She had to lower her eyes. She could not bring herself to look at Cole any longer. The memory of that passion-filled night made her shame overpowering.

Cole's fingers bit into her shoulder. She knew by the way he touched her he was angry, but his face was cloaked by the night shadows. His answer was sharp, stabbing through her like a knife. "Naturally you were the picture of naive innocence. That is why you responded so freely to me," he spat.

"I . . ." she faltered, "It must have been because of the drugs . . ."

Cole abruptly turned away from her. She was a picture of loveliness and she was driving him mad with desire. Her hair was still wet and it hung down past her waist. The length in itself was sensual. He could envision his hands becoming entangled in it during a moment of passion. He could still see the way her breasts thrust rigidly against the damp fabric of her dress, and the way her clothing clung seductively against her wet body. She was beautiful! And, Cole thought angrily, she claimed to be innocent. An ugly grin touched his face as he thought about her deceitfulness. He knew she was not speaking the truth and there was a way to prove it!

With a muffled groan, Cole spun and swept Jessica into his arms, crushing her to him in a powerful embrace. He would make her respond to him, then he would show her exactly how innocent she actually was.

In one fluid motion, Cole had her pressed down to the

ground and onto a soft carpet of grass and leaves. His lips were hungrily nibbling at her mouth and lovely throat. A pounding fire suddenly surged through his loins. He had not intended to actually make love to her. His intentions were to simply arouse her, then he would have confronted her with her so-called claim to innocence; but now, his plans had quickly gone awry. In an almost dreamlike trance, Cole unbuttoned the bodice of the dress that had been so hastily buttoned a few minutes earlier.

His fingers glided up and down her back until he was tingling with excitement. Just the touch of her silken skin was pushing him past the point of reason. He had intended to drive her wild with longing, now it was his body that was betraying him. At first when Cole took Jessica into his arms, she knew she shouldn't respond to him. She wanted to, but she knew it went against all of her principles. However, the longer his lips plundered her lips and shoulders, the greater her desire grew. She did not know what charisma Cole possessed to make her so weak where he was concerned. Shrugging aside the last shreds of reason, Jessica answered his burning kisses with a flaming tempo that matched his desire.

Somewhere in the reality of the moment, Jessica could hear Cole quietly curse as he tried to remove his sodden boots. Impatient to have Jessica, Cole finally gave up. He simply slipped down his pants and mounted her. The instant his throbbing flesh touched her moist womanhood, Jessica squealed in pleasure.

It was all happening too quickly, almost like the loving was nothing but lust. Jessica wanted Cole to whisper words of love and tenderness in her ear. She longed to hear the words that would bind them together, instead, all she could hear was his ragged breathing, or was it hers?

She knew she did not want this moment to end. This man was practically a stranger. She did not know his likes and dislikes, his moods or temperament, but she knew she loved him. She knew her life would be incomplete without him, and she would do anything to get him, even to the point of allowing him to make love to her. True, he had made love to her previously, and she *had* responded freely to his advances. But that was a different time and different circumstances. She wanted *him!* She wanted his hardness to enter her body. She wanted his kisses to plunder her mouth and breasts, and she also wanted his heart to return the love she felt for him.

When Cole's lips found hers, Jessica eagerly parted her lips to accept his invading tongue. Then, almost shyly, Jessica felt her tongue enter his mouth and respond wholeheartedly. With one swift plunge, Cole plummeted deep into the very core of her being. He took her almost savagely, and just as fiercely, Jessica accepted him.

Time flew by, but it passed in a fleeting moment, or was it an eternity? Cole moved in and out with a frenzied crescendo of passion. The intensity of the moment was building to a gigantic molten release.

Jessica cried out in pleasure as she felt her insides churn in a violent, delicious eruption, and Cole's breath came in ragged, heavy gasps when he exploded inside her.

For a moment, all time and movement were stilled. Jessica thought she would burst, her happiness was so complete. She ran her long, sensual fingers through his heavy mat of hair, then her hands cradled his head while he sought to recapture his breath.

"Oh, my darling!" she panted, "I am so happy. You have made me complete. I never knew it could be this beautiful!"

Cole raised his head and stared darkly at Jessica. His inner being was a turmoil of feelings. He was so drawn to this beautiful creature. She was everything a man would want in a woman. She was soft, easy on the eyes, she seemed to have a loving nature, and she was a hellcat of passion. But something was missing. If she had been a real lady, she would have spurned his advances immediately. She would have never allowed him to make love to her. If he had had any doubts before, now he had none!

"So," his voice came in a raspy growl, "Do you still claim you are innocent?"

Jessica recoiled in horror. Cole should be taking her back into his arms and whispering sweet words in her ear. "I . . . I don't . . . understand," she whispered. The pain that was suddenly shooting through her was too painful to bear.

"No decent woman would have allowed me to make love to her!" he jeered bluntly. "Get up and cover your body, you shameless hussy!" he shouted as he rose from her.

Jessica's mouth gaped in surprise. This terrible scene could not be happening! Cole was supposed to love her as much as she loved him. "Cole! Please don't!" she cried.

"No, Jessica," Cole's lips curled into an ugly snarl. "You should have protested before I made love to you, not now. If I had any doubts before, you've now made up my mind for me. You're a tramp! You women are all alike! You try to act so innocent, when all along you are simply playing a man for a fool. Well," he stabbed at his chest with his thumb, "this is one man who will not be made a fool of again!"

"No!" Jessica cried, her voice filled with shock and dismay. "You have judged me wrong."

Cole's steel blue eyes snapped with an unjustified rage. "I don't think so, Jessica. You say you are an innocent victim of circumstances, I say you are nothing but another scheming woman. I will admit what happened at the Golden Slipper was an unfortunate incident. You may have been innocent when we first made love. But how do I know you did not take other men after I left?" Cole knew he was being unreasonable, but the cruel, hurting words would not stop flowing.

"You know I was being held prisoner there, and you know there has not been anyone else!" she cried.

"Maybe so, but you were mighty eager."

"I thought you . . . loved me," she accused. It was difficult for her to understand Cole. Why was he so insistent on hurting her?

"Hell!" Cole spat. "You probably decided I would be a worthy catch. After all, you are looking for a husband aren't you?"

"No! I am not looking for a husband!"

Cole smirked cruelly, "That's right. Your kind doesn't want a husband. Any man will do!"

Jessica could not ever recall being so angry and frustrated. Cole had simply used her to prove to himself that she was not what she claimed to be. Her words were barely audible as she said, "I don't know who hurt you so badly, but somehow, and I don't know why, I feel sorry for you, Cole." Tears threatened to spill from her eyes.

She was angry yes, but the agony which was in her heart overrode her anger. She gazed up at Cole, and hoped the truth was evident in her eyes. "Yes, I let you make love to me. Not because I had my sights set on you, not because I thought you would be a good *catch,* but because I thought I was in love with you." She shook her head disgustedly, "I see now that there is not such thing as love. Maybe lust, but not love. I will tell you this, because it doesn't matter what you think of me now. You could have had my heart with no questions asked. However, you have so much hatred inside you, you cannot accept anyone at face value, nor can you allow any feelings in your heart." Jessica placed her hands on her hips and stepped boldly up to Cole. "I will say one thing more, I have been used by you, but so help me, you will never use me again! This I swear!"

Cole raised one eyebrow. He had not expected this verbal assault. He had almost expected a demand for money, not this, quiet, hurt anger. Why did she look at him with such huge, rounded eyes? Why did he feel a sudden stab of pain through his heart?

Finding it hard to throw off his old inhibitions, Cole threw his guard up once again. Forcing a sneer to his voice, he asked sullenly, "And just what will you do if I decide I do want you again?"

Jessica's nostrils flared in anger. She raised a hand and struck Cole soundly across his cheek. "There, Mr. Smart, that is only a sample of what I will do!"

Cole grabbed her wrist and pulled her closer to him. "No one has ever done that before!" he growled.

"Maybe not!" Jessica tossed her head and jerked her hand away from his grasp. "I'll warn you now, Cole Robertson, lay another hand on me and I'll . . . I'll . . ."

"You'll what?" he sneered.

"I'll kill you, so help me, I will!"

Cole whistled through his teeth. "My, my, you certainly sound tough. Now you are making threats!"

"No, Cole, that was no threat, it was a promise!" With those words, Jessica turned and marched stiffly back toward the camp. She was so angry, she was actually shaking. To think that she had actually thought she was in love with that despicable cur! He was a terrible man. But a part of her had been shattered. She had cared for him. She had been in love with him her entire life. Now, that part of her life was over. Gone were the naive dreams of youth. Dreams were for children, and she was no longer a child. She had been forced to grow up very rapidly. Jessica knew her shame would come later, but out of that shame would come a maturity, a wisdom, and a different outlook on life. She made a silent vow that no man would ever hurt her again.

Chapter Thirteen

Jessica sighed as she tucked her knees beneath her chin and idly wondered which perilous direction her life was taking. She had been back at camp for what seemed like hours, and sleep still had eluded her. Fearful that her restlessness would awaken Helen or June, Jessica had picked up her blanket and walked down to the edge of the creek and now sat staring moodily out across the small stream.

The moon was bright, lighting up the entire area as brightly as streetlights in a lonely city. Her color deepened as she recalled how easily she had gone into Cole's outstretched arms. No wonder he thought her to be a harlot. She had done nothing to dispel his doubts. Perhaps all was not lost, though. Cole had shown her his true colors. He had shown her exactly what an untrustworthy despicable person he actually was.

"Do you want to talk?" Helen's soft voice broke into Jessica's private thoughts.

"What are you doing here?" Jessica gasped as she looked up sharply. "I didn't wake you, did I?"

Helen chuckled. "No, I had to take Aaron to the privy," she motioned to a large bush with her head. "And I noticed you were gone. When I got him back to sleep, I decided I would find you and see what was the matter." She sat down beside her friend.

Jessica shrugged her shoulders, "Nothing." Her voice betrayed her though. It trembled with the agonizing pain that wrenched her heart.

"I understand you may not want to talk, but there is no need in you wallowing in misery. If you want to get it off your chest, I'm ready to listen."

Jessica lay back on the grass, resting on her side and toyed with a small wildflower, twirling it between her fingers until the stem lay limp on the ground. Finally, in a small, hushed voice, she said, "I suppose it would feel good to be able to tell someone about it." Abruptly sitting up, Jessica let her head collapse into her hands. She cried for a moment, then admitted tearfully, "I . . . let myself believe I was in love with Cole."

Helen, not realizing how deeply Jessica's feelings ran, laughed. "Honey, I can imagine you are in the same boat as many other women, especially as handsome as he is."

"No, Helen! You don't understand!" Jessica sobbed.

Helen looked at her strangely. A slow light of realization dawned on her. "Jessica?" she spoke hesitantly, "Exactly what happened between you and Cole back at the Golden Slipper?"

Jessica stared down at the ground. "He made love to me."

"And I take it you responded?"

Jessica, unable to speak, simply nodded her head.

"And now you are feeling guilty?"

Again, Jessica nodded, then she blurted, "It sounds worse when it's spoken than when it happened." She looked up at Helen and pleaded, "Will you let me explain how it actually happened?"

Helen patted her shoulder. "Jessica, I'm not sitting in judgment on anyone. Go ahead and talk and get it off your conscience."

Jessica's head bobbed wordlessly at first, then she started telling her friend about the experience at the Golden Slipper. She also told her about her daydreams, and how many times she had escaped into the world of make-believe, and how surprised she was to discover that Cole had actually been real, that night in the bawdy house.

"I can certainly understand why you are so hurt," Helen said when Jessica paused in her recounting of her experience.

"But . . . that's not all," Jessica admitted shamefully. "Tonight . . . I went down to the creek to take a bath and wash my hair. I . . . stepped into a deep hole and he pulled me from the water . . . and it happened again."

"You mean he made love to you?"

"Yes."

"Did he say he loved you?"

"That's the horrible part!" Jessica sobbed miserably. "He hates me! He thinks I am nothing but a harlot, a cheap tramp! He claimed to have made love to me tonight to simply prove what I really am!"

Helen exhaled a deep breath. "I can see why you are so terribly upset. Although it may not be as bad as it seems."

"I don't see how you can think that!"

"I may be wrong," Helen stated honestly, "but it sounds to me like Cole is hurting as badly as you are. It sounds as if he doesn't want to be attracted to you, and he is, and he is fighting it."

"It makes no difference now!" her steel gray eyes settled on her friend's comforting face. "I would never be able to trust him again. I would always be wondering when he would turn on me with more terrible accusations!"

"You may be right, although I have a feeling you are wrong. If I can make a suggestion . . . ?"

"Of course you can. I would not have told you what had happened if I did not value your opinion."

"I think I would let matters lie for the present time. I am getting to know Mr. Baker . . ."

"Who?"

"Ed Baker, one of the men who works with Cole. He mentioned that they were very close. Perhaps he will tell me something, then I in turn can pass it on to you."

Jessica had noticed Cole and the sandy haired Irishman pairing off the way some men do who are good friends. She had also noticed the appraising glances he had been casting in Helen's direction. She sighed deeply, obviously troubled, "I am happy that you have met someone you can possibly grow fond of, but I would rather the matter be dropped between me and Cole. It would be foolish of me to tell you I no longer loved him. The fact still remains that he is not interested in me as a woman or a possible wife, and to be frank about it, I don't think I would ever be interested in another man for a husband. Only another woman would know how badly his actions hurt me." She raised her gaze to meet Helen's troubled one, "I don't believe any information could take away that hurt. I don't know what Ed could possibly tell you that would make me change my mind."

Helen shrugged. "You may be right, I don't know. I will say this, if I were you, *and* Jessica, if I cared for Cole the way you claim, I would not close my heart to any of his advances. Nor would I close my heart or my mind to any explanation that might come along to explain why he has acted this way toward you."

Jessica nodded slowly, "Perhaps you are right. I know I am too emotionally upset right now to come to any kind of conclusion. I do know how much he has hurt me, and if I can help it, I will not allow myself to be hurt this badly again!" With those words, Jessica stood, picked up her blanket and raced back toward the camp, feeling Helen's worried eyes following her all the way.

The journey to Utopia continued without incident. Cole would leave camp very early in the morning. Each evening when he returned, he would be carrying some sort of wild game. Sometimes it would be venison, wild turkey, or rabbits and squirrels. He did provide amply for the women. Whenever one of them tried to flirt with him, he would merely shrug his shoulders and walk away, clearly uninterested.

Helen stepped into a small hole the third day out of San Francisco spraining her ankle. She appeared to be none the worse for wear. Because of her slightly incapacitating injury, she was able to ride in the huge, Conestoga wagon with Ed. Their friendship began to grow and blossom with each passing day. And Aaron seemed to worship Ed. His childish eyes would light up every time the man spoke to him. One night, Helen excitedly told Jessica and June that Ed had very shyly took her hand and held it for a brief moment. Youthful lights of excitement would flash in the woman's eyes each time she mentioned Ed's name. It became evident to all concerned, she was falling deeply in love with the good-natured Irishman.

Everyone liked Ed. Just as Cole was adamant in his feelings about the women, Ed make it a point to show them he was proud of their decision. He had been in California since the beginning of the gold rush, and for one, he was looking forward to female companionship. And Ed was always playing practical jokes on the women. Nothing that was harmful, or cruel, but simple little things. Ed was very talented when it came to silly little drawings. If a woman did something silly, she was sure to receive a picture of it the following day. Once, a woman had rushed to the bushes, and had almost squatted on a snake. Ed knew she had a good sense of humor and it did not bother him a bit to present her with the drawing. His manner was such that no one was offended by what he did. In fact, it came to be as a status symbol for a woman to possess such a drawing, and it pleased them even more when they received more than one of the pictures.

With each passing day, the women became more excited about reaching Utopia. Ed and Helen's romance grew into something deeper than a casual affection, and Aaron's love for the man grew by leaps and bounds. It soon became obvious to most of the women that bitter feelings lay between Jessica and Cole. Whenever he passed by the line of women, he would always nod politely and tip his hat to everyone but Jessica. She merely ignored him. It was apparent to all the women she was avoiding him, and many wondered why, especially since he had rescued her from the bordello in San Francisco. How they found out about the bordello, Jessica did not know and she didn't think her close friends or Cole told anyone.

They traveled for ten days before starting the climb up into the mountains. A road had gradually been hollowed out through the trees and brush, but the going was still slow. In several places, the wagons had to be unloaded before the eight-horse teams could pull the wagons up the steep inclines. The air became much crisper, not cold; however, a noticeable difference was present.

Nervous anticipation filled the women the night Cole told his charges they would be arriving in Utopia the following afternoon. A hushed silence drifted over the camp as each woman became lost in her own private thoughts as they wondered what lay ahead in their immediate future.

Chapter Fourteen

When they were an hour away from Utopia, Cole left the caravan to ride on into town. He knew the men were aware the women would soon be arriving. He had seen several scouts, and look-outs, who were now on their way back to town to tell the men the good news.

The closer they came to Utopia, the more nervous the women became. There were thirty or so clustered around Ed's lead wagon. He tried to dispel their nervousness by telling them about the pits which dotted the area.

They were *Mexican arrastres*. Essentially, they consisted of circular pits about eight feet wide and two or three feet deep, side-lined and floored with flat slabs of rock. A stout vertical post in the center of the pit supported a horizontal pole balanced across its top and pinned to revolve. One end of the pole extended over the edge of the circle far enough for a mule hitch or a burro, and the slowly plodding animals circled the outer rim of the pit endlessly.

Ore was dumped into the rock-floored pit and

crushed by a drag stone which was fastened to the horizontal pole with rawhide thongs. The drag stone was heavy enough to smash the huge chunks of ore.

After the ore was crushed, it was scooped out of the *arrastres,* and taken to the drywashers located in Utopia. There the gold was separated from the gravel, then the gold was transported to a huge safe until the time when they had enough gold to process through the mint, then taken to the vaults in San Francisco where is was deposited in the mining company's name.

Ed explained further that the men were issued stocks, and every two months, each man received his share of the profits. Ed boasted proudly that over three million dollars had already been taken from the three sunken mines they were operating.

Ed's soothing voice put the women at ease, and before they knew it, they had crested a craggy hill and Utopia lay nestled below in a small valley.

Over a hundred small log cabins were lined in neat rows around a general store, and one extremely large building.

They were able to see clotheslines in the back yards, and several large gardens. A huge corral was a good distance from the town, and in it were fifty to sixty head of horses. In another pen, burros lined the troughs, eating. A livery stable was also close to the animals' pens. The women were also able to see a huge banner strung up across the long building saying, 'WELCOME'.

Men stood in the town square, anxiously awaiting the women's arrival.

As they were directed to the town square, Jessica couldn't help but notice how many pains the men had taken to make themselves presentable. They stood self-consciously, shifting from one foot to the other, clutching sweated hats. Some had rolled up their shirt sleeves to reveal faded red union suits. Some wore beards, some had mustaches, and some were clean shaven. The anticipation was so heavy it could have been cut with a knife. Excitement could be seen dancing from the men's eyes.

Captain William Stockard stood on the veranda of the building that was commonly referred to as the community house. He had his hands placed upon his hips and a proud smile graced his weathered, but handsome face. He was an extremely tall man, and other than the age lines upon his face and his dark hair streaked with silver, he appeared to be as lithe and young as most of the miners who had slowly clustered around the building.

Swooping low, with his hat making a graceful sweep, William straightened, held out his arms and said, "Welcome to Utopia! I hope your journey has been a pleasant one. My name is William Stockard, but my friends simply call me Cap'n." He started to stroll the length of the porch, never breaking the speech he had prepared. "I know how tired all of you must be so I won't keep you long. I do want all of you to know how pleased we are to have you here. I hope I can soothe any fears any of you might have. I know many of you have wondered if you would be placed on a block like they do the slaves down in the south. I know I have heard rumors about men handling their brides in this manner, but this will not be the case. I want all of you to be happy, and to enter into good, solid relationships with my men. My plans do not call for an automatic pairing off, and I'm sure my right hand man, Cole Robertson has already told you this, but I only want to make it clear just in case there are any questions. I want you women to be able to meet the men and have a say in your choice."

William continued to pace back and forth on the porch. "I will tell you that we have made preparations for a dance to be held tomorrow night where most of you can be properly introduced. Now, like I said, I know you are all tired. If you ladies would like, you can go to the cabins on my left and make yourselves comfortable. You will not be bothered or annoyed because my men have graciously consented to move their belongings to the other cabins, and in some instances, into tents and other shelters. I know you are all weary from your journey, so I will not hold you any longer. Please feel free to prepare whatever food there is in the cabins; I'm sure you will find them well stocked with supplies." William started to turn away, then as an afterthought, he addressed the women once again. "Ladies, the ones with children, please caution them to stay close. It has been an exceptionally harsh summer and food in the wilds is in short supply. Grizzlies have been coming very close to town, and it could be dangerous if the children happen to wander off."

Ed helped Helen to dismount from the wagon. Offering her his shoulder, she was able to hobble to the nearest cabin. Jessica, carrying Aaron, Linda, June and Brenda followed closely behind. When they entered the cabin, Ed gently placed Helen on the bed.

"Now, you stay here," he commanded sternly. "Your ankle won't get well if you're up and around on it."

"Ed!" Helen sighed, forcing irritation into her voice, "You are treating me like an invalid. There is nothing wrong with my trying to walk." Even though she was scolding him, she was thrilled at the attention he was showing her. It had been so long since she had been treated like someone special. "What about Aaron? Someone has to watch him!"

"I'm sure Jessica won't mind, will you Jessica?"

"I sure won't," she readily agreed. "In fact, I thought I would take him outside after a while so he could play. You know, the kind of playing a little boy likes, dirt, throwing rocks, dirt, looking underneath stones and bushes, dirt," she giggled as he tousled the little boy's hair affectionately.

"Can we go out and play right now, Aunt Jessica?"

"In just a little bit. Let me freshen up first."

"Aaron," his mother said, "Jessica is tired right now. Let her rest a while."

Disappointment flashed across his freckled face. "Aww, shoot, I never get to have any fun."

Ed tried to hide the smile playing at his lips. "Now, son, that is no way to talk to your mama. Tell you what, you can come with me and help me unhitch my horses."

"Yippee!" the boy shouted. He slipped his hand into Ed's and looked up at him seriously. "I like you," he stated matter of factly. "Are you gonna be my new daddy? I sure do hope so!"

"Aaron!" Helen shouted.

"I was just wondering out loud, Mama," he explained.

A huge grin spread across Ed's face. He ruffled Aaron's hair. "We'll have to see about that, son. Although," he looked at Helen wistfully, "I guess that is more or less up to your mama." He ducked his head sheepishly, grabbed Aaron's hand and together, they hurried out the door, leaving Helen propped up on the bed, her mouth gaping open in surprise.

Jessica looked at her friend and smiled, "Well, it looks like that's settled. Shame on you, you didn't tell me he had proposed," she scolded.

"He hasn't," Helen sputtered. "I . . . had no idea . . . I thought, I . . . knew . . . I was under the impression . . . he liked me, but I didn't know if it was merely friendship . . . or whatever," she shrugged. Her eyes betrayed the excitement she was trying not to reveal. They were round and huge, and dancing with lights Jessica had not seen before.

"How do you feel about him?" Jessica asked bluntly, although she could tell by the expression on Helen's face what her answer would be.

"Why . . . I don't know . . . I've never given it much thought."

"Now, Helen, I don't believe that." Jessica knew her friendship with Helen allowed her to be frank. And with the other women in the kitchen preparing an early supper, Jessica felt free to speak her mind.

Helen blushed and lowered her eyes. "All right," she admitted hesitantly. "I do care for him. It was too much for me to hope that his feelings would be the same."

Jessica patted Helen's hand, "I think I can understand, but I've seen how he looks at you, and I don't think there is any reason for you to worry."

"Really?"

Jessica laughed, "Yes, really." Glancing toward the door, Jessica said, "I guess I had better see if they need any help in the kitchen. I'm a good cook," she added.

"Wait a minute, Jessica. There is something I think I should tell you."

Jessica reluctantly turned around and walked over to sit at the foot of the bed. Almost unconsciously, Jessica's small white teeth had begun to worry her lower lip, and her smoky eyes had turned a shade darker. "If it's about

Cole, I don't think I want to hear it."

"That is utter nonsense!" Helen snapped irritably. "I think what I have to say will help you undestand Cole."

Jessica couldn't help but be interested. She could have climbed the tallest mountain and shouted how much she hated him, but it would not have made any difference in her *true* feelings. She knew she was hopelessly in love with the man whether she wanted to admit it or not.

"All right, I'll listen. What about Cole?"

Helen raised up on her pillow and leaned forward. "It seems that Cole was left standing at the altar several years ago."

"What?"

"Yes, she left him standing at the altar." Helen nodded to emphasize what she had said.

"When?" Jessica's mind was busily working. Perhaps Cole was still in love with this woman.

"It's sort of long, but bear with me," Helen gestured with her hands. "Cole was only twenty when he asked Melissa to marry him. Melissa, that's the girl's name. It seems they were practically raised together, and Cole had always loved her. He had claimed her for his sweetheart when he was only a child, and Melissa had always seemed to care for him. But she was flighty, always craving thrills and excitement. Cole's father had given him a section of land for a wedding present. Ed said that Cole had worked, building a house and putting in a crop. The day of the wedding, Melissa's father met him at the church and told him Melissa had run off with a traveling drummer the night before. She had even left him a note telling him she would be bored to death on a dirt farm in the middle of nowhere. She wanted the excitement of a large city and she wasn't going to bury herself on a farm and be old before her time by having babies every year."

Helen's eyes grew wide as she continued. "Melissa also told him in the letter that he was a fool, that she and his best friend had been intimate. Cole went looking for this so called best friend. They got into an argument and the young man was shot. It wasn't serious, but it really did something to Cole. He started asking around and discovered Melissa had been sleeping with half the county. Cole was so hurt and ashamed, he left his home and has never returned, even when his folks died. Of course, in all honesty, Ed did say that Cole didn't know his parents were dead until it was much too late. Still, he didn't return even then. He simply had an attorney to arrange for the sale of the land and holdings. Then it seems Cole drifted around for several years, building a reputation with a gun. He met that nice man who welcomed us to Utopia, William Stockard, and the captain took him under his wing so to speak, and they've been together ever since. Now, Jessica," she cautioned, "Please don't repeat what I've told you. Ed said that Cole was very close-mouthed about this, and he had only told Ed after a few too many drinks. I'm afraid Cole would get very upset if he knew Ed told me what happened."

Everything started to drift into place. There was a reason why Cole disliked women, especially women who claimed to be innocent and naive. Melissa had probably claimed innocence too. That was why Cole was against women being brought in here as brides. He figured they would soon become bored with a simple life and cause trouble. At that moment, Jessica realized if she wanted Cole, she would have to fight for him. And she did want him. That much she knew for certain.

Rising slowly to her feet, Jessica turned to Helen. "I

want to thank you. What you've said has opened my eyes."

"I thought it would."

Jessica could not say anything else. She wished desperately to be alone and collect her thoughts, but with the other women chattering endlessly in the kitchen, there was no place she could seek privacy. Jessica walked out onto the small front porch, only to find many men milling around outside. She went back into the cabin to listen helplessly to the other women's joyous laughter and gossip.

Finding a chair to sit in, Jessica worried about the coming dance. Mr. Stockard had said that the men and women would be properly introduced. She knew as far as looks went, she was fairly attractive. What would happen if one of the men became interested in her? She knew she would never be able to go into the arms of another man, not after knowing Cole. He had not only taken her body, he had taken her heart and soul. No man would ever measure up to him.

After being called several times to come and eat, Jessica sighed, and walked wearily to the table and fixed her plate. She only picked at her food, barely able to force a few bites down. The women did not notice her quiet and pensive manner. Later, after the meal, nothing was said as she gathered the dishes, cleaned them up, then walked back outside.

Ed had bought Aaron back, and even his childish questions did nothing to shake her from her thoughtful mood. Finally, unable to stand the happy chatter inside the cabin, Jessica threw a shawl across her shoulders and stepped outside. She walked with a purpose toward a sure destination, oblivious to the men and their admiring glances.

Jessica walked out of town with a sure, steady stride. She carried her head high and proud, every bit the lady her mother had raised. She had no intention of leaving; the walk was a simple way of escaping from the questions flooding through her mind and through her heart. After leaving town, Jessica found a well hidden obscure trail beneath the branches of a cluster of tall pines. She climbed for what seemed to be hours over the trail that twisted and wound its way past the flatlands of the meadow, to the higher plateau of the mountainside. The shawl was removed when tiny rivulets of perspiration trickled down her sides and between her breasts. The mountain air became thinner, making it difficult for her lungs to suck in as much air as she needed, but still she climbed. Coppery tendrils which had escaped from her hair ribbon, flickered across her face. Jessica simply tucked her upper lip inward, pushed her bottom lip out, and blew the hair from her eyes. Finally, Jessica stepped out into a clearing and realized she was close to the top of the mountain. She made her way toward a steep wall on the side of a cliff, and finally stopped. She could go no farther. The mountain wall jutted upward into the heavens.

Jessica took her shawl and brushed dirt off the top of a flat rock and sat down. The view from the high elevation was astounding, a vast panorama of glorious sight. She could turn her head and see in every direction. Although the names of the surrounding mountains were not known to her, Jessica slowly scanned the horizon and drank in their loveliness. To the east lay an ancient volcanic crater, its gray-black rocks jutted through the lush, green vegetation, enhancing the greenness, making it appear as brilliant emeralds shining in the sunlight. To the north, a towering red-pink shape loomed high above all of the others, and to the southwest, a hundred mountains or more graced the cumulus-studded cerulean of the sky. They were tipped and streaked with the last remaining bits of snow left from the previous winter's storms. Jessica did not know that these mountains were never clear of the white icy wonder.

Jessica was oblivious to any sounds other than the ones her heart made. She did not hear the footsteps which approached her newly found, secret hide-a-way.

"Hello," a strange voice called out. "Are you all right?"

Jessica jumped, startled to hear someone else. Glancing up sharply, she was relieved to see the older man who had welcomed them to Utopia. "I beg your pardon?"

"Are you all right?" Captain Stockard asked as he walked over to where the girl was sitting. He sat down beside her. "I assume it's all right if I join you?"

Jessica replied, her words not rude, nor did she mean them to be, "Yes, I guess so, after all, there is no other place."

The man rested his arms across his knees and scanned the countryside for a moment before speaking. When he did talk, his voice was deep and mellow, almost in awe. "It's the most beautiful sight I have ever seen. I come here often. How did you find it?"

Jessica drew a deep breath. "Oh! Am I intruding on your private place?"

William laughed, "No, Ma'am. I wouldn't be so selfish as to claim this spot for myself. It's too pretty. I guess I'm glad someone else found it too, someone who will appreciate the beauty."

"I feel more at peace here than I've felt for such a long time," Jessica admitted openly. It was strange. She did not feel the usual awkwardness that generally came with a stranger interrupting a private moment.

"You know, you really should be more careful," he said quietly. "I followed you all the way up here." He had not attempted to look at the girl. And she had not acknowledged his presence other than speaking.

"Why?"

Only then did William allow his gaze to be torn from the mountains. "Because I was afraid you would get hurt. I was standing out on my porch when you walked outside the first time. I could tell you were restless. There was just something about the way you were carrying yourself. You were acting mighty miserable. Then, in a little while, I saw you coming out of the cabin wearing your shawl." William squinted one eye and grinned at Jessica. "I said to myself, that little gal is probably feeling awfully homesick. She doesn't have the look in her eyes that says she wants to go exploring. She looks like she's running away from something." William raised his brows, "I decided to follow you and make sure you didn't get into any trouble."

Jessica smiled at the way the man described his conversation. "You are very observant."

"By the way, my name is William Stockard." He extended his hand.

Jessica returned the introduction, "My name is Jessica Tate. I am pleased to meet you."

William frowned momentarily. "Tate, Tate, Jessica Tate. Where have I heard that name before?"

Rolling her eyes upward, Jessica slumped back against the rock outcropping. "Oh, God! Not again!"

"Pardon?" William said, obviously confused.

"I have already been through this episode once before. I'm sure Cole must have told you about me."

"No, Cole and I have not discussed any one of you ladies in particular."

"Are you serious?"

"Of course I'm serious. Is there a problem?"

Jessica swung around abruptly, her shawl clutched tightly in her hands. She stared at the man a long moment before her heart stopped its ferocious pounding. There was something about the man's manner that made her believe him. Taking a deep breath, she said, "I guess I must leave the impression that I am quite mad. I can assure you, I'm not. I merely went through a similar experience and the results were very disastrous."

"Would you like to talk about it?"

Jessica stared deeply into William's warm brown eyes. He seemed to be a trustworthy man. If she told him how she felt now, perhaps he would be able to assist her if one of the miners claimed her for his wife. Jessica found her voice with difficulty, "Yes, I believe I do want to talk about it." She started a the very beginning, how her mother and sister died, the year she spent with her maiden aunt, and how she ran away. Then she told him about stowing away on the *Sea Nymph,* about the deep and lasting friendships which were formed on board the ship. Her voice became faltering and hesitant when she told him about leaving the ship and searching for her father, and how Berny Timbers deceived her. She had too much pride to reveal the intimate moments she shared with Cole, though. Jessica finished her sad tale by saying, "It is a rather lengthy and complicated story, but somehow, Mr. Robertson rescued me from the

Golden Slipper. But surely you can see, Mr. Stockard, I am here under false pretenses. I can not accept marriage between one of the men here. I merely came to California to find my father!" Huge, rasping sobs tore through her. She dropped her head into her hands and cried.

William was beside himself. "There, there, Miss Tate, I assure you, there is nothing to worry about," he soothed, as he patted her shoulder. "Please, dry your eyes and listen to me. I hate to get your hopes up . . . just in case I'm wrong, however, I . . . you're not going to believe this!"

Jessica wiped her tears with the back of her hand, "Believe what, Mr. Stockard?" she sniffed.

"It was right after Cole left, a tall red-headed fellow came to me looking for a job. He knew horses inside out. I needed a good man, and I hired him. If I were to hazard a guess, I would say he is your father, because his name is Jess Tate, and you bear an uncanny resemblance to him!"

Chapter Fifteen

"My father is here!" Jessica squealed. She could not believe it. All of this time she had been searching for him and he had been here, right here in Utopia! Jessica leaped to her feet. "I've got to go back. I have to see him for myself to make sure!"

William grabbed her arm. "Wait, I'm afraid that's not possible right now."

"Why not?" Jessica could not understand why William did not want her to return to town. "My father is there, isn't he?"

"Well, not exactly," William admitted.

"But, you said, you said . . ."

"I know what I said," William soothed, trying to calm the frantic girl down. He didn't blame her for being so upset, especially after hearing her sad tale. "Yes, I did hire a man whose name is Jess Tate, and I am sure he is your father. However, he is not in Utopia right now. I sent him over to Cresent City a couple of days ago to pick up three teams of mules. He won't be back until the end of the week."

Jessica was crestfallen. "The end of the week?" she repeated.

William nodded, "Yes, I'm afraid so." His manner brightened, "Look at it this way, tomorrow night we'll be having a dance, and many things will be happening. Time will pass quickly, you'll see," he reassured her.

Jessica clutched at his hand excitedly, "Tell me, is he well? Has he been sick? How did . . ."

"Whoa!" William chuckled, the sound masculine and hearty. "One question at a time. From what I could tell, he looked absolutely fine." William stood. "I have an idea it is going to be dark before long. Why don't we start back and finish this discussion over dinner at my house?"

Jessica glanced around in surprise. The afternoon was fading rapidly. Dark shadows had already started to form on the surrounding mountains. A sudden chill enveloped her. She did not want to be caught in the wilds after dark, even if she was in the company of this brave man. "You're right, it is getting late. We should be starting back."

"And, supper? You'll have supper with me?" he asked eagerly.

The laughter Jessica felt bubbling in her heart was the first giddiness she had felt in a long time. "Yes, I think that would be delightful." It was strange how comfortable she felt in the presence of this man. He was easy to talk to, and very understanding. In many ways, he reminded Jessica of her father.

The walk down the mountainside was pleasant. Jessica marveled at the beauty she had missed while climbing. The smell of pine needles rose around her. She noticed the play of chipmunks as they darted in and out of the path, also the fanciful flight of butterflies as they fluttered their tiny, multi-colored wings. Before Jessica knew it, they were in the flat meadow surrounding Utopia. She could not believe the time had passed so quickly. William walked with her to the cabin in which she was staying and told her he would be calling for her within the hour.

Jessica's friends were exuberant over her wonderful news. They were amazed over the coincidence of fate bringing Jessica and her father back together. When she told them she had been invited to William's house for dinner to discuss her father, they all pitched in and helped her to get ready. Brenda pressed her dress, Helen shone her scuffed slippers, and June rummaged through her small trunk looking for the perfect ribbon for her hair.

While Jessica sat in front of a fading mirror, Helen deftly brushed the coppery tresses, allowing a few tendrils to curl casually around her oval face. The rest was simply brushed back and tied with the mint green ribbon June had discovered in the bottom of her trunk.

"Well? How do I look?" Jessica asked twirling around the floor.

"You look beautiful!" June said. "You'll set that man on his ear."

Jessica stopped abruptly. "Oh! I don't want to do that." Looking at the circle of her friends, she said, "Do you think I'm seeing him romantically?"

With raised brows, Brenda replied, "It certainly looks that way. I've never seen such color in a woman's cheeks if a man wasn't involved."

"Oh, you have it all wrong. William is a very nice man, and I thoroughly enjoy his company, but I have no romantic inclinations toward him."

"Well, I don't know . . ." Brenda's voice trailed doubtfully.

"It's true. We are going to discuss my father," Jessica protested. Seeing the doubtful expressions on some of the women's faces, she continued. "I think it's a sad day when a man and woman cannot enjoy each other's company without someone trying to make a romantic interlude out of it. It's . . . as simple as this, William treats me like I'm a person instead of just . . . just a woman."

Helen stepped forward, "Aww, come on girls, leave her alone and quit your teasing."

At that moment a knock sounded at the door. Jessica breathed a sigh of relief as she answered the door. There was no need of them making more out of this dinner engagement than there was. A person would have thought they were about to elope or something. "Hello William," Jessica smiled as she opened the door.

"My, you look lovely tonight, my dear."

"Why, thank you," she stammered, feeling her face suddenly color. Darn, she thought when she heard Brenda snickering behind her. Giving the women a withering glance, Jessica slammed the door behind her.

"Is something the matter? Are you angry?" William wanted to know.

"No . . . yes, I suppose I am a little angry," she admitted.

"Why? Did I do something wrong?"

"Oh, no, not you, William. One of the girls was teasing me about you."

"And that made you angry?" disappointment sounded in his voice.

"You are misunderstanding. She hinted I was becoming romantically involved with you," Jessica stated honestly. "She couldn't understand that we are merely going to discuss my father over our dinner."

"I was hoping we could talk a little about you."

Jessica laughed. "I'm sounding terrible, aren't I. Let's pretend this conversation did not take place."

By that time, they had reached William's porch. He opened the door and waited until Jessica had entered before following her inside the foyer and closing the door. William's house was much nicer than the other cabins. For one thing, it was much larger, and tastefully furnished. Jessica's eyes swept over the parlor, taking in the huge stone fireplace, the horsehair sofa, and the several overstuffed chairs. An enormous bookcase filled one entire end of the room, and in front of it sat a huge desk with various papers scattered over it. The windows had heavy, dark green velvet drapes hanging over them, and several lamps were resting on various tables, giving the room a well rounded and cozy look. It was masculine, but not overly so, a woman could very well appreciate the decor. Jessica turned as William helped her off with her shawl. She spied an intricately hand carved chess set on the table nearest to the fireplace.

"Oh! A chess set, how beautiful!" she said after she had walked over and picked up one of the pieces. "Did you carve this yourself?"

"Yes, I did . Tell me, do you play?"

"Oh, yes, my father and I used to play all the time."

"Good! I'll have to challenge you to a game."

"Challenge accepted," Jessica said firmly.

William tilted his head slightly and nodded. "I feel honor bound to warn you now, I'm ruthless. I like to win and I will show you no mercy."

Jessica fidgeted under his barrage of words with double meanings. Silly, she told herself. You're merely being self-conscious because of what Brenda said earlier. Forcing a laugh, Jessica retorted drily, "Perhaps it will be I who will show you no mercy, Captain William Stockard."

"A warning well heeded, Miss Tate. Now," he extended his arm, "If you will come with me, I believe dinner is ready, and hopefully, I have a delightful surprise for you."

"Oh? I like surprises."

William escorted her into the small dining room, held her chair for her, then sat down himself. "Ching Lee, you can serve supper now." He explained ot his guest, "I have a Chinese cook. He's very good around this place and a very good cook. He's made something special tonight."

Jessica watched eagerly as Ching Lee brought in a huge tray of food. She was suddenly ravenous. Barely touching her food when they arrived at Utopia, then the long mountain hike, and the wonderful news that her search for her father was over, had definitely improved her appetite. She leaned forward curiously upon seeing a huge potato that had been baked, cut open and filled with various ingredients.

"What is it?"

What does it look like?"

"A baked potato," she stammered, feeling very foolish.

"That's what it is, however, the secret is, cream; Soured cream that has been whipped, plus a bit of chopped parsley, shredded cheese, and finely chopped pieces of crisp bacon, which will be served with a steak that is so tender you can cut it with your fork."

Jessica's eyes widened when Ching Lee placed a huge piece of meat on her plate. It smelled delicious. It had been such a long time that she had eaten a good serving of beef, it was hard to remember how it tasted. A huge serving of fresh green beans were also placed beside the meat and potato.

"My goodness, I can't eat all of this."

"We won't know until we try, will we?" William teased. He had seen how she had looked at the food. He also knew what kind of food was served on the ships which sailed around the Horn. He also knew this food was very different from the food served on the trail. "Go ahead and eat," he urged as he filled her glass with wine. "We can talk later."

Jessica ate until she thought her sides would burst. Surprisingly, the plate was empty before she pushed it back. "I didn't know I was so hungry," she said, blushing.

"I knew Ching Lee's cooking would make you a convert. Now," a dark expression crossed his face, "Before you misunderstand anything, I would like to explain a few things to you. First, I don't want you or any of the other women to think I consider myself above my men because my house is nicer. This house," he gave a sweep of his arm, "goes with the job. I am Mayor of our fine city, and the men insisted upon building a house such as this as partial payment for the responsibility. The men eat just as good as we've done tonight. I will admit, I did tell Ching Lee to go to a few extra pains, but for the most part, our fare is all the same."

"Oh, but I didn't think . . ."

"I really didn't believe you did. I simply wanted to clear the air just in case there were questions later. Now there is something else I would like to say. For a good part of my life, I was a Captain in the Texas Rangers, but I originally came from the east. I have a very good education, I was an attorney for a short period of my life, but the glamor of the open trail enticed me away from the doldrums of a tedious office. I can speak as properly as a polished gentleman, or shoot the breeze with the roughest cowhand."

Jessica was embarrassed. She had never been spoken to so frankly before. "Thank . . . you, but . . . why are you telling me all of these things?"

William picked up her hand and kissed it lightly, "Because I am very attracted to you. There is something about the way you carry yourself, the way you look . . . " his words broke off. "Am I making you uncomfortable?"

"Yes, you are," Jessica admitted freely. She had been taught not to bandy words with anyone, to speak her mind as long as her frankness didn't border on cruelty. "I thought we were going to talk about my father."

"All right," William nodded. "What do you want to know?

Jessica grinned, thankful that William's feelings were not hurt. It was amazing how much he was like her father. "I would like for you to start at the very beginning."

William told Jessica how Jess had come into town seeking a job. He told her how he looked and how he had acted. His conversation was easy. It lasted for almost an hour. Finally, when he was finished, he looked longingly toward the chess board. "It's still early, may I invite you to a game?"

"All right," she readily agreed, feeling a little smug. Mr. Stockard seemed to think he was a good player. He did not know her father had been the best in New York State, and had taught his daughter everything he knew. Jessica had just put William into check when the front door opened and Cole walked in.

"Excuse me, Cap'n. I didn't know you had company." A sullen look flashed across his face when he saw Jessica.

"You're not interrupting, Cole. In fact," he chuckled, "You're saving me from being very embarrassed. Do you know she is an excellent chess player?"

"No, but then, I'm sure this young . . . woman has many hidden talents." He raised one eyebrow in that less than tactful manner of his that made her feel as though she was little better than dirt.

"By the way, Cole, I want to thank you for rescuing Jessica from that hell-hole she was trapped in. It would have definitely been our loss. Did you talk to the sheriff or the vigilante committee about it?"

"I . . . er . . . uh, no, sir. Did you tell him *all* about the Golden Slipper, Jessica?" he asked coldly as he glanced sharply at her.

"No . . . ." she stammered, white spots suddenly appearing on her cheeks. Surely he wouldn't be so callous as to blurt out the shared intimacies between them. "I simply told William how you gallantly rescued me."

"William?" he mouthed slowly, making it somehow sound dirty.

William did not catch the implications of Cole's tone of voice. "I told them all to call me Cap'n but I guess she preferred my given name," he said with a shrug of his shoulders.

At that moment, Ching Lee came rushing into the parlor. "Cap'n, Cap'n, you must come!" the Chinaman shouted, tugging on William's sleeve.

"What is it?" Irritation was evident in William's voice.

"Misser Baker needs you down at the stables. Your hoss is having baby!"

"Jessica, I'm sorry, I have to leave. It's my prize mare," he explained sheepishly.

"That's perfectly all right. I understand. You are forgetting how excellent my father is with horses. I can see myself home."

"Nonsense! Cole, would you please walk Jessica home? I'm sure it would be safe is she went alone, but with the men all excited over the women coming in today, we can't be too careful." Not waiting for Cole or Jessica to protest, William grabbed his hat, jammed it on his head and disappeared out the door.

Cole stared at the closed door for a moment then said, "No, William, we can't be too careful where Miss Tate's virtue is concerned."

Jessica threw her shawl around her shoulders, "You don't have to get nasty, Cole!" she spat angrily.

"What's the matter, disappointed because Cap'n got called away? Are you planning on sinking your hooks into him?"

Jessica was determined Cole would not get to her, she would control her temper. "No, Cole, for your information, I was Mr. Stockard's guest tonight because we found out my father is here in Utopia."

"He's here?"

"Well, not actually, but he is expected back at the end of the week. It seems he went to Cresent City after some mules."

"There was no one here with his name when I left to go to San Francisco."

"No, he was hired while you were gone."

"I see you've managed to change the subject!" he growled unfairly.

"I didn't change the subject to start with!" Jessica took a deep breath to try and help calm the terrible pounding of her heart. She was certain Cole could see her dress top move with each beat. "Look, Cole, I don't know why you hate me so badly. I have done nothing to you. By rights, I should be the one with a bushel of complaints. After all, I am no longer a virgin because of you. You see, I happen to recall sitting at the table right after I drank the drugged coffee, and you were the one who insisted upon having *me!* So there, Mr. Robertson, I am the injured party. Now," she added icily, "I want you to know I have no designs on William. I simply find him, pleasant, and a charming man. I guess . . . I'm drawn to him because he reminds me of my father."

"Yeah, I'll bet!" Cole drawled in an ugly, surly voice. God, why couldn't he stop trying to hurt her? Wasn't it like she said, hadn't he done enough to her?

Jessica knew the reason Cole was so bitter, but somehow, during this heated argument, it didn't help much. She wanted to shout and tell him exactly how much she loved him, but she knew that would only prove diasterous. Instead, she said, "Cole, I realize you dislike me. I realize you have a wrong impression of me." She held up a hand to silence his protest, "You are wrong about me, whether you will admit it or not, you are wrong." Taking a deep breath, she continued. "However, you should be pleased to know, you will not have to worry about me much longer. My father will be back by the end of the week. I plan on convincing him we should leave. I've seen this land and know we could start a small farm somewhere. Then both he and I could go about rebuilding the shambles of our lives. So, you see, Cole," huge tears tore at her voice. "I plan on never having to see you again!" With these words, she whirled and ran blindly out of the door, leaving Cole staring silently, almost broodingly behind her.

Chapter Sixteen

The following morning, Utopia was converted into a bustling melting pot of activity. A steer had been slaughtered and placed over a huge spit. It was attended to by a man who stood and constantly turned the crank. There was still the smell of gunpowder in the air where a party of men had gone on a hunting trip for quail. They claimed the small delicate birds rivaled the excellent taste of pheasant.

The women were as eager to prepare for the festivities as the men. From each cabin wafted the delicious smell of rich cobblers, cakes, pies and cookies. They were delighted to find such well stocked pantries, and proved it by the delectable morsels taken from the ovens.

Jessica had decided not to attend the dance. She saw no reason to go. She was not looking for a husband, and she hated the thought of seeing Cole again. She intended to stay out of his way until her father returned; then she would use all of her persuading abilities to convince her father to leave. Cole had made it plain to her how he felt. She did not fit into any of his plans, and she would not torture herself by living in the same town with him. Just the thought of seeing him each day and not shouting how much she loved him was more than she could bear. Jessica had even fantasized Cole falling in love with another one of the women. She knew her heart would surely break if she ever saw another woman in her love's arms.

Helen walked into the cabin from the clothes line. Seeing Jessica sitting calmly at the table, making no obvious preparations, Helen demanded irritatedly, "Jessica! Why aren't you getting ready?"

"Because I am not going."

"Not going! You can't. You have to go."

Jessica frowned, opened her mouth to argue, then suddenly laughed, "I have no business there, Helen. I'm not looking for a husband."

Helen placed her arms akimbo, "Well! I certainly hope I'm not either, but I still want to go. This is going to be my home and I want to meet everyone and make friends."

"That is where we differ," Jessica stated firmly, wagging her finger in her friend's direction. "I do not plan to live here any longer than possible. My father will be here by the end of the week and I hope he will take me as far from this place as possible."

"Why, Jessica?"

"Because Cole is here," she answered matter of factly.

"You love Cole."

"I know I do, that is why I want to leave. Can't you see, Helen, I love him too much to stay around him when there is no future for us. He hates me, he can't stand the sight of me!" Tears were glistening in her eyes.

"Pshaw. He walked you home last night, didn't he?"

"Sure, after William put him in a position where he could not refuse. Then we still had a terrible argument."

Helen shook her head, "I didn't think you were a quitter."

"I'm not a quitter," Jessica snapped.

"Yes you are, you are refusing to stay and put up a fight for the man you love. You are a coward, you're proving it by running away."

"I'm not running away!" Jessica stood and walked to the window; Helen'ts direct statements were bothering her, because they had a ring of truth to them. "Look, Helen," she said, spinning around to face her friend, "Can you blame me for wanting to avoid additional heartache. Cole has made it plain he has no feeling for me except hatred. Why torture myself?"

Helen shook her head sadly, "Don't you realize there is a thin line between love and hate. If Cole hates you, which I sincerely doubt, he can be made to love you."

"But I don't want him to be made to love me, Helen. I want him to love me because he wants to!"

"Perhaps he does love you! Perhaps he is as busy fighting his emotions as much as you have been. Are you going to chance throwing it away?"

Jessica stepped over to Helen and grasped her shoulders. "Tell me, do you honestly think there is a chance for us?"

Helen shook her head, "I don't know. I do know, however, you have nothing to lose by going to this dance. He just might accidently say something to encourage you. If you don't go, though, you will never know."

Jessica thought for a momen, stunned by the impact of her friend's words. "Perhaps you are right," she said slowly. "Perhaps I should go. As you have said, it certainly will not do any harm."

"Atta girl!" Helen smiled happily, then suddenly frowned. "Now that we have that settled, I'll admit I'm worried."

"Why? Is it about Cole?"

"No, this is my problem. It is about Ed."

Jessica knew how deeply Helen cared for that happy go lucky Irishman. "What about Ed?

"I haven't seen him all day. I thought he would have at least come by." Disappointment settled over her face as she added, "but he hasn't."

"I saw him once today. He was down at the stables grooming the horses, and complaining very loudly about all the blasted cockle-burrs."

"He did say he was coming tonight?" Helen asked in a worried tone.

"Yes, he did," Jessica smiled. "He even went as far as to say, wild horses couldn't keep him away."

Helen found herself laughing. "I guess it is no secret how I feel about him."

"No, no secret."

"I have many things to consider when it comes to another man," Helen seemed to be arguing with herself. Not getting an answer nor expecting one, she added after a moment, "I have Aaron to consider. I couldn't give him a stepfather who would be cruel or too harsh with the child."

A smile teased at Jessica's lips. "I thoroughly agree."

"I have debated with my conscience for several long, hard, hours, and I have reached a conclusion."

"Oh?" Jessica tried to pretend surprise. "And what is it?"

"If asked, I will marry Ed."

Jessica placed her hand over her mouth and giggled. "What is the secrecy surrounding that decision? I assumed it was a certainty already."

"Well!" Helen puffed haughtily. "he hasn't asked me to marry him yet."

"He will," Jessica reassured her, "He will. I would wager my last dollar."

"Do you have a dollar?" Helen asked, adding some light hearted teasing.

"Humm, no, but if I had one, I would wager it."

Both women broke into gales of laughter over their silliness. They were relieved laughter could come so easily when both of them were faced with very serious decisions. Helen had staunchly made up her mind, while Jessica's destiny remained hanging on fate.

Excitement hung in the air of the community hall. Checkered curtains hung over the windows, and matching cloths had been draped over the long and narrow tables. The tables had been placed in the center of the hall and ran the entire length of the building. Some enterprising soul had gathered wild flowers and each of the tables held a beautiful bouquet.

A massive fireplace was at one end of the building, and several pot-bellied stoves had been placed at intervals along the length of the hall to assure the occupants of abundant heat during the long, harsh winters. Several rows of benches lined the wall. There would definitely not be room for everyone to be seated, but the men who had planned the affair doubted if a seat for everyone was necessary.

An enormous amount of food had been placed upon

the tables, everything from fresh garden vegetables, meats of all kinds, the desserts the women had prepared, and even pitchers of iced lemonade and cider.

At the other end of the building a small platform had been erected. Lanterns had been strung on wires outside for the dance that would come later.

The women were awed over the forethought that had gone into planning for their arrival.

After everyone had arrived, Jessica was amused to see the men and women still segregated. The men lined up awkwardly against the right wall and the women stood on the left. Not a soul broached the no man's land in the middle of the room.

A sound of restlessness began to run throughout the hall. Everyone was beginning to wonder when the party would start. William made his way through the throng of people and stpped up on the stage.

"Ladies, gentlemen, may I have your attention please." After silence settled over the hall, William continued, "I'm sure many of you thought this moment would never arrive, at least," he grinned, "I know you men did. I have been thinking about how to handle the introductions. Since there are so many of us now, I have decided it might be wise for everyone to introduce themselves. I realize it may take a long time, but if we proceed in an orderly manner, I'm sure it will work out fine. I'm going to ask for you women to form a line, and those with children, please come to the front so you can go first. I would like for you to briefly state your names, ages, and any special interests you may have. Now please don't be nervous . . ." His words were interrupted by a commotion at the door.

The embarrassed silence was soon transformed into

loud hoots of laughter and muffled giggles as a repulsive and unsightly woman pranced haughtily toward the platform. She wore a homely calico dress that was too short. Her ruffled bloomers did not quite meet the high topped scuffed brogans on her feet. She wore a bonnet with wilted flowers stuck into the band, and underneath the bonnet, her hair could be seen protruding in every direction, and it was the strangest color. A make-believe mole had been drawn on the atrocious creature's face and her lips had been painted a bright garish red. Her bosom was overly endowed and her buttocks were so large that her dress stuck out in back instead of falling smoothly over her hips. She was ugly!

Jessica, Helen and June craned their necks to get a better look at the weird creature who was now climbing upon the stage. It dawned on them at the same time that this was no woman, it was a man dressed up like a woman! It was Ed Baker! The trio, along with all the other occupants roared with laughter at the hilarious spectacle on the stage. Ed pranced back and forth, then did three pirouettes, spun once again, then curtised toward the crowd. A stupid grin spread across his face.

Helen gasped and dropped her head into her hands, "My God, that's a horse's tail he's wearing for hair!"

Jessica and June clutched their sides as they rolled with laughter. Ed was the funniest sight they had ever seen.

Ed batted his eyelashes and motioned for the crowd to be quiet. He dantily stroked his face, then smoothed his hair before saying, "My name is Agmirillo Deliverworst," in a falsetto voice.

After that round of laughter stopped, Ed continued, "I am here from New York and I am looking for a husband."

Virgil Morris, a miner who had hatched this hilarious idea with Ed, fell to his knees and moaned in a baleful voice. "Oh, Agmirillo, Agmirillo, I have fallen deeply in love with you. Will you please consent to be my bride?"

Ed pursed his lips and stared thoughtfully at Virgil before answering, "Well, I really don't know. I have had so many other offers . . ."

"I can not live without you, my love. You must marry me!"

"Oh, my," Ed touched his cheek thoughtfully, "Decisions, decisions."

"Oh please," Virgil wailed, "Say you will be my bride and take me out of my misery."

A voice called from the back of the room, "For God's sake, Agmirillo, tell Virge you'll marry him and get us *all* out of our misery!"

Ed glanced up, smiled and said simply, "Okay, I think I'll quit while I'm ahead."

When the laughter subsided and Ed had left the stage, William stepped forward wiping the tears from his eyes. "Thank you er . . . Miss Deliverworst . . . I hear the miners over in Crescent City are looking for brides if the er . . . er . . . if Virge backs out on his proposal." Turning his attention back to the men and women William said, "I suppose we ought to start these proceedings. I know everyone has been patient, and if Ed is an example of what loneliness can do to a man, we certainly need to do something about it before it's too late." He motioned for the first woman to step forward, "Go ahead Ma'am, and tell the gentlemen your name."

By the time Helen reached the center of the platform, Ed, who by this time had changed back into his own clothes and washed the mess from his face, stepped forward and announced, "Gents, I hate to dissappoint you, but I have had the privilege of getting to know this lady." He slipped his arm protectively around her shoulders. "And, if she will have me, I would dearly love to make her my wife." He gazed tenderly into her eyes, revealing all the love he felt for her.

Helen swallowed hard before answering, "Ed, if you had not proposed, I don't know what I would have done."

"You mean you accept?" he asked incredulously.

"Of course I will," she answered with fervor. They were oblivious to the hushed silence which had settled over the men and women. Ed and Helen did not realize their happiness was a culmination of all the crowd's hopes and dreams.

The entire scene had been so awesome and so dramatic, Jessica and many of the other women brushed tears from their eyes. Ed and Helen stepped from the platform. The next lady walked forward and the procession continued.

At first, Jessica had refused to get into the line. After accusations she was being unfair, she reluctantly took her place. When her turn came, she hesitantly walked onto the stage. Trembling under the ardent attention of the men, she said, "My name is Jessica Tate. I believe some of you know my father, Jess Tate. He started working here recently, but is in Crescent City at the moment." Lifting her chin a little higher, Jessica continued, "I will be honest with you. I am not seeking a husband at this time. I merely came to California to find my father . . ." her voice trailed off quietly. Shyly ducking her head, she stepped off the platform and darted outside. She ran blindly into Cole.

"I didn't think you meant it, Jessica."

"Meant what?" she retorted coldly.

"I was under the impression you *were* looking for a husband, but on the other hand, and I think I've said it before, perhaps *any* man will do!"

"Why can't you leave me alone! You have succeeded in ruining my life. Why do you keep hounding me!"

A man standing nearby stepped forward, "Are you having problems, Ma'am?"

"No." Jessica forced a smile. "This gentle . . . this man was commenting on the fact he thought he knew my father." The lie rolled glibbly off her tongue, and immediately she was disgusted with herself. Why did she continue to protect this man?

"Oh, it's you, Cole," the man said in surprise. "I didn't recognize you. I thought someone was getting out of the way with this young woman."

"Perfectly all right, James," Cole said. "We can't be too careful with our womenfolk." He smirked and shot a blazing look at Jessica. "We should be on guard just in case one of the women's virtue is placed in question."

Jessica glared at Cole, but managed a sweet smile as she answered crisply, "I feel so fortunate to be in the company of men who care so deeply about a woman's honor. You know, I will have to admit, at first I thought perhaps we might be at your mercy, for instance, like the farmer who let a wily fox guard his chickens." With those words, Jessica gave Cole a disgusted look and strode angrily away.

Someone had thoughtfully pulled a bench outside. Jessica sat down. She tried to push the ugly confrontation with Cole from her mind, but was unsuccessful.

She couldn't help wonder what kind of thoughts she would be having if she had never met Cole.

"You certainly look sad," William said, settling down beside her.

"Oh!" she gasped, "You startled me. I was thinking."

William beamed, "I'm very pleased about tonight. It's gone nicely, and I was especially proud of the way Ed and Virgil's little comedy scene was received. I didn't know a thing about it, and for a moment there, I thought they might have carried it a little too far."

"Oh, no, it was perfect. It was the right thing to make everyone feel at ease."

"I didn't know Ed was serious about that woman. Helen is your friend, isn't she?"

"Yes, she is. I don't know what I would have done without her during the voyage. She offered quite a bit of encouragement. She's a very special lady. Ed made a good choice, and from what I've been able to observe about him, he will make Helen a good husband."

William looked at her strangely. He had detected a sound of uncertainty in her voice. He couldn't understand the aura of sadness which surrounded this young woman. He knew she should be happy, but tiny frownlines were etched on her brow. He turned his head and glanced back into the hall. "They're moving the table with the food out here. I'm glad, because I'm hungry as a bear," he said, patting his stomach. "I'm also anxious for the dance to start. It's been a long time since I've twirled a pretty girl around the floor." He looked questioningly at Jessica, "That is, if you will dance with me?"

"You want to dance with me?" Jessica gasped in surprise.

"Of course, you are the prettiest girl here."

Jessica blushed. It felt very good to be complimented so nicely. For the most part she had only heard insults from Cole and, unfortunately, his opinion was very important to her. "Thank you, William," she lowered her eyes and blushed.

"Why should you thank me for telling the truth? You are not only pretty, you are beautiful." William sensed he was embarrassing her. He quickly changed the subject. "I would imagine you're getting anxious to see your father."

"Oh, yes, I am. It seems forever since I've seen him."

"It sounds as though you were very close."

"We were. There was a special bond between us. Oh, I loved my mother, don't get me wrong, but when father was home, it was him I ran to when I needed someone."

"I'm happy everything is working out for you, Jessica. You are too lovely to wear such a look of sadness. Perhaps a different light will shine in your eyes when he returns."

"Do I look sad?"

"Not now." William's voice had dipped low, almost to the point of intimacy. Suddenly realizing Jessica was becoming uncomfortable with this line of conversation, William took her arm and began walking through the crowd, introducing her, and mingling with the other people.

When everyone came outside, William proposed a toast to Ed and Helen, then the music began. The captain swept Jessica into his arms and began moving his feet in time with the music. Jessica did not have a choice except to follow.

With shouts and laughter, the men broke free of the restraint they had been showing. It was as though they suddenly realized these were flesh and blood women and not some goddesses from afar. The music became louder and more boisterous as the night progressed. The hard ground shook with the pulsation of stamping boots and slippers. The air drummed with the sound of well tuned guitars and fiddlers. The night was alive with enthusiastic anticipation.

Jessica had been dancing for what seemed like hours. After the first two dances, she had lost sight of William, but had gone shyly at first into the eager arms of the men as the band struck up dance after dance. She finally had a chance to slip away unseen, so she cautiously moved to the shadows which surrounded the community hall. Resting her flushed cheek against the coolness of the outer wall of the building, she gasped in surprise when she heard a familiar voice.

"I can't believe you are stopping for the night. Or, are you simply catching your second wind?"

Jessica whirled around and searched the shadows for Cole. Seeing the fiery glow of his cheroot, her eyes narrowed slightly. She was determined she would not allow Cole to make her angry. She was also tired of his brow-beating. She might not be able to change his opinions of her, but she had made up her mind not to flinch or cower under his assault. She had always been sharp-witted as a child, being able to match a slurring retort with one just as sharp. It was time she started to stand up for herself. "Who said I was stopping?"

"Hummmph!" he grunted, "I figured as much."

"And what is that remark supposed to mean?"

"I didn't think you would give up this easily." He gave a wave of his hand, "There are a lot of men out there. From the way you were going into the arms of one and then another, it looks as though you can just about take your choice."

Jessica gritted her teeth as she bit back an angry reply. All of the women had been dancing with a variety of men and he wasn't condemning them. Instead, he chose to seek her out for slanderous remarks. Then a satisfying smile pulled at her lips as she thought of the perfect argument. In her sweetest voice, she replied, "Why, Cole! You noticed. I do believe you are jealous!"

"What?"

"Apparently so," she shrugged her shoulders indifferently. "Each time I see you, you have some smart remark about me and other men. The only thing I can read into your actions is jealousy."

"Me jealous of you!" Cole sputtered indignantly.

"Why, Cole, I never thought you would admit it."

"I have not admitted a thing." He threw his cheroot onto the ground and stamped it out. "You are wrong, Jessica, I am not jealous of you."

Jessica placed her arms akimbo. "Then, you *will* stop making these insulting remarks."

"I didn't know my remarks were insulting."

"You know they are, Cole. You made snide remarks about me dancing with the men, yet nearly all of the other women were exchanging partners." Not giving him a chance to reply, Jessica stepped forward, placed her arms around his neck and pressed her lips to his.

Cole, stunned, could not respond for a moment. Then, when it dawned on him, his arms encircled he tiny waist and his lips answered her passionate kiss.

Breathlessly, Jessica pulled back, gazing intently into his eyes, she said, "I love you Cole Robertson. If you have no feelings for me, then I can accept that. However, I cannot live with the way you have been treating me. I realize I must sound as though I have no shame. I do. I also have pride, feelings, and every other emotion a woman feels."

"Damn-it, Jessica if only . . ."

"If what, Cole? If circumstances had been different and if I had never been at the Golden Slipper, if I had never gone back into your arms that night when I nearly drowned. Yes, it might be different between us right now. I doubt it, though. The ghost of Melissa is standing between you and any woman, regardless of who or where she is.

"Melissa! How do you know about Melissa?"

"A woman has ways, Cole." A frown touched Jessica's brow. "Tell me, Cole, why do you condemn women? Why did you condemn me for being at that . . . horrible place? Are you not to blame? After all, you were there. What does that make you, Cole? Are you *that* much better than me? But then it seems as though men have always been better than woman, or at least they think they are. What is morally right for me should be morally right for you." She searched his eyes for a reaction to her words, but was faced with a stony, piercing glare. "Let me tell you now, you will treat me like the lady I am. You will not make any more snide remaks in my presence, and you will talk to me decently, or *don't come near me!*" With a rustling of her skirts, she whirled and ran toward her cabin.

Cole stared after the woman. As badly as he hated to admit it, she was right. He was no better than she. Why should a man be placed above a woman? And he *had* searched for words with which to taunt her. He had been cruel, almost driven by a wild desire to hurt her. Was it really because of Melissa? He felt torn with indecision. Her words kept ringing through his mind. She claimed to love him. How could she love him after the way he had treated her?

Now he had been proven wrong. His opinions of the women were wrong. He had thought they would be consorting in the streets with the men after their arrival, but they had acted like ladies. If he had been mistaken about the women, perhaps he had been wrong about Jessica. He knew he was attracted to her. Perhaps he ought to try and make peace with the firey red-head. Then maybe he would be able to sleep at night, instead of restless tossing and turning. At least it was an idea, Cole thought to himself as he turned and made his way into the shadows of the night.

Chapter Seventeen

The next few days passed quickly. Life in Utopia seemed to settle down into a near-normal existence. Romances started to bud, and several impending marriages were announced. During this passage of time, Cole had not approached Jessica. In fact, it seemed he had gone out of his way to avoid her, while William's actions were the opposite. He had appeared bright and early each morning, eager for a leisurely stroll with the young woman.

Jessica, in a short period of time had grown very fond of the captain. He was so much like her father, friendly, charming, and handsome in a mature sort of way. She was not romantically attracted to him, but simply felt comfortable with his company.

In the meantime, Jessica was finding it difficult to be patient. It seemed as though her father would never arrive. It was as though she was caught in a vacuum, a never ending vortex of time and space. She felt like a young child at Christmas, knowing it would come, but impatiently wondering when. At times, she doubted if the end of the week would ever arrive.

A couple of evenings before Jessica's father was due back she went to bed early, hoping the night would pass quickly and in turn ease the suspense of agonizing, endless waiting. Finding sleep impossible, Jessica climbed out of bed, dressed, threw a shawl across her shoulders and walked outside. She thought a stroll would help to soothe her restless spirit. Seeing the community hall well lighted, Jessica decided to go inside and talk with some of the women she had not had a chance to visit with in a while.

She was astonished to see so many people inside. Some people sat at tables writing letters since men were going to San Francisco in a few days to make a gold deposit. Many of them were engaged in conversation, and there were a few tables with only men sitting around them. They were playing poker. Intrigued, Jessica walked toward them. Although he father used to play, Jessica had never seen the game before, but had heard about it. It was supposed to be something evil and wicked, but most men usually managed to have a game every so often. She walked quietly up to a table, not paying attention to the players, instead, her eyes were rivoted on the cards which were spread out on a green covered table.

"Well, look here, seems like we have an audience." One of the men chuckled.

"Oh, I'm sorry, I didn't mean to disturb you," she said as the men all turned to look at her. Jessica felt a sinking feeling plummet all the way to her stomach when she saw Cole. She had been standing directly behind him and had not noticed because her attention had been so fixed on the game. "Please continue with your game," she stammered, "I'll leave."

Cole spoke, "Why leave, Miss Tate? I seem to recall a conversation we had the other night and you pointed out there should be more equality between men and women." He gestured with a wide sweep of his hand, "Sit down and join us. You don't mind do you, boys?"

"Heck no! Might accidentally liven up this place," a man said.

"Oh, I couldn't!" Darn Cole, anyway! she thought. He knew as well as she did what she had been talking about, and it had nothing to do with a card game.

"Sure you can!" Cole spoke mockingly as he rose and offered her his chair. "Here, take mine, I'll get another."

"I . . . I . . . can't. I don't know to play, besides, I don't have any money. Then too," she lowered her eyes, "in my opinion, ladies do not play poker."

Cole's mouth quirked as he shook his head at her, "Now, Miss Tate, we can understand your reluctance, being from New York and all, but out here in California things are different. Just think, you can help keep your father company during the long winter months if you know how to play."

Her eyes turned a deep smoky color, as they did when she was angry. "I told you, Mr. Robertson, I have no money." Nodding her head at the table, "I see you gentlemen are not playing for fun." The table was littered with chips of different colors.

"Think nothing of it, if you want to join us, I'll loan you some money," Cole offered.

Why was he being so insistent? Was he deliberately trying to make a fool out of her, or could he have taken their conversation to heart and was only being polite. Somehow, she doubted if the latter was the case. Feeling a burst of courage, she brazenly replied. "What if I lose the money you loan me? I have no job, and no way to repay you. Your repayment terms *may* be too high."

The men guffawed. "She's got you there, Cole."

Cole's blue eyes were laughing at her, but his face was solemn. "All right, Miss Tate, I'll loan you fifty dollars. If at the end of the game, and we are quitting at eleven o'clock tonight, you can not repay me, I'll expect you to clean my cabin and cook my meals for one week."

Jessica could feel her face flush with color. "Are you sure that is all?"

"On my honor," he swore solemnly.

"You can believe him, Ma'am. Ol' Cole may be a rounder, but if he gives you his word, he'll live up to it or die trying."

Jessica looked at the four men around the table, staring at them hard. What did she have to lose? If she did lose, it would give her an opportunity to get to know Cole better. He would also see that she knew how to care for a home. The old saying, 'you can catch flies with honey better than vinegar' went through her mind. However, if she won a little bit of money, she could buy some badly needed material for some new clothes. She had filled out considerably since her last dress had been made. "All right, gentlemen, tell me how to play," she said suddenly, sitting down in the chair.

It was explained about the different suits, the order in which the cards ran, and what rank. After asking several questions, and a simple game was played, Jessica found herself receiving five cards face down. Cole was dealing. They cautioned her not to let anyone else see her cards. She passed her deal, wanting to get a little more familiar with the game. She won one pot and folded early on the next one, then lost in the next two hands.

Cole's turn came to deal again. Jessica was fascinated over the way his strong hands manipulated the cards so easily. He dealt the cards and Jessica had a difficult time keeping her expression calm and not betray her hand. She had been dealt three tens, a king, and a four. The betting was boisterous around the table. Jessica drew two cards, Richard drew one, Rylie took three, Andrew drew two, and Cole dealt himself one. Jessica's eyes widened when she saw her cards. She bet ten dollars. The other men except Cole, dropped out. Cole raised her bet by ten dollars. Jessica studied his face for a moment, then raised Cole's bet by another ten dollars.

"Hot damn!" Andrew shouted, then he realized his language had gotten carried away. "Sorry, Ma'am," he apologized, "Let me see your cards, what are you holding?"

"Oh, no, Andrew, all of you said I should not reveal my cards before the hand was over."

"You sure must have a good hand to bet so much."

Jessica smiled sweetly, then stared hard at Cole. "I do have a good hand. I believe I have a winner."

Cole placed his cards face down on the table, teetered back in his chair, and said, "So you think you have a winner?" He cautiously looked at his cards once again and a broad smile spread across his face. "I think I have a winner too, Miss Tate." He peered at the chips in front of her. "I see you have twenty dollars left, I'll raise you the twenty."

Jessica swallowed hard. She looked at the remainder of her chips. She hated to put all of the money in this one pot, but she *knew* her cards were good, very good. Taking a deep breath, she said, "All right, Cole, I will call you." Tossing in all of her chips, she asked, "Now, what do you have?"

Cole took a long draw on the cheroot he was smoking, then smiled. Slowly, one by one, he turned over his cards. Ace of hearts, ace of spades, ace of clubs. Cole's smile grew broader as he continued to turn over the cards, a nine of spades, and a nine of diamonds. A full house!

Jessica could feel the familiar sinking feeling in the pit of her stomach. "I see," she said slowly. Looking at Richard, she inquired hesitantly, "Would you please tell me what beats what?"

Richard's brows shot up, "Ma'am, you would have to have . . ."

"Please," she interrupted, "Just tell me what beats what."

"Miss Tate," Cole said politely, "Well now, I guess we can be a little more relaxed, I suppose I should call you, Jessica, that is, if it's all right."

"Of course it is."

He was enjoying this immensely. He had not expected her to run out of money so soon. "We're not professional gamblers, this is only a friendly little game." He explained, "In the stricter games where they play for blood, you have to call your cards, but here," he looked around the table, "we let the cards speak for themselves."

Jessica blinked, obviously confused. "How do cards talk?" she wanted to know.

That innocent remark brought gales of laughter from around the table.

Cole patiently explained, "Jessica, that was simply a figure of speech. For instance, if you were to place your cards down on the table and said you only had an ace high, but in reality, you actually had an ace-high straight, then the cards would speak for themselves instead of what you called your hand."

"Oh, I see," she nodded. She was so embarrassed. The smirking arrogance on Cole's face made her feel ridiculous. If only she had not bet all of her money on this hand. Disappointment showed clearly on her face as she asked once again what series of cards beat another series of cards.

Cole took his time in explaining. He spoke so slowly and so deliberately, Jessica knew he was making fun of her. "An ace high, beats a hand with no pair, a pair beats an ace high, two pair beats a pair, trios beat two pair . . ."

Jessica leaned her forehead against her hand, "I believe that is far enough Cole." She turned over her cards. "You see, I only have two pair of tens."

Cole stared dumbfoundedly at the cards, while pandemonium broke out around the table. Richard yelled, "Hot damn, Cole, she sure showed you which way was up and back!"

A slow swell of color began to spread across Cole's face. Bested by a woman! What was worse, she was an amateur card player. Cole shook his head. He knew he would never hear the last of this from the men.

Jessica gasped, her hand flew to her mouth. "What is it? Why are all of you laughing?"

Andrew, still chuckling, "Well, Miss Tate, you done won yourself a pot. Ya got forty-miles-of-railroad, there. Ain't no two pair, that's four of a kind. Beats the fire out of Cole's hand!" he cackled gleefully.

"You mean I actually won, but . . . I thought I only had two pair."

"No, Ma'am," he said firmly. "It's a good hand, pull your money."

Jessica glanced questioningly at Cole. Apprehension settled over her. She had wanted to form a better relationship with this man, now he had been embarrassed by her. All her hopes had suddenly been dashed by her stupidity. She should never have played with them. For a man to be beaten by a woman in a man's game, was surely the ultimate in humiliation. "I guess . . . I was lucky," she choked, wishing the other men would shut up and quit teasing Cole.

Cole grinned sheepishly and passed the cards to Jessica, "It's your deal." His male ego had been wounded, but the only thing left for him to do was to shrug it off and go on with the game. There was plenty of time left. Perhaps he could still be able to win enough money back so she would be forced to come to his cabin. That had been his ultimate goal in the first place.

Jessica took the cards and began shuffling them. An idea dawned on her. She recalled their agreement. At eleven o'clock, she would have to have the fifty dollars to repay Cole. If she didn't have that much left, she would still be honor bound to clean his cabin and cook his meals for the entire week. A sly smile spread across her face. She would make it a point to be short when quitting time came.

The next two hours passed slowly. Jessica caught on rather quickly to the game. She began to go against the odds and draw for hands she had a slim chance to make. A few times she hit it lucky and managed to catch the cards which made her an inside straight, or a two card draw to a flush but for the most part, she lost fairly steadily.

At eleven o'clock, they began to count their money. Jessica forced a worried frown to appear on her brow. Looking earnestly at Cole, she said humbly, "It looks as though I only have thirty-two dollars."

"Do you remember our agreement?" A strange gleam appeared in his eye.

"Yes," she nodded, "I do remember our agreement."

A devilish smile spread across Cole's face. He leaned back in his chair and rested the back of his head against his clasped hands. He drawled slowly, "Looks like I have a cook and someone to clean my cabin for a week." He delighted in taunting her. He had been thinking about what she had said the night of the dance. This mere snip of a girl had waltzed into his life and now everything had changed. Even when he was able to fall into a restless sleep, his dreams were filled with the vivacious beauty.

Jessica pushed the remainder of the money toward him. "Here, this is all I have left." It was difficult to hide the smile about to erupt.

Cole, misunderstanding her actions refused the money. He thought she was trying to renege on her bargain. "No, you keep it. Our deal was for one week, and I demand full payment."

"I was only offering this back to you. I have no intention of backing out on our agreement. I simply thought you would want as much of your money back as possible."

"No, you keep the money. Our deal was for fifty dollars, or a week's work. I'll have to take the week's work."

Richad said eagerly, "Shoot fire, Cole, if it's the fifty dollars, I'll pay you back and let Miss Tate work a week for me!"

Cole grinned and shook his head, "Nope, my deal was

with Jessica." Although he had very badly wanted her to lose, he couldn't resist teasing her a little bit. "You *can* cook?"

"Of course I can cook."

Cole's blue eyes took on a new gleam. "Let's see, I think I would like to have a venison steak about this thick," measuring with his thumb and forefinger, "creamed potatoes, gravy, fresh bread, coffee, and a huge slab of apple pie."

Jessica raised her brow. This time it was her manner that was mocking. "One question, Cole. Do you prefer the wild taste in your venison, or do you like it soaked in milk before it's cooked?"

Cole's mouth formed a tiny oh as his glance went around the table. "I guess that answers my question as far as Jessica knowing how to cook. Only the smart ones know about that."

Andrew spoke up, "I recall a time when I was so hungry, I didn't care if the meat had a wild taste to it or not. Fact is, I almost et the whole thing raw! You young whipper-snappers have it too easy now-a-days. Now, I remember a time . . ."

"Not now, Andrew," Cole said laughingly. He liked his whiskered old friend, but some of his tales lasted for hours. "I think I ought to walk Miss Tate home. She is liable to have a very busy day tomorrow."

As they walked out the door, Jessica couldn't help but feel a little smug over her brilliance. Now, she would have a chance to show Cole how nice she really was, and how well she could cook and clean.

Cole was glad the night was dark. Jessica would have seen him smiling and surely thought the worst. For a few minutes during the card game, he thought she was actually going to win, or at least break even. That would have spoiled all of his plans. He stole a glance at her. The silhouette of her delicate features could barely be seen. He was mystified by the firm jut of her chin, the way her nose turned up just the slightest bit, and the smooth line of her brow. She was a beautiful woman, and soon he would know the truth about her. He would find out if his first opinion of her was correct, or if he had been badly mistaken. If he had not been mistaken, then maybe he would be able to get her out of his system. Either way, it would be a relief one way or the other.

Jessica thought her heart would leap from her chest it was beating so rapidly. She loved Cole, she knew she did. It could not be a mere physical attraction. The nearness of him was enough to drive her wild with longing. She was also aware of the danger of being so close to him in the coming week. She would have to muster all of her will power not to swoon into his arms if he embraced her. She would not again make the mistake of showing her love so freely.

Jessica smiled when she noticed the way their steps blended together while they walked side by side. A moment of easy silence passed between them as they continued on toward the cabin where she was staying.

Jessica suddenly stopped. "Oh! My father will be here day after tomorrow. What about him?"

"What about him?"

For the first time that evening, Jessica sounded upset. "I will want to see him."

"Of course you will," Cole readily agreed. "Believe it or not, I am not as mean as you might think. Besides, you will not be my prisoner, you will simply be repaying a debt." He turned to look at her, his voice became softer,

"I can understand how anxious you are to see him. It sounds as though you love him very much."

"I do love him. We were always so close, and Cole," she returned his urgent stare, "I didn't mean to imply you would try to prevent me seeing him, I was just wondering who would cook and take care of him."

Cole threw back his head and chuckled loudly. "How long has it been since you've seen him?"

"Almost two years."

"Who do you think has been taking care of him during this time?"

Jessica folded her hand over her mouth and giggled, "I suppose he has, and I guess I sounded terribly silly."

Cole's long legs began to step along the well beaten path. He turned expectantly and answered, "No, not silly, but you did sound like a typical female."

Jessica hurried to catch up with him. "And is that so horrible?"

Cole stopped, thought a moment and smiled, "Now that I think of it . . . no."

They had stopped in front of the cabin. Jessica stared up at Cole, gazing deeply into the endless depths of his eyes. She wanted to stay there forever. She wished the moment would never end. Before she could say another word, Cole leaned over and gently placed his lips on her inviting mouth. His kiss was not urgent nor demanding. It was tender and kind, sweet and loving, it was heaven, it was bliss.

He whispered gently, "Good night, my sweet, I'll see you in the morning."

Jessica crept quietly inside. She slowly removed her clothes and slid her gown over her head. She was tingling with excitement. She flung open a window and attempted to cool her burning cheeks in the crisp mountain air. She felt a cleansing feeling sweep over her. Gone was her guilt about Cole, and gone was the resentment she had bottled up in her heart. For the first time since she had met the man of her dreams, she actually admitted to herself that she had resented him. She had resented the fact that they had not met properly. She had resented the fact that he had turned on her so viciously, when she had not been in the wrong. If she had not known before, she now knew she was painfully aware of him as a man, of his blatant sensuality, and of the wild abandon of earthly bounds which lay beneath the surface of every glance they happened to exchange, and every spoken word. Lulled by the calmness of the night, Jessica sat on the window sill and gazed up at the twinkling stars into the wee hours of the morning.

Cole was going to fall in love with her, that was the one thing in her life she knew for certain. She wanted him, and by all that was holy, she would have him!

Chapter Eighteen

The following morning came early. Surprisingly, even after getting only a few hours sleep, Jessica was filled with boundless energy. Her life was becoming exciting. All of her dreams were coming true. She was getting a second chance to capture Cole's love, and her father would be home the following day. What more could a woman ask for.

She longed for a leisurely bath, but decided to spend the time on her hair. It was so long, it took a great deal of care just to keep it looking nice. She took a quick sponge bath, then looked at the rack which held her pitifully few dresses. She finally decided upon the silver-dove muslin with black piping trim. It was her favorite dress except for her really nice one she wore only on special occasions. She loved the way the sleeves fit her arm. They were designed quiet simply, straight until they reached the bend of her arm, then tiny gathers almost making them puffed, but not quite, and the cuffs were wide with lace and black piping trim. The bodice was elegant in its simplicity. Tiny rows of lace and black trim ran from the shoulders to the waistline. The cut of the dress revealed her petite waist.

Jessica was putting the finishing touches to her hair when a knock sounded at the door.

"Yes, I'm coming," Jessica called, thinking it was Cole, she rushed to the door. Opening it wide, Jessica gasped when she saw William, she had forgotten about their morning walk.

"Good morning, aren't you expecting me?" he asked confused.

"No—well, not actually—I was . . ." she stopped, feeling very foolish. "I'm sorry, William, I was on my way out. I will not be able to go walking with you this morning."

William's face fell in disappointment. "I'm sorry, are you feeling bad today?" He was puzzled over the fact she was dressed and appeared to be very excited.

"Oh, I'm feeling fine. I am simply having to repay a debt." She felt awkward and wondered why she was hesitant to explain in detail to William. "I really must be going now, will you excuse me?"

"Sure," he mumbled, stepping out of her way. He was very disappointed. He had grown fond of their morning strolls, and of Jessica's company. When he had first seen her as she opened the door, he thought her extra grooming pains had been for him. He knew he should not be so enamored with the girl, he was nearly twice her age, but still, he was in good health and had taken good care of himself. Jessica seemed to enjoy his company; why at times, he thought she was downright attracted to him. He knew she was fond of him, and only hoped that fondness would grow into something deeper. He stepped back from the foor to let her pass. She bid him a cheery farewell before walking toward the edge of town. Watching until she passed out of sight, William turned and walked back to his house. Suddenly the morning did not appear as inviting as it had a few minutes earlier.

Jessical timidly knocked on Cole's door. Upon receiving no answer, she hesitantly pushed open the door and called his name. He was not there. She pushed the door open and was immediately overwhelmed by the simple yet masculine appeal the cabin held. Two huge stuffed chairs sat in front of the fireplace with a table in between them. A gunrack holding four rifles hung by the door. On one wall was a Mexican serape, its circle being perfect. On another wall was a bookshelf, which held a surprisingly large number of books, not as many as William's held, but Jessica was still impressed.

She walked slowly into the bedroom. It was stark and simple. A huge four poster bed dominated the room. Her eyes grew wide with wonder when she saw it. She could imagine Cole carrying her to it and making mad, passionate love to her. She shook her head and scolded herself for having such torrid thoughts. Gingerly touching the side of the bed, Jessica smiled, realizing it had a downy soft feather mattress. She recalled the cold New York winters and how she and her sister would run and jump into bed with her parents early each morning until their fireplace warmed up the house. It was strange how an insignificant item could touch the long forgotten memories of her childhood. Jessica touched the colorful patchwork quilt, admired the delicate stitches and wondered who had taken the pains to sew it so well. Jessica quickly decided she was discovering a lot of hidden mysteries concerning Cole.

Examining the room further, Jessica noticed the wash stand with a pitcher and basin, and in another corner was a tall, highboy chest, its rich mahogany wood gleaming in the morning sunlight. Turning, Jessica noticed Cole's saddle rack was empty. He must have had to go somewhere very early, she mused. An amusing smile touched her lips when she saw Cole's dirty clothes had been hastily kicked underneath the bed. Just like a man, she thought as she knelt to retrieve them.

Jessica walked over to the wash table and put up Cole's mug and razor. It gave her a feeling of well-being, of closeness to handle his intimate possessions.

Ambling slowly into the kitchen, Jessica walked in a dream-like trance. She had expected a stack of dirty dishes, but surprisingly, the room was tolerably clean. The aroma of fried bacon still hung in the air. Jessica's eyes widened when she saw a bouquet of fresh field flowers sitting on the table. Beside the flowers was a note.

> I thought these might brighten your day. Please have supper with me tonight. I will expect you. Had to go up to one of the mines, and will not be back until supper.
>
> Signed
> C.R.

A tear fought its way into Jessica's eyes. This was a side of Cole she had never seen before, but it was a side of him that did not disappoint her, and she was not surprised. She knew he could be kind and considerate and this deed proved it.

The fragrance of the flowers mixed with the masculine aroma in the cabin. It was a pleasant scent. She could smell the faint aroma of one of his black cheroots, and almost expected him to enter the room at any moment.

Sighing, Jessica decided she had wasted enough time. If she wanted to complete all of her chores, she had better get busy. Jessica stirred the ashes in the cookstove and added some kindling, then a couple of pieces of split wood. Soon, a huge boiler was steaming with hot water. She rolled up her sleeves and began working. The table was scrubbed until it sparkled, and the plank floor was mopped and scrubbed until she could almost hear its squeaky cleanliness as she walked across it. Next came the front room, and when it was thoroughly clean, she moved on to the bedroom. She had just finished it and had walked into the front room to sit down when she heard someone at the door. It was too early for Cole. Who could it be, she wondered as she opened the door. It was William standing outside and he looked angry.

"Jessica! There is absolutely no need for you being here! I talked to Rylie a few minutes ago, and he told me what happened last night at the poker game. You don't have to be a maid for anyone, not even Cole."

"Why, William, you don't have to be so upset. I really don't mind doing this. After all," she laughed and shook her head, "I made a deal with Cole and I didn't have enough money to repay him. I am simply living up to our agreement."

William stared at her. His brow was creased into a stern frown. "I don't like this, Jessica. I don't want anyone getting the wrong ideas about you."

Jessica glanced over William's shoulder, "Please come

inside and we can discuss this. There is no need in letting the entire town hear our conversation."

William crossed his arms stubbornly, "There is nothing to discuss as far as I'm concerned. If you brought a shawl, get it and I'll see you home."

"No, William. This is a debt I owe, and I intend to repay it."

"Cole has not gotten out of the way with you, has he?" William narrowed his eyes and stared at her inquiringly.

"William!" Jessica gasped. "Don't be ridiculous! I thought Cole was your friend."

"He is, in fact, that boy is more like a son to me. I don't want him making any improper advances toward you though. I don't want the entire town gossiping about you either."

"But . . . William, many of the other women have started cleaning the men's cabins and cooking for them and no one is gossiping about them!"

"That's right!" William's face had suddenly grown ashen, "But those men and women have an agreement between them. Tell me, do you and Cole have an agreement?"

It dawned on Jessica what William was getting at. He was interested in her! Her mind flew at a furious pace. It came with a screeching awareness that all of those innocent inquiries and those early morning walks, and William's solicitous attention had been because he was attracted to her! She did not love this man. True, he was kind and considerate, and he was a wonderful man, but it was Cole she loved. But because he was all of those things, kind, considerate, wonderful, she had to be truthful with him. "No . . ." she said slowly, "There is no agreement between Cole and me, but I have to be truthful with you, I . . . have feelings for him."

"Does he feel the same way about you?" William asked quietly.

"I don't know. I wished to God I did know," Jessica admitted, lowering her eyes. She could not bear to see William's pain any longer. He started to turn to leave. "William, wait, please wait." She touched his arm. "Please answer me, I never gave you a reason to think . . . did I?"

"No, Jessica," he patted her hand. "I was simply a foolish old man to even . . ."

"Please, William," she took his hand, "Please come inside so we can talk." He followed reluctantly, but sat down in Cole's chair. "William, please, you don't know how much I respect, admire, and cherish your friendship." Her eyes dropped to the floor. "I don't know if there can ever be anything between Cole and me. And as for my being here, it has absolutely nothing to do with my feelings. I made a silly mistake by borrowing money to gamble on. I don't think I would be a very nice person if I backed out on our agreement." Dear God, why couldn't she simply say she was deeply in love with Cole and let this wonderful man go on about his life. She realized she was giving him false hope. She never intended for William to fall in love with he. True, he had not mentioned the word love, but she had seen the look in his eyes and the expression on his face. Had Jessica been an older and more experienced woman, she would have realized all of these men in Utopia were starved for female companionship. Even the mature men were susceptible to a woman's charm.

"Are you sure Cole hasn't declared his love for you?" William asked. "I would never do anything to hurt him."

Jessica shook her head, "No, he has not given me any indication he feels anything for me." There was no way Jessica was about to tell William all that had happened between them. "Please, William, can't we remain friends?"

William smiled, "Of course we can still be friends. I'm terribly sorry I created a scene, my dear. I would never hurt you, or embarrass you."

Later, a glimmer of tears appeared in Jessica's eyes as she watched William leave Cole's cabin. He carried himself so tall and proudly. She was probably a fool for discouraging his attentions, but she could not live with her conscience if she led him on and gave him false hope that there could never be anything between them.

William was furious with himself. He had barged in on the girl and had acted like a fool. He reminded himself of a gangly school boy. He should have realized Jessica would have been interested in one of the younger men. Why, he was old enough to be her father. William made up his mind to watch the relationship between Jessica and Cole, and if it did not develop, then he would approach Cole and sound out his feelings about Jessica. If Cole gave the indication he did not care for her, then he would begin to court her and try to win her heart. He knew he could never do anything to hurt the man he loved as a son; he would live out his life alone before allowing that to happen.

Chapter Nineteen

Jessica managed to ward off her foreboding feeling. She pushed William to the back of her mind as she walked out to the cold storage room and cut two thick steaks from the venison that was hanging from the rafter. After placing them in a bowl of milk to soak, she walked back over to the cabin she shared with the other women. She desperately hoped June or Helen was there. She needed to talk to someone she could confide in.

June was busy kneading bread in the kitchen table. She had flour all over her, and smiled when she saw Jessica. "I may not be neat as a pin, but I sure am a good cook. We're having company for supper tonight," she bubbled happily. "I guess you might as well know before you hear it from someone else. I have met a man! He is everything I could hope for."

"Oh?" Jessica smiled, "Do I know him?"

"I don't know, his name is Stuart Hall."

Jessica shook her head, "I don't know, perhaps if I saw him, I would recognize him, but the name isn't familiar."

June looked strangely at Jessica, "What is the matter?" she demanded to know. "You look as though you have something serious on your mind."

"I do, I don't really know how to explain it, though."

June placed a clean dishtowel over the bread and placed it to rise on a small table near the stove. She poured two cups of coffee and sat down, "All right, tell me about it. Does it have something to do with your being over in Cole's cabin?"

"You know about that?"

"Sure do," June nodded. "In fact, the entire town is talking about it, especially the men. They never thought Cole would get that interested in one woman."

"Can't they understand it was a silly loan . . . or have you heard *why* I am over there?"

"I heard something about a poker game," she chided Jessica, "and here I was worrying about you. Looks like you can take care of yourself. When did you learn how to play poker?" she added bluntly.

Jessica laughed, "I haven't learned, that's why I am having to cook and clean for Cole for an entire week. But that isn't why I want to talk. It seems as though William has heard the gossip too. He came over earlier this morning and demanded I leave."

"Leave town?" June gasped.

"Oh, no, he demanded I leave Cole's cabin." Jessica searched her friend's eyes for understanding, "June, I did not realize it. William is falling in love with me."

June took a sip of her coffee, then placed her hand over her mouth thoughtfully. Finally, she said, "Now, I'm beginning to see what you are getting at. Cole and the Captain are as close as father and son. You love Cole, and the old man is in love with you."

"June, don't call William an old man!" Jessica scolded.

"Well, it's the truth. Older men have been marrying younger women since the beginning of time, and I doubt seriously if that practice will cease tomorrow. However, you are now faced with a problem, a problem which could become very sticky."

"More than that," Jessica admitted. "William asked me if there was anything between us and I could not lie. I was truthful. I told him that I cared for Cole, but did not know how Cole felt about me." Jessica stared intently into the cup of steaming brown liquid. "There is something else I have been thinking about. I know many of the women gossiped about me when I had to be rescued from the Golden Slipper, now it seems as though I have added fuel to the fire. I certainly don't want my father to hear the ugly rumors, and I don't want my reputation to be damaged. What do you suggest I do?"

"God, I don't know, Jessica. If you'll pardon the expression, it sounds like a hell of a mess to me!"

Jessica nodded thoughtfully, "Me too."

June met Jessica's stare with an unwavering gaze, "There is one thing I could do to help. I could talk to the women and let it be known exactly *why* you're going to Cole's cabin. Maybe that would stop some of the rumors."

"Do you really think so?"

June shrugged, "I don't know, but at least it's worth a try. After all, what do you have to lose?"

"Apparently, not much," Jessica forced a smile. "There is something else, June, about this situation between Cole and William. I would never do anything intentionally to hurt either one of them or their relationship."

"I know that," June mused. "The most important thing though, is how you feel about them. You admitted you loved Cole, and you also said you were not sure how he felt about you. Has he given you any reason to hope he shares the same feelings for you?"

"Not really," she admitted.

"Then it looks to me like you have a big decision to make." June's brow wrinkled into a frown, "Wait a minute, I recall you saying something about leaving Utopia after your father returned. I take it those plans have been changed?"

"If there is a chance Cole has feelings for me, I'll not say a word to father about leaving." Jessica stood and made her way to the door. "Thanks a lot, you've been a big help to me."

"I don't know what I've done," June said, shaking her head.

"For one thing, you listened. That means a great deal to me." She turned the doorknob, "I'll see you later."

That afternoon, Jessica decided to strip the curtains from the windows and wash them. She needed to keep busy. Her mother had always told her busy hands didn't allow the mind to wander. She had just put them into the huge black wash pot when she heard a horse whinny at the front of the cabin. Looking to see who was stopping, Jessica's heart began to beat rapidly when she saw it was Cole.

"Cole . . ." she stammered, "You're back early. From your note . . . I wasn't expecting you until later."

"I finished sooner than I expected," he said, a subtle hint of humor was evident in his voice. He looked around the cabin. "Certainly looks like you've been busy here."

"Yes, I have been living up to my agreement." Jessica kept her eyes averted from his direct gaze. She knew the power hidden behind those blue shards of steel. She was aware of Cole's nearness. She sensed him stepping closer to her. If he takes me into his arms, I don't know what I will do, her inner voice screamed. Please, dear God, give me the strength to resist his charm.

Cole took a deep breath, "Mumm, something smells good."

"I believe you ordered an apple pie," Jessica stammered, relieved Cole had nout offered to take her in his arms. "Have you had anything to eat?"

"Yes, we have a chuckwagon up at the mines, I would like a cup of coffee though."

A fire was still blazing in the stove from where she had baked the pie. She put on a pot of coffee, then sat down at the table. Cole joined her.

Jessica removed a flower from the vase and toyed with it. Feeling somewhat harrassed by Cole's relentless eyes, she began unsteadily, "Cole, I . . want you to know . . . I appreciate this truce."

"Truce?" Cole was deliberately baiting her.

"Yes, truce," she met his eyes.

"Do you think we were having war?"

"Weren't we?" she replied in a strained whisper.

Cole chuckled, "Yes, I suppose so." He was not a person to apologize, but he did offer, "I guess I did carry it a little too far. And about that night a Coyote Creek, I never meant for that to happen."

"Neither did I, Cole." Her heart was soaring into lofty heights. Cole actually sounded as though he cared. His manner indicated he would possibly court her. Dear

God, please let him fall in love with me. Please let me have the strength to resist temptation.

Cole got up from the table and was pouring the coffee. "What in the world?" he mouthed when a piercing scream sounded from outside.

They rushed ot of the cabin and ran in the direction from which the scream came. They were joined by several other people rushing from their cabins. As they neared the community hall, they saw a woman crying hysterically and wringing her hands.

"It's my Tommy!" she gasped. "He's nowhere to be found! He's disappeared! Oh, Tommy . . . Tommy . . ." she cried, burying her head in her hands.

Cole took the woman by her shoulders. "Now, calm down," he soothed, "Getting hysterical will not help."

The woman was frantic. "My Tommy . . . you have to find him!" Her face was contorted, twisted in a demented horror. She continued to scream and moan convulsively. Cole raised his hand and slapped her into silence.

"Cole!" Jessica breathed unbelievably, "that wasn't necessary!"

Cole was alarmed. A child was missing and his mother was hysterical. It could be serious. He pointed a finger at Jessica, "Stay out of it, Jessica! I didn't hit her to hurt her, I've got to calm her down and that was the only way to do it." He turned his attention back to the woman. "Listen to me, lady," Cole shook her, "you have to calm down. We won't be able to find the boy until you tell us what happened!"

The woman's voice came in gasping sobs, "I was over there," she pointed to a clothesline, "Hanging clothes. Tommy was playing at the edge of the woods. I looked . . . one minute and he was there . . . the next minute he was *gone!* I went looking for him and . . . I saw . . . Oh, God . . . I saw . . ." She began crying again.

Cole glanced up to see William running toward them. "What is the matter?" he gasped.

Cole ignored his question, instead, he shook the woman again. "You have to get a hold of yourself and tell what you saw. Tell us, damn-it!" Cole's voice was breaking with urgency.

"I saw . . . a big, black, furry thing . . . I think it was a bear!"

William's eyes met Cole's. "I'll get the guns!" He raced to his house and was back in a matter of moments.

In the meantime, Cole barked orders. "Jessica, get this woman in the house and give her something to calm her down. There is some laudanum on the top shelf in my cabin. You," he pointed to another woman, "Go ring that bell hanging by the hall. The men will hear it from the mines and come to help."

"Let's go, Cole, we're wasting time," William urged, handing Cole a gun and extra ammunition. "You women gather up the children and go to the cabins, *and for God's sake, stay inside!"* The men took off running in the direction where the woman had pointed. When they approached the woods, Cole and William stopped and studied the signs the child had left. There were also huge bear tracks present. Each one of them looked grim when they saw a trail of blood leading off into the dense underbrush.

"Damn!" Cole swore softly.

William felt the same as Cole. It would be a miracle if they found the boy in time.

They proceeded cautiously, moving as quietly as possible. They were both seasoned hunters, regardless of whether their prey was man or beast; they were well versed in the art of tracking. Many times, back in Texas, the two of them had tracked Indians for days on end. They knew one moment of carelessness could bring certain death.

It was a wild, lonely country. The further they climbed, the more difficult the terrain became. The wind was brisk, blowing off the snow on the top of the mountains; still, the men continued to follow the trail.

The two men worked in perfect unison, prescience flowed between them easily. They were always alert, knowing at any given moment a huge giant could come roaring down upon them.

Finally, William signaled for Cole to stop. He pointed to something lying in the underbrush. Cole moved cautiously forward. He stopped and slowly picked up a pair of bloody trousers. The muscles in his face twitched as he handed them to William. From the size of the pants, the child couldn't have been more than three or four years old at the most. They knew the child would not be found.

Cole's lips settled into a thin, white line. He said grimly, "Looks like we've got a killer bear on our hands." Sorrow was evident in his voice as he said, "I think we ought to keep going instead of waiting for the other men. It looks like rain. If we turn back now, we might lose the trail."

"I agree," William's strong voice trembled with emotion. "The mother has a right to know, but we can't let that bear get away. If we do, he's had a taste of blood, he'll be back." His words were ominous in the quiet of the forest.

Deep in the brush, the bear peered through the leaves and vines. His eyes glowed red with madness. A growl came from deep within his chest. His nose rose high into the air as he sniffed the new and different man smell. His mouth foamed, mixing with the blood on his chin, then he turned back to his prey.

Darkness fell quickly over the woods. William and Cole knew they would have to find shelter for the night. They discovered a cliff with a twenty-foot drop at the bottom of a long, steep mountain. They knew they would be safe for the night. Cole found two pieces of iron pyrite and after gathering twigs, dried leaves, and small branches, he built a smokeless fire. Then finally, for the first time since they had left Utopia, William spoke about the seriousness of the situation. "You know if we don't get that bear, he'll keep coming back to town. He's had a taste of human blood, there will be no stopping him until several lives are lost unless we do it now."

Cole nodded, "I know. It gives me a sick feeling, right here!" He felt the bile of nausea rise into his throat.

"You know, Cole, I wanted everything to be so perfect! Now, the devil has invaded my Eden!"

"William," Cole looked at his friend strangely, "Utopia is filled with flesh and blood men and women. It's not going to be a perfect existence."

"I know, I know. It's just . . . all of those people are under my care and now, I've let them down. You know yourself, while we were riding for the Rangers, we saw horrible things. We saw men, women, and children who had been butchered so badly by the Indians, they no longer resembled human beings. We've even come across bodies when the buzzards were still picking their bones clean, but never have I felt as helpless as I do now. And I know part of it is the way I feel about Utopia." He looked at the man he loved as a son, "I don't think you are understanding what I'm saying."

"I think I do, William, and it bothers me. Man, you can't live their lives. Utopia is not a garden of Eden. It isn't Paradise!"

"I realize what you're saying, Cole, and I agree with you. However, I have poured so much of my soul into that place, I feel it's a part of me. I believe if Utopia stopped existing, I would too, and I guess that's why I want it so perfect." He laughed ruefully, "In fact, I made fool out of myself today. I heard the rumor that Jessica was taking care of you and I went over to your cabin and demanded she leave. I guess I tried to make something dirty out of a simple situation."

"What do you mean, William?" Cole suddenly felt a tightness in his chest.

"I thought there was something between you and Jessica, and I was mad, because I wanted her for myself. But, to be honest, I don't know if it is Jessica who attracts me, or if it's the fact that Jessica reminds me so much of my own Anne."

Cole nodded. He had never met William's wife. She had died a long time ago. But his friend had talked about her many times. "What did Jessica tell you?" Cole asked, wanting an answer, but dreading to hear it.

"She told me that she was simply repaying a loan or wager, whatever," William gave a wave of his hand. "But when I asked her if there was anything between the two of you, she said no, however, she did say . . ."

"Listen!" Cole said sharply. He had heard a noise down at the bottom of the cliff. From the sound of it, it was a large animal.

"Do you think it's the grizzly?"

"I'd stake my life on it, and we both will if we go down there in the dark. We had better lie low until morning, don't you agree?"

"Yep," he answered firmly. They leaned back against the cliff. There was only one way the bear could come, and that was by following their trail. The thought crossed both of their minds, that perhaps now, they were the ones being tracked.

William knew he had left Cole under the wrong impression. He had meant to tell him about Jessica's declaration of love for the man. He would have to set the record straight later. Right now, their lives and the lives of untold men and women depended on their alertness.

Chapter Twenty

Like a pale blush, drawn stole slowly across the mountain peaked sky. Summer was in full bloom, but a hint of crisp autumn was already in the air. Squirrels and chipmunks worked tirelessly, gathering acorns and other nuts for the coming harsh winter. Birds sang from the highest treetops, and flowers eagerly turned their faces toward the warmth of the morning sun.

The man took a stick and stirred the coals in his campfire. He had driven a small metal rod into the ground. On the rod was an arm which was able to swing back and forth. The man filled a pot with water, placed the wire bale on the handle and swung the pot over the fire to heat. When the water began to boil, he sprinkled a handful of coffee in it and waited for the grounds to settle. While waiting, he went over to his wagon and sliced some bacon from a jowl. Returning to the campfire, the man placed a fire-blackened skillet on it, waited until he could see the heat rise, then placed the pieces of meat in the pan to cook.

The man cast a worried glance in the direction of the

mules that were staked a few hundred feet from his camp. He took a deep breath, removed the skillet from the fire and went over to investigate. His brow creased into a frown. The mules were becoming increasingly skittish. Their ears were pointed straight up, and their hooves pawed at the ground. They strained at their ropes, trying desperately to free themselves from their bonds. They were frightened of the menace that lurked in the near-by woods.

Cole and William knew they were getting close. The tracks the bear was leaving were fresh. The grizzly couldn't be over ten minutes ahead of them. They were alert, they were cautious. If the wind changed direction, the bear would be aware of their presence. He was a crafty old giant. There was no telling his age, but he was smart. It was as though he sensed someone was on his trail.

The grizzly had the scent of man all around him. He paused and lifted his nose into the wind. Flecks of foamy blood dripped from his mouth. The bear scratched at the burning in his side where a careless hunter's bullet had accidently found its mark. The bear moved gracefully. Patchy sunlight filtered through the trees and glistened on his shiny coat. The bear paused again and sniffed. He had been running since the first light of dawn and he was angry and thirsty. The pain in his side intensified. The scent in his nose grew stronger.

The man tried to calm his mules. They grew more restless by the minute. He glanced uneasily toward the wagon where his rifle was leaning. He cautiously worked his way through the mules. He needed to get to his gun. The man stopped suddenly. He heard a soft growling noise behind him. Turning, the man's eyes widened in fear. An eight foot grizzly stood a few feet from him.

The man swallowed hard. He knew that to turn and run would mean certain death. He inched backward, silently cursing himself for leaving his gun. He had known better. The bear slowly started waddling toward him. The man took several steps backward. He knew he was looking death in the face.

William and Cole heard a frenzied scream of terror. Not even pausing to glance at one another, they began running. They burst into the clearing in time to see the bear make one mighty swipe, sending the man flying across the ground. Cole shouted, averting the bear's attention, drawing it to himself.

It was as though everything happened in slow motion. Cole raised his rifle and took careful aim. The bear charged at him, towering several feet above his head. His eyes glowed red, maddening foam dripped from his mouth. With a steady finger, Cole pulled the trigger on his gun, but it did not fire.

Thinking quickly, Cole shouted, "William! I'm in trouble!" He tossed the gun around to get the barrel in his hands. He drew the gun back and when the bear was in range, Cole swung with all of his might. The stock of the rifle shattered against the bear, but it kept on coming. With one swipe of its front paw, he knocked Cole away.

William saw what was happening, "Bear! Look here, you mean son-of-a-bitch!" William raised his rifle, took careful aim and fired. The bear kept coming. The bear clawed at the stinging pain suddenly tearing at its chest.

His slavering jaws shook with fury, but he still kept coming. William took a deep gulp of air, aimed the gun and fired once again. This time, the bear staggered back and went to all fours. The bear heaved upward trying to rise, but only fell back on his haunches. The grizzly gave one last screaming roar, then fell over dead.

William ran to where Cole was lying crumpled on the ground. He gently turned him over and a look of horror crossed his face when he saw the gaping wound across his friend's chest. He knew he had to get Cole back to town where he could be taken care of properly. Remembering the other man, William rushed to where he lay. A quick glance told him the man was beyond help.

William swiftly harnessed a team of mules to the wagon. He lifted Cole and placed him on the wooden planks, then he carried the other man over to the wagon and hurriedly draped a blanket over his body. The man was not a petty sight to see.

He knew Cole was in a bad way. He had to get some help for him and soon! From what he had been able to see, the grizzly's blow had ripped his flesh and crushed some of his ribs. It was possible the broken ribs had punctured Cole's lungs.

Although concern for Cole was the most important thought in William's mind, he couldn't help but wonder about the man the bear had killed. He knew him. He was Jess Tate, Jessica's father. Not only would he have to tell the little boy's mother what had happened to him, he would have to see the heartbreak on Jessica's face when she learned her father would never return.

The ride to Utopia was a hellish nightmare William thought would never end. He had never taken a whip to a team of horses or mules in his life, but he did that day.

He flicked the whip over the mules' heads, and when they did not go fast enough, he criss-crossed the whip across their flanks. William drove the mules like a madman over the high mountain pass. It was barely a decent trail, much less a road. It would have been unsafe for the wagon to proceed with caution, but the way William was driving, the wagon nearly careened over the the mountainside several times. The wagon reeled along at such a wild, rocking pace, William had to slow up several times for fear of hurting Cole worse than he was already injured.

Finally, Utopia came into sight. William felt a great rush of relief. He brought the animals to a stop in front of his house. William shouted for help and he was instantly surrounded by men and Cole was gently lifted from the wagon and carried inside.

The women lining the street could see the form of a body underneath the blanket. They stood clustered in tight little circles, talking and wondering aloud who had been killed. No one knew what had happened. Not a word had been heard from Cole and William since they had left the previous afternoon. There was still a party of men out in the woods hunting for the bear.

Someone ran to Cole's cabin and shouted to Jessica that William and Cole had returned. She looked down at Mary, Tommy's mother, sleeping restlessly from the drugs she had been given. Hoping the woman would stay asleep until she found out what had happened, Jessica rushed over to the community hall. When she neared the rear of the wagon, she stopped. She had been told William and Cole had returned, but in what condition! One of them had been killed! Jessica could feel all color drain from her face. From where she was standing, all she could see was the soles of a man's boots. Who was it, the man she loved, or was it the man whose friendship she treasured most in the world?

"Jessica!"

Upon hearing her name, Jessica spun around. Her eyes widened in horror when she saw William. Her mind had registered the sound of his voice, and now she was faced with the stark moment of truth; William was alive and Cole was the one underneath the blanket!

William took a hesitant step forward. "Jessica, please don't look at the body." His eyes lowered in nervous apprehension, then it dawned on him what she was thinking. She had no way of knowing the man was her father. She thought the dead man was Cole.

Her voice froze. She heard a deep roaring in her ears. Her lips moved, but no words came. *Dead! Dead!* Her beloved Cole was dead! No! It could not be true! He was too vibrantly alive to be dead! Jessica could feel blessed darkness slowly envelop her.

"Jessica!" William shouted, catching her before she fell. "Don't . . . Jessica, it isn't Cole!"

The words snapped Jessica out of her faint. "Wha . . .! It *isn't* Cole!" she repeated incredulously. "But . . . who?" Her eyes flew to the covered body. "Who . . . what about . . . Tommy?"

William scooped her easily into his arms. "Let me take you inside, my dear." He was desperately concerned someone would raise the blanket and Jessica would see her father before he could tell her.

"Cole? What about Cole? Where is he?" she cried.

"They have already carried Cole inside. He's been hurt, Jessica, but he's going to be all right!"

Jessica slumped into William's arms in relief. Tears of

relief slid effortlessly down her ashen cheeks. She was docile in his arms as he carried her into the house and to the spare bedroom. She could hear voices coming from the other bedroom. "Cole?" she whispered, searching William's face for some kind of reassurance.

"Ed's working on him now. He's had some training in medicine. Cole's in good hands, Jessica."

"My God, what happened?"

William knew she would have to be told the truth. He could not delay it any further. He slowly started at the beginning, telling her about them tracking the bear through the woods, and how they had found the bloody trousers. He noted the sheer terror on Jessica's face when she realized what had actually happened to the child. Then he explained how they had camped through the night, afraid they would lose the animal's trail if they had come back to Utopia. His voice had a soothing effect, he slipped into the details about the other man so easily, Jessica did not realize the implications until he paused and looked directly into her eyes. "Jessica," he sighed deeply. There was no easy way to tell her. "I'm afraid . . ." he could not bring himself to look at her. "The man outside is your father."

The roaring sound came once again in her ears. The room began to spin crazily. Her mind cried out in protest. She trembled and pressed back against the bed, squeezing her eyelids shut as if that would somehow blot out the pain twisting her heart. The loss she felt was so great, it was like a searing flash of fire rippling through the very essence of her soul. The thought of never seeing her dear father's face crinkle with joyous laughter, his lips never breaking into a gladdening smile, and his large, strong hands never caressing or touching her again was more than she could bear. Gratefully, Jessica could feel herself slipping into the welcoming void of oblivion.

Later, Jessica awoke. She could hear voices coming from the other room. The shock of hearing about her father's death had left her weak, drained, empty, and with a sense of foreboding loneliness.

"Jessica, are you all right?" a soft voice asked.

Looking up sharply, Jessica saw Helen sitting on the chair beside her.

"William asked me if I would sit with you." Her eyes were filled with compassion. She reached out and stroked Jessica's brow. "My dear friend, I am so sorry. You are so young to have suffered this much heartache. Is there anything I can do?"

Jessica's bottom lip trembled. She fought back the tears. "No, nothing, not unless you can turn back the clock . . ." her voice broke with grief, "Not unless you can undo every terrible thing that has happened . . . and I know you can't do that. You can only do what you are doing. Oh, Helen," she cried, "Why does God have to take the good ones and leave the evil people alone? My father was such a good man! Where is the justice?"

Helen patted Jessica's hand, "Friend, we do not have an unjust God. Oh, I remember the pain and heartache I felt when my husband died and I asked the same questions you are asking. However, I did not find *one* clear cut answer. I simply had faith that God in his infinite wisdom, knows best. And he does not place too great a burden on anyone. You are young and strong and your grief will fade. Jessica," Helen's voice grew strong with conviction. "I know I am not overly religious, however, I strongly believe in God and in the hereafter. Perhaps . . . God called your father home because he needed another angel in heaven. I . . . cannot offer any explanation other than that."

Jessica sank back against the pillow. Maybe it's true, she thought. She remembered how close her mother and father were in life, perhaps they could find this closeness in death. Jessica's eyes misted, then huge tears began falling. It was as though the tears were cleansing, washing away the grief which tore at her heart. She knew a certain part of her would never forget the love or the goodness instilled within her by her parents. She knew through her, a part of them would live forever, that they would have a part of immortality. Their blood would run through the veins of her children and her children's children. Yes, the loss of her father had brought back the pain she had suffered when her dear mother died, and that loss would never be diminished. But it was a loss she could accept, and eventually come to terms with. Life was for the living, she must pick up the shattered pieces of her life and continue. She knew she must strive for happiness—that is what her parents would have wanted.

It would be hard, but Jessica knew she could face the following days with a wisdom and with the strength to endure. The coming days would be difficult, but at least God had spared Cole. Perhaps this was all part of God's master plan. Perhaps it had been written in the great book that one of Jessica's loved ones must depart the weary bonds of earth on this precise day, and Cole had been the one chosen to live.

"Jessica," Helen asked, concern rippling her voice. "Are you all right?"

Jessica raised her head, and through tear dimmed eyes, she answered, "No, not really, but I will be. I guess I need a little time to cry, to scream, and to shout how unfair life is, then I believe I will square my shoulders and face the terrible blow fate has dealt me." Jessica drew a rasping, tear choked breath. She reached out her arms. Helen wrapped her arms around Jessica and together, they wept.

Chapter Twenty-one

Jessica sat by Cole's bedside, watching the steady rise and fall of his chest. Huge tears glistened in her eyes, then stole quietly down her grief stricken face, dropping and forming two dark circles on her skirt. She was unaware of the clock chiming in the hallway outside, she was unaware of the colorful afghan covering her legs, she was unaware of anything in the room except Cole.

The oil lamp flickered, causing the shadows to deepen on his face. His skin, burnished by the sun, now appeared pale and ashen as he lay against the sparkling white of the pillows. A blanket had been drawn to his waist and had become twisted as he had thrashed about on the bed, thus restricting his movements. The fever which had consumed him for several days had finally broken, but Cole had shown no signs of regaining conciousness.

The ill-fated tragedy had happened four days earlier, and it was as though Cole was fighting a raging battle with the angel of death, and did not quite have enough strength to return to the land of the living. From time to time, he would raise his head, open his eyes, and mutter a few incoherent words, then sink back into the dark and dreary pits which possessed him.

Jessica took his hand and gently caressed it against her cheek, "Oh, Cole," she whispered softly, "Please don't die. Please be all right. I love you so much. I don't know what I'll do if I lose you too! Now that my father is dead, I have no one!" An expression of anguish flashed across her face when she realized what she had said. "Oh, God, forgive me," she cried. "I must sound terribly selfish. It seems as though all of my thoughts are concerning me. I know I should pray for Cole's life for his *own* benefit instead of mine. Dear Lord, just like Helen said the other day, you wouldn't place too heavy a burden on anyone." Tears flooded down her face, "I really don't think I can take anymore heartache. I have lost everyone who was dear to me. If you let Cole die, then please, oh, please, take me too!"

For how long Jessica prayed, she did not know. The lamps grew weak as the wicks lapped at the remaining drops of oil. Ching Lee brought in fresh lamps, but Jessica did not acknowledge his presence, she was so intent in her prayers. Finally, she raised her tear-streaked face, suddenly feeling the cage of her despair slowly ebb away, much like the pounding surf soothing and washing the sandy beaches by the sea.

Cole's dark lashes flickered, then he slowly opened his eyes and looked around the room. His gaze finally rested on Jessica and he asked softly, his voice weak and faint, "What happened? Where am I?"

Jessica jumped up, dropping the lap robe to the floor. "Oh, Cole! Thank God!"

"What happened?" he asked once again.

Jessica sat down and leaned forward, "The bear attacked you, Cole. Don't you remember?"

His eyes widened with an unspoken terror. He asked falteringly, "Willliam? Is William all right?"

"He's just fine," Jessica reassured him. "You have to be still, Cole. The bear tore a huge, gaping hole in your chest and you *must* lie still. You'll start the wound bleeding again." She gently pressed him back on the bed.

"Where's William?" Cole asked, his expression revealed he did not fully believe her.

"He's in the study trying to get a little bit of rest. We've all been keeping an around the clock vigil for you." She knew she should go for William, but she desperately hated to leave Cole's side. Reluctantly, she said, "I'll get him for you."

"No, Jessica, please don't go." Although Cole's mind was still hazy, he knew he wanted her to stay near him. Her closeness was comforting and reassuring. "The bear? Was it destroyed?"

"It's all right, Cole," Jessica soothed. "William killed him. The animal will never hurt anyone else again!" her voice broke with bitter anger and remorse.

Cole shook his head, his brow dipped into a puzzled frown, "It was so strange. I've never seen a wild animal attack without some kind of reason. I've seen she-bears attack whenever their cubs were threatened, but I've never seen anything like that before. Does Tommy's mother know?" he asked, his eyes revealing his unspoken misery.

"Yes, William told her as gently as possible. He also told me afterward that someone had shot the animal and only wounded him. That's why he had gone mad." Jessica paused, the rhythmic pounding of her heart seemed to echo throughout the entire room. She did not want to talk about that monstrous bear. That terrible creature had taken her father's life, the life of an innocent child, and had nearly destroyed Cole. She was glad he was dead. If it was within her power, she would have gone into the woods and destroyed each and every one of the ferocious creatures until there were none left, so great was her rage and anger.

Jessica forced her rage to abate. She must not dwell on the past and what could have been. She had to put her grief and anger in its proper perspective. She had to go on with her life, especially now that she had someone to live for. Cole was alive. He was going to be fine. She knew she could now face any obstacle thrown in her path.

Cole's eyes fastened unseeingly behind her. A cloudy opaqueness gradually lowered over his blue eyes like a curtain being drawn. He was reliving each tormenting moment of that horrible day. His face revealed many emotions; horror, fear, and uncomprehending rage. Then slowly, he brought his gaze to Jessica. "There . . . was a man . . . in the clearing . . ."

"Yes, Cole, there was a man," she whispered. She pulled her gaze from Cole. It was as though he was looking into the very depths of her soul. She took a deep breath and commanded her eyes to find his again. She noticed the saddened expression on his face. It dawned on her Cole seemed to be avoiding something. She gasped, "You know, don't you. Somehow, you know he was my father! But, how?"

Cole had listened carefully to Jessica. He winced inside over her words. She had said the man *was* her father. Yet, all along, he had known he was dead. He shouldn't have been surprised. In his anxiety, he had raised his head from the pillow. The force of his realization sent him slumping backward.

"How did you know, Cole?" Jessica asked once again. Her question held no importance, William had already explained everything that had happened. He had told her how they had arrived a moment too late to save his life. What was now important, Cole was awake at last. She desperately wanted to keep him talking. She was afraid he would slip back into unconsciousness.

Cole's voice trembled with emotion. "Everything happened so fast. I guess . . . I knew your father was due back here today. When we burst into the clearing, I caught a glimpse of him . . . and I automatically knew who he was. And now, I can see by the expression on your face that he's dead, isn't he?"

Jessica could not speak, she merely nodded, confirming his worst fears. She could not even bring herself to tell him how much time had actually passed.

"I'm so sorry, Jessica," he said softly.

In one fluid motion, Cole raised his arms and Jessica went willingly into them. It was a long moment before she could trust her voice enough to speak. "Oh, Cole, I'll miss him so much!" she cried bitterly, laying her head on his unbandaged shoulder. "It is so unfair. Why couldn't we have at least been able to see each other again before he died."

Cole gently wrapped his arms around her. There was nothing he could say to make it easier for her. He could feel the racking sobs which tore through her body as she buried her face into the muscular hardness of his shoulder. He could feel rivers of tears streaking across his flesh, but he did not care. With his arms wrapped around her, and even in her hour of grief, a sudden feeling of peace and love swept over him. He wanted to hold her forever. During that moment, he realized how deeply her loss, her agony, and her grief, affected him. A foreign feeling surged through him. It had been so long since he had held a woman in his arms in a truly loving moment. He couldn't quite understand the rash of emotions sweeping over him. Cole wondered briefly if these emotions were nothing but compassion, but deep within his heart, he knew better. He was experiencing the stirrings of love. No! No! He didn't want to fall in love. He wasn't ready for the mental entanglements that came with a relationship with a woman. Besides, William had already declared his love for her. Nothing he could say or do now would change that fact.

Even the memory of Melissa's face was a blur to him, and in her place, the picture of Jessica was firmly etched into his mind.

Cole could not bear to let Jessica go. He continued to hold her tenderly as he gently stroked the coppery tangle of her long, beautiful hair. "Jessica, my sweet," he whispered to her silently, "I want to hold you in my arms forever . . ."

Jessica raised her tear-streaked face and gently traced her finger along the firm jut of Cole's jaw. "What did you say, Cole?"

Cole was startled. "I didn't say anything," he answered quickly. He thought he had silently declared his love for her. Had he actually spoken it out loud? That would never do. She must never know how he really felt about her. He couldn't interfere. William loved her. Thinking quickly, Cole said, "I was only wondering about your father's services. When will it be held?"

"Services?" Jessica mouthed numbly, forgetting that Cole had been unconscious for so long.

"Yes, services for your father."

Tears crept into her eyes once more. Cole had no way of knowing how much those words tore through her heart. "Cole," she said slowly, "You have been unconscious for four days now. We have already buried my father. William spoke the words over him."

Cole could not believe it. He felt himself sag against the bed. Four days! It didn't seem possible.

Jessica's eyes riveted on Cole's face. His breathing had become heavy and labored. "Cole, please rest. You are overtiring yourself. You've been very very sick. In fact, I overheard Ed say that he didn't think you were going to make it there for a while. I heard him tell William you . . . might even die. Please lie back and rest. Don't overly excite yourself!" The urgency in her voice made it tremble as she pleaded with him.

"Four days!" he repeated incredulously, not heeding her cautious words. "You mean I have actually been out for that long?" It was still difficult for him to believe.

"Yes, Cole, I'm being honest with you. Ed said this morning that the reason why you were remaining unconscious for so long, was because you had lost so much blood."

For the first time since awakening, Cole allowed his hand to stray to his chest and other side of his shoulder where it was tightly bandaged. With the tip of his finger, he could trace the gaping wound. Cole realized what his chest must look like. He had seen men whom bears had ripped apart and they had not been pretty sights. Then the memory of what Jessica's father had looked like crossed his mind. At that moment, Cole realized exactly how close he had come to death, and William had been the one to save his life. It was ironic, all in one fleeting moment, to realize he loved the same woman as the man who saved his life. The scene unfolded before his eyes once again, how William, risking his own life, had pulled the bear's attention away from him. That thought and that thought alone gave Cole the determination to never stand in William's way to gain the love of this beautiful young woman.

"William," he muttered weakly. "I have to see him." His newly discovered feeling for Jessica was something he could not face at the moment. Just the sight of his old friend might give him enough courage to carry through his plan of sacrifice. William must never know of his feelings for Jessica. He knew if William even had an inkling, he would step aside, his love for Cole was so great. "William, please get him for me," he whispered harshly.

"Don't get excited," she patted Cole's shoulder. "I'll get him for you." Her smile was genuine as she rose and hurried for the door. "William, come quickly!" she called anxiously.

William had been dozing in his chair by the fireplace. A raw slice of terror ripped through his heart when he heard Jessica call out. He had been expecting the worst. He had seen Cole's wounds and he agreed with Ed. He doubted if Cole would live. Jessica's voice had trembled when she called him. William knew he couldn't stand the thought of losing Cole. He was the son he would never have. William hurried toward the bedroom. A stab of terror raced through him when he saw Jessica standing outside of Cole's bedroom door with tears streaming down her face. "My, God, Jessica," he croaked, "Cole . . . is he . . ."

A broad smile spread across her face. She could not contain her happiness. "Oh, William!" she squealed happily. She was so thrilled, she ran to meet William, and threw her arms around his neck. "Cole's awake! Oh, William, he's going to be all right!"

William simply buried his head in the heady aroma of Jessica's hair when he heard the good news. He felt himself go limp with relief. He did not see the crestfallen expression which swept across Cole's handsome face when he saw them embrace through the open doorway.

"He's awake!" William shouted happily as he uncoiled Jessica's arms from around his neck. He raced into Cole's room and stopped short at the bedside. "Cole?" he spoke softly. "Cole, answer me son, do you hear me? Are you all right?"

Cole's eyes flickered and a smile tugged at his lips. "I'm fine," he rasped. "It'll take more than a mangy ol' bear to do me in."

Sudden tears glistened in William's eyes. "I sure was worried about you, son. We thought we were going to lose you several times."

Even though Cole was in severe pain, he managed to smile again. "If I had known I would be getting this much attention, I would have tangled with a bear sooner." Cole touched his throbbing chest, "However, I think I would have picked out one that was a little tamer." Then Cole's mood sombered, "I'm sorry it was all on you to have to tell Tommy's mother, and Jessica. By the way, how is she taking her father's death?"

William shook his head wonderingly, "She's simply amazing. Yep," he nodded, "That little gal is quite a trooper. Not only has she faced the loss of her father, she has also insisted upon staying right here by your side. Finally, I had to put my foot down and make her get some rest last night. I was afraid she was going to get sick. She agreed . . . with only one stipulation."

"Yeah? And what was that?"

"That I let her use my room. Since I was sitting up with you, I didn't think it would hurt her reputation too much."

"I was worried about her," Cole admitted. "I knew how much she was looking forward to seeing her father again, then when he got killed, I didn't know if she could handle it or not."

William shook his head and smiled. "We don't have to worry about her, Cole. She'll be fine." William paused and stared down at Cole. There was a lump so big in his throat, he thought it would choke him. He awkwardly patted Cole's arm, "Yopu don't need to fill your mind with worries about Jessica. She's handling everything all right. The most important thing for you to do is get well and back on your feet."

"I'm going to be fine," Cole said as he pulled himself up on his pillow, grimacing at the sudden stab of pain. "You don't have to worry about me. William, would you please shut the door? There are a few things I want to say to you in private." Even though Jessica wasn't visible through the doorway, he knew she was near, and his words could carry. After the older man had closed the door, he walked back to Cole.

"William, I don't want to alarm you, so don't get the idea that I am making a death bed request. It's just that . . . I was talking to Jessica before she called you in." Cole knew he was pressing the issue about Jessica, but the sooner he set William straight about a few matters the better off everyone would be. "She needs somebody like you, William, someone who is strong and who can give her the security she needs. You need to encourage her to return the love you feel for her."

"Why this sudden concern?" William asked cautiously.

"Because she's been batted around long enough." Noting the puzzled expression on William's face, Cole added, "I've kind of grown fond of her myself. After all, who wouldn't feel sorry for the kid after everything she's been through." Cole hoped his ramblings made sense. The last thing he wanted William to think was that he was talking out of his head.

"You mean . . . there's nothing between you and her?" William asked slowly.

Cole forced a grin, although smiling was the last thing on his mind. "Not from my standpoint, there isn't. Oh," he gave an indifferent wave of his hand, "I'm not trying to flatter myself by saying this, but she could have been a little infatuated with me there for a while, after all, I am the one who rescued her from that bordello. But no," he shook his head, "I have no feelings toward her other than friendship." His words sent a searing flash of agony through him. They had been the most difficult he had ever spoken, but it had to be done. With him out of the way, now maybe William could be happy. Cole did not feel guilty about lying to William. His and Jessica's happiness was the most simportant thing in the worlds to him. He didn't feet guilty about Jessica either, he knew she was genuinely fond of William, and given time, she would fall in love with him.

William gruffly cleared his throat, "I really think we can talk about Jessica some other time. You are very weak and you need your rest. Now, you lie back and quit your fussing!" he said sternly, shaking his finger at him, scolding Cole like he would have a small child. "I'm leaving now so you can get some rest, but I'll be back in a little while. I would imagine you are getting hungry. I'll have Ching Lee to warm up some soup for you. While he's doing that, I'll go get Ed, I think he will want to look you over. Now, you be sure and lie still," he cautioned as he turned to leave.

"Wait a minute. Could you change that soup into a beefsteak about that thick?" Cole measured with his fingers.

"Nope," William smiled. "If someone doesn't eat Ching Lee's soup, he'll get his feelings hurt and before you know it, I'll have to look for another cook, and you know how hard good cooks are to find." William chuckled as he closed the door to the bedroom. It was great to have Cole back again!

Jessica had been waiting in William's study. When he walked in, Jessica got to her feet. "Doesn't he sound great!" she exclaimed happily.

"He sure does! He's hungry, that proves he's going to be all right. Listen, Jessica, I'm going over to get Ed. I think he ought to look at Cole. While I'm gone, would you have Ching Lee warm up that soup?"

"Let me go get Ed," Jessica injected. She took a deep breath, "For the first time in days, I think I would love to have some fresh air. The walk would do me good."

"But . . . you shouldn't be out after dark."

"Nonsense! You know perfectly well the streets are safe, especially after you posted the guards on the outskirts of town and set up patrols. If we're not safe here in Utopia, then we'll never be safe."

"Well, I suppose you are right," William drawled, "but, you be careful."

Jessica assured him she would be fine as she walked over to the coat rack, removed her shawl and tossed it around her shoulders. She stepped out onto the porch, and marveled over the chill in the air. She had heard the first frost of the season was due soon, and from the nip in the air, she didn't doubt it. She stepped off the porch and twirled around and around, her shawl flew through the air like giant wings about her shoulders. She was so happy! Cole was awake and all was right with the world! Well, almost, she thought as she gazed wishfully at the small hill where the graveyard was located. Jessica shook her head determinedly. She would not think about her father right now. She would try to ignore the dull ache in her heart, and for the rest of the night, she would only think about Cole and the future.

Her steps were lively as she made her way to Ed's house. She rapped on the door and it was opened instantly. Ed paled when he saw Jessica standing there.

"Jessica! What in the world are you doing . . ." His eyes widened, "Cole? It is Cole?" He grabbed for his jacket hanging on the peg beside the door. "Is . . . he worse?"

"Oh, no! He's fine. He awoke a little while ago, and apparently, he's doing fine. William simply sent me to tell you so you could come and look at him."

"He's awake! You mean he actually came out of the coma he was in!" Ed shouted with glee. "Thank God!" he said, breathing a deep sigh of relief. "I was really worried about him." He jammed his hat on his head and was off the small porch in one single bounce. "Well, come on, I want to see him." He hurried Jessica along.

"I'm coming, don't walk so fast. Cole isn't going anywhere."

Ed deliberately shortened his stride in order for Jessica to keep up with him.

"Tell me, Ed, have you known Cole very long?"

"Only since I have been out here in California." Ed explained about their first meeting as he and Jessica walked to William's house. "When I first drifted in out here, I did some panning in creeks. Had a pretty good poke salted away, but some dry-gulchers jumped me and stole everything I had. I bummed around for a while, stayed drunk most of the time. I was in a saloon in San Francisco, drunker 'n hell, and mooching drinks. One man threw some money in a spittoon, and dared me to fish it out. I started to, but Cole stepped in. That was the first time anyone showed me any compassion in a long time. Cole hauled me out of that bar, got me cleaned up, shoveled some self-respect back into me, and I've been dry ever since. There's nothing I wouldn't do for that man, Jessica."

"That story really surprises me, Ed," Jessica said softly. "You seem to be a much stronger man than that."

"I thought so too. But when I got into that trouble . . . well, never mind."

Jessica sensed he was starting to tell her about his past and then changed his mind. She knew a lot of the men and women out here were starting their lives all over and didn't like to talk about their yesterdays. She tried to change the subject. "You certainly seem to know a lot about medicine. Tell me, were you a doctor?"

"Why do you ask?" Ed asked abruptly.

Jessica shrugged her shoulders. "Because, like I said, you certainly seem to know what you are doing. In a way, it seems like you are wasting yourself here."

"Jessica," Ed started hesitantly, "Sometimes there are things a person shouldn't ask about. That part of my life isn't open to discussion. There are three people here who know about me. They are William, Cole, and Helen. I would rather have it stay that way."

Jessica nodded. She wasn't surprised. "I'm sorry, Ed. I shouldn't have pried." She smiled up at him. "Matter closed. And I promise never to ask again. All right?"

Ed nodded sheepishly and smiled. "All right, Jessica. I know you and Helen are very good friends, one of these days I may tell you all about my sordid past."

"Knowing you," Jessica chuckled, "I doubt if it can be all that bad."

They rounded the corner of the community house, and Jessica stopped and gasped. "Look Ed!" she tugged at his arm. "Look at the mountain, my God, it's on fire!"

Ed threw back his head and guffawed.

"Hurry, do something, sound an alarm!" Jessica shouted.

Ed caught Jessica by her hand and laughed again. "Calm down! Don't get excited. The mountain isn't on fire."

"But . . . it is! Just look!" Jessica's mouth dropped open in surprise when at that moment, the full moon crested the top of the mountain, lighting up the valley as bright as day.

Jessica placed her hand over her rapidly pounding heart. "Oh, my, you must think I'm a hysterical fool! When I first saw it, it really looked as if the entire mountain top was on fire."

"I know. I thought the same thing when I saw it for the first time," Ed admitted. "It's nothing but a harvest moon, but out on the plains, the Indians there sometimes call it a planting moon. Regardless, it's beautiful, isn't it."

"Oh, it's the loveliest sight I have ever seen," she gasped in awe.

A smile touched Ed's lips. "Hummm, after I check on Cole, think I'll go over to Helen's and see if she wants to go for a walk. Reckon she would like that?"

"I'm sure she would. What woman alive could resist a moon such as that, especially if she was walking with the man she loved." Jessica stared wistfully at the moon. Tiny moonbeams danced on the ground, and sparkled on the newly fallen dew. The entire town, valley and mountains looked as though it belonged in a fantasy fairytale. The tops of the fir trees sparkled like shiny jewels, and fluffy white clouds played chase with golden night magic. Jessica's eyes grew soft and misty. Oh, Cole, she thought. How I wish you were here by my side instead of lying so helplessly on that bed. How I wish you and I were the ones going for a walk. How I wish you were able to take me into your arms and whisper sweet words of love to me. And yes, how I wish you would even hold me passionately in your arms and make love to me. I can almost feel your body pressing close to mine, loving me, ravishing me, and even possessing me. How I wish I could feel your hard, muscular arms holding me as tightly as possible, and your masculinity inside of me, driving to a passionate frenzy. "Oh, Cole!" she whispered. "Please hurry and get well. I will win your love. By all that's holy I will share your life!"

Chapter Twenty-two

The days slowly passed into weeks. Cole's wounds continued to heal, and before long, he was up and around. He was still very weak and had to take it easy. He was gradually building up his strength by taking walks, which with each passing day, lasted longer and longer. Jessica offered to walk with him, but he always managed to come up with some sort of feeble excuse to walk by himself.

After Ed and Helen's wedding, and after June married Stuart Hall, Jessica was the last woman remaining in the cabin. There were only five women left in Utopia who were not married, and arrangements had already been made for them to return to San Francisco.

Jessica was confused. A short while before Cole was attacked by the bear, he had acted as though he was starting to feel something for her, but now, it was as though he was an entirely different person as his strength returned. It seemed to Jessica he was deliberately avoiding her, while William was exactly the opposite. He showered her with gifts and small trinkets and acted delighted to spend his leisure time with her. It became a ritual for them to play a game of chess every night. Cole never joined them. He would sit out on the front porch and smoke one cheroot after the other. He was truly a changed man after the attack.

Utopia was beautiful in the autumn. The elms, cottonwoods, and oak trees began to turn into their fall foliage. Their amber, brown and golden leaves brightened the entire area, while the pines turned greener. Grass in the meadows became brown, and the mountain peaks became white capped. Winter loomed ominously close when the snow crept closer and closer toward the small valley. Every three or four days, supply wagons would bring additional food to be stored for the coming winter. All the signs showed it would be a harsh one.

Jessica walked over from her cabin to William's house. She had promised him she would bake a cake. Although Ching Lee was an excellent cook, he had not mastered the art of baking. After no one answered her knock, she stepped inside and made her way to the kitchen. She added some wood to the huge cookstove, tied an apron around her waist, and started taking the cake ingredients from the cupboard. She began humming a tuneless little song as she added more milk to the batter.

"Well, if this isn't a homey little scene," a voice drawled lazily from behind her.

Jessica recognized the voice instantly. "William!" she gasped, spinning around. "I thought you were up at one of the mines?"

Tossing his hat onto the table, "I was, but I finished early so I thought I would try to catch you. I stopped by your cabin and figured you were over here."

"I hope you don't mind me making myself at home. I did promise you a cake, and the oven in my stove doesn't work very well. It gets too hot." She busied herself by pouring two cups of coffee from a pot that been sitting at the back of the stove.

When Jessica placed the coffee cup in front of William, he took her hand. "Please, sit down, I want to talk to you." His eyes were warm and loving.

"What is it? Is something the matter?"

"Oh, no, nothing is the matter. It's just that . . . I do wish you would make yourself at home."

Jessica was puzzled. "What do you mean?"

"I would love for you to make this your permanent home." William gazed tenderly into her eyes, drew her into his arms and kissed her. It was the first time he had ever taken her into his arms and his expression showed he did not want to let her go.

"William!" she gasped, pulling from his embrace and pushing back a stray wisp of hair. "You shouldn't have done that."

"Why not?" he asked boldly. "Only a fool would say I didn't love you. Jessica," he said tenderly, "I want you to be my wife. I want to marry you and take care of you for the rest of our lives," he said in a rush of words.

Jessica could not believe what she was hearing. "William . . ." she stammered, "I had no idea."

"Yes, you did, Jessica," William accused. "I told you how I felt about you that night of the party when you women first came here." Now that his courage was up, William wasn't about to let it lay. Not that he wasn't brave, he was, but when it came to Jessica, it was difficult for him to talk to her. He added, "I fell in love with you the moment I set eyes on you. Jessica, forget about

Cole. He'll never make you happy."

Jessica stared at William unbelievingly, then she turned and walked over to the window and stared out at the snow capped mountains. Finally, she spoke. "No, I am telling the truth. I really had no idea you still had feelings for me except that of friendship." It was true. She had been so wrapped up in her own thoughts and problems, she had not paid attention to anyone other than Cole. Cole, just the thought of his name was enough to bring tears to her eyes. Oh, God, why wasn't it Cole standing in front of her, proposing? Why? Why? "William, you don't want me!" she cried. "You know I don't love you! And please, let's leave Cole out of this," she added defensively.

"But, Jessica, Cole has already told me he doesn't love you. I would have never said a word if I thought I was coming between the two of you." His eyes implored her to understand.

Jessica could feel the color drain from her face. "What do you mean . . . he told you he didn't love me? Have you been discussing me as though I was nothing but a . . ."

"Now, Jessica, don't take it the wrong way," William interrupted.

Jessica searched William's eyes. All of her intuition told her something was very wrong. "Tell me," she said icily, "Do you and Cole sit around discussing my future as though I was nothing but a chattel? Did he say, I don't love her, William, you can have her?" Jessica's voice rose hysterically.

William placed his hands on Jessica's shoulders and forced her to sit down. "Now, will you calm down and listen to reason." He knelt beside her chair. "Jessica, we had the talk the night he regained consciousness. He was worried how you were coping with the fact that your father was dead. I don't know how the conversation swung around to the fact that I loved you, it just did. I asked him how he felt about you, and he said he couldn't help but feel sorry for you. But everybody does because you've had such bad breaks."

Jessica refused to remain sitting any longer. She leaped to her feet in a rage. "So! Now I'm just a poor little orphan that gets nothing but pity!" I don't want any pity! she screamed. Jessica stared at William bitterly. She bit her bottom lip, determined not to cry. Cole didn't love her! Cole had verbally handed her over to William without as much as a backward glance. No wonder he had been avoiding her all of these weeks. He was ashamed, and he had every right to be! Poor William, he had thought there was a chance she would fall in love with him. Cole had used them both! Used them as if they were something dirty to be discarded after he was through with them. These thoughts raced through her mind.

"William," she choked, "How dare you be so inconsiderate of my feelings. I told you a long time ago that I didn't love you."

"Inconsiderate of your feelings?" William shook his head miserably. "How can I be inconsiderate of your feelings by telling you how much I love you? I want nothing for you but happiness. I want to take care of you. If you want to call that inconsiderate, then so be it." He drew her back into his arms. "I love you, my darling. I want to marry you. If you're not happy here, I'll take you away. We can travel. We can see Europe, the Far East, anywhere."

Tears began to form in Jessica's eyes. "You mean . . . you would actually leave Utopia? Your life is here, William. Are you really saying you would leave your dream behind?"

"For you, I would sacrifice anything." He gently stroked her cheek. "If I didn't know before, I do now. Cole still has your heart. But he doesn't love you, Jessica. He was hurt so badly, I seriously doubt if he could ever love anyone. No, Jessica, I couldn't ask you to remain here. I couldn't bear for you to have to see him every single day and know he did not return the love you felt for him. I would gladly take you to the four corners of the earth if it would help to make you happy."

Jessica cried, "But how could you marry me if you know how much I love him?"

William's large hands tenderly cupped Jessica's face. "In time, you would learn to love me. I would be willing to wait until that day came. And you would fall in love with me, my darling. I know you would."

"Oh, William, I couldn't treat you that way."

"You would not be doing me an injustice. Don't you see," he said eagerly, "I know your heart, and I'm very willing to accept you any way I can get you. And . . . another thing, my love, I wouldn't expect you to be a complete wife to me until you were ready."

"Oh, William," Jessica rubbed her suddenly throbbing temples, "I don't know. I'm so confused." her brow wrinkled into a worried frown. "You're so good, you don't deserve someone like me, or a friend like Cole."

"I don't know how good I am, Jessica, but Cole is my friend, and I do love you. And I really don't want to hear you refer to yourself in a demeaning manner again. You are a beautiful young woman, inside and out. Do you hear me?" he demanded forcefully.

Jessica simply sank further into the chair. "I don't know what to think anymore, William."

William realized she was full of indecisions. He got to his feet. "I think you need some time by yourself to think things out and hopefully, you will make the right choice."

"Yes, perhaps I do need some time," she agreed, taking off her apron and placing it over the back of the chair. "I think I'll go for a walk up on the mountain. Maybe there, I'll be able to collect my thoughts." She started for the door, then glanced back over her shoulder. William looked so pitiful, she ran back to him and threw her arms around him. "Oh, William," she cried, "I'm so miserable. I wish you were not involved, then it wouldn't be hard. You're so good and kind. I don't want you to get hurt!"

William patted lovingly, "Now, Jessica," he soothed. "Everything will work out all right, you'll see. Go on, take your walk, and when you get back, I know you'll have the right answer for me."

Jessica nodded. "You're right. I will feel better after a walk. When I'm up on the mountain, things are suddenly clear, and large problems turn into small ones." She stared up at him determinedly, "There's one thing, when I come back, I will have an answer for you. If I do decide to marry you, I will hold you to your word about leaving here. However, if I decide I can't marry you, then I'll leave so we can all start rebuilding our lives."

"That's fair enough," he answered solemnly.

At that moment, the entire area started shaking. The windows started rattling, and the dishes jingled together in the cupboard.

Jessica's eyes grew round with fright. "My God!

What's happening?"

William held her reassuringly. "It's all right, Jessica. We have these earth tremors quite often." He glanced around, "See, it has already stopped. There's nothing to be afraid of."

"I've never experienced such a strange feeling in my life!"

"I know. I felt the same way the first time one struck this area. But there's nothing to be worried about. The ground shakes for a few seconds, then everything returns to normal. Oh," he added off-handedly, "Sometimes we have to replace a few broken windows, but so far, that has been the extent of any damage."

Jessica placed a trembling hand over her heart, "Well, it certainly scared me."

William cautioned, "If you take that walk, you watch out for falling rocks. Sometimes, after a tremor, the ground becomes loose."

Jessica nodded, her brows worried. "I think I'll go back to my cabin and pick up a heavier shawl, it is liable to be colder up on the mountain."

"I agree, and you should pack a picnic lunch too. There is food left from breakfast. Why don't you go get your shawl, and I'll pack you something to eat."

"You don't have to do that, William."

"I know," he smiled. Smoothing his hand across her cheek, he added, "It's something I want to do. If I leave you to do it, you'll probably go off without anything."

Jessica turned numbly and walked toward the door. "William," she said nervously, "I never meant . . ."

In a few easy strides, William was standing by her side. "Now, I don't want to hear anything sad right now. You are a kind, sweet woman, and very warm and loving. I simply want to make you my wife and spend the rest of our lives together. Surely I can't be so bad that even the question of being my wife is distasteful?"

"Oh, no! There is nothing about you distasteful. I just . . . I simply . . . don't want anyone to get hurt because of me."

William smiled. "My sweet, Jessica, you could never deliberately hurt anyone. Go on now," he urged. "You have some serious decisions to make."

Chapter Twenty-three

The morning slipped lazily into the afternoon. The livestock came in from the pastures by themselves and huddled close to the fences, while the calves bawled loudly. The roosters paraded around with ruffled feathers and the hens roosted early. In the western sky, shafts of vibrant color reflected through the mottled clouds that hung over Utopia. The clouds hanging precariously over the mountains were dark and heavy.

William came out of the warehouse and turned his collar up against the crisp, sharp wind as it blew off the snow covered mountains.

"It sure looks like snow," a man said as he passed by.

William did not answer him, instead, his worried glance scanned the streets, hoping to catch some signs of Jessica. He turned and walked over to her cabin. Finding it empty, he then hurried back to his own house. One of his men came after him right after Jessica left to get her heavier shawl. He had no idea what time she had actually left, or when she had returned, *if* she had returned. Throwing open the kitchen door, the first thing

William saw was the picnic basket he had packed earlier that morning. Good! She was back! William breathed a sigh of relief. He had been afraid she was caught out in the threatening weather.

"Jessica? Jessica, are you here?" he yelled. Receiving no answer, William stepped over to the table and picked up the picnic basket. A flash of aggravation went through him when he realized it was still full. Jessica had not taken it with her. She had gone for her walk without any food, and an early storm was threatening! Watch it, William, he said to himself. There is no reason to panic. She's probably visiting with one of her friends. Surely she saw the clouds and returned. I'm just worrying for nothing.

Regardless of his own reassurances, William was still worried. He quickly decided to search for her. He went over to Helen's, then to June's. At each place he asked them if they had any idea where she was, and each time the answer was negative. After asking at several more cabins, William felt a sinking feeling in the bottom of his stomach. Jessica was not here. She was either on the mountain, or in one of the meadows, still taking the walk he had encouraged her to take. It would be his fault if she was lost!

William forced himself to remain calm. He hurried to the stables, saddled a horse and rode up the mountain as far as he could, then he dismounted and continued on foot. The wind became colder the higher he climbed. The only place he knew she went occasionally was the secret hide-a-way, high upon the mountain. William reached the high peak a few hours before dark, only to find it barren of life. The wind picked up in its intensity, blowing rain and tiny flecks of snow. William's hopes were dashed. It was as though Jessica had completely disappeared. He couldn't help but wonder if her disappearance was by choice or by fate.

William came down from the mountain as fast as he could. A search party had to be organized before darkness set in. With the storm coming, if Jessica was out in the wilds, lost, she was in perilous danger.

"Men, I know the weather is threatening, but that's all the more reason I've called you together." William said. He had pushed his horse past his endurance to reach Utopia before dark. The bell of the community hall had once again been rung, calling the inhabitants together in a time of need.

"What's the problem, William?"

"Miss Tate went for a walk this morning and she has not come back yet. She's out there, men, probably not dressed warmly enough to withstand this storm that's brewing. It's already snowing a light snow in the lower meadows. And, ladies, I would appreciate it if you would stay close by your cabins. We certainly don't want to have to search for several lost souls. Men," he addressed the congregation, "You all know what we're up against. We've had lost people out there before, some we were able to rescue in time, and some . . . well . . . there were some we couldn't find." He scanned the gathering of men very carefully, "You all use your heads, dress warmly and stay in groups. I also don't have to warn you about gun shots up in the high country. You all are aware that the noise could trigger an avalanche because the snow is too loose." William's eyes darted around the room. He hoped to see Cole. He had not seen him since early morning. A nagging thought ate at William. Perhaps he had seen Jessica. Perhaps they were even together! No, no, he should not think such things. Cole would never do that to him, and neither would Jessica.

"You men plan on who you will search with while I start gathering up supplies." William stepped off the platform and made his way through the throng of people.

Helen placed a worried hand on William's arm. "Please find her, William. I am so worried."

"Helen! You are the person I wanted to see. I know I was over at your place a little while ago, but . . . did Jessica mention to you . . ."

"No, William, I haven't seen her since last night when she ate supper with us. She seemed to be in very good spirits though." She thrust her hands deep into her apron pockets. "I cannot imagine what could have happened to her." Helen seemed to be gripped by uncertainty. Finally, she asked, "William, did she have an argument with someone?"

William considered her question a moment before answering. "No, Helen, as far as I know, there was no argument. However, I did ask her to marry me."

"And what was her answer?" she pressed.

William shook his head, "She didn't give me one. She did have a lot of things on her mind, several problems to work out before she could give me an answer." William pounded a fist into his opened hand. "Like a fool, I suggested she take a walk. I really thought it would help her come to a decision."

Helen patted his shoulder, "Now, let's not start placing blame and feeling guilty. In all likelihood, she took the walk, wandered a little too far, and has become lost. Why, any minute she is liable to wander in, mad as a wet hen because of all of the fuss."

William's usually warm eyes were sad as he shook his head doubtfully, "I certainly hope so . . . I certainly hope so."

Ed stepped up to Helen and took her by the arm. "I think you ought to be getting back to the cabin. It's dark outside and it's starting to snow harder. You need to get Aaron inside before it starts freezing. He might catch a cold."

"Ed," William interrupted, "Have you seen Cole?"

"No, not since early this morning." His eyes found Helen's. It was apparent they were thinking the same thing. Both Jessica and Cole were missing. Could they be together?

Their question was answered almost immediately when the door to the community hall flew open and Cole stepped inside. He stamped the snow from his feet and brushed off his coat. His mouth tightened and a sharp awareness hardened his eyes. He asked brusquely, "What's going on? What's happened?"

William hurried to him and clasped him on the shoulder. "Cole, it's good to see you! Have you seen Jessica?"

"Jessica?" Apprehension settled over Cole. "No, I haven't. What's the matter?" he asked again, this time his manner was demanding.

"She went for a walk this morning and has not returned yet. We're organizing a search party now." William turned a baleful eye toward Cole and tried not to sound too hopeful. "Were you on any of the trails? Think, Cole, could you have seen some sign of her and not realized it?"

Cole walked over to one of the pot-bellied stoves and poured a cup of steaming hot coffee. "No, I don't think so. Why . . ."

"Wait a minute, Cole. Let's start from the beginning. Where have you been?" William asked.

Cole eyed him warily. It was obvious the captain was trying to conceal a hidden anger. "I went for a ride this morning and was checking on some high pasture land. You know me, William, I really don't have to have a reason to go riding. Anyway, when the earth tremor hit, my horse got a little skittish. It had been a while since he was ridden." Cole smiled sheepishly, "That scoundrel threw me. When I caught up with him, he had lost a shoe and I had to walk him back. I didn't see any signs of Jessica, or anyone else for that matter." He waved his hand, "but enough about me. What about her? How long has she been missing?"

William breathed an inward sigh of relief as he explained about the girl. He omitted the part about his proposal. Now was not the time or place to go into such detail.

"You mean to say, she's out there in this storm that's brewing, without food or warm clothing!" A bitter tightness gripped at his insides. Jessica lost! She would never be able to survive the threatening elements. "What are we wasting time here for? Let's get started!"

"Now, wait a minute," Ed injected. "We can't go off half-cocked. We need to get organized or we'll be missing a lot more people than Jessica."

Cole nodded, "You're right, I don't know what I was thinking about."

"You're just worried—just like all of us."

"I was going to get some supplies," William said. "Do you want to help me? We need to pack several survival kits."

"William," Helen said, "Why don't you tell us women what you'll be needing and we can pack them; you can get the search party organized."

"Would you mind?"

"Of course not," Helen replied eagerly. After getting a list of what the men would be needing, she asked several of the other women to help her.

William called for the men to assemble around one of the long tables and quickly drew a sketch of the surrounding area. He then divided it into sections, and appointed groups of five men to each section.

"Men, I don't have to tell you how dangerous this could be. Fortunately, you all have wintered here before and I believe you know how to take care of yourselves. If the weather doesn't get any worse, we might have a chance to find her."

"Wait a minute, William," Cole interrupted. "You haven't assigned me to a group."

William sighed, "I know I haven't because you're not going." He stared Cole straight in the eye.

"Why?"

"Because only a few weeks ago, you were nearly dead. You don't have the strength to battle this storm." William shook his head, "we don't need two people missing."

"He's right, Cole," Ed agreed. "You can't walk the length of this town without huffing and puffing. Of course, those damned cheroots don't help much."

"Cole! Ed! Cut the nonsense!" William growled. "Let's get back to the matter at hand. After all, Jessica's safety is much more important right now! Cole, I'm not asking you to stay here, I'm *telling* you!"

The men suddenly felt ill-at-ease. It was strange to hear sharp words between Cole and William. Many of them shuffled their feet and pressed forward to the table and awkwardly peered at the map William had drawn.

The muscles in Cole's jaw worked furiously. Damn! He was being dismissed from the search as if he was nothing but an invalid. Sure, his breath was a little short and he didn't have the strength he used to, but he really felt fine considering his chest muscles and been ripped open. He was as able-bodied as any man in the building. Why did William feel as though he could not contribute something to the search party? It was Jessica who was lost out there in the woods where it would soon turn into a freezing hell. Dear sweet Jessica, the woman he loved with all of his heart. If only he could see her right now, he would take her into his arms and beg her if necessary to return the love he felt for her.

Cole stared silently at the group of men. All right, he thought to himself. Go ahead and make your plans. You don't think I can help, William. I'll show you I can. I'll find her myself. Cole knew he could have argued with William about going along, but he knew it was useless. If there were two men on earth who were more stubborn than he was, it was William Stockard and Ed Baker.

"Now, let me warn you," William cautioned as Cole opened the door and stepped outside. "If the storm turns worse, take shelter. Use your own judgment about trying to make it back here. I . . . simply do not want lives lost needlessly."

Cole staunchly marched toward his cabin. He knew he would have to hurry, time was of the essence now. After reaching his cabin, he lit a lamp and began gathering supplies. He tightly rolled several warm blankets together and tossed an old musty buffalo robe onto the bed. Then he took a pillow case into the kichen and started throwing food into it. Candles, sugar, tins of canned milk, coffee, bacon, dried beef jerky, beans, two loaves of bread, and blackberry jam. He knew from experience a diet of rich food would help to sustain a man from the cold. He also knew whiskey wasn't good for you when it was freezing cold, but sometimes, a good stiff belt didn't hurt a thing. He gently placed the bottle in the sack along with the other supplies. After making sure he had plenty of matches, Cole blew out the lamp, tucked the blankets and robe under his arm, and threw the sack of supplies over his shoulder.

He walked quickly to the stables. Cole decided not to take his own horse, it would take too long to reshoe him. Besides, if it was gone, William would know he had joined the search. Instead Cole chose a horse he knew was a good mountain climber and was familiar with winters in the high country. He swiftly saddled the horse and fastened the supplies to the straps of the saddle. He wanted to be well on his way before the men came out to begin their search.

Chapter Twenty-four

Cole left Utopia under the unwelcome cover of darkness. The wind had stopped blowing, but he knew it was just a lull before the storm hit in full fury. He tried to put himself in Jessica's place, to reason in his own mind what he would do and where he would go if he was her. Would she try to find shelter, or would she try and make it back to Utopia? A nagging worry was foremost in his mind that she could be hurt and lying somewhere, unable to reach shelter.

Cole let the stallion follow the ruts that had been cut into the ground by wagons hauling ore down from the mines. Then a short while later, he turned the horse up a long meadow. It was senseless to go anywhere near the mines because Jessica had not been seen since she had left that morning. As he rode along, he could hear the dead frozen grass crunch underneath the animal's hooves. Cole had a plan. It was a slim one, and it could have been called a hunch. He had seen Jessica ride around the meadows before. It was possible she had taken a horse. If that was the case, she might have let the animal have its head. The stallion Cole was riding had been ridden all over these mountains. He knew all of the trails. He just might follow the same trail the other horse took.

Soon, Cole was among the tall pines and poplars, a few birch and cottonwoods also dotted the area but not many. It wasn't long before they reached the double pine, where two trees had grown into one gigantic one. Cole knew exactly where he was.

Apparently, many years ago, someone had marked the tree by loading a shotgun with gold dust and blasting a cross on it. There were eleven other such markings along the trail. Legend had it that there was a thirteenth cross. Whoever found that last cross would find a gold mine worth more money than could be imagined. But Cole was not seeking that kind of wealth, he was searching for the wealth that money could not buy. He was searching desperately for the woman he loved.

The area abounded in unwritten history. Old weapons with intricate carvings had been found along the mountain streams. Dates and names had been discovered carved into the walls of the granite cliffs, much higher up, past the timberline. Ancient trails had been beaten down and worn through the cliffs, going where no white man had the courage to go. There were ancient dwellings somewhere up ahead. They were caves made by nature, and some had even been carved out of the granite mountain by the old ones who walked the earth back before the time of Christ. Cole had never seen it himself, but he had heard rumors about the ancient one's ghosts roaming the area, keeping it sacred by protecting it with spectral guards.

The stallion turned toward a steep and narrow draw.

His hoofs stepped firmly and as sure-footed as if it had been broad daylight. Even though it was very dark, Cole's eyes had adjusted to the blackness of the night. However, he wished the snow had covered the trail, he could have seen any signs that might have been left. Although there was no reason behind his thinking, Cole had a certain feeling Jessica wouldn't be found in the lower pastures and meadows. Instinct told him, she had been deeply troubled about something, and she would have tried to escape her problems by leaving them far behind. Not that she was running away, he was sure that wasn't the case. He had known William a long time, and there was something he wasn't telling. He was hiding an important fact, but it would not be as important as where Jessica was. Cole had no idea how close to the truth he actually was.

The trail grew steeper and more difficult to climb. Although Cole could not see them, huge mountains jutted upward, almost as if they were reaching out for God in his magnitude. To his knowledge, the mountains had no proper names. The largest one was simply called God's mountain. Even on a clear day, it was difficult to see the top of the tall one, it was so high. Clouds continually covered its peak. But the dark granite face always seemed to beckon to the people below, almost as if it was daring them to trespass on its sanctity and splendor.

The trail took a turn and Cole topped out on a narrow rim. On one side was a huge gaping canyon. He could see the snow covered outlines of boulders and scrubby outgrowth. To his right lay a vast, glacial gorge, its ice dark and black with age. For a moment, Cole was filled with indecision. Perhaps he was wrong in letting the horse have his head. Would she have had the courage to come this far? Would she have had the courage to continue climbing? No, he couldn't weaken now. The caves were not too far ahead. Besides, he had caught a glimpse of the map William had drawn. This area had not been covered. He had to press onward.

It was bitterly cold. The wind picked up again, bringing huge snowflakes with it. He stopped the horse and climbed down. He removed a woolen scarf from his saddle bags and tied it around his head. His ears had become so cold they were stinging. He did a few deep knee bends to get the circulation going back into his feet. The cold was a bitter enemy, if you didn't treat it with respect, a man would soon die.

Cole also removed a piece of beef jerky from the sack, cut off a chunk and put it in his mouth. It had frozen solid and was impossible to chew. He slipped the rest of the jerky into his coat pocket, then he wallowed the cud in his mouth, wetting it with saliva until it became pliable enough to chew. Cole slipped off one of his gloves and felt his face. He realized it was all right, that there was no danger of frostbite yet. He left the icy shield which had formed on his eyebrows, beard and clothing. To have brushed it off would have meant losing some of his precious body heat since the ice helped to insulate by forming a barrier against the driving wind.

Cole remounted his horse and together, they carefully made their way upward, constantly climbing. He knew they should reach the area of the caves in a short while. He also knew he would not be able to stay out in the weather too much longer. When he reached the valley of the caves, he would have a few minutes to search for her, then he would have to take shelter or die. He dreaded to think of what he would have to do if he did not find her.

He would have to have hope and faith that some of the other men would have better luck.

It was so cold. He had never been this cold before. It felt as though he had ice running through his veins now. What would it be like in another hour? Cole refused to let his mind dwell on how Jessica was managing to hang onto the slim margin of life. He tried his best not to think about her delicate body fighting the elements of the storm. Cole bitterly shook his head. He could not allow himself to think about such things. She was all right. She *had* to be all right. He had been so foolish. He had rebuffed the only woman who had really loved him. But, if given a second chance, he would make it up to her and spend the rest of his life trying to make her happy.

The trail showed no signs of recent use. In places, it was almost impossible to pass, but the stallion continued onward with a steady pace. To a certain degree, Cole was glad he could not see on either side of him. He knew the trail was very dangerous, that there were drop-offs and deep canyons. One misstep and he would fall hundreds of feet to the canyon floor. The horse stumbled once and nearly lost his footing. Cole could feel his heart pound rapidly in his chest. The horse was his only way out, his only way to safety. Suddenly, the stallion stopped, threw back his ears and whinnied. Something had scared him. Cole dismounted, picked up a large stick and made his way forward. He poked the stick into the ground, knowing that sometimes, the trail dropped off into nothing. Cole saw a huge mound blocking the trail ahead. He stopped and knelt down. Cold fingers of fear clutched at his heart when he brushed the snow from the mound. It was a horse! And on the horse's flank was the common brand of Utopia's livestock. Jessica had come this way. Cole's breath caught in his throat as he looked around for Jessica. He was afraid he would find her body too. Cole quickly explored the area. She could not have fallen over a cliff as there were tall boulders around the carcass of the horse. Also, from the position of the horse, they had been returning. Could he have passed her on the trail? Surely his stallion would have sensed her presense. Why had the horse died on the trail? What could have happened? Did Jessica use her head and go back to the caves? She had to have done that! Surely she wouldn't have tried to make it back.

After he satisfied himself he wasn't overlooking anything, Cole led his mount past the dead horse and continued on to the caves.

"Jessica! Jessica!" Cole yelled, cupping his mouth and shouting, turning as he called. "Jessica! Please answer me!"

The valley of caves was an eerie place. Although the wind wasn't too strong on the valley floor, it whistled through the higher caves. Now he knew why it was rumored to be haunted. "Jessica!" he called once again. He was so cold he could barely hold his hands to his mouth.

Surely if she had made it back here, she could have built a fire somehow. He would have to pass by each one of the caves and search them, because she would have moved back away from the mouth. But wait, Cole reasoned. Think, man, think. Try to think like she would. She would not be at the back of the valley. If she came back here, she would have probably stopped at the first cave she came to. Cole turned his horse around and went back to the valley's entrance. Snow had already covered any signs she might have left. He dismounted, broke off a stick, cut off a piece of one of the blankets and wrapped it around the stick, then he lit the blanket, making a haphazard torch. It wasn't much, but it would help him to see.

Cole entered the first cave, and it was too shallow. She would not have taken shelter here. The wind blew in too strongly. He then went into the second cave. It was deep, running several hundred feet back into the mountain. He constantly called her name, "Jessica, Jessica," but still no answer. He led the stallion into the second cave and tied his reins to a rock. He couldn't chance the horse spooking, and running off, then he went back out into the terrible cold, still calling, still searching.

Pausing near a huge rock outcropping, Cole thought he had heard something. Then he felt a splattering of small rocks hit him from above. Looking up, he saw her leaning over the edge.

"Cole!" her weak voice cried. "Cole, please help me!"

Cole scaled the heights as quickly as he possibly could. Gathering her into his arms, he whispered, "Thank God, Jessica! Thank God, I found you!" Her tiny body shivered underneath her thin shawl. Scooping her into his arms, he carried her back down and made his way to the cave where the horse and supplies were.

Cole sat her on some rocks, took off his coat and draped it around her pitifully thin and shaking shoulders. Then he relit the torch in order to see how to unload the horse. His first step was to untie the blankets and wrap her securely in them. Then he put his coat back on.

She was shaking violently. He had to get her warm and quick! His own numb limbs could barely carry him, but Cole went back out into the night and gathered firewood. There was enough leaves and scattered debris in the cave for him to use as tinder for the fire. It took him seemingly a long time to get the fire to catch because the wood was wet, but soon it blazed, and before too many minutes passed, it was roaring and crackling with much needed heat. Cole turned his attention back to Jessica. She was shaking so violently, she had not attempted to talk.

Cole spread out the buffalo robe by the fire, then removed the bottle of whiskey from the sack. He sat Jessica up and held the bottle to her lips. "Here take a drink of this, it'll help get you warm," he said, holding the bottle for her.

Jessica drank eagerly, then gasped and coughed as the whiskey left a trail of blazing fire all the way to her stomach. She coughed again and pushed the bottle back to Cole.

"No, take another drink," he ordered.

This time, she lifted the bottle to her lips. It did not burn quite so bad, but she still coughed. Cole took a long pull from the bottle, then stuck the cork back into the top. It helped to revive him.

He hurried and draped a blanket over the mouth of the cave to help block the wind from whistling in, then he unsaddled the stallion and fed him some grain he had thoughtfully brought along. Cole knew he should help get Jessica warm, but he also knew he had to gather more wood to last through the night. The longer he waited, the wetter the wood would get and the harder it would be for it to burn. Cole braved the storm once more. In his cold and weakened condition, he staggered under the burden of the firewood, but in a few minutes, he hopefully had enough wood gathered to see them through the night.

The flames cast eerie shadows on the walls of the cave, flickering and dancing, magnifying the size of the boulders and his own shadow. He quickly removed his wet clothes and boots. He draped his clothing across a stick and placed it near the fire, then he crawled in between the blankets with Jessica. Not only was it important he warm her, he had to be warmed too. Lying together, their body heat would gradually increase. Cole swore under his breath when he realized Jessica's dress was also wet. He had to toss back the blankets and quickly remove her clothing, which he placed on the stick alongside of his clothing, then he snuggled back down beneath the blankets.

Lying beside Jessica was the same as being beside a freezing chunk of ice. She shuddered and shook violently. Cole pressed his body close to hers. Thank God, he had found her in time.

Silent tears crept down her face. "I thought I was going to die," she cried.

"Hush, Jessica," Cole soothed. "Everything is going to be all right." He had many questions he wanted to ask, but they would have to wait until she was able to talk.

For hours, they lay huddled underneath the blankets. Jessica's violent shaking finally eased, and she managed to doze off into a fretful sleep.

Cole continued to hold her tightly in his arms. If he had a choice, he would never let her go. Her firm breasts jutted into his chest. The tips seemed as though they were burning into him. Even though he was still cold and in a weakened condition, he wanted her badly. He could feel his maleness grow firm with desire, but it was a desire he dared not satisfy. He refused to take advantage of her. Cole managed to doze, only to awaken a short while later. The fire was dying down. He would have to get up and add more wood.

Cole eased out from underneath the covers and when the fire blazed again, he crept over to the mouth of the cave and peered outside. The wind had increased in its velocity, and the storm whipped in its fury. It had turned into a full scale blizzard. Cole placed more rocks around the blanket to hold it securely, then raced back to the bed and its warmth.

Jessica drew her breath sharply when Cole crawled in beside her. "Oh! You're so cold!" she whispered, drawing him nearer to her. She gasped again when she realized he did not have on any clothes. "Cole!"

"Now don't get alarmed," he cautioned. "I promise I won't hurt you."

"But, why . . ."

"Jessica, use your head," Cole said, but the tone of his voice was not sharp or scolding. "My clothes were wet and so were yours. We were both freezing to death. We had to get warm," he added matter of factly.

"Oh," she said in a small voice. "I thought . . ."

"Well, don't. I wouldn't take advantage of you."

"I know that Cole." She paused a moment. "You risked your life for me."

"Do you feel like talking?" Cole asked.

"About what?"

"Why did you come way up here? What happened to your horse? Why didn't you come back when the storm . . ."

"Wait a minute, Cole," she chuckled, but the laugh fell flat. "I couldn't help but notice that you had a bag full of food. Could I have something to eat before I explain?"

Cole mentally kicked himself. Of course she was hungry. She had been without food for hours, and the cold would automatically deplete her body's nourishment. He got back out of bed and checked his clothes to see if they were dry.

Jessica peered through lowered lashes as Cole dressed. She marveled over the animal sleekness of his body. His muscles were firm and taut, rippling with strength. She was amazed at the sheer size of him. His shoulders were broad and muscular, his belly firm, and his hips were narrow, powerful and splendidly masculine. Her heart wrenched when she saw the scars left by the bear's vicious attack.

Cole hurried outside, scooped up a pot full of snow and brought it back into the cave and placed it on the fire. He then fished out a skillet and began slicing bacon while the skillet heated. When the snow melted, he dumped a handful of coffee grounds into it, then placed the bacon in the skillet. Soon, the aroma of the food wafted through the cave, making it impossible for Jessica to remain in the bed. Cole tried to keep his eyes averted while Jessica dressed, but he too, found it impossible to do so. He cast shy glances in her direction, taking in her firm, jutting breasts, the downy hair below her stomach, and her shapely limbs. She glanced up nervously, and Cole ducked his head. It embarrassed him that she caught him watching her. Taking the fork, Cole turned the bacon, then he broke off huge chunks of bread and spread them with the blackberry jam. Both their mouths were watering in anticipation, the food smelled so good.

Even though the cave was warm compared to what they had previously experienced, it was still cold. Jessica took one of the blankets and tossed it across her shoulders and huddled close to the fire. Her smoky gray eyes danced with joy when Cole poured the coffee and handed a plate of food to her. The next few minutes passed quickly as they ate hungrily. Finally, Jessica set her plate down and poured another cup of coffee.

Cupping her hands around the steaming ambrosia, she looked up at Cole, took a sip of the coffee then asked, "Now, what was it you wanted to know?"

"I'm just curious about how you became stranded up here."

She nodded, "I can imagine why."

"I found your horse back on the trail." His voice seemed overloud, almost to the point of echoing in the cave. The muscles in his cheek tensed then flexed as their eyes met. Electrifying tension charged the air around them.

So many things had happened since she had left Utopia, it was difficult to find a place to begin. Cole was beginning to look impatient. She knew she must start somewhere, but there was a reserve in her, a reserve that commanded her not to tell him about William's proposal.

"Some of the things are a little hazy," she began. "It seems as though it all happened a lifetime ago."

Cole raised his eyebrows. "I would imagine so."

"To put it briefly, I decided to go for a walk. I went up into the lower meadows, and I found that double pine, you know, the one that has grown together with the golden cross blasted into the trunk."

Cole nodded. Apparently, he had retraced her steps.

She chortled, "Now, I feel rather foolish about the entire thing."

"Go ahead and tell me," Cole urged.

"Well," she drew a deep breath, "I had heard the old legends about the lost mine. I simply went back to the stables and saddled a horse. I decided I would try and find it." She would have never admitted why she had wanted to find the gold mine. The money from it would have allowed her to go far away, to forget about the past, and for time to help heal her broken heart.

Cole nodded, everything was falling into place.

Jessica continued, "I rode further than I had intended. Before I knew it, I was way up here in the high country. Then it started to rain, and I knew I was in trouble. I had started back home when a mountain lion spooked my horse. He ran away with me." Tears started to form in her eyes as she remembered. "The horse stumbled and fell." She looked up at Cole with tears glistening in her eyes. "Cole, the horse broke his leg when he fell!" her voice caught in a sob. "I couldn't leave the poor animal to suffer, so . . . I . . . picked up a big rock and hit him in the head." She began crying so hard, it was difficult for her to talk, but still, she continued. "I had to hit him in the head several times before he stopped kicking."

Cole felt so sorry for her. He imagined how terrible it was. It would have been a hard thing for a man to do, much less a tiny, delicate woman. He quickly went to her side and comforted her. "There, there, Jessica. You did what you had to."

"I know, but it was horrible!"

Cole let her cry for a while. He realized it was something she had to get out of her system. And her crying went beyond having to kill the horse. It was a culmination of everything that had happened to her. Cole doubted if she had cried this hard when her father had died. Finally, when her tears were spent, Cole unfolded his arms from around her, and freshened her coffee.

"Drink up," he ordered. "It's good for you."

She obeyed his command, then continued with her story. "I knew I would never make it down the mountain before the storm hit, and I had to do something." She looked around the cave, "I came back here, but I could feel something watching me. It was so scary! I was afraid it was the mountain lion, so I climbed up in one of the upper caves. I gathered as much firewood as I could, then, I remembered father teaching me how to light a fire without matches. I think I worked for hours trying to get the sparks to catch fire."

Cole looked at her and simply shook his head. Bless her heart, she didn't realize it, but if a mountain lion was after her, it wouldn't have done her any good to climb to an upper level of the caves.

"The wind kept blowing harder and harder," she continued, "And I began to get sleepy. I knew I shouldn't go to sleep, but I did. When I woke up, the fire was out and it was pitch black. Oh, Cole! I knew I was going to die!" she heaved a ragged sigh. "I really thought I was going to die!"

"Well," Cole said gruffly, "I'm here now. Everything is going to be all right. You're safe with me."

"How long do you think we'll have to stay here?"

Cole shrugged, "I don't know. It depends on the storm. It may blow over by morning or it could last for several days. This high up, it's hard to tell. I've heard of storms lasting from mid-winter all the way until spring. Up here, after the first bad snowfall, winter is usually here to stay."

"Are you telling me we will have to stay here until then?" Jessica asked, alarm filling her voice as she glanced at the small sack of food Cole had brought along.

He laughed, "No, I didn't mean it that way. The storm will break in a few days time, at least long enough for us to get out of here."

"What about Utopia? Will many people leave?"

Cole shook his head, "I doubt it, especially since the men aren't lonesome anymore."

"What about those women who are going back to San Francisco, will they still be able to leave?" Jessica asked earnestly.

Cole stared at her. It was hard to read what was going through her mind. Was she also considering going back?

Jessica shivered, "I'm getting cold again."

Cole agreed. The cave was indeed getting colder. Although the fire still blazed high, and the blanket remained snug over the mouth of the cave, the bone-chilling wind and frigid air continued to creep in. Cole doubted if anything could ward off the chill that penetrated every nook and cranny of the dark gray granite walls of the cave.

"I guess we ought to go back to bed," Cole suggested.

Jessica had a feeling Cole was silently laughing at her, but she did not see any amusement in the situation. She found the entire episode rather uncomfortable. "Yes, I suppose we ought to." She looked at Cole expectantly, "Cole . . . I don't think . . ."

He grinned sheepishly at her, "Relax, Jessica. I'm not going to hurt you."

"I didn't think you would!" Jessica's trembling chin lifted proudly, defying him to think otherwise. "I believe we are two reasonably mature adults, caught in a perilous life or death situation. For either one of us to be intimidated by the other would be ridiculous." Although she spoke brave words, Jessica was scared. She was scared he would take her in his arms. She was scared he would want to make love to her. She was not afraid of Cole, she was afraid of herself. How could she go through life without his love? How could she go back and face William with the answer she must have for him. She knew she could not live a lie. She could never pretend to love a man she did not love. But how could she hurt him? How could she turn aside from her own feelings? A chilling shudder enveloped her body. She could not bear to think about the mess her life was in at this time. It was something she could not face. Too much was at stake.

Chapter Twenty-five

"At least you can look at the bright side," Cole remarked trying to put Jessica at ease, "At least, we can keep our clothes on this time." The moment he said it, he felt foolish. He had only meant the remark in lighthearted teasing, but the words had sounded empty and brash.

Jessica glanced sharply at Cole. She felt the warmth of his gaze more firmly than the heat of the blazing fire. She started to snap a sharp reply, then she noticed he was actually blushing. The sight of a grown, masculine, sensual man blushing was amusing. Jessica clapped a hand over her mouth to muffle a giggle while a deeper color rose in Cole's cheeks.

Cole grinned and toed the ground with his foot. He could see the humor in his remark too. "Well? What else could I say?" he asked.

Jessica groaned and rolled her eyes upward. "Cole, please," she laughed, "you're making it worse."

"Yeah, I guess I am. Oh, hell, Jessica, you know what I meant!"

"Yes, I know what you meant," she replied. Suddenly, Jessica felt elated. It felt so good to sit with Cole and to be able to carry on a light hearted conversation, even if they were trapped in a blizzard high upon a mountain. The laughter was good for both of them. It helped to alleviate the seriousness of their predicament.

Cole decided to change the subject. He pulled on his boots and slipped on his coat. "I think I'll go out and get some snow so we can have water in the morning. Also, the horse will need water too. While I'm out there, I'll pick up a few more pieces of firewood." He couldn't believe what he was saying. He was actually running away from Jessica. If he had stayed in the cave another minute with her, he would have had her in his arms.

It took longer than Cole had expected. The wood around the immediate area of the cave had already been gathered. He saw a large piece of wood sticking up out of the snow. He walked over for it, and promptly sank up to his waist, and slightly turning his ankle in the process. Realizing how dangerous it was not being able to see, Cole pulled himself out of the snow and made his way back to the cave. Unless it was absolutely necessary, he would not go back out into the blizzard until he could see better. They would simply have to ration what wood they had until morning, then he would attempt it again.

When he came back into the cave, Jessica was already in bed. Cole brushed off the snow, took off his coat and boots and crawled in beside her. Jessica gasped sharply and jerked away.

"Cole!" she scolded. "You did that on purpose!"

"What?" He was confused. What in the world was she talking about?

"You deliberately went outside! Your clothes are wet! You knew that would happen!" she accused.

Cole's mouth flew open as he stared up into the darkness. She was right! His clothes were wet again. Stifling a groan, Cole realized he would never be able to convince Jessica his actions had not been on purpose, that he had simply gone outside to do the chores he had mentioned. Now he felt foolish again. "Jessica," he snapped, "Regardless of what you think, I did not go out there to deliberately get my clothes wet! Why don't you just turn over and go to sleep, I'm tired and I happen to have a terrible headache!" He turned his back on her and snuggled down into the blankets, but sleep was impossible. Jessica kept giggling.

"Jessica, I'm warning you, if you don't hush up, I'll . . . I'll make you sleep outside!"

That remark brought gales of laughter from Jessica's side of the bed. "Oh, Cole!" she laughed hysterically, "If you only knew how that sounded! Do you really think I believe that when you risked your life to rescue me?"

"It might have been the biggest mistake I ever made in my life!" he growled.

Jessica continued to giggle. It wasn't really funny, it was the simple fact that she had been so close to death a few hours earlier. Her giddiness was a form of hysterical release.

"Jessica! Would you please go to sleep?"

She punched him on his shoulder and pulled the blankets off him.

Quick as a flash, Cole turned over, pulled the blankets over their heads, and crushed Jessica beneath him. He wove his fingers through the long tangle of her hair and whispered hoarsely, "Jessica, so help me, you have no idea how hard it is for me to lie here beside you and not take you in my arms. I want you more than I've ever wanted a woman in my entire life. If you don't leave me alone, I . . . I . . . can't be held responsible for my actions!"

Words of denial and protest froze in Jessica's throat. Although her mouth opened, no words formed. She could only stare unseeingly at him, helplessly caught in the web of her own desires. She could feel his breath hot against her face. She had not intended for this to happen.

"Answer me, Jessica. Do you want me?" Cole asked, his words rasping and muffled with passion.

Jessica knew she had only one fleeting moment to make a decision, a decision that could haunt her the rest of her life. Her hesitation lasted but a flickering instant. She did not say a word, instead, her arms went around his neck as she pulled him closer to her. William Stockard was completely forgotten.

Their lips melted in common union, searching, spiraling, devouring, until their needs became a greedy quest for more. Passions flared, and all caution was thrown to the wind. Their tiny corner in the world toppled into a chaos of ecstasy. The flaming torch of their desire blazed fiery hot with wanton flames of passion. Even under the confines of the blankets, their clothing was removed with ease. The scalding heat of his mouth made her catch her breath as he lowered his head to taste the rose-colored hue of her passion-taut nipples.

Jessica's hands threaded through his coal black hair. "Oh my God, Cole, I love you so much!" she murmured fervently. "Kiss me," she begged in a whisper. "Love me!" Those words were her last conscious moments of sanity before being swept into the land of paradise.

Her teeth found his shoulder when he complied with her request. The heat of his fullness melted deep inside her, throbbing and driving to a supreme intensity, a supreme intensity that had driven them wild.

Cole raised up, pulling her with him. Her hair formed a cascading flow of tousled silk that spilled to the bed. Without ever breaking stride, Cole turned to where she was on top, riding him. With freed hands, he cupped one breast and savored the tastes of the other with his mouth. The flames of rapture devoured their souls. Cole lunged forward burying himself deep within her, while she responded with a fervent pitch of intensity.

The crescendo of their passion grew, far beyond the bounds of mortal pleasure. They soared until they tasted the nectar of the gods.

Later, Jessica lay snuggled close to Cole. She walked in the misty land of dreams, thoroughly satisfied and thoroughly contented. This was her place in life, her destiny she had to fulfill. Nothing so perfect could be wrong. They had blended into oneness. No spoken words could ever unite them more than they were already united.

"Cole, my darling, I love you," she whispered.

Cole did not answer, his unspoken reply came in the form of tightening his grip and pulling her even closer to him. His lips sought hers, and again, his love lifted them beyond the land of reality.

The following morning, Cole slowly eased out of bed, being careful not to awaken Jessica. He slipped on his clothes and stepped over to where the blanket was stretched across the opening of the cave. He didn't have to look outside, he could still hear the wind howling fiercely. He seriously doubted if the storm would abate and enable them to leave that day.

Cole added more wood to the fire and put on morning coffee. He waited until it had boiled before waking Jessica. Instead of calling her, he knelt down beside her and gently nuzzled at her neck. Her eyes flew open instantly.

"I wasn't asleep," she informed him as she coiled her arms lovingly around his neck. "I woke up the minute you left my side."

"Oh? Playing possum with me?" he teased.

"No," she chuckled, "I was simply being lazy. I wanted to wait until you had the fire going again and the coffee made before I braved the cold."

"Why, you sneaky little thing!" he raged playfully. "I'll teach you!" He yanked back the cover exposing her beautiful nakedness. He could not hold back the gasp that erupted from his throat. She was beautiful! The muted light of the fire reflected on the dark walls of the cave, throwing the cast of bronzed shadows on her magnificent body. "My God," he muttered harshly, "I still want you! It's as though every time I have you, it only leaves me wanting more!"

Jessica raised up to her knees. She guided Cole, urging him to follow her. She stared up into his steel blue eyes, devouring his features, burning into her memory the way his eyes caressed her. Her arms inched slowly around his neck. She said not a word. She didn't have to. Her eyes told him exactly what she wanted. Jessica could not believe she was actually contemplating making love to Cole. Not making love *with* him, but *to* him!

He started to ease her down unto the bed but she refused. "No, Cole, not yet," she whispered. "I want to do it."

Cole looked at her in surprise. This was indeed a surprise. A surprise he thoroughly enjoyed.

They stood face to face, kneeling on their knees, their

eyes riveted to each other. Jessica, methodically began to unfasten his shirt. Her long sensual fingers toyed with each button. She could feel the beat of his heart as her hands caressed the heavy mat on his chest. When she had the shirt removed, she leaned forward, her tongue flicked out to touch his nipples. Cole exhaled in a mighty groan of pleasure.

Her hands sought his trousers, she slowly undid the fastenings, and allowed her hands to dance lightly on his upper hips. Cole could not stand it any longer. He quickly slipped out of his pants and rejoined Jessica on the buffalo robe.

"Jessica, my love, we ought to get under the blankets, it's cold in here."

Her brows raised mockingly, "Is it? I didn't notice." Although she was scared, the fright did nothing to hamper the supreme pleasure she was deriving from her love-making attempt. She swallowed hard. Although desire for Cole was building, her courage was fading rapidly. How would she find the nerve to continue?

She entwined her arms around Cole's neck. Her gaze drifted downwards, and her eyes widened in amazement. She had never seen an aroused man before! Her eyes flew to Cole's face. He had sensed her sudden reluctance.

"Relax my love, I won't hurt you." Cupping his hands around her face, he drew her to him. When her lips were but a breath away from his, with the tip of his tongue, he traced around the outer edges of her mouth.

"Oh, Cole!" she moaned, "Take me, love me!"

Cole stood, fitted his hands around her waist, and lifted her to her feet, then he brought her higher until her feet were off the mat, and their cheeks were touching. She felt him manipulating his hands around her waist, then she felt herself sliding downward, downward, until she was impaled on his shaft of love.

Her eyes widened in surprise, and she gave a gasp of delight. Nothing separated them. He was all hers, and she was all his. Like one possessed, Jessica willed her legs to coil around Cole's waist, as she took him completely.

Deep in the warm, secret place between her thighs, Jessica felt a wildfire start to blaze through her loins. Cole thrust upward with languid deliberation, while Jessica writhed in pleasure. Her arms wound tightly around his back, feeling his muscles stir and strain beneath her hands as he plunged into her faster and faster with a passionate all-consuming fury. It was a flaming moment of ecstasy that lasted for an eternity.

Later, Cole and Jessica snuggled underneath the blankets. The pot containing the coffee had boiled dry and had been long since forgotten. The wind continued to shriek and howl in the fury outside, while a fury of passion and desire unfolded in the flickering shadows inside the cave.

Jessica and Cole were like naughty imps basking in the delights of boundless pleasure as they sampled the forbidden fruits of love throughout the day and on into the darkness of night.

They would sleep, make love, sleep, then get up to gather more wood, then the same scene would be repeated. They seldom stopped for food. Their lustful appetite for each other demanded to be sated before their body nourishment could be considered.

Finally, during the dawn of the second day, the storms, the one raging outside and the passionate one which raged inside finally abated.

Cole awoke to an eerie silence. Regret filled him. He

looked over at the woman he loved more than life itself. She had curled into a tight ball beside him, snuggling as close as she could possibly get. He hated for it to end. They would have to start back immediately. Suddenly, he felt very possessive toward Jessica. It dawned on him that he would have to share her again. Share her with Helen, June, William, everyone in Utopia! A sadness engulfed him.

Cole smoothed a tangle of hair back from her face, He made no move to mount her. Instead, he gently played with her, caressing, softly titillating, cupping her breasts and placing kisses all over her body. He was not demanding or passionate, simply loving and tender.

"Mmmm, Cole, my darling," Jessica murmured, winding her arms around his neck.

"Get up, my sweet, the storm is over. We have to go back. They'll all be looking for us."

"Oh, Cole, do we really have to leave?" Jessica knew they did. They would have to face the platonic idea of reality.

Cole chuckled, "Of course we have to go back. You know that."

"I know," she whispered, stretching, arching her back and making a soft mewing sound. "I just hate for all of this to end." She deliberately baited Cole by leading the conversation to where he could have said, it didn't have to end. She waited a moment, knowing he would propose at any minute, but Cole did not say a word.

Cole was not a man of many words. He took it for granted Jessica knew he loved her. He took it for granted she knew he wanted to spend the rest of his life with her. Cole spatted her on the buttock and with a stern but loving tone to his voice he said, "Get up lazybones! Time is wasting!"

"Ouch!" she yelped as she took a swing at Cole.

"Oh, no, we can't start that again," he muttered huskily, drinking in her beauty, becoming mesmerized by her loveliness. Groaning, Cole swung his long legs out from underneath the cover. "We have to get up," he urged again.

Jessica reached out her hand for support as she too, climbed from the bed. Her eyes widened as she grasped Cole for support. "Oh!" she sighed weakly.

"What's the matter?"

"My legs! I don't know if they will hold me!" she uttered, her gray eyes wide with wonder. "What is the matter with me, Cole?"

Cole helped her over to a rock and sat her down. His brow was creased into a frown, as concern for her filled him. Then, it dawned on him what had happened. Up until a couple of nights ago, Jessica had only had a man a few times. They had gone wild with their lovemaking, feasting on each other's delights a countless number of times. She was sore from that! When he explained what he thought the problem was, she agreed, although her face flamed over the idea.

"Come, I'll help you get dressed, then we'll have to eat a hearty breakfast before we leave." His eyes were concerned as he asked, "Are you up to leaving now? The trail back to Utopia will be rough, and it's freezing cold outside."

"We have no other choice, Cole. If we stay here, the men will intensify their search. I . . . don't think William will let them stop until I'm found, and he's bound to be worried about you too."

Cole silently agreed. Although Jessica had no idea exactly how worried William would actually be. For a moment, he wished he had left his friend a note or message.

Now that Jessica had mentioned it, William was probably beside himself with worry. To hell with William! Cole thought suddenly. If I hadn't left Utopia to come look for Jessica, she would have been dead by now. There was no way she would have been able to survive the storm.

Cole started making preparations to leave. After they had eaten, he showed Jessica how to pack a bed roll. He left out two blankets and the buffalo robe, and his ground sheet which was made from rain slicker material. Taking his knife, he cut the ground sheet into wide strips and wrapped them around his feet. He would have to walk back, and let Jessica ride the horse. He would have to keep his feet as dry as possible. The cold would be severe, but if his feet became wet, he could be in trouble.

After giving the cave one final search, Cole was satisfied he had gathered everything they would need. He had deliberately left behind several items to lighten the load on the horse.

Looking down at Jessica, he gave her one last kiss before leading her and the horse outside into the bitter cold.

Chapter Twenty-six

The valley of the caves looked like an icy wonderland. Muted rays of sunlight reflected on the snow making it glitter and glisten. Rain had mixed with the snowstorm, and now, prisms of light illuminated from the icicles hanging over the many caves entrances like stalactites. A few granite boulders showed their gray faces through the snow. Both Jessica and Cole stared at the beauty in awe.

"I've never seen anything like it in my life!" Jessica whispered reverently. "It's so beautiful!" This made the entire affair seem as though it all happened in a wonderful fairyland of make-believe.

"It's almost as beautiful as you," Cole murmured in her ear. He could not resist brushing her cheek with his lips. "I suppose we ought to get started." It was apparent Cole hated to leave their winterland paradise as much as Jessica. It wasn't so much actually leaving the enchanted place, but the fact they had experienced such happiness and had really discovered each other.

Cole readjusted the pack and they were off. The trail was difficult to travel even under perfect conditions.

Now that the snow was deep and a thick sheet of ice lay beneath the snow, made it all the more hazardous.

Cole led the way, carrying a long stick to probe the snow with, and holding the reins with his other hand. He stepped carefully, and each time the horse balked, Cole would proceed with extra caution. They passed the place where Jessica's horse had died. The animal could not be seen.

Sheer cliffs jutted into the crystal azure blue sky. A few lacy white clouds drifted lazily across the horizon. The sun was brilliant against the clarity of the fresh snow, but it did not provide any heat, it simply gave light.

Jessica snuggled deeper into the warmth of the ancient buffalo robe. Only her frosty breath, misty in the frigid air could be seen.

Cole continued to proceed with caution. One misstep, and they could all go plummeting over the side of a cliff, never to be seen again. Once, when they rounded a bend on the mountainside, Cole stopped in surprise. Ahead lay a natural stone bridge, spanning a deep and dangerous canyon. He turned to Jessica and asked, "Did you actually cross that when you went to the valley of the caves?" The idea crossed his mind that they might have taken the wrong trail.

"Yes, Cole. But it didn't look that dangerous when I crossed it." Her worried gaze passed over him.

Apprehension settled over Cole as he thought about his journey to the caves. He had actually crossed over that thin margin of rocks during the darkness of night and during a driving storm. He looked once again at the bridge. It was not safe to cross. The rain and snow had formed a slick glaze over the surface. One misstep and they would careen over the side and fall to their death on the rocks below.

"Jessica, you are going to have to dismount," he said cautiously.

"Tell me, Cole, do you think it is safe to pass?"

"No, but we have no other choice. Look," he gestured with his hands, "You stay here, I'll lead the horse across then come back for you."

"Oh, Cole! You'll be killed!" she cried.

Cole touched her cheek with his gloved hand. "Don't fret, Jessica. You know as well as I do, there's no other way." He took the blanket from around his shoulders and draped it around hers. "Here, just in case I don't make it across, this will help to keep you warm."

"Oh, Cole, no! You can't go!"

"I have to Jessica. We can't stay here, we have to cross. Only . . . if I don't make it, don't worry. Now that the storm has broken, someone will come looking for you." With those words, he turned and slowly started making his way across the rocky, ice covered natural bridge.

"No, Cole! There has to be another way!" she shouted. Cole ignored her as he cautiously placed one foot in front of the other. The stallion snorted in protest, but he followed as Cole tugged on the reins. They finally made it to the other side. Cole turned back and smiled across the bridge at Jessica. "It's all right! I'll be back after you as soon as I tie up the horse." Cole had to lead the horse several yards up the path before finding a suitable place to stake the animal. When he turned back around, Cole saw a sight that made his blood run cold. A mountain lion was perched upon a ledge over Jessica. Cole inched slowly back to the horse and quietly removed his rifle from the scabbard. Jessica's eyes grew wide when she saw what Cole was doing. She started to question him, but he silenced her with a shake of his head. "Please, Jessica, don't move!" Although his words of caution had been quietly spoken, alarm was evident in his voice.

Jessica's eyes widened in fear as Cole raised the gun up. It looked as though he was pointing it right at her. An unbelieving smile touched her lips, then she felt snow as it sifted down on her head. It all happened at the same moment. As she peered upward, the cat jumped and Cole fired the rifle. The huge mountain lion screamed as the bullet struck him. He leaped past Jessica and fell headlong into the deep canyon.

Her mouth agape, Jessica spun around to stare wordlessly at Cole. Finally, she sputtered, "What if you had missed?"

Cole, without thinking, was so relieved, he had started back across the bridge. When he realized what he was doing, he was only a few feet from the edge. Taking one giant leap, he pulled Jessica into his arms. "Jessica, my darling," he breathed, "You could have been killed."

"I know," she whimpered, "You could have missed and hit me!"

"Me miss?" he asked incredulously. "No, I wasn't worried about that, I was afraid the cat would lunge at you and make you lose your balance." He continued to cradle her in his arms.

"I didn't know what to think when I looked up and saw you aiming that gun at me!" she sobbed.

Cole pulled back and looked at her. "What do you mean? Did you really think I was going to shoot you?"

"No, I didn't. I simply had no idea what you were going to do," she admitted honestly.

Cole thought a minute about what she had said. It was a reasonable assumption. What would he have thought if he was with someone and then out of the clear blue, saw *them* aiming a gun in *his* direction! Cole walked to the edge of the cliff and peered over. He could see the huge cat lying in a crumpled heap, with blood staining the snow. "You know, I really didn't believe you when you said a mountain lion was stalking you. I would say he's been lying in wait for you all this time."

Jessica gasped, "You mean he actually waited through the storm for me?"

"No, I didn't mean it that way. He probably holed up in one of the caves and when we left, he left too, tracking us, and in an animal's way, hoping one of us wouldn't make it. Then he would have had an easy prey."

Jessica gasped once more. "I didn't realize animals were that smart."

"You'd be surprised how smart they really are," he admonished her. "Jessica, you have to start remembering that you're not back in New York. This is a raw, wild country. If you are going to survive, don't ever underestimate anything, man or beast."

A fire of defiance snapped in her own eyes as she faced Cole. "You almost sound as if that was a warning . . . a threat."

"No, of course not," he answered, although his reply was slow in coming. Jessica had read more into his words than he had meant. But it wouldn't hurt for her to be extra cautious. The past had proven how gullible she was. He nodded toward the bridge. "I suppose I've proved how safe it is. We had better get on our way if we're going to get home before nightfall."

After they crossed the bridge, the trail became easier. At noon, Cole stopped, built a fire and made coffee which he laced heavily with the tinned milk and sugar. They ate the remainder of the bread and beef jerky, hastily broke camp and were on their way again.

The cold bit deeply into Cole as he walked, leading the horse by the reins while Jessica sat on the saddle. Even though he had taken precautions to keep his feet dry, he could gradually feel the dampness seeping inside his boots. He had to press on. To have stopped would have meant spending the night without shelter or enough supplies since many had been left behind at the cave. As they traveled into the lower lands, Cole could see signs where men had been searching for them. He thought about firing his gun into the air, but decided against it. They were still too high. Any unnecessary gunshots could still trigger an avalanche.

It was late afternoon before they reached Utopia. As they came into town, Cole could see window curtains hastily jerked aside, and the people began to file out on their porches. Some of the women ran toward the horse and two weary travelers, but Cole ignored them and their questions. Jessica had become so cold, she had fallen asleep several miles back up the trail. Cole knew she was not in any danger even though she was sleeping.

As he was leading the horse up to the community house, William came from the stables. He stopped in surprise when he saw Cole. Breaking into a run, he rushed up to Cole.

"Cole! My God, where did you find her? We've been combing the hills for both of you! Is she all right?" he asked, his eyes slowly going to the bundled figure on the horse.

"She's fine," he whispered, lifting the reins to William. "You'll have to take these out of my hands. They're frozen to my gloves."

William stared at Cole. His hands appeared to be frozen in claw-like shapes. His face was crusted with ice.

"You'll have to help her down from the saddle," he whispered before toppling over face first into the snow.

When Cole awoke, he was in his own feather bed. Warmed bricks had been placed under his feet and blankets were piled high on top of him. He glanced wearily around the room. He saw Ed sitting in a chair with his head bowed in his hands. "Man, could I ever use a stiff drink right about now," he muttered thickly.

"Cole!" Ed said with a start. "Thank God! I was beginning to wonder if you would ever wake up!"

Cole struggled to sit up, glancing out at the dark night, he said, "I guess I was exhausted. How long did I sleep?"

"You've slept for about twenty-eight hours straight! You must not have slept since you left."

Cole's thoughts went to how he and Jessica had made love in the shelter of the cave. "No," he admitted with a wry grin, "I didn't get much sleep." He looked at Ed, "Jessica? Is she all right?"

"She's fine. William had her taken to his house. Apparently she was just as exhausted as you. I was told she could barely walk."

Cole had to know if everyone was all right. He asked hesitantly, "Ed, the search party? Did everyone make it back okay?"

Ed nodded. "They sure did. There was one group that

was a little slow coming in, and we were beginning to get worried, but everything's just fine now." Ed seemed to be uneasy as he said, "I believe William wants to see you. He asked me to let him know when you woke up."

"Yeah, I want to see him too." Cole said, swinging his legs over the side of the bed.

Shaking his head, Ed stopped him. "No, he said he would come over here to see you. I'll go get him while you shave and do whatever you need to do."

Cole had just sat down to a meal of thick sliced ham, scrambled eggs, and steaming black coffee when William entered the front door. "Cole? Cole? Where are you?"

"Come on in, I'm having something to eat."

William walked into the kitchen. He stared hard at Cole for a moment before asking, "Do you mind if I have a cup of that coffee?"

Cole smiled, "Now, William, when have you ever had to ask? Help yourself." He gestured with his hand.

William poured a cup then sat down across the table from Cole. His mouth was set into a firm line. He said bitterly, "Apparently there are several things I need to ask about."

Cole shoved back his plate and lit a cheroot. "All right William, we've known each other far too long to play cat and mouse. And, I damn sure don't like to be the mouse. So let's get it out in the open. What do you have on your mind?"

William glared at him. "I'm glad you feel that way, Cole, because I have a lot on my mind. The main thing is Jessica!"

Cole toyed with the small black cigar, "All right, what about Jessica?"

"Why did you lie to me, Cole?"

"Lie?" Cole repeated, the hair on the nape of his neck started to bristle. Very few men had had the nerve to call him a liar. His eyes became cold and sharp. "Suppose you explain?"

"I never thought you would treat me this way, Cole. Damn it!" He slammed his fist against the table, "You've been just like a son to me!"

Cole was starting to get angry. "Now wait a minute, William, I have no idea what in the hell is stuck in your craw, but I would suggest you tell me what's eating you instead of beating around the bush. I would like to know what I've done to get you so mad at me?"

William spread his fingers wide apart and looked at his hands. Then he glanced up at Cole and stared at him, almost as if he contemplating his next move. Finally, he said, "You lied to me, Cole, and I damn sure don't like it!"

Cole took a long draw from his cheroot then exhaled loudly, he needed a moment to cool his rising anger. "Look, William, I'm not asking you this time. Would you please just tell me what in the hell is bothering you?"

William's eyes gleamed dangerously as he spat, "You certainly ought to know what I'm talking about. It's Jessica! You knew how I felt about her and you deliberately went after her!"

"It's a damn good thing I did go after her. If I hadn't, she'd be dead by now!"

"That's the point I'm trying to make, Cole. You knew where she was all along!" he uttered through gritted teeth.

"You're wrong, William," Cole said, shaking his head. "I had no idea where she was."

"And you expect me to believe that? What kind of fool to you take me for? You made a beeline for her as soon as you left here!"

Cole scrutinized William very carefully. He could see why his friend was angry. He realized he did look guilty of William's accusation. "Regardless of what it looks like, William, I had no idea where she was. Call it blind luck—fate, whatever, I let my horse have his head and he picked out the trail."

"Hell, Cole, you didn't even take your own horse. You simply picked one out at the stables."

"Yes! You're right! I did *simply pick a horse!* And by God, you ought to realize why I picked that stallion. He knows these mountains better than any man. I figured if any one of them could get me through, he could!"

A shadow of doubt slipped across William's face, but it was soon replaced by his burning, jealous anger. "Uh, huh, sure. I still say you had it planned. You could have told me your idea, and I could have been the one who went after her. But, hell no, you had to play the gallant hero and rescue her yourself! And God only knows what kind of ideas you filled her head with, and it wouldn't surprise me in the least if you didn't take advantage of her!"

"Those are fighting words, William!" Cole uttered coldly. "For one thing, that night when I asked what I could do, you dismissed me like I was a little boy you were sending to his room. You didn't even ask me my opinion. And as for my taking advantage of her, that's a damn lie! Who said I did?"

"No one had to, Cole," William muttered icily, "I know you. You'd bed anything that wore a skirt. I've got eyes in my head. I've seen how you watch her." He shook his head, "I never thought you would treat me this way. You waited until I had fallen in love with her, then you tried to move in." William leaned back in his chair and eyed Cole intently. "I think we ought to have an understanding right now." He took a deep breath, "I think it's time we parted company. I've asked Jessica to marry me, and she has agreed to become my bride. There's no place for you here. I don't want her to have to look at your face everyday and remember. I don't want to have to look at your face everyday either . . . and remember. I know you have a partnership here. I'm buying your share right now. I'll deed that thousand acres I own in Texas over to you." William stood on his feet, placed his hat on his head and started for the door. "I'll expect you to leave by first light in the morning!"

Cole sat in his chair, too stunned to move. Jessica had agreed to marry William. It didn't matter when she had agreed, whether it had been before she went up on the mountain, or after. Either she had responded to his love making, knowing she was going to marry William, or else she had gone into William's arms after she had spent all that time in his. Cole sat there, feeling like a fool. Jessica had played both of them for fools, played one against the other until she came out with the winning hand. A sarcastic grin spread across his face. William had even shown his true colors. True, he could try to warn him. He could try to tell him exactly what Jessica was, but he knew William would never listen to him. After those ugly things the captain had accused him of, he deserved everything Jessica could dish out. Cole glumly decided they deserved each other.

Cole slid his chair back, knocking it over in the process. He didn't stop to pick it up. He stormed to his bedroom and took a small box out from underneath the bed. In it was a lock of blonde hair tied with a red ribbon. He threw it into the floor and ground it with the heel of his boot. Then he mentally threw Jessica out of his heart, and crushed her alongside of the lock of Melissa's hair. He removed a packet of envelopes from the box, envelopes containing a record of the money he had been saving. He smacked the packet against his thigh. "All right, William," he said aloud, "I'll take that land. I figure you owe it to me. With this money, I'll stock it full of prime beef. One of these days, I'll be rich enough to buy and sell your soul if I so choose!"

The following morning, just as the sun was lighting up the eastern sky, Cole rode up to William's house. He slammed through the front door without bothering to knock. William and Jessica were sitting at the table, being served breakfast by Ching Lee.

"I came after my deed, William," he snarled, curling his lip insolently at Jessica.

"What makes you think you have the right to barge into my house, Cole?" William asked angrily.

"Until you pay up, I have the right to go where I damn well please!" Turning to Jessica, who was sitting wide-eyed over the scene that was unfolding before her eyes, Cole said, "Good morning, Miss Tate. I trust you slept comfortably last night."

Jessica's eyes darted between them. "Cole, William, what on earth is the matter with you? Why are you angry?" she demanded to know.

Cole's eyes widened innocently, "Why, no reason at all, Miss Tate," he slurred sarcastically.

"Jessica," William interrupted, "Please go your room. I'll explain as soon as this man leaves."

Jessica sat dumbfoundedly. "I don't believe this! What is the matter?"

Cole ignored her. "Where is my deed, William?"

"I don't have it here, it's in the bank at San Francisco. I'll have to send a man for it."

"Then I'll ride along with him to make sure I get it." He glanced down at Jessica and leered, "While I'm there, I'll see about getting me a woman . . . a *good* woman. In fact, I think I'll make a stop at the Golden Slipper while I'm there. They usually have choice stuff there, although a bad one does slip in now and again." Without giving her a chance to answer, he spun on his heel and marched to the door. Tossing a look of hatred over his shoulder, he said to William, "Have your man meet me at the stable, I'll give him fifteen minutes." Then Cole slammed the door soundly behind him.

Chapter Twenty-seven

Almost in a daze, Jessica rose from her chair and walked to the fireplace. She was numb with shock. Holding her hands out to the fire, she tried to warm herself, but the chill she was feeling crept into the very pit of her soul.

William watched her anxiously. "I'm sorry you had to hear that, my dear," he said softly.

"Can you please tell me what is going on?" she pleaded, turning to face William.

William's face was gray from worry and fatigue as he replied, "I will, but first I have to send a man to go with Cole. And, Jessica, I seriously doubt if he'll be back." He hurried to the door, slipped on his coat and followed Cole out into the yard.

My God, what has happened? Jessica cried to herself. Why is Cole acting this way? Had she done something? No! No! She would not allow it to end like this. She would find out what was bothering Cole and what the argument was about. Racing into the guest room, Jessica threw her shawl around her shoulders and ran after them. Only she was minute too late. Cole had already mounted his horse and was riding away from Utopia.

"Cole! Cole! she screamed running after him. "Come back! Cole, please come back." Her voice trailed off into a painful whimper as Cole continued to ride. He never even looked back.

Jessica could feel the earth spin. It tilted one way and then the other. Then mercifully, she slipped into a painless void.

Much later, Jessica's eyelids fluttered slowly open as a warm cloth was pressed gently against her face. She fought against returning to the unpleasant world of reality. In her world of misty haze, everything was perfect, and there was no pain. Her mind was in a tangle of confusion. She could make no sense of where she was.

"Jessica, speak to me, please speak to me," William commanded. "You have to wake up!"

"Why should I?" she muttered thickly as the terrible memories flashed back. Memories of how Cole's final words had cut into her heart like a knife, its blade honed razor sharp. Memories of how hatred filled his blue eyes and masked the handsome qualities of his face. Memories of how she had lain in his arms and how they sought and found the flaming ecstasy of love. Now, he had turned his back on her without so much as a backward glance. Her knuckles turned white as she clenched her hands into fists. Over a strident objection from William, Jessica rose from the bed and stumbled back into the main room in the house. She felt the heat from the fireplace on her cheek, but it failed to stop the coldness spreading throughout her heart. Cole had used her. He had never loved her. He had simply taken what she had offered in the name of love, and twisted it into something ugly and sordid. Deep rasping sobs shook her entire body.

"Jessica, my love, please don't cry. He's not worth it." William tried to soothe her. Standing there, he gently took the girl into his arms and comforted her. He gently caressed her flaming locks of hair, appearing more crimson in the flickering glow of the fire. Holding her so intimately, William knew he had made the right decision when he had lied and told Cole she had accepted his proposal. While Jessica had been lost out in the storm, he had come to realize she meant more to him than life itself. He would not want to continue living if Jessica were not at his side. Then, when Cole brought her back from the clutches of death, he saw the look of love on their faces, and the choice had been made. Even if it meant forsaking the love and friendship he had shared with Cole for all of these years. William gazed at Jessica tenderly. She was hurting now, but he would soon make her forget Cole. This treasure, this shining jewel among the rough was worth any sacrifice he had had to make.

"Jessica!" William snapped gruffly, "You have to snap out of it. He's not worth your tears!" William knew he would have to lie again, something that was more than distasteful to him, but once started, he would have to carry through. Grasping Jessica by her shoulders, he stared at her intently, his eyes piercing the unseeing barrier she had defensively raised, masking the torment which was screaming through the very essence of her being. "Listen to me! Cole is gone. It is all over, you have to accept that!"

"But, why, William? Why? I thought he loved me," she cried.

William took a deep breath. He knew he would have

to do it now while he had the courage; he realized it would take a lot of courage to break her heart. "Jessica, listen to me, I told you he's not worth it." He guided her to a chair and helped her to sit down, then lowered himself down to bended knees. "My dearest, sweet, Jessica, you deserve much more than Cole could have ever offered you. Believe me my dear, it'll hurt me as much as it does you for me to tell you this, but Cole is a scoundrel. Do you remember how upset I was when I returned last night?"

Jessica nodded. When she and Cole had returned, William had brought her here and put her to bed. She had slept for hours. Then when she awoke William had firmly refused to let her go outside. She had asked and asked about Cole, but had been constantly reassured he was fine, that he would see her this morning. But last night, William had gone out, and when he had returned, he was in a rage. When questioned about it, William had refused to answer. Jessica had a feeling she did not want to hear what William now had to say, but she also had the feeling it would clear up the mystery of why Cole had treated her so badly.

"Yes, William, I know you were upset and angry. I suppose you and Cole had an argument?"

William nodded and swallowed hard. "Yes, I guess you could call it that. I went over to Cole's house and he wasn't there. I found him in the community hall . . . bragging about how . . . he . . ." his voice trailed off.

Jessica's face had blanched, a wretched expression flashed across it. "He bragged . . . about . . . what?"

"He . . . bragged about . . . you and the . . . relationship you shared while . . . trapped out in the storm." William pulled his gaze from hers. He could not bear to see the pain.

"Oh, God, no!" she mouthed. "Surely you misunderstood him?"

"No. I'm afraid not," he answered slowly, shaking his head. "He was saying some very ugly things, Jessica. But let me explain a few things to you about Cole. Several years ago, he was hurt very badly by a woman. Since then, he apparently hasn't cared who he hurts or why. It almost seems as though every woman is merely a conquest to him." He sighed deeply, "You're not the first woman, and I'm sure you won't be the last he'll treat this way."

"You mean he . . . actually bragged about what happened between us?" she asked. She tried to stop the memories from coming. But they were too firmly etched in the chasms of her mind. How Cole had held her in his arms, how he had whispered sweet endearing words of love and passion to her, how he had caressed her body and made it his.

"Yes, that's when I stepped in. My darling, you know how I feel about you. When I overheard Cole boasting, I felt a rage I didn't know possible. I even called him out to defend your honor, and he refused. We ended up having a rather heated argument. I finally told him to leave Utopia, that we didn't want his kind here, that we were trying to build a town that men and women would be proud to call home, and a decent place where they could raise their children. He flatly refused at first, said he had a partnership here. That's when I offered him the land I owned in Texas. I suspect Cole has always wanted that land, because he snapped at the chance. That's why he came by this morning."

Jessica bowed her head in shame. Her hurt ran so deep, tears would not even come. "Oh, William," she whispered in a small voice.

"Now Jessica," he hastened to say, "I want you to forget about him. My offer still stands. I would be greatly honored if you would consent to become my wife."

"Oh, no, not now, William." She gazed up at him painfully, "I couldn't do that to you . . . not after what Cole did. I could never dishonor you."

" How could you dishonor me?"

"Because . . . of what he told those men."

"Listen, my love," William thought fast, "All of those men know Cole very well. We all know several instances where Cole was with a woman and absolutely nothing happened, and he still boasted about his affair with them. It's just something we overlooked. Now," he took a deep breath, "I want to set this straight. I don't know what happened between you while you were up on the mountain. I don't care to know. If you were intimate with him, then well, I think I can understand how a man such as Cole can turn an innocent young woman's head. If you were not intimate with him, then you can chalk it up to another one of his lies."

"But . . . but . . . what about the men? Wouldn't they gossip behind your back? How could you hold your head up. How could I hold my head up? How could I cheat you in that manner?"

"You wouldn't be cheating me, Jessica," William argued. "I want you in any form, shape, or fashion. If we marry, the men would realize there was nothing to what Cole said. They all have too much respect for me to gossip behind my back."

Jessica dropped her head into her hands in confusion.

"I don't know, I simply don't know!" Her head was spinning in turmoil. Too much had happened. She would have to think.

William sensing her reluctance, spoke softly, "My dear, I'm not pressing for an answer now. I realize you need time to think." He forced a laugh, "But please, don't go for another walk to clear your mind."

Her head bobbed numbly, she felt like disappearing into some dark hole and dying. Never had she been so completely devastated.

William gathered her into his arms and stroked her cheek, "My darling, it hurts me to see you suffering so much. Surely there is something I can do to help?"

"No," she whimpered. "There is nothing anyone can do. But, William," she searched his eyes, begging him to understand, "I really don't think I could be so unfair to to you. How can you ask me to marry you and not know if you were getting what another man had rejected?"

"Jessica, my love, don't you understand? I don't care what happened. To me, you are as innocent as a spring flower, a fragile rose bud, blossoming into a beautiful woman. Please don't feel guilty about Cole. And don't worry about being a wife to me in the full sense of the word. I promise to be patient. I fully realize it would be hard for you to have a relationship with a man after the way you have been treated. But Jessica, let me impress this upon you. I told you I would not push for an answer. However, a prompt answer would help to dispel any ugly remarks. I know what I said about the men not gossiping because they knew Cole, and because of the respect they have for me. But if we could announce wedding plans very soon, I'd bet it would convince them that Cole was lying. They would see that I had accepted you.

They would see you the way I do, how sweet and innocent you really are." William was becoming quite frantic in his attempt to convince Jessica. He could not take a chance on losing her now, not after coming this close.

"Oh, William, you're so kind." Jessica pressed her fingers to her throbbing temples. "I'm so tired," she muttered thickly. Too much had happened. She could not bear to face the reality of it all.

William sensed he was winning. A strange light flashed in his eye. He stood and hurried into the kitchen only to return in a few minutes with a glass of water. Thrusting a tiny slip of paper at Jessica, he said, "Here take this, it is a powder that will help you to sleep. Take it," he urged. "It will be good for you."

With trembling hands, Jessica accepted the small packet. She raised it greedily to her mouth, and tasted the bitterness with her tongue. After washing it down with the water, she looked up at William, "I don't know if I can make it to my room or not." She was tired. So tired.

William scooped her easily into his arms. He couldn't help but notice how light she felt. She must have lost several pounds while suffering through the ordeal she experienced while in the mountains. He carried Jessica into the bedroom and tenderly placed her on the bed. After snugging the afghan under her chin, he drew the drapes and softly closed the door behind him.

Jessica lay on the bed. Her eyes were wide in spite of the drug William had given her. She had just been proposed to by one of the kindest men she had ever known, but she could not hug herself in girlish anticipation over the prospect. Her nerves were screaming with emotion, Jessica felt drained, and old—old long before her time. She had only started to blossom into maturity, and now she wished she was of an age where she could look forward to the blissfulness of eternity. It was a bizarre fact, she was eighteen years old, and her life was over. She did not care to live. Deep down inside, she did not know if it was because Cole had treated her so badly, had toyed with her affections then callously betrayed her, or whether it was the fact that she now faced a life without him by her side. She loved him; she hated him. Her gray eyes darkened with rage. Hate! She suddenly liked the sound of that word.

She felt every turbulent emotion known to man as the drug started to take effect. She fought against the surrender her body was forcing upon her. It was her desire to rant, scream, gnash her teeth, and fling herself from the bed. But it was as if she was paralyzed. Her limbs would not obey her feeble commands. Instead, a drowsiness took control of her body, forcing her into the darkness. One last fleeting thought was to stop fighting the drug. It was meant to help her relax. Yes, sleep, sleep was what she needed. It would be a way to escape the pain thundering through her heart. Her long sooty lashes fluttered and cast a shadow against her pale cheeks as she settled into the land of infinite oblivion.

In her drugged slumber, Jessica rose above her body and looked at the sleeping form upon the bed. Suddenly, she was thrust into an unreal world of gray and black. She did not know why, but the need to run, to escape, overwhelmed her. Glancing over her shoulder, her eyes widened in fright. Two mighty beasts were chasing her, flames were snorting from their nostrils. Their hooves were misshapen into long, grasping claws. The sounds of the beasts' high-pitched screams echoed in her head. Jessica knew she was still asleep. She struggled for release from her nightmare, but something kept pulling her back into the clutches of the beasts. She was in agony. Her heart was racing at a thunderous pace. The terror was so intense she could not scream. She saw her throat constrict and her mouth work furiously, but no sound came forth. She found herself running, scrambling for safety, but all she found were jutting gray walls that towered above her. They became as hot as molten lava to her touch. She could feel one of the beasts slipping its talons into her long streaming hair and grasping, pulling her closer to him. She turned and the beast was smiling at her, revealing long, sharp pointed teeth. Then both of the ferocious beasts perched above her. Their faces took human form before they swooped down to devour her. At that moment, Jessica knew she was in the fiery pits of hell!

Chapter Twenty-eight

Sleet battered its way through the early morning sky, pelting the trees and rooftops, and quickly forming a crusty layer of ice over the windows. Steady puffs of wood smoke climbed through the chimneys and flues and disappeared into the driving wind. All of the men who had wintered in Utopia before were amazed at how quickly winter had arrived. Many claimed it was there for the duration, while others swore there would be a relief in the weather, that they would have a spell of Indian Summer before the frosty breath of winter showed its true and lasting face.

Jessica tossed restlessly on her bed. She struggled to awaken, but something seemed to hold her back. It was almost as if she hated to face the world of reality.

"Jessica, Jessica, you have to wake up now," William said repeatedly. "You have slept long enough. Come on, wake up," he gently nudged her shoulder.

"No! No!" she screamed, coming awake, but not enough to push aside the monsters chasing her.

"What's the matter?" William asked, concern shadowing his face.

Jessica sat up in the bed. Her face was blanched from fright, and perspiration poured from her brow. The look of relief was evident on her features when she saw William standing beside her bed. Her hand flew up to help calm the terrible pounding of her heart. "I was having a nightmare. One that was so horrible, I pray I will never have the likes again."

"My poor darling," William soothed, handing her a glass of water. "Here, drink this. It will help calm you down."

She eyed it suspiciously, "There isn't anything in it, is there?"

"You mean, sleeping powders?"

Jessica nodded.

"No. I wouldn't give you anything like that unless you either asked for them, or was so upset you had to have something." He took a deep breath, "Other than the nightmares, are you feeling better this morning?"

She looked up at him, "I really don't know. I haven't had much of a chance . . ."

"I'm sorry, Jessica, here I go again, rushing you, or so it would seem."

Jessica forced a smile. "No, that's all right, William. Regardless of what you think, I'm much stronger than you believe I am. I seriously doubt if any woman has died from shame or a betrayed heart before."

"Atta girl!" William beamed. "Are you hungry?"

She shook her head. "No, coffee or a cup of hot tea would be fine." She glanced around the room nervously, "I need to get up. Is my robe in here?"

William beamed proudly. "I thought you would never ask." He stepped over to a finely crafted cedar chest and removed a long, flowing woolen robe. It was beautiful. It was pearl gray, and silver stitching decorated the pockets, the collar had flowers the color of cinnabar and russet embroidered on it. The sleeves were long, and the cuffs were buttoned by tiny, delicate pearls. "This is a mere token of my affection," William smiled. "As soon as you consent to be my wife, I have a few more gifts in mind."

Jessica managed a weak smile, "Are you trying to buy my affections, William?"

"Of course not," William answered, he had the grace to toe the floor sheepishly, "I simply wanted to give you something that was pretty. I've seen your clothes, and you could really use some more. Tell me, do you sew?"

"Yes, I do," she stuttered.

"I have ordered yards and yards of fabulous material. Velvets, silks, fine linen, and because I know how practical you are, a few pieces of gingham."

"William, that isn't necessary!"

"But it is. I'm far from being a pauper. I can afford it, so I'll buy it for you."

Jessica stared at the afghan, she was tormented by uncertainty and struggled to retain control." William, please, I have to have a moment . . . no, not a moment, but time, time to sort things out in my mind."

William walked to the door. "Of course you do, my dear," he said tenderly. He grinned self-consciously, "I guess it seems like I am being inconsiderate, believe me, I don't mean to be."

"I know," she answered. Inwardly she was screaming to be left alone. She desperately had to have a few private moments.

"Tell you what, there are few things I need to check

on. I'll leave you alone for a while, and who knows," he added brightly, "you may have some good news for me when I return."

Jessica stared at the closed door a few minutes before tossing back the covers and stepping out of bed. As she went about her morning toilet, she was locked in the grip of numbness and indecision. It was difficult to believe what had happened in her life. She had absolutely no reason to doubt William's word, Cole had proved what a scoundrel he was. But still, she would have placed her life on the line that Cole had returned the love she felt for him. It did not seem reasonable that he had risked his life by braving the storm to rescue her in order to have another conquest to brag about. After all, he had taken her innocence back at the Golden Slipper. That fact would have given him a reason to boast unless he was ashamed of the fact that it was a bawdy house, and he was expected to pay for the woman's services. Cole was a proud man, perhaps he thought he would be accused of taking advantage of her, that the conquest had not been a victory won. That still did not account for him risking his life to save her.

Jessica pressed her fingers to her temples. Why was everything so complicated? It sounded as though she was trying to make excuses for Cole. If Cole was innocent, then William had to be lying. She recalled the cold, cutting words Cole had spoken to her, and she knew William was not lying, and even felt ashamed because the idea crossed her mind. But why did these unanswered questions keep nagging at her? Could she merely be trying to find a reason to doubt Cole's actions? She should hate him with all of her heart. No, Jessica mentally shook her head to get her thoughts straight, she did hate him. It was the kind of hatred that left her feeling empty.

Jessica knew she should be relieved to have discovered what kind of man he actually was before becoming committed to him. Deep down inside, Jessica knew she had already pledged herself to him. She would have never willingly entered into such a brazen affair if she had not been ready to make that total commitment.

The young girl sat down at the dressing table and began to brush her glorious mane vigorously, wincing as the bristles became ensnared in the tangles received during the long, nightmare filled sleep. She peered curiously at her reflection in the mirror. What was it about her that caused men to act foolish? She saw nothing unusually spectacular. True, her hair was pretty. The only time scissors had touched it was to trim off the dead ends. And her skin was nice, it was not marked by pockmarks or unsightly freckles. Her eyes? She supposed their unusual color was attractive. She had never paid much attention to how she looked before, in fact, she seldom formed opinions based on anyone's looks, that is, until Cole happened along. She had been drawn to him because of how he resembled the man in her dreams.

Jessica gave her image a disgruntled smile. She was procrastinating and she knew it. She was doing everything to delay the obvious, and that was to make a decision about William. William, just the thought of him set her to thinking seriously.

Would she be cheating him and herself if she entered into a marriage feeling the way she did? She did not love him. She seriously doubted if she could ever love anyone else again. Oh, she was sure she would be able to form a respect for whomever she decided to marry, but nothing could ever compare to the emotions she had felt for Cole. No one would ever compare to him. Jessica flashed a wry smile at the wan reflection in the mirror. Lord, she hoped no one would compare with Cole. She could never go through such an ordeal again.

She eyed herself warily, "All right, Jessica," she spoke aloud, "You have come to the conclusion that Cole is a cad and a scoundrel. He is completely without honor or virtue. You have to put him from your mind and forget he ever existed." Her eyes darkened momentarily, only a few days ago, she had doubted if she could face life without Cole. Now, remembering the wicked gleam in his eyes, his scowling remarks, and with what William repeated, she felt gladdened over the fact she would never have to see him again. True, her thoughts had first leaned in the direction of why he had acted the way he did, but the longer she thought about it, the angrier she became. "All right, Jessica, you have wasted enough time on that scoundrel. No matter how much you try to make him into a decent person, he isn't one. It is time to direct your thoughts toward a more positive course. You will simply have to consider William's proposal." Jessica got up from the chair and walked over to the window. Peering outside, she gave thought to her relationship with William.

She had discovered the hard way there was no such thing as love. Love was a word for misty-eyed girls with nothing but dreams and stardust in their heads. Yes, she supposed there was a certain fondness that developed between married people. And, she was fond of William. Her knuckles whitened as she tightly clutched her hands together. There was another problem. What about her reputation? Was it ruined beyond repair? She certainly didn't want her friends to think she was bad.

Jessica glanced wildly around the room. This would never do! She could not reach any decision here. She would go to her friends and talk to them. They would be able to help.

Jessica hurriedly left William's house. She went to June's but did not find her there, so she continued on to the cabin where Helen now lived.

Helen admitted her immediately. "Come on in, Jessica, June and I were having coffee. We were discussing you."

Jessica shrank under her friend's innocent remark. Her face was blazing when she sat down at the table. She waited until Helen poured her coffee before saying anything. "I . . . certainly hope were giving me the benefit of the doubt."

June and Helen exchanged a confused look. "What do you mean? June asked.

"Helen said you were talking about me. Before you form an opinion, I would like for you to hear my side of the story."

Helen laughed nervously, "Wait a minute, Jessica. I didn't mean to imply we were talking *about* you. We were simply discussing and wondering what was going on."

"You mean you haven't heard the ugly rumors?"

"We've been hearing a lot of things, but I wouldn't go so far to call them ugly rumors," Helen said truthfully. "Naturally, we are very curious as to what happened between Cole and the captain. I never thought they would part company. I have asked Ed, but he has no idea what happened." Both Helen and June looked expectantly at Jessica.

Jessica took a deep breath. "All right, since I have come for advice, I will tell you what is going on." She began hesitantly, stumbling over the scene that transpired at William's house the morning before. She purposely did not go into details about the mountain interlude. When she finished, tears were glistening in her eyes.

"Let me get this straight," June said slowly. "The day you disappeared, William proposed to you. You thought there was no chance you and Cole would get together, so you took a long walk. . .ride, whatever, and became stranded in the mountains. Cole found you and brought you back safely. I can certainly understand how you were close to a complete collapse when you got back. I know Helen and I were very curious as to why William refused to let you have any visitors. Then, William overheard Cole bragging about what happened in the mountains." She raised her brows and nodded affirmatively, "As far as that goes, what happened, if anything, is none of our business."

"Ed sure hasn't said anything about ugly rumors!" Helen stated firmly.

June continued, "then Cole and William had an argument when William confronted him about the slanderous remarks. The following morning, Cole stormed into William's house and was very sarcastic to you. Right, Jessica?" she asked.

Jessica nodded. "Yes, unfortunately, everything is all correct. However, there is one other thing. William again repeated his proposal." Jessica lifted her chin and looked at both of them. She had hardly expected it to be so difficult. "My friends, I desperately need to talk, for you to help me decide what to do."

June laughed uneasily, "Well, Jessica, it looks to me like you are the one that will have to make up your mind. You know your heart, not us."

"I know, but it helps to talk about it." She looked June squarely in the eye, "As far as knowing my heart, you can forget that. I loved Cole, and actually thought he returned my feelings."

"Jessica," Helen interrupted, "I can't believe Cole would say those ugly things. If he's that vicious, then why did he risk his own life by attempting to find you?"

"That question crossed my mind also. But wait a minute!" Jessica screwed her face into a frown and waved her hands wildly. "Listen to us! We are all trying to make excuses and apparently, we are attempting to find some way to clear Cole of William's accusations. Don't get me wrong, I'm not fussing at you because I am guilty of the same thing. I think we are all confused because it is unlike Cole to have done this. But on the other hand, we are being unfair to William. We have just about called him a liar. Think about it, he loved Cole like a son. He would never do anything to harm him. He had absolutely no reason to fabricate a story."

Helen said firmly, "I still say Ed has not mentioned a word about the men gossiping."

"Think about it, Helen, Ed *wouldn't* say anything!" Jessica stated bluntly.

"And I think we are also forgetting how Cole talked to me yesterday morning. He sounded like an *arrogant bastard!"*

"Jessica!" the women chorused in unison, their tone of voice scolding.

"Well, he did! Let's just forget Cole! My dilemma is whether or not to marry William!"

June shook her head, "Jessica, that decision will have to come from you. It's your life, you will have to decide. However, I think I know how you feel. You probably want to reason aloud why you should or should not marry him."

"That's right," Jessica breathed a sigh of relief over her friend's understanding attitude. "I don't want to cheat William. I want to be a good wife to any man I marry. I simply don't know if I can enter into a marriage feeling the way I do."

"Exactly how do you feel?" Helen asked.

"I am over the foolish notion that a person should marry for love. I realize it works with a few people, but it's not for me. I'll never love again." She recognized the path ahead of her. She was doomed to be unfulfilled. "On the other hand, it is difficult to accept a marriage proposal from a man who deserves more than I can give."

Helen and June exchanged worried glances. They hated to see Jessica so acquiesced to her self-imposed fate. June spoke, "Why do you think it would be unfair to William?"

"Because he loves me and I have no feeling toward him other than friendship."

"Does he know this?"

"Yes, of course, I had to be frank with him."

June sighed heavily, "Jessica, speaking of being frank, I'm going to be frank with you. I think it's too bad you and Cole didn't work out. I really believe the two of you could have been very happy. However, it did not work. Now, you face marriage to a man you do not love. Let me ask you this. Does the idea of marrying William appear so distasteful to you? You need to ask yourself if you would want to spend the rest of your life with him."

Jessica shook her head slowly. "I am not overly fond of marrying anyone right now. But I see no other way to survive. I realize the circumstances, even though it makes me look as though I would consider marriage for the sake of convenience I am really very fond of William. Too, I have to face the facts. I am out here in an uncivilized land. I have no money. I seriously doubt if I could look after myself without someone taking advantage of me, or should I say, some man taking advantage of me again," Jessica added thoughtfully.

June raised her brows, a warm blush had spread across her cheeks. "Jessica, I can't believe I'm hearing you say all of this. I may make you mad at me, but I'm going to tell you my opinion." Her voice raised a note higher. "Here you are, crying on our shoulders. I say, grow up! You sound like a whining brat!"

"June!" Helen gasped. "There's no need to talk to her like that!"

"Yes there is," June stated firmly. "Jessica, you claim you can never love again, then in the next breath bawl about marrying William because you don't love him! That does not make sense! Do you actually think I married Stuart because I felt the rapturous flames of love? No! I married Stuart because he is a good, kind, and decent man. I had an affection for him, because he is so good! Now, take Helen," she pointed at her, "She married once for love. Look where it got her, on a marriage ship. She had to sign away any right she ever had to even legally board. She had to promise to marry a man, a man she didn't even know if she would like, much less love! I did the same thing, just like all the other women who came with us! Luckily, Helen fell in love with her husband before she married him. I was was not in love with Stuart, and I'm still not. But with each day that passes, I grow more fond of him. So tell me, Jessica," June asked, placing her hands on the table, "What makes you think you are better than us?"

Jessica flinched. She stared down into her cup of coffee while Helen protested heartily.

"June! That's cruel! Jessica came over here asking for our advice, not a lecture." Helen gathered Jessica into her arms, "She's young, she has fanciful ideas."

"Then it's high time she learned the facts of life!" June crossed her arms stubbornly.

"Wait a minute!" Jessica cried irritably. "Please don't fight on my account." She looked up at Helen, "She's right," she said pitifully.

June rolled her eyes upward. "For God's sake, I didn't mean to start a war." Although her eyes were sad, a smile touched at her lips. She hugged Jessica to her ample bosom, "Look, kid," she said affectionately, "I never had a sister, so you'll have to pardon me for acting like one. And that's what I did," she said, wagging a finger in Jessica's face. "I simply acted like an older sister and tried to set you straight on a few things. And as usual, I got a little too carried away. Let me make it clear that I'm not mad at you. I merely wanted you to hear what you've been saying. As for my advice or opinion, I'm going to give that to you too." She paused and took a deep breath. "You loved Cole, but that didn't work out. I think many women have had a Cole in their lives at one time or another. Now, you take William," June raised a brow and squinted thoughtfully at her. "You could certainly do a lot worse. If you actually think you want to enter into a marriage without love, then marry him. That man is crazy about you, he has money, and you will never have to want for anything. But it all comes back to point one; do you want to marry without love?"

Jessica timidly cast a glance in Helen's direction. "What do you have to say?"

Helen pursed her lips and raised her brows significantly, "I will have to agree with June. I will say, I think her tactics were too harsh though."

Jessica managed a weak smile. "Well, it looks like I got what I came after."

"Tell me," Helen asked, "Have you made up your mind?"

"Well," Jessica began slowly, "I think it would be redundant of me to go back on what I said about love, so there is one thing left to do, and that is to accept William's proposal."

June and Helen looked at each other. "Are you sure?" Helen asked. "Do you think you're rushing into a decision that could wait for a while?"

Jessica's teeth worried with her bottom lip before she answered, "No, actually I feel better now that I have made a decision." She slammed her fist down on the table. "It's time I started living my life the way I want to live it. I'm tired of being at the mercy and whim of everybody else!"

June chuckled, "Then dear, you shouldn't be considering getting married then."

Jessica appeared to be confused. "Why?" she asked amidst gales of laughter from June and Helen.

"Because," Helen said, "being married is the same as having a small child to care for. Don't get us wrong, but most men are very helpless, until it comes to telling a wife what to do. Believe us, if you want freedom, then you don't need to get married!"

Jessica blushed shyly, "I didn't mean it that way!" Her mood sobered, "I guess I should be going. I want to tell William I have reached a decision." She smiled once again, "I do want to thank you. You've been a lot of help."

Helen shrugged. "I don't see anything we've done."

"You were here, that's the main thing." Jessica took one last swallow of her coffee, "I'll see you later."

Jessica tried to keep her steps light and cheerful as she made her way back to William's house. She knew she would not get over Cole quickly. Even though he had hurt her very much, she had loved him with all of her heart. It would take time for her wounds to heal. William would have to realize how deeply she had been hurt, he would have to be patient with her.

Her hand trembled as she opened the front door. "William?" she called. "Are you here?"

The tall ex-captain sauntered into the parlor holding a steaming mug of coffee. His face lit up when he saw Jessica. "Well, hello," he could not conceal his expression of relief. "I was wondering where you were. Been to see Helen?" he asked curiously. He did not dare tell her he had assigned a man to watch her. He dared not admit, even to himself, that he was afraid she would try to leave.

"Yes," she answered curiously. "How did you know?"

William hastily gulped his coffee. "Oh, I didn't know for sure. It was a lucky guess."

Jessica accepted his answer without question. She turned and walked over to the fireplace to warm her hands. Suddenly realizing she had been holding her breath, Jessica released it haltingly. Whirling around to face William, she said, "I have an answer for you."

"You do?" William's eyes widened in surprise. His heart began to beat faster. "Am . . . I going to like what it is?"

"I certainly hope so."

"You mean . . ."

"Yes, I will marry you, William."

He was across the room in a fleeting moment and had Jessica in his muscular arms. "Oh, my Jessica, he said, cradling her close to him, "You won't be sorry. I'll make you happy. I promise I will."

Jessica accepted his affection with a total submission. She could not help the tears which flooded her eyes. She did regret them though. The feeling inside of her made her resent Cole even more than she had thought possible. William was such a good man. It was so hard to see him so happy, when she was only giving him a tiny part of her. And it was all Cole's fault. As William's arms wrapped around her waist, she tried not to remember the feel of Cole's arms around her, and the feel of his hands on her body. For an instant, she wanted to bolt and run, but it soon passed. Just as the memory of Cole would dissolve into the misty shadows from which he came.

Chapter Twenty-nine

Brilliant rays of sunlight streamed through the windows of the bedroom, filling it with an abundance of light and surprising warmth. Indian Summer had indeed arrived in the village of Utopia. Jessica stretched in the luxurious comfort of her bed. Turning on her stomach, she plumped up the pillow, basking in the peace and quiet in the final few moments before having to rise and face the day. She could not believe the time had passed so quickly. After accepting William's proposal, a whirlwind of activity had begun. Along with all the other normal routines, plans for their wedding were made.

Jessica had adamantly protested over all the fuss, claiming that the other women's weddings were not so elaborate. William countered that their wedding was different. With him being the leader of Utopia, it was expected. Besides, a fancy wedding would help to alleviate any rumors that could still possibly exist.

When William had shown Jessica the material for her wedding gown, all satiny white and pure, she had tried to tell him she could not wear such a gown. She felt unworthy of the purity the color implied. William had refused to listen to her protests, even to the point of being obstinate. He did not want to know what happened between Cole and Jessica. He told her what was in the past was over, they had a bright future to look forward to.

Jessica climbed out of bed and walked to the window. She stared out across the meadow. She was swept away in the relaxed beauty of the magnificent land. One would never have known only a few weeks earlier, snow had covered the area completely. Now, it was a splash of color right from an artist's palette. The trees were dotted with a few traces of green, but it was the golden slashes of brown, amber, russet, and cinnebar, which praised the lazy blue sky.

Jessica's gaze moved to the community hall. A commotion was coming from that direction. A smile teased at Jessica's lips as she imagined the scene unfolding around the hall. Chinese lanterns were being strung, a white arbor was being erected and hearty winter roses were being entwined through the arbor. William had spared no expense to make this a memorable day.

Jessica knew she would have to start getting ready soon. The minister was due to arrive by noon. It was odd, she mused, how she had accepted the inevitable, once she had made up her mind. She couldn't say she was actually looking forward to marrying William, but she had accepted the fact that fate could have dealt her a sharper blow.

She was determined not to let any lingering memories of Cole creep into her mind and spoil the day for her. She would not do that to William. He was too kind and good.

Jessica paused in front of the mirror. Staring at her reflection, almost as if she was seeing a stranger, she made a silent vow. "I will be a good wife to you, William. I know I can never live up to your expectations, but I will certainly try very hard. This I promise, the moment I accept your ring in marriage, the moment I accept your name, I will be completely committed to you. From that moment on, I will be your helpmate, standing by your side through any adversity. I will make a home, cook your meals, and clean your clothes. I shall also share your bed and bear your children. I may never feel the burning flames of love, but William, you will never know it. My life will be, at first, a lie. But one day, I have all the faith in the world that it will change. I have a fondness, and admiration for you now. Perhaps, one day that will change. I also swear that I will never cheat you. I will never see another man in my mind's eye when you take me into your arms." Jessica took a deep breath. It was with a sigh of relief that she had come to terms with her future. She felt better now that she had made her secret vows, vows she would never be able to repeat to any man alive.

Jessica padded leisurely through her small cabin. Most of her belongings had been taken to William's house the night before. Only the items she would need to get ready for the ceremony had been left behind. William had at first insisted she go ahead and move in with him, but Jessica had stubbornly refused. She had not wanted to add fuel to the flames of slanderous gossip. She wanted their marriage to start out as near perfectly as possible.

Knowing there would be a huge wedding feast later

on in the day, Jessica decided to have only a cup of coffee for breakfast. The fire in the monstrous stove was just starting to catch when an earth tremor shook the cabin. It was not a violent quake. Jessica went on about her business. When the second one hit, she grasped the table for support. Glancing uneasily at the stove pipe when black sooty ashes drifted down on the stove, Jessica became alarmed. Since experiencing the first one, many weeks ago, several quakes had struck Utopia, but none had trembled as badly as the one that just happened. Jessica started to dress and go outside to see if anything had been damaged. She walked to the door first and opened it a tiny crack. Not hearing any shouts of concern, Jessica shrugged her shoulders and went on about her business at hand.

Cole rode hard toward Utopia. He wanted to hurry up and get there, get William's signature on the deed then start out for Texas as soon as possible. The first few days he had been in San Francisco, had been a blur to him. The moment he had hit town, he had proceeded to get roaring drunk. It was as if he did not care what happened to him. He felt a bitterness he did not know was possible. Twice, a woman had taken his heart, twisted it, abused it, then callously discarded it when she was finished. Not only had Jessica betrayed him, she had cost him the dearest friend he had in the world. Now, as Cole rode along, he couldn't help but be curious.

A few days ago, he woke up in a strange hotel room, with Ed Baker scowling at him. Cole remembered their conversation down to the letter.

"What the hell are you doing here?" Cole growled as

he pulled the quilt up over his head.

"I'm trying to find out what is happening to my friends." Ed rose from the chair, walked outside for a few moments, then came back into the room with a huge pot of coffee. "Here, drink this," he said, pouring a cup and shoving it at Cole.

"I don't want any damn coffee! I want a drink of whiskey!" he thundered.

Ed made a lunge toward the half empty whiskey bottle sitting on the dresser top. He was callous in his victory of having reached the bottle before Cole. He sauntered toward the window, raised it, and tossed the bottle down to the street below. "By God, I came up here to get you sober and that's exactly what I intend to do. Drink that coffee!" he commanded in an angry voice.

Cole scowled at him, but reached out with a shaking hand for the mug.

"Damn!" Ed swore softly, "you look like hell!"

"I didn't ask you for an opinion," Cole retorted, sipping the scalding liquid carefully.

Ed waited until Cole had finished the cup. As he refilled the mug, he asked him, "Now, will you tell me what in the world is going on between you and William? He won't tell me anything."

Cole stared at him through blood-shot eyes, "I don't see that it's any of your business," he said finally.

"I'm making it my business."

Cole swung his legs off the bed and grabbed at the headboard for support. "Go ask William," he snarled fumbling in his shirt for a cheroot.

"I have. He tells me the same thing. Look, Cole," he sighed heavily. "You and William have been through too much together for it to end like this. Out of respect and friendship for me, would you at least tell me what happened?"

Cole slumped back on to the bed. "I don't know what happened."

"Don't hand me that line. It has something to do with Jessica."

Cole's eyes became hard and glinted like cold shards of steel when Ed mentioned her name. "Since you know so much about it, suppose *you* tell me what happened!"

Ed drew a deep breath, "All right," he said firmly. "I suppose you do remember that I saw you with her when the ship first docked here in San Francisco. I also saw your face that night you went after her. Only thing was, you had already rescued her. You simply went back to even up some kind of score. I saw how you watched her in that crowd of women, how your eyes would get soft-like when they settled on her. Oh, I felt the tension that was going on between the two of you. But I knew she had you, Cole. She could wiggle her little finger and you would have come running. I also saw how William watched her. I knew then, that there would be trouble between you." He raised one brow and peered at Cole. "Does it sound about right, so far?"

"Go on. Tell me more of this . . . fairy tale you're inventing," Cole said slowly.

"I was aware of the fact that William didn't want you to look for Jessica when she got lost. I also saw how he acted when he realized both of you were gone. We nearly had to hog-tie him while the storm was at its peak. He was bound and determined to go after you. Then, when you brought her back, William wouldn't even let the women attend to her." Ed shook his head, "It just seems . . ."

"Seems like what?"

"William has changed. He's not the same man he used to be," Ed stated firmly.

"A lot of people are not what they appear to be, Ed. You of all people should realize that." Cole's voice was not as surly as it had been.

"Are you referring to me being a doctor and how the townspeople turned on me when Senator Blake died?"

"Yes, I am. After all the good you did for them, they nearly ran you out on a rail when the big-shot senator died."

This time, it was Ed who winced while Cole spoke. Ed bit on his lower lip then said, "I was out of line by trying that new technique. I should have never attempted surgery under those conditions." He slammed his fist into his hand. "Damn it, I didn't come all this way to talk about me. Did you know William and Jessica are getting married in a few days?"

The muscles in Cole's cheek tensed, then relaxed as he answered, "No. I had no idea they would marry this soon." He looked Ed straight in the eye, "I hope they're happy. I don't know who deserves whom the most."

"The only problem is, I've been hearing some things that bother me."

"And what is that?" Cole was torn between finding out what was going on back in Utopia and wanting Ed to leave him alone. He would have been happy just to have been left alone in his misery.

"There are supposed to be rumors, ugly rumors floating around Utopia about you and Jessica. It seems like you were boasting about . . . the . . . situation between you and Jessica."

"I what?"

Ed nodded, "Yep, that was my reaction. Then, a day or two after you left, Jessica showed up on our doorstep asking Helen's opinion about her marrying William. Seems as though she couldn't quite make up her mind."

Cole shook his head, confused, "But . . . that can't be right. Jessica had agreed to marry William before I even left."

"That's the same story I've pieced together. Oh," Ed offered off-handedly, "It's not so much what I have actually heard. Part of it is doubts that Helen has expressed to me. She can't figure it out any more than I can." Ed worried with the tips of his fingers, "I don't know, but I think if I were you, I'd go back to Utopia and see what is going on. I sure would hate to see some of my best friends make a bunch of mistakes. I know from experience, once you've committed yourself in one direction, it's damn sure hard to change."

Cole ran his hand through his hair. "All right!" his voice carried louder than he had intended. "So there is something strange going on. Someone isn't telling the truth. Who do you think it is? Tell me, is it Jessica, or is it the man I have known for a long time, the man who has saved my life a countless number of times, the man whom I thought of like a father! Tell me, is Jessica lying? Or is it William?"

Ed shook his head, "I don't know. I don't know that anyone is actually lying, but something's not right."

Cole rubbed his knuckles in the palm of his hand, and began to pace the floor, slowly as he sought some answers to the questions hammering inside of his head. He stopped suddenly and threw up his hands in surrender. "Why did you come to me with your suspicions? Even if something is wrong, there's nothing I can do about it!"

Ed shook his head, "I don't know why I came . . . unless it's because I thought I owed you. I remember what you did for me. I simply hated to see you sink as low."

Cole sat down on the side of his bed and watched the smoke of the cheroot as it curled upward. "I haven't got that deed yet. I suppose I could go back to Utopia and get William to sign it." He glanced up at Ed, "I guess you think I'm wrong to accept that land?"

"I really don't know what you're talking about."

"That thousand acres William owns in Texas," Cole said casually, as if Ed knew exactly what he was talking about. "When William and I argued he told me to get out of Utopia. I didn't feel he had the right to tell me that since I have a partnership there. He knew I always wanted to have a ranch so he offered me his land instead of money. I accepted it, even though its value doesn't equal what I have in the mining partnership."

Ed stood to leave. He twisted his hat nervously in his hand, "I have to get back now, Cole. I'm leaving it with you. The decision is yours to make. I simply could not stand idly by and see the people I care about wreck their lives."

"Thanks Ed," Cole bit on the inner edge of his mouth. "I've got some thinking to do." He grinned sheepishly, "And I doubt if I can find any answers in a bottle."

Ed smiled. "Adios, my friend, I'll see you soon."

Cole thought about the situation for two days before he took action. He had decided Ed was making more out of it than necessary. He knew Utopia, it was filled with many good men and women, but they were only human, they were bound to have gossiped when he left so abruptly. Ed must have misunderstood some of the rumors. But Ed's visit had started him thinking. Jessica had been the only woman he could ever love. There had been something about her, her quiet mannerism, her innocence, her wit and charm, and yes, even her beauty. It was too bad it was all a deceptive front. Perhaps that was why he had been suspicious of her in the beginning. And William? That man was as hard-headed and stubborn as he was. There would be no way to convince him Jessica had used them both. The way he saw it, there were two courses of action he could take. He could either leave California and start all over with the money he had saved, or he could take the land William had so scornfully offered. His first instinct was to throw the deed into William's face, but that would be foolish. He had ridden every acre of that land, and there was none finer. There were larger ranches in Texas, but not a one could be compared to it. The Trinity River ran right through the heart of it, there were also plenty of timber, and the meadows stood abundant in tall grass. Cole could imagine cattle grazing as far as the eye could see. No, he would take the land, nurse and nourish it until he had a ranch that was second to none.

Cole's mind snapped back to the present. He suddenly reined in his horse. Something was wrong. In his haste to reach Utopia, he had not paid attention to the sudden stillness. There was an eerie silence surrounding him. Now that he thought about it, he had not seen a single animal for a long time. He glanced up, birds flew in a frenzy from treetops, and a huge deer crossed the path in front of him. The animal pawed the ground frantically then leaped through the air. At first, the tremor was slight, then the intensity grew. Earthquake!

Cole spurred his horse clear of shaking boulders. A cold grip of terror clutched at his heart. This was a big quake, not the slight tremors they had experienced before! He was only a few miles from Utopia, what if there were men down in the mines? They would be trapped! They were his friends!

Cole gouged his spurs hard into the horse's flanks, dodging falling rocks, and leaping over sudden cracks which appeared in the earth. The earthquake lasted seemingly for hours, but in reality, only a few minutes.

Cole's eyes were wide in horror when the holocaust stopped. Huge trees, hundreds of years old, lay toppled by the magnitude of the quake. Deep crevices, tens of feet wide were now splitting the ground. In the distance, Cole could see that one side of a mountain had been completely changed, and dust was still rising from it.

He had to cautiously make his way on to Utopia. When he at last topped the rise overlooking the small town, he was appalled at what lay before him. A deep fissure had cut right down the middle of the town. Cabins lay in splintered heaps. People lay like broken toys on the ground. Cries of despair swelled upward.

As Cole rode closer, he could see the damage was even worse than he had first thought. If Utopia had been hit this hard, what had happened to the men in the mines! A woman clutched at his leg.

"Please, help! My husband is trapped in the cabin! I can hear him! Please, he's calling for help!"

Cole leaped from the horse and raced toward the shambles. Gathering strength from an inner source, he began tossing aside splintered logs. Trying to discern where the muffled cries were coming from, Cole glanced around frantically. Through the debris, he could see a bloody hand. He began working at a frenzied pace to free the man. The woman worked alongside Cole. When they at last had the man clear, Cole left him with her and ran for his horse. Others would need help also. His animosity toward William was forgotten during this horrible time of tragedy.

Jessica sat on the ground. She was in a stunned daze. Her satiny white wedding gown was splattered with crimson specks of blood. Numbly looking around, Jessica saw the tattered paper lanterns fluttering in the gentle wind. The many long tables which only a few minutes ago had been piled high with their wedding feast were now scrambled on the ground. Cakes had mixed with pies, meats of all kinds were scattered among the vegetables, and bright red cherries stained the white linen cloths which had covered the tables. Jessica was in a stupor. She did not seem to hear the cries of fear and pain around her. She was definitely in a state of shock.

"What is the matter with everybody?" she mumbled, staggering to her feet. "William? William? Where are you?" A woman ran by and knocked her back to the ground. Jessica numbly got to her feet once again. She pressed trembling hands against her head, trying to drive out the moans and cries of pain.

"Jessica, Jessica, are you all right?" a worried voice asked.

"Yes. No . . . I don't know. What is the matter? Why is everybody crying? Where is William? Where is my husband? Cole?" she asked in confusion. "What happened to Cole?"

Helen grasped her shoulders and shook her hard. "Jessica, you have to snap out of it! Are you hurt?" she asked worriedly, taking in the blood splatters on her friend's dress.

Jessica looked down at her hands, then she rubbed her arms. "No, no, I don't think so? Why should I be hurt? William promised to take care of me."

"Jessica! Get hold of yourself! If you're not hurt, we need you. The women are setting up a hospital for the injured."

"Injured?" Jessica mouthed numbly, "Why should anyone be injured? We just had a wedding."

A scream welled from deep within Jessica's throat when the earth began to tremble again. The buildings that still stood, swayed with the tremor. Helen was thrown to the ground. Jessica struggled to help her up. She could hear the word, "aftershock," swell in her ears.

"Jessica, it's all right!" Helen muttered.

Who had been screaming? Jessica wondered. Why was everyone running around in confusion? She pushed her hair out of her face and her hand came back sticky with blood. She held out her palm to Helen. "Look, look at my hand. It must be hurt."

"No, it's not your hand, dear," Helen said, peering at her head. "You must have been hit by something."

"Why would anyone want to hit me?" Jessica asked. She was so confused.

"Jessica," Helen explained patiently, "You have to snap out of it. There was an earthquake. Many people were hurt. We need your help."

Jessica frowned. "An earthquake?"

"Yes," Helen extended her arm, sweeping it in front of her. "See, it completely destroyed our homes."

Jessica's eyes took on a sharper gleam. She was beginning to come to her senses. "Aaron! Is Aaron all right?"

"He's fine," she reassured her, "So is Ed."

"William?"

"I don't know," Helen answered truthfully, "I haven't seen him."

"June? What about June?"

"She's helping to set up the hospital. Come, Jessica, please. June needs our help. So many are badly hurt."

Jessica picked up her skirts and began running behind Helen. All of the terror and horror had come back to her. Her mind raced frantically as she hurried behind her friend. Where was William? He had been right beside her when the first tremor struck. Everything ran together. Buildings began collapsing, trees toppled, and Jessica remembered the ground opening up and actually swallowing some of the people. The last thing she had remembered, was a tree falling, how she had looked up in terror right before it had hit her. After that, she had no recollection of anything until Helen began talking to her.

Chaos unfolded around them as they made their way to one of the few buildings that remained standing. Jessica numbly saw people stagger by calling for loved ones, some who would never again answer any call, except that of their Maker.

A line of sheet covered bodies was in front of the cabin. A few women and men knelt beside them. Some were openly crying and some merely had a glazed expression of terror stamped on their faces. Horrified voices began echoing throughout the town.

"Stretcher, stretcher, please bring a stretcher over here! Please help my husband! He's buried underneath the cabin! Has anyone seen my child? For God's sake, somebody please help me!"

But it was as if God had momentarily turned his back on their mountain paradise.

Jessica entered the dimly lit cabin. Men and women were lined up on the floor. June was kneeling beside a child who lay on a blanket on the floor. She shook her head, "There's nothing else that can be done for her," she muttered sadly, as she pulled the blanket up over the tiny blonde curls which framed the little girl's face. An expression of relief flashed across June's face when she saw Jessica. "Thank goodness you're all right. I was afraid . . ."

Jessica placed a hand on June's shoulder. "Stuart?" she asked simply.

"I don't know. I haven't seen him."

Ed came charging through the front door. He began barking orders, "Get a fire going in the fireplace and start boiling water. June, Jessica, start looking at the wounded and see who's hurt the worst. I'll attend to them first." His worried gaze caught Helen's eye. "—Helen," he asked hesitantly, "Where is Aaron?"

Helen nodded to a corner where he sat, his huge round eyes wide in fear.

In a few easy strides, Ed was by his side. "Son, are you all right?"

Aaron nodded.

"Son, now listen carefully. I want you to go outside." He grabbed at a woman's hand, "Brenda, take Aaron outside. Gather up all the children and find a cabin that is not damaged. Keep them inside. They don't need to see this. But if another quake hits, get 'em outside, it'll be safer there."

"But . . . but . . . don't you need me here?" she asked, her voice breaking with unshed tears.

"We need someone to take care of the kids. All of them like you, they'll mind you good. Brenda," he added in a softer voice, "Have you seen Virgil?"

"Yes, he's out there . . . helping . . . to dig out the people who are trapped underneath the rubble."

"Good!" Ed's relief was evident. "Please take the children," he asked again, "They don't need to see what's going to happen in here." Ed knew many people would die. He also knew he would have to amputate limbs and God only knew what he would have to do before the day was over.

Ed turned his attention back to the wounded. He, along with Jessica and June, and several other women worked hand in hand, bandaging wounds, treating cuts, and comforting badly injured people.

Outside, the scene unfolded into a grisly nightmare. Several of the cabins had caught fire when the earthquake tore them apart. They were now nothing but smoldering ashes.

Women worked alongside the men as they formed lines to remove the splintered logs.

Cole desperately searched for William. When he could not find him, he took charge. He assigned men to find out who was missing and where they had last been seen. When he had asked about the men in the mine, he had been told that no one had been working that day, that they had all been here for the wedding. Cole knew without asking whose wedding it had been. Instead of feeling bitter as some men would have, a surge of relief flooded through him that no men had been in the mountains. At least they wouldn't have to worry about digging through the rubbled heap of destroyed mines.

When things took on a resemblance of organization, Cole made his way to the building designated as a hospital. It was too bad the community hall had been destroyed. It would have been larger, it would have held many more of the wounded. He opened the door, and the first person he saw was Jessica, in her blood spattered wedding gown. His breath caught in his throat. Even though her hair streamed with dirt and grime she was still beautiful. His eyes hardened momentarily when he caught a glimpse of the golden wedding ring on her finger.

"Cole! Thank God you're here!" Ed said, stepping over a man in the floor and wiping his hands on a bloody rag. "Have you seen William?"

Cole shook his head, "No, I haven't. In fact, no one has seen him."

Ed looked worried. "That's not like him to disappear when there's an emergency."

"I know it," Cole muttered, still not taking his eyes off Jessica.

"Do you think he's been hurt?"

Cole nodded, "I came to see if he was here." He twisted his head awkwardly, "It looks really bad out there."

"It's bad in here too. We're losing people right and left. There's forty known dead, and there's no telling how many more we'll find when all the rubble is cleared away."

Jessica glanced up, "Ed . . . this man . . . needs . . . help," she stuttered when she saw Cole standing there.

Cole took a step toward her, "Jessica?"

Jessica could feel her heart pounding in her chest. It

took all of her will power to keep from running and throwing herself into Cole's arms. Then she remembered how he had scorned her. She remembered she did not have the right to go to Cole. Twisting her ring with trembling fingers, she said, "Cole, please, I don't know where William is. He may be . . . injured. Please find him."

Cole ran his fingers through his hair. He had seen something in Jessica's eyes. Something he could not explain. He glanced at Ed. Ed placed a restraining hand on Cole's arm.

"Please do as she asked. Find him, Cole."

Cole nodded brusquely. "All right," his voice sounding strained. "Where did you see him last?"

"We were in front of the community hall. It was . . ." she lowered her eyes then raised them defiantly, "after the ceremony. We were starting to eat. When the first tremor hit, I recall him shouting and running after someone . . . than . . . a tree hit me. Helen found me later . . . I was terribly confused. I didn't know what had happened."

Cole and Ed stepped outside. Cole said worriedly, "It isn't like William to run . . . unless he saw something . . ." He shook his head, "Perhaps he saw someone injured?"

"That's what I would think. Cole," Ed said, "You know I can't leave. I have to help as many of these poor souls as I can. I . . . know you and William aren't on the best of terms right now . . . but would you please try to find him? I'm worried."

Cole raised his brows thoughtfully, "Regardless of our differences, William is still William. He was the best friend I ever had. There's no way I could turn my back on him now." His gaze slowly took in what was left of Utopia, "I can't turn my back on this place either."

"All right, let's try to figure this out," Ed said. "The last time I recall seeing William and Jessica, they were standing close to the front door of the community hall. Like she said, they were starting to serve the food. So I guess that would be the most logical place to start looking."

Cole slowly made his way through the rubble. It was difficult to believe how quickly the town had been annihilated. Not only was he surrounded by death and destruction, Cole knew he was witnessing the extinction of their way of life. Utopia could never be rebuilt, at least not on its present site.

He finally reached what remained of the community hall. The roof had caved in, and the walls stood like jagged skeletons reaching toward the sky.

"William! William! Answer me!" Cole shouted, cupping his hands around his mouth to make the sound carry farther. "William, William, I said, answer me!" Cole remained silent for a moment, turning his ear, hoping to hear something, some sort of reply. But all that could be heard were the wailing cries of distraught men, women and children.

His eyes narrowed as he glanced toward William's house. It was still standing. He made his way over to it, and after a quick investigation, he stopped a man running by.

"Mark, I need you to take a message to Ed. Can you do it?"

The man looked at Cole in a stupor. "Yeah, I guess so." He didn't tell Cole he had just found his wife. She was dead.

"Tell him William's house looks to be in pretty good shape. It's still got a roof and the walls and framework are strong. A few windows are out, but we can hang blankets over them. He's going to need a lot larger place than where he is for a hospital."

Cole desperately wanted to search for William, but chaos once again reigned in Utopia. More lives could be saved if he showed leadership. Pulling his gun from its holster, Cole fired a few shots into the air. He stepped up on an overturned crate and shouted for their attention.

"Come on, you people," he waved at them with his hand. "We have to have some order. You're wasting valuable time by running here and there. Many people are trapped in cabins and by falling trees and logs. We're not going to be able to save their lives unless we get better organized." As soon as most of the people had gathered around, Cole began. "Has anybody seen William?" He scanned the shocked and numb faces, desperately hoping for an affirmative answer. When one did not come, he continued, "William is probably trapped underneath debris. I am taking charge until he's found. As soon as he is found, I want to know." Cole's eyes narrowed. His hand streaked back to the revolver he had just replaced in his holster. He drew the gun and fired it over the head of a man who was coming out of one of the warehouses with a huge bundle of food. "Mister," he growled dangerously, "I'd suggest you put that right back where you got it." Glancing at a couple of men he knew he could trust, he asked, "Thomas, Zeke, have you found your wives?"

"Yes, sir," they answered.

"Then get your shotguns and stand guard at those storehouses. If anyone tries to remove goods or food without my authorization, shoot 'em."

He turned back to the general crowd. "How many collapsed buildings have been searched?"

The men looked uneasily at each other.

"You men break into groups of three or four. John, you take a detail of men and make sure those fires don't spread. Walter, you take nine other men and go to the stables. Harness ten teams of mules and horses. We may need help raising some of the beams and fallen logs. The rest of you men split up. Half take the right and the other half take the left. Form groups of two or three and do a systematic search. Once a destroyed building has been searched, mark it with a red or white flag. All right, men, we're wasting time. Let's get started."

A woman stepped forward. "Wait a minute, Cole. What about us? What can the women do to help? This is our home too, you know."

Cole nodded, "You're right. First things first," he told the women as soon as they had gathered closer. "Those of you who have children, take them . . ."

"I believe Brenda is gathering the children together. Her cabin wasn't destroyed. She's taking them there," a woman said.

"All right, those of you who have children, take them to Brenda's house. You other women, we need food prepared." He pointed to women he recognized, "You, you, and you, get a team of women together and start cooking. We will probably have to work night and day until everyone is accounted for. I will also need several groups of you to check the cabins that remain standing. If the building appears to be safe, check them out. However let me warn you, if the building is shaky, don't take any chances. If a building is questionable, mark it . . ." He craned his head to shout at Zeke and Thomas, "Men, let the women have any supplies they need within reason. Some of the women will be preparing food for the entire town so don't be alarmed if those three ladies take out a large quantity of food. If one of you would look inside the warehouse and find some whitewash and brushes, also hammers and nails." He turned back to the women, "If the cabins are questionable, take a bucket of white-wash and mark it with a question mark. If it's unsafe, paint a huge X on it. Now, when you find cabins that are safe, get them ready for tonight. It's going to get cold. If windows are broken sweep up the glass and tack blan-kets, boards, anything that you can find over the win-dows. Now, there's one other thing," Cole rubbed his chin thoughtfully. "We need to save as many supplies as possible. We don't know how long this weather will hold. I would like for a couple of details of women to form and scavenge through the destroyed cabins that have been flagged by the men. Save as much as possible. Food, blankets, clothing, anything you can find. I have been away for the past few weeks and have no way of knowing if winter supplies have been passed out yet. If I know William, he has already made sure the cabins were well stocked." Cole felt a sinking feeling when the women said that supplies had already been distributed. He scanned the women once again. "Is there anything I've missed?"

One woman stated, "Cole, we appreciate what you're doing, but I have a question. Why can't we help the men try and find survivors? It looks like that's more impor-tant."

Cole firmly shook his head. "No, it isn't. We've been having a spell of Indian Summer. You don't know this country as I do. It could start snowing tomorrow. It's true, time is crucial for the people who are injured and lying beneath the rubble. However, it is also crucial that we also survive. It will not do any good to rescue those people if we don't have the facilities to care for them. So don't sell yourselves short. What you will be doing is very important." He asked the women once again, "Is there anything else? If not, then please carry out my orders."

Cole stepped down from the crate and walked over to the warehouses. Thankfully, they had not been destroyed. "Zeke, Thomas, let them have it if it's within reason. You saw what that man was trying to carry off a while ago. He was simply trying to prepare for his family. After the worst is over, perhaps we can allow things to go back like they were, I doubt it though. Take care now, you hear?"

Cole hurried over to the community hall. He fished in his pocket for a cheroot, squared his shoulders and joined the other men to help search for survivors. He breathed a silent prayer that William would soon be found, and that he would be all right.

Chapter Thirty

The Indian Summer's sun proved to be unmercifully hot. Mules and horses strained against their harnesses as they pulled heavy beams away from the rubble. Soon, piles of broken timbers, cracked beams and wooden planks began to stack up in front of each destroyed cabin.

Cole couldn't understand why so many people had been trapped in the cabins since a wedding had just been performed. It was explained to him that many of the people had gifts for the newlyweds, and had gone to get them when disaster struck.

Not all of the people injured were found in the destroyed cabins. Many had been hurt when the cabins had collapsed and were crushed by falling debris.

Cole joined the detail of men working on the community hall. Several people were found uninjured, only dazed but had been trapped underneath the wreckage and had not been able to free themselves. Cole was helping one man to his feet when someone called out, "Cole! Come here! Quick! We've found him!"

Someone else thoughtfully took the man's arm as Cole ran. He leaped over splintered logs, jumbled furniture and part of the collapsed roof. When he saw William, his breath caught in his throat. A heavy beam was across his legs, and a huge rounded sliver of wood had pinned him to the floor. It had stabbed him right through the stomach. William clutched at the stub protruding from his shirt. Cole had seen that kind of wound before when they were Rangers. He knew William did not have long to live.

"Cole, thank God you're here," William panted. His eyes widened with pain. It was an effort for him to talk. "Jessica, where is Jessica? I have to see her!"

Cole spoke softly, his voice trembled with choked tears, "I'll go get her for you, William."

"No, no . . . please don't leave me. I have . . . things to tell you."

Cole looked up at the man who had found him. "John, please go get Jessica. Tell Ed to come too. He may be able to help."

A thin smile pulled at William's lips. "I don't think Ed will be able to help me. I . . . think I've bought it, this time." His eyes widened, "Jessica! Is she . . . all right?"

"She's fine," Cole reassured him. "She's at the hospital helping Ed."

"Cole, be honest with me . . . Were many of my people . . ." His voice trailed off questionably.

"No, no," Cole lied. There was no need to break a dying man's heart. "Injuries are very minor considering the damage." Cole took William's hand in his. He felt so helpless; there was nothing he could do except try to comfort his friend until Jessica arrived. Seeing William near death, their quarrel suddenly seemed insignificant. A stabbing pain pierced his heart. He knew he was losing a vital part of his life and he was powerless to stop it.

"Don't look so sad, Cole. I've had . . . a good life. Cole?" his face contorted with pain.

"I'm here, William, I'm here!" Damn-it, God, why did you have to take him? he thought. Why not someone else? Why not me?

William's breath was beginning to come in short gasps. "Cole," he reached blindly for his hand, "I have many things to . . . tell you . . . and I don't have much . . . time left. I have to set it right . . . about Jessica."

"No, William, there's nothing to set right." Cole realized now was not the time for bitterness. Let William die peacefully, there was no need for him to know how Jessica had used both of them.

"But, you're . . . wrong. You don't . . . know what I did. Have to wait . . . until Jessica . . . here . . . before I tell . . . you. Don't think I have . . . strength to . . . say it twice."

Cole looked around wildly. What was keeping Ed? The man had been a first-class doctor. Maybe he could help William if he arrived in time.

Jessica and Ed came running, out of breath and huffing and puffing. When Jessica saw her husband, she gasped and her hand flew to her mouth in horror. John had said William was hurt very badly, but she had not expected to see him like this. Ed quickly knelt by his side and examined the wound. Cole had to hold Jessica back in order for Ed to tend to William. He rose hesitantly, and shook his head, and mumbled, "I'm sorry, Jessica. There's nothing I can do." A sheer look of desolate helplessness was written on his face as he stepped away.

The distant sound of muted voices drifted on the wind as Jessica knelt by his side. It was almost as if the world stopped turning. Everything slowed down. Time and movement passed by in slow-motion. Jessica's hand clutched for William's. She paid no mind to the crimson smear that suddenly inched between her fingers. All she could see was William, poor William, desperately struggling for the last thread of life.

"Oh, God, no!" she whispered in anguish. "Oh, William, my husband . . ."

"Hush, Jessica, my love. Please let me speak. I am dying, I know I . . . am dying, and I don't . . . have much time. I have to clear my conscience. I have to tell you . . . and Cole how . . . I wronged you." He drew a sharp breath and silenced the protest Jessica was starting to make. "No, let me talk. I *have* to tell you this. First, thank you for becoming my wife," his voice was growing weaker with each moment that passed. "I shall die a happy . . . man."

She flung her head wildly as she sought Ed. "Please do something for him! Don't just stand there!"

"No, my love . . . there is nothing he can do. I have made my peace . . . with God, please let me make my peace . . . with you and Cole." His eyes pleaded with them to understand what he was about to say, "Cole . . . Jessica . . . I lied." An echo of a weak smile touched his lips. "God, it felt good . . . to say that. I was afraid . . . I would die . . . before . . ." his voice trailed off.

"Before what?" Cole pressed. He did not hear what William had said about lying. He simply urged his friend to speak, to clear his conscience, to right any wrong, real or imaginery. He knew how important death-bed confessions were to their souls.

"Before I could . . . tell you . . . the truth."

Jessica did not seem to hear him. She was desperately clutching at his hand and pressing it against her lips.

"Jessica . . . Cole . . . please listen to me!" he commanded. "I cannot stand . . . this pain any longer. I *have* to tell you!"

Jessica snaped out of her daze. "Oh, William," she cried, "I'm listening."

"Cole, I . . . lied to you." His eyes were suddenly crisp and alive with a renewed strength. It was as though he had reached down into some reserved inner source for the stamina to continue. "I lied to Jessica too." His hand struggled to reach up and caress her face. "My sweet, darling, Jessica. Please forgive me. I wanted you so . . . much, I deliberately lied. Cole never said . . . any of those things. He . . . loves you . . . as much as . . . I do."

"Oh, no, William!" she gasped, reeling under the impact of the words. "Why?" she cried.

"Because . . . I wanted you . . . more than . . . life itself. I loved you enough . . . to completely destroy . . . my . . . with Cole." William's speech was beginning to slur together. He knew death was imminent. "Cole, please . . . look at me my . . . friend." His request had been needless. Cole's attention was riveted on him. "I . . . she never . . . promised to marry me . . . until you had already left. I was wrong. Even Utopia was . . . wrong. I envisioned many great things. But they . . . were not for the good . . . of everyone except . . . my own glory." Blood began trickling from his mouth, his eyes grew wide as searing pain tore through him.

Cole was stunned. He would have sworn William was not capable of a lie.

William made a last minute desperate appeal, "Cole, please take care of Jessica . . . please don't let what I . . . did come between you." He begged frantically, "Please swear that you will take care of her!"

Cole clutched William's hand, "You have my word, old friend."

William gave a smile, radiant, with relief. "You can still call . . . me, friend? After what I . . . did to . . ."

"You'll be my friend forever, William." Tears suddenly clouded Cole's vision.

William turned his head toward Jessica. "My darling . . . remember, please . . . remember how much . . . I loved . . ." All of the pain and misery left his face as he slumped forward and died.

"No! No! No!" Jessica cried, collapsing against William's chest. "Don't die! Please don't die!"

It was Ed who pulled Jessica away. Cole continued to kneel, while staring at the man who had been his friend. At that moment, nothing else mattered except the fact that William was dead. How could he condemn William for his deeds when his only guilt was loving a woman too much. Cole staggered to his feet and lifted Jessica from Ed's arms. He had to get her away before she went into hysterics. She was crying so hard, her entire body was shaking miserably.

Ed instructed the other men to take William's body down to the hospital, then he quickly followed Cole as he carried Jessica to William's house.

"Oh, Cole," Jessica cried, "Why did he have to die? I don't care what he did to us, he was still a good man." She buried her face in his wide, muscular shoulder.

Cole could feel his arms tighten around her. It was as though he was trying to protect her from the agony that was ripping them apart. His heart was filled with love and admiration as he carried Jessica across the road. It was amazing she harbored no bitterness toward William. If she had been a lesser woman, she would have hated him. Cole's steps slowed considerably as a chilling thought swept through him. What if she really did love William? What if she had loved him enough to have willingly shared her life with him? During Cole's tormented thoughts, he forgot about the romantic interlude they had shared in the mountains. Then he recalled the hateful bitter words he had flung at her early that morning when he left Utopia.

Cole shook his head, shrugging off his gloomy thoughts. He ought to be ashamed, he must now think of Jessica as his friend's widow. William had just died, and he was already coveting her. This was not the time nor place to rake up the past. Maybe later, when both of them had had time to sort out their feelings. He pushed the front door open with his boot and carried her into the spare bedroom. Sensing Ed was behind them, he asked, "Ed, I know many women have lost their husbands today . . . however, Jessica seems different. Could . . . you give her something to make her sleep?"

"Sure!" Ed readily agreed. "I'll give her something."

"No you won't!" Jessica protested adamantly as she struggled out of Cole's arms. "I'm not any better than anyone else. No other woman has had to have sleeping powders." She placed her arms akimbo, "As soon as I wash my face and compose myself, I'm going back to the hospital. I'm needed there!" Her bottom lip trembled defiantly.

"Are you sure?" Cole wanted to know. "You know you don't have to go."

"Maybe not, but I want to go back, I need to go back, Cole. I have to keep busy." Jessica was rigid in her decision. "I don't even want to have a spare minute to think." Her resolve seemed to crumble as she looked first at Cole, then Ed. "Oh, God, I don't know what to think about what William did!" Silent tears started to fall effortlessly down her weary, drawn face.

Cole's face was a stiff mask. "I know, neither do I." Deep lines were chiseled on his brow and around his eyes. All of a sudden, he felt so tired. It was a weariness which ran all the way into his soul. "Jessica, there is one thing we will have to remember, William was a good man. In fact, there was none better."

Jessica nodded, her gray eyes raised hesitantly, "For once Cole, we are in total agreement." She nodded at Ed, "I believe we should be getting back. They'll be needing us," she said as she walked toward the front door. She would freshen up at the hospital, every moment spent in this house was torturous, and too full of memories. She tried to keep her eyes averted from William's easy chair, but it was impossible to ignore all of his personal items scattered in an orderly fashion around the house. She stopped at the door and gasped as men carried a sheet draped body past them. She knew it was William.

Cole watched with saddened eyes as Ed and Jessica fell in behind the tiny procession. He waited until they were out of sight before turning back to the grisly tasks that still lay before him.

The townspeople of Utopia worked through the long anguish-filled afternoon and on into the late hours of the night before all of the cabins had been searched. A few tents were raised, blankets were spread on the ground, and makeshift beds were hastily prepared for the weary survivors. The women and children were allocated the space inside the cabins where it was warmer.

When dawn broke the following morning, the scene was even more heartbreaking than it had been the day before. Rows and rows of blood stained sheets lined the main street of Utopia. Every so often, a heartwrenching wail pierced the eerie silence as another one of the bodies were identified.

The dead numbered; forty-two men, thirty-eight women, and four children. Plus twelve women and eight men were missing completely. It was suspected they had been swallowed by the earth when it had split open. But, by dawn, the wide crevice was only a thin crack in the ground since the aftershocks had gradually let the earth slide back together.

The minister who had married Jessica and William, had been kept busy the first day, performing last rites and comforting grieving souls. The second day was filled with conducting funeral services. All day long, the men worked digging graves, while the women prepared the bodies for burial. Time was of the utmost importance. Although the nights were very cool, the days were filled with the warmth and heat of the Indian Summer.

A numbness settled over everyone. They went about their unpleasant tasks mechanically. No one was left untouched by the tragedy. It was impossible to have been left untouched as friends helped to bury friends that they had worked side by side with for months, and in some cases, years.

The following day, after the last person had been buried, a group of men approached Cole; they requested he call a meeting. After all the people who were physically able, gathered together, Cole stepped up on a crate and called the meeting to order.

Cole gazed out over the people, he saw the heartache and misery written on their faces. They were a desolate and beaten people. "Folks," his voice carried strong and clear. "As you know, we have been tested with an adversity that goes far beyond the endurance of mortal men. Each one of us has been touched in some way or the other by this calamity. Many of us will recover and rebuild our lives; however, there will be some that will never get over this tragedy. I was asked to call this meeting. Apparently there are some of you who have something to say. We've had enough chaos to last a lifetime, so let's keep this meeting to an orderly gathering. Who would like to talk first?"

Ed was among the first to raise his hands. Cole stepped down from the crate and Ed took his place. "Folks, I will try to be brief. I've heard many rumors about you wanting to leave. In a way, I don't blame you, but this is our home. We can rebuild. We can learn from this terrible thing that happened. I really hope each and every one of you will stop and consider what we have had here. We can have it again," he added as his eyes scanned the crowd.

John Thompson took the crate when Ed stepped down. "I'll agree with Ed, we did have something good here. But I doubt if we can rebuild." He gestured, "My wife is terrified another one of those earthquakes will hit before we can get out of here. I don't know about the rest of you folks," he shook his head, "But me and my wife are leaving first thing in the morning."

another man stood before the gathering when John finished. "I will go as far as to say that I believe we will all agree we've had a good life here." He removed his hat and scratched his head thoughtfully, "However, I can't help but wonder how safe this general area will be. I saw the crack that split this town apart. Sure, it's closed up now, but what about the ground underneath? Nope!" he shook his head firmly. "You can count me out if you're taking names on who's staying."

Amidst a clamor of noise from the crowd, Cole stepped back up on the crate. Motioning with his hands for them to calm down, he said, "Wait a minute. It sounds to me like many of you are forgetting about your livelihood. If you leave, what about the mines? Are you going to turn your backs on that?"

John stood up and faced Cole. "I'm not going back in the mines. I feel like I escaped with my life, and I'm not about to tempt fate again. Like he said," nodding in the direction of the man who had just spoke, "That quake ripped this town plumb in two. I can't help but wonder how it broke up the earth down in and underneath the mines. In fact, I wonder if we even have any mines left?"

Cole was not about to let William's dream die without a fight. The people were consumed by fear, and that fear could be conquered if he tried. "Then we need to check the mines before we rush into a decision. I'm willing, how about you men?"

John shook his head, "Nope! I've said it once and I'll say it again, I'm not staying, and I'm not about to go back into those mines, even to check them!" He looked around, searching the expressions of the men and women, "I think this meeting is even senseless. But since we're all here, maybe we ought to take a stand on our feelings. I say; if some of you want to stay, then fine! But if some of you want to go to Frisco with me and my wife,

I would like to know so we could make preparations. What do you say, Cole? Any objections to our taking a vote?"

"Of course you can take a vote. You know we've always run this place very democratically. I can't or won't stop anyone who wants to leave. And, yes, I do agree with you, John. I think we ought to know how everyone is feeling." He ran his fingers through his hair nervously, "Those of you who want to stay and help rebuild Utopia, please raise your hands." Bitter disappointment swept over him when only a few hands went up into the air. He laughed, only the sound was without joy. "Perhaps you didn't understand me, I asked for you to raise your hands if you wanted to stay and rebuild."

Jessica saw what was happening. She hurried through the crowd and stepped up on the crate to stand beside Cole. "I can't believe this! You're turning your backs on a way of life that has been good to you. Think of the freedom you've had here. When we first arrived in San Francisco Bay, it was nothing but a slum. And, most likely, there is where you would be this very day if it had not been for William and Cole. Sure, each one of you have put in a lot of work here in Utopia. You know as well as I do, it was William who inspired you, and who led you, and yes, even helped to make you wealthy men. Are you going to betray him by turning your back on his dream?"

John nervously fingered his hat. "Ma'am, I mean this with all due respect, William ain't here no more. Even if he was here, I doubt he would ask what you are asking us to do. We all realize how rich those mines still are. We had just hit a vein in the number two mine that is big as a tree trunk." He shook his head, "That still don't entice me to go back and work it. The money wouldn't do me no good if I was dead. My widow might enjoy it, but I sort of figured on helping her spend my money. Which, by the way, I do have quite a pile of sitting in the bank at Frisco. No, Ma'am, I'm leaving."

Jessica's lips settled into a thin line as she glanced at Cole. She stood proud as she tossed her flaming red hair defiantly. "All right, John. No one will try to stop you or anyone else who wants to leave. I hope all of your new lives are successful." A frown creased her brow. "There is one thing, though, I know all of the supplies should be split equally. However, I would appreciate it if those of you who leave would share part of the supplies with the ones who remain behind. You will soon be where you can buy more, and we will be busy preparing for the winter. I am taking it upon myself to say that you are all welcome to the wagons, except one. Leave that behind for us. You can see Ed about the injured and find out when they will be well enough to travel. I . . . speak for myself," she added hesitantly, "It has been a pleasure knowing all of you, and I wish you well in the start of your new lives."

Cole acted as though he was going to protest, but Jessica silenced him by placing her hand on his arm. "Cole, you can't change their minds. We don't even have the right to try. They want to go, let them leave without any hard feelings."

Cole laughed in sharp derision. "You're right. I was wrong to even try to stop them." His shoulders slumped, he was completely devastated as he stepped off the crate and disappeared into the crowd.

Jessica stared after him with remorseful eyes. She couldn't help but wonder what his plans were now. She was aware of the fact that he was going to take the land in Texas. Would he stay, or would he continue with his plans? Jessica was confident he would remain until everything was settled. Then what? What about them? What would she do if he came to her and declared his love? Jessica pressed her fingers against her throbbing temples. Dear Lord, what did the future hold for her? Did Cole fit into it anywhere? What about the woman he claimed he wanted to see in San Francisco? Was he in love with her? Could he possibly want that sort of woman? Jessica knew she would have to have many answers to her questions before she could even begin to plan her life.

Chapter Thirty-one

Jessica was in the warehouse helping to allocate supplies, when the door to the small office opened and June walked in. "June!" she exclaimed happily as she rushed from the desk and hugged her friend close to her. "Where have you been? I've been looking for you. It's been several days since I've seen you."

June stared at Jessica, her bottom lip began to tremble. "I've been avoiding you," she said simply.

"Why?"

"Because I feel like a deserter." Her eyes evaded Jessica's piercing question. "I'm going back to San Francisco with the others."

"Oh, no, June. I was hoping you would stay. Is it because of Stuart? Does he want to go back?"

June stared at her uncomprehendingly. Tears began to seep into her huge brown eyes. "I guess you don't know."

"Know what, June?"

"Stuart . . . is dead."

Jessica gasped, "Oh, no! I'm so sorry, June. Honestly,

I didn't know. Why didn't you tell me?"

"Well, you were so busy . . . and I really thought you knew."

"I didn't know," she cried. "If I had, I would have made sure I found you. I wouldn't have let you face it alone."

"It's all right, Jessica, really it is. I could have found you and told you, but I knew that William had been killed . . . and I really didn't want to put any more on you. You had enough burdens of your own."

"My burdens will take care of themselves. What about you?" she wanted to know. "Are you sure you want to go to San Francisco? Could I persuade you to stay here?"

"No," June shook her head sadly. "It's best if I leave. I'm going to go to Ohio. Stuart had folks there. You see . . . I am going to have his child, and I think I should live in a place where the baby will have a family. I never had much of one, and I do want more for this baby than I had."

"A baby!" she whispered in awe.

June nodded, a terse smile touching her lips. "Yes, thank God, I will have someone. I will have a part of Stuart with me. This way, I feel like I haven't lost him completely." Her teeth worried with her bottom lip. "Jessica, do you recall that conversation we had several weeks ago when you were debating whether or not to marry William?"

"Of course I remember it. It helped convince me to accept his proposal."

"Well, I remember making a statement that I have regretted making."

"What is it, June? Please tell me," she whispered.

"I recall telling you that I didn't love Stuart. Only . . .

I did love him! I simply did not realize it until it was too late!" Her shoulders jerked as she crumpled into a chair and cried.

Jessica wrapped her arms around her friend in a comforting manner. She was at a loss for words. She knew from her own personal experience, words did not help much, however, the presence of a friend was greatly needed in the dark hour of grief.

When June had cried her fill, she looked up at Jessica. It was as though she was bursting with the overwhelming need to talk.

"What is it, June? Please tell me what you have on your mind."

June came from her chair quickly. Her need was desperate. "Jessica, please don't make the same mistake I did. I know you didn't love William. Please don't tie yourself to his memory. Don't bury yourself here in this God-forsaken place, simply because it was his dream! You must not let the circumstances surrounding his death prevent you from being happy. I know, regardless of what you say, you still love Cole. You have never stopped loving him. Go to him! Make him listen to you! Convince him that you love him! Don't let a silly misunderstanding keep you apart. If he leaves Utopia, hitch up a buggy and follow him to the ends of the earth if necessary." Her words broke off, and she blushed gracefully. "I'm sorry," she said with a shrug to her shoulders. "I got carried away. I didn't mean to preach to you. I only want you to be happy. I don't want you to waste a precious moment." Misery contorted her features, "When I think about all the time Stuart and I wasted. . . when I think about how much happier we could have been if he had only known how I felt about him . . . Oh,

Jessica, please don't make the same mistake!" she pleaded.

Jessica felt as though her heart was being ripped from her chest. She could not bring herself to tell June about William's deathbed confession. She had no way of knowing what had happened. Only, how could she approach Cole now? Yes, even in the tangled emotions of her mind, she knew she loved him, but William was not even cold in his grave. How could she dishonor the man who had married her? How could she bring shame to his memory by throwing herself at another man? A man who might not have the same feelings that she did. No, she would have to bide her time. She would have to wait and let Cole make the first move.

Jessica was saved from having to continue the conversation when a man came into the office.

"Mrs. Stockard, I have a list here with the people's names on it who's staying. They told me to tell you to figure out how much it will take for each person through the winter, and add a little bit more in case there's some kind of emergency. We'll need to take the rest because . . ." the man had the grace to appear embarrassed, "Supplies might be running short in Frisco. I mean . . . we'd use the supplies even if we stayed here."

"Look, Mr . . ."

"Deveraux," he answered.

"Look, Mr. Deveraux, you don't have to apologize." She glanced at June. "Excuse me for a moment please. June, I'll think about what we were talking about. Don't worry," she managed a smile, "I'm sure I'll make the right decision."

June walked to the door but Jessica stopped her. "Wait a minute, I . . . I am sorry about Stuart. You have my deepest sympathy."

"Thank you."

"When will you be leaving?"

June shrugged, "I'm not sure. I guess as soon as everyone has gathered their belongings. Probably tomorrow."

"Then I'll come and see you tonight. We can talk some more. Oh," she added, "Be sure and provide me with the information about where you'll be going. Who knows, I may make it to Ohio one of these days."

June grinned, "Yeah, sure."

Deveraux was beginning to get impatient. He loudly cleared his throat. "Look, Mrs. Stockard, I really need for you to check that list so I can start loading supplies."

"I'll be right with you, Mr. Deveraux. I'll see you tonight," she reminded June.

After June left, she turned her attention to the man in front of her. "Let me have about an hour, Mr. Deveraux, I will have to calculate how much it will take to feed each person who stays. If you will come back then . . ."

"All right," he agreed. "Be back in a little while."

Jessica opened the list and began to read it. Her feet became riveted to the spot when she saw Cole's name was missing. Apparently, he must still be planning to go to Texas, she thought. All of those words he had spoken had been nothing but a farce. He had tried to convince everyone else to stay when all along, he had no intention of trying to rebuild the destroyed town. He never intended to help. Silent tears flooded her eyes. Damn you, Cole Robertson, she thought blindly. How could you do this to me, to everyone who had faith in you?

When Jessica had composed herself, she examined the list further. A huge wave of relief washed over her when she saw Ed, Helen, and Aaron's name on it. Turning the paper over, Jessica was shocked to find it empty. The only people who were staying were listed on the front of the paper, there were four more couples other than Ed and Helen. Counting her, that made only twelve out of the hundreds who lived there! It would appear they were doomed to fail before they ever started. Fourteen people could never rebuild Utopia into the thriving town it once was.

At that moment, Ed walked in. When he saw the crestfallen expression on Jessica's face, he asked, "My God, Jessica, what in the world is the matter?"

"Look at this!" she flung the list at Ed. "I'm afraid we will not be able to rebuild with such a small number of people."

Ed examined the list carefully, sighing deeply, he remarked, "Perhaps it isn't as bad as it appears. I have a hunch that some of the people will be back in the spring, after the shock wears off. I think we'll all be surprised at how a winter in San Francisco will change their minds."

"Tell me, is it bad there?"

Ed bobbed his head, "It sure is! Of course, it was several years ago, but supplies ran short. What there is of them are so high it's ridiculous. William had the right idea when he arranged to buy entire shiploads of goods. Since there was so much of the supplies destroyed in the earthquake, they can't possibly take enough with them to last through the winter." He patted Jessica's shoulder reassuringly, "Don't worry. Many will be back. You'll see."

"That's encouraging," she replied in a gush of relief.

Ed watched her for a moment as she bent her head over the figures that were in front of her. "Come on, Jessica, tell me what else is bothering you."

She glanced up sharply, "What makes you think something else is bothering me?"

"Your face is like reading a book," he laughed. "It's very expressive. Come on and tell me," he persuaded.

"It's the list, Ed. Didn't you miss someone?"

"No, I can't say that I did."

"Cole is not staying," she snapped bitterly. "I thought surely he would remain. I am very disappointed in him, especially after the way he tried to talk the other people into staying."

"Why, of course Cole is staying. He wouldn't leave now."

"He isn't on the list though! I was asked to mathematically divide the supplies up, so I had to have a list of people who were staying. I'm sure Mr. Deveraux was very thorough when he prepared it."

"Well," Ed thoughtfully rubbed his chin, "There's one way we can find out. Cole's up at the stables, I'd suggest you go up there and ask him what he's planning on doing?"

"Me go? Oh no," Jessica shook her head firmly. "It would be better if you went."

Ed jammed his hands into his pockets, "Can't right now. I'm going to keep an eye on the supplies and make sure more is not loaded than there is supposed to be."

"Do you mean you think they would take more than their share?" she gasped.

"It's a good possibility. I don't want to take a chance. Men are strange when it comes to food out here in the wild country."

"I suppose you're right. Especially if supplies are hard to come by in the city." She paced the floor a few moments, aware that Ed was staring at her. She stopped and suddenly placed her hands on her hips. "Someone is going to have to find out if Cole is going or staying. I can't figure the supplies if we do not have the right count."

"Like I said before, you need to go because I feel I have to stay here."

Jessica eyed him warily, "Are you sure you're not using devious means in order for me and Cole to talk?"

"Me be devious?" Ed chuckled as he raised his brows in mock surprise.

"Yes, you! Helen has warned me about you, Ed Baker!"

"All right! All right!" Ed ranted suddenly. "You stay here and I'll go. Just tell me one thing. What will you do if someone pulls a wagon up front and starts loading in supplies? Supplies that will mean the difference between life and death for us this coming winter." He grabbed a gun from the rack hanging on the wall and thrust it into Jessica's hands. "Here, only be prepared to shoot it, and be prepared to make each shot count!"

"Oh, take your gun!" she shouted. "You know I could never shoot one of my friends!"

"I know you couldn't, that's why I suggested you should go find Cole and asked him about his plans. Besides," a quick grin spread across his lips, "One can never tell what will happen when you see each other."

"I don't know," she said flippantly, "One might just be surprised!"

Jessica slammed out of the door and marched determinedly toward the stables. She dared not let her womanly emotions cloud her judgment. She would approach Cole on a strictly business-like manner. If he said he was leaving, she would do nothing to try and change his mind. It would be a decision he would have to make without any influence on her part.

She rounded the corner of William's house and ran smack into the middle of Cole. The force of the impact sent her reeling to the ground.

"Jessica! Are you hurt?" Cole asked worriedly as he helped her to her feet.

"No, I'm fine!" she snapped, brushing the dirt from her clothes. "You should be more careful. You should have been watching where you were going!"

"Well, now, perhaps the same could be said about you!" he spat angrily.

Oh, darn, Jessica thought. She shouldn't have been so quick to snap at Cole. There was something about him, she mused as she stared at him intently. He appeared to be very angry. Surely it wasn't because of their running into each other.

"Wait a minute," she said firmly. "I didn't mean to snap at you. In fact, you were the one I was looking for."

"Jessica, I'm really very busy right now . . . I . . ."

"Please, Cole," she placed her hand on his arm. "I have to talk to you. It will only take a minute."

He stared down at her with a burning intensity. It seemed as though he was debating with himself whether to comply with Jessica's request. Whatever argument raged through him was quickly lost. Perhaps it was the way she looked at him with her large, sad, gray eyes, or perhaps it was the frightened aura that surrounded her, or it could have even been the way her bottom lip trembled ever so slightly. "All right, Jessica," he sighed, "What is it?"

Jessica spoke before losing her courage. "Mr. Deveraux brought me the list of people who are staying here. Your name wasn't on the list. Ed . . . seems to think . . . even though your name isn't on it, you were still planning to stay."

"Why, of course I'm staying. I couldn't leave now. I couldn't leave you," he added softly.

Jessica could feel her face color with a sudden rush of emotions. Her heart had started pounding very rapidly. Cole was staying! Cole was staying! Those words ran repeatedly through her mind.

Without giving Jessica a chance to say anything else, Cole blurted, "Jessica, I'm in a hurry. I have to go. I don't have time to talk to you now." Seeing a strange expression cross her face. Cole rushed to say. "Jessica don't look at me like that." He brusquely took her by the arm and led her in the direction he was heading. "Jessica, like I said, I really don't have time to stop and explain," he said as they walked hurriedly, Jessica practically running to keep up with him. "The day I returned to Utopia, the day the earthquake struck . . . I had a lot of money in my saddle bags. I had withdrawn all my money from the bank in San Francisco. During all of the excitement . . . I forgot about it, and now, it's gone!"

"Gone! You mean stolen?" she stopped abruptly.

"Yes, stolen!" Cole spat bitterly. "If you don't mind, go on back and tell Ed I am definitely staying." He stopped short. "I may not have time to talk to you now, Jessica, but I'm sure you'll understand. It was all the money I had in the world. However, when things get settled around here, I would like to talk to you . . . that is, if you're agreeable. I believe I owe you an apology. Only now is not the right time or the right place." His eyes begged her to understand.

Jessica had never felt such anger in all of her life. She would have never thought anyone would have treated Cole this way. He had ridden in and helped save so many lives. He had given so much of himself, now for him to be treated so terribly, was almost more than Jessica could stand.

"Of course," she agreed. "Do you need some help? I think it's horrible" she exploded.

"So do I, but no, there's nothing you can do. There's nothing anyone can do, except I do plan on asking many questions before the first wagon pulls out of here!"

"I'll tell Ed. Maybe there is something he can help you do," she said determinedly, watching as Cole strode angrily down the wagon cluttered street.

She hurried back to the warehouse, and when she told Ed what had happened, he stormed out of the building in a blind rage, ranting about the dog that would do something like this to a mutual friend.

Later, when Jessica had finished her calculations, she went out into the storage area and instructed the men on how much to load and how much to leave behind. Ed had returned by this time, and when she questioned him with a silent, piercing glance, he merely tightened his lips and shook his head, indicating they had not had any luck in recovering Cole's money.

Jessica realized she should not attempt to see Cole now. She would wait until the last wagon had left, then make herself available. One thing was certain though, she was determined not to throw herself at him. If they were going to have any kind of a future together, Cole would have to make the first move. Then too, she would have to remain loyal to William's memory. Even though he had married her under false pretenses, she could never dishonor his name. She could only hope Cole felt the same way.

Chapter Thirty-two

The hour just before dawn darkened as the earth rotated and swept away the brilliance of the stars while the sun waited in the universe's theatre wings, impatient to make its magnificent debut of the new day. The autumn winds swept across the snow covered mountains, its freshness washing the face of the valley below.

That morning, Utopia was anything but a sleepy village. Campfires lit up the area and the smell of fresh bacon drifted on the wind. Voices rang throughout the darkness. Lanterns danced like fireflies as they bobbed and twinkled as the light helped to chase away the predawn gloom. The sky gradually turned from midnight black to the muted color of dapple gray, then the sun finally spread its glorious smile on the season of mists and mellow fruitfulness.

Many wagons, their white canvas tops billowing in the gentle wind, formed a perfect line. Travois attached to spare horses and mules held many of the injured. People lined up alongside the wagons. They were walking in order to have room for supplies and personal items. The first wagon began to roll. The exodus from Utopia had begun.

Jessica, Cole, Ed, Helen, and the four other couples stood on the front porch of William's cabin as the procession slowly creaked and lumbered past them. A few of the people threw up their hands in a farewell wave and shouted goodbye, but most stared stonily ahead of them. June broke the formation by walking up on the porch and hugging Jessica and Helen. It seemed as though she desperately hated to leave, but circumstances prevented her from doing as she wished. Their muffled tears soon turned into smiles. Each one of the women hated for the other to see her cry. They promised to somehow keep in touch as June ran to resume her place. Before too long, only a cloud of dust remained, practically choking the men and women standing on the porch.

Ed broke the eerie silence. "Well, I guess that's that." he said, staring wistfully as the last wagon disappeared over the small rise. He wrapped his arms around Helen, "Come on, little Mama, let's have some coffee."

The others trailed self-consciously back into the house. Somehow, the valley had never seemed more lonesome at that particular moment.

Later, when the coffee was ready, the group huddled in front of the fireplace.

Cole stepped in front of the hearth and said, "Why all the long faces? Everyone of you looks as though you've lost your best friend."

Helen glared at Cole, "Some of us have!" she snapped.

"Wait a minute, Helen," Cole spoke in a soothing voice. "I was only teasing, merely trying to snap all of you out of the depressed mood you're in."

Helen blushed, "I'm sorry, Cole. I shouldn't be wearing my feelings on my sleeve."

"That's all right . . . I guess it was a pretty callous remark." He forced a wry grin, "Not to change the subject, but we need to make plans. What do you men think?"

Ed, Virgil, Andy, Ralph, and Paul, all chorused an agreement.

Cole continued, "We have two things pressing us. One, we need to get everyone's cabins situated, and secondly, we need to go hunting while the weather holds in order to replenish the larder. I don't know about you all, but I hate to think of spending the winter on a diet of beans and cornbread. In my opinion, the animals are still fidgety from the earthquake. If we could pick us up a few wild boars, several turkeys, and maybe four deer, we'd be in pretty good shape. We were left two cows. I don't know what you think, I would kind of like to save them for fresh milk and butter. One thing about it, we have plenty of hay. They didn't have enough room to carry that with them," he added bitterly.

Virgil, thinking aloud, "Yep, we can save the cows. Only thing, when the snow gets too deep, we'll have to move a stable in closer to one of the cabins to make it easier to take care of them."

Cole nodded to Virgil and Paul, "I think we're the best hunters. What say we get an early start in the morning?" He glanced over at the other men, "That is, if it's all right with you?"

The others readily agreed since they were better at carpenter work. By splitting into two small groups, they would be able to finish winterizing what was left of the town before winter hit.

"Well, what can we do?" Barbara, Paul's wife asked

testily, as she placed her hands on her hips. "We can help too!"

"Sure you can," Andy said. "It doesn't take long for turnip greens to grow. Since the fall garden was destroyed, it might not be a bad idea to get some turnip and mustard greens in the ground. And, I'm sure there will be plenty to do."

Jessica laughed, "Yes, there is. I was raised in a small community in New York State, and my mother always made sure all of the blankets and linens were washed and sunned before cold weather. Also, there's still berries in the upper meadow. Jellies and jam will help through the winter too. It was my understanding that food like that was left up to the individual families, and much of it was destroyed. I know there is only one jar of jam left in the panty," a smile lit her face, "But there are several crocks of honey. It's my guess Ching Lee was planning to buy their jams and preserves from some of the women. Jessica's voice trailed off as she realized the men did not care about such things. She could see they were only listening out of courtesy. "Well," she said hesitantly, "I suppose we ought to get started." She dared not look at Cole, although she could feel his burning gaze upon her. There would be time for that later.

The men refilled their coffee mugs and stepped out on the porch. They discussed the situation and decided the best thing they could do and still insure everyone's privacy, was to use the scrap lumber and logs and completely rebuild at least four cabins. They would place them close to William's house to where they could all have easy access to each other when the winter snows grew deep and severe. They decided it would be for the best, since William's house was so large, Ed, Helen,

Aaron, Jessica, and Cole would live there. All six men began working on the cabins.

While the men were busy discussing their plan of action, the women were not idle. It was decided that Barbara and Helen would work on the fall garden, Jessica, and Brenda, Virgil's wife, would start on the laundry and blanket sunning, while Gloria, Ralph's wife, and Nita, Andy's wife, would go to the upper meadows and start picking berries, then make jellies and jam from them.

The first day passed quickly. They all gathered together that night for a large meal consisting of a venison roast, boiled potates, beans, sourdough bread, gravy, and succotash. After the meal, the women started to clean the kitchen while the men gathered in the parlor and began molding bullets for the hunt.

Cole kept his eyes glued to the kitchen door. He simply had to talk with Jessica. It was important to him to find you her feelings. He had to know if she still loved him.

Jessica finished drying the last dish. She glanced toward the door leading into the parlor. She knew Cole was in there with the other men. She had to talk with him.

Helen was aware of the turmoil Jessica was suffering. Ed had told her about William's dying declaration. She also knew Jessica and Cole had not had a chance to be alone and talk since the terrible tragedy. She knew Jessica still loved him. She loved him even though she married William. Helen decided she would not stand idly by and let her friends ruin their lives. She hung her dishtowel on a rack and announced, "I don't know about you ladies, but I think I'll step outside and get a breath of fresh air."

"Oh, no, I'm too tired, I'm going to bed," the other women said.

"Come on, Jessica, go outside with me," Helen urged.

"As if I needed more fresh air," Jessica laughed, referring to the fact that she had spent the day outside, washing.

"Yes, fresh air," Helen insisted. "Come on, I won't take no for an answer."

"Oh, all right." Jessica replied as she untied her apron and hung it on the rack beside the dishtowel.

They walked into the parlor and Helen leaned over Ed, placed a kiss on his forehead, and asked him to keep an eye on Aaron while she and Jessica got some fresh air. She deliberately spoke loud enough so Cole had no trouble hearing her. After donning shawls, the two women stepped outside.

It was only a matter of minutes until Cole made a flimsy excuse about checking on his horse.

"That sure was a good supper," he stated as he shut the front door behind him. "You ladies really outdid yourselves."

"Why, thank you, Cole," Helen replied, looking up surprised. She glanced at Jessica. "However, perhaps you ought to tell Jessica, after all, she was responsible for the venison roast and sourdough bread."

"Helen!" Jessica laughed, embarrassed.

"Well, you did cook them!"

Cole sauntered over to the porch railing and propped a boot up on it. He avoided looking at Jessica, but he realized she was staring unseeingly at the ground. He glanced around and was surprised to see Helen grinning at him.

"Oh, my," she shivered. "I didn't realize it was this cold out here. I'm going to have to go back inside."

Jessica turned hesitantly to follow her.

"Wait a minute, Jessica," Cole stammered. "If you have a moment, I would like to talk to you."

Helen, not taking the chance that Jessica would use the cool night as an excuse to go back inside the house, quickly removed the shawl from around her shoulders and handed it to Jessica. "Here, take this," she offered, "It's chilly out here."

Cole flashed Helen a brilliant smile as she disappeared through the front door. He stepped to the edge of the porch and peered up at the sky. "Nice night out, isn't it," he remarked casually.

"Tell me," Jessica asked, trying to conceal the smile threatening to spread across her face, "How long did it take you and Helen to plan that?"

He smiled, "It didn't take long, in fact, there wasn't even a plan. Things that are meant to be rarely take plans. It seems they simply fall into place."

"You're sort of smug about it, aren't you?"

"No, not smug. I think that's a too strong a word, although I do think . . ."

"Oh, look!" Jessica interrupted, pointing up at the star shrouded sky as a shooting star streaked across the heavens. "Quick, make a wish!"

Cole moved closer to her. He placed both hands on her shoulders and forced her to look directly at him. "I have my wish already. It was granted the moment we were left alone," he whispered tenderly.

"Oh?" she choked.

"I also have another wish, but I doubt it will be granted."

"Oh?" she said again. "Why do you have doubt?"

"Because I wish we could walk arm in arm throughout eternity. I see it now," he whispered reverently, "Our souls high upon the plains above the endless sand of time." Cole's lips came closer to Jessica's lips with each word he spoke. "I wish you were my wife. I wish . . ."

"Hush, my love," she placed a finger across his lips. "If you continue, there will not be another star left in the sky." Jessica could feel his maleness pressed against her. She tried to free herself from his grasp, but his hands tightened on her shoulders. "Cole, please. We have to talk. We have to talk about us, William, and our future plans, if any."

Cole let his hands fall down by his side. "All right, Jessica. I agree, we do have to talk," he decided firmly. "Only," he laughed jerkily, "I don't know where to begin."

"Neither do I." Jessica strolled to the outer edges of the porch and stared up at the star filled sky as if she was searching for an answer, searching for a place to begin. "Cole," she spoke softly as she turned to face him. "Please, don't hate William."

"Like I said before, I could never hate him. And what is so unusual, I really can't blame him for what he did."

"Cole! How can you say that!"

"Because he loved you," he answered simply. "How can you fault a man for falling in love with a woman? You can't," he said, not giving her a chance to reply.

She shivered. "Somehow, all of this makes me feel . . . dirty."

"You shouldn't," Cole said as he placed his arms around her.

"No, Cole, not now," she cried, pulling from the near-embrace. "There are some things we have to settle first."

"Like what?"

She brought her gaze up to meet his. "I feel like William cleared any doubts that might exist between us. However, I am curious to know . . . if . . . there is . . . another woman you care for . . . in San Francisco?"

Cole nodded. "I was afraid of that. Jessica, you have to believe me," he gazed deeply into her eyes. "There was not another woman. I was simply trying to hurt you as badly as I *thought* you had hurt me. I was being spiteful. For that, I owe you an apology."

"Actually, Cole, it goes much deeper than that." She turned her face away from him and started crying.

"What's the matter? Why are you crying?" he asked, concern filling his voice.

"Because it's all our fault. I feel so much guilt over William's death. I really believe it could have been prevented."

"How?" he asked incredulously. "Could you have prevented the earthquake? No, of course not! And neither could I!"

"That's not what I meant! His death could have been prevented if only we had trusted each other. Tell me, would he have been in the same place as he was when the earthquake struck if you had not believed him? Would he have have been there if I had not believed him? Tell me!" she cried.

"Wait a minute, Jessica. You're wrong by trying to place the blame on us. You tell me one thing, would he be dead today if you had not stowed-away on the ship? What if your father had never decided to leave home and try to find a new home for his family. What would have happened if he and your mother had never met and had you? No, Jessica," he shook his head. "If you have to blame anything, blame fate, blame circumstances, but don't blame us!"

"Oh, Cole," she cried as she buried her face in his shoulder. "I don't know what to think! I only know I hurt so badly inside of me."

A tiny morsel of fear gripped at Cole. It was a minute before he could bring himself to speak. "Tell me, Jessica, and be honest. Did you love William?"

"No, I didn't," she was quick to reply. "But I think I respected him more than any man I have ever known, even my father. I respected him because his thoughts were always on others. And I guess I'm trying to find a place to put blame because I was so disappointed in him! There! I said it! I actually said something bad about the great William Stockard!" She angrily swiped at a tear running down her face. "I can't believe I said that," she whispered after regaining her composure.

"It's incredible," Cole muttered. "I had no idea you were feeling the same way I do. I feel such an anger inside of me. I am like you. I am mad at him, I am mad at me for not having more faith in you. And I'm mad at you for not having any faith in me."

Jessica took Cole's hand and pressed it against her cheek. "My darling, I honestly think I am relieved."

"Why?"

"Because I have been fantasizing what would happen when we had this meeting. I was afraid you would ask me to marry you immediately."

"And, what if those were my plans?" he asked softly, his lips a mere breath away from hers.

"Cole, tell me. Do you love me?"

"Yes, with all my heart." He nodded and smiled, "And

what about you? Do you love me?"

"Yes, I love you more than life itself."

"Then, will you marry me?" his words fell soft and gentle against her skin.

"No."

"What? Why not, Jessica? You just said you loved me!"

"I do, and I do want to marry you." She turned and walked away from him. Sitting down on the steps, she asked him to join her. They sat in silence for a moment before she began to speak again. "I was afraid you would ask me to marry you when we finally had a chance to talk." She glanced at him and smiled, "I was also afraid you wouldn't."

"You're not making much sense, Jessica."

"Cole," she turned toward him, imploring with her eyes for understanding, "If I married you now, we would be haunted by William. He would always be a barrier between us. Oh, don't you see, we have to rid ourselves of the guilt we have surrounding his death." She ducked her head, "And regardless of all of our spoken words, we have to stop hating him for what he did to us."

Cole started to adamantly deny that he hated William, but the words would not come. It hit him so hard, the knowledge practically sent him reeling across the wooden planks of the porch. Jessica was being truthful. Not only that, she was right. William would stand between them. They would never be able to find true happiness as long as their marriage stood in the shadow of his memory.

"You're right," he finally admitted. His face was stricken with remorse when he looked at her. He realized he would not be able to go through life without her by his side. "Jessica?" the word came in a strangled gasp. "What are we going to do?"

Jessica slipped her hand into his and leaned her head against his hard, muscular shoulder. "I have been thinking about that too."

"And . . ."

"Cole, why can't we start all over? Why can't we nurture our love, let it grow and mature? I really think if we waited a while, our love would be stronger, strong enough to face any test." She squeezed his hand and whispered softly, "Next spring, if I am asked to be your wife, my answer will be different than it was a few minutes ago."

Cole swept her into his arms and placed sweet, tender kisses on her lips, cheek, and throat. "Oh, my darling," he murmured, "I don't know if I can wait that long."

"Yes you can, Cole. You can wait," her face blazed at the meaning. Her face turned even redder when she admitted how badly she wanted him. "But," she explained, "it wouldn't be right. Don't get me wrong." She pleaded for him to understand. "I want you very much, however, I want our love to be *right,* more than I desire you. A marriage has to start out right or it's doomed from the very start."

Cole laughed in his own special way, a way Jessica found almost impossible to resist. "You know," he said honestly, "I would really like to rant and rave, pace the floor and shout at you." He spread his fingers wide apart and flexed them. "But, I'd be wrong. I agree with every word you've said." He glanced at her and grinned cockily. "You know that you, me, Ed, Helen, and their little boy are going to be living together, don't you?"

Although she had not heard the men's conversation

earlier that evening, she admitted that the thought had crossed her mind as the most logical thing to do.

Cole groaned. "Then you realize how hard it will be for me to remain a gentleman?"

"My darling, I trust you completely. Besides, there will be safety in numbers, and since you will have to sleep in the parlor, and since Ed and Helen will be sharing William's . . . I mean the larger bedroom, that means Aaron will have to share my bedroom." She propped her chin on a cupped fist. "Somehow, I don't see you willing to have Aaron as an audience to your displays of heated passion."

Cole's handsome face crinkled as he guffawed with laughter. "You little minx! You planned this deliberately!"

"Yes, I did!" she readily admitted. "You see, I was a very spoiled child. I usually got what I wanted." Her voice turned from a teasing manner to a huskiness, "I want a proper courtship, and I want a proper marriage, but most of all, I want you, and I do want it to be right."

"It will be my love, you'll see."

"I know," she whispered softly.

He crushed her in his arms. "Do you realize how many walks I will have to take in the cold this winter simply to keep you an honorable woman?"

She smiled. "Yes, I guess you will. Although, for our marriage to be perfect, it'll be worth it."

Cole twitched his mouth grimly. "Well, I sure hope time passes quickly."

"Oh, it will! Before you know it," she snapped her fingers, "Spring will be here like that!"

Time did pass quickly. The following days were filled with the thoughts of survival. The men's hunt was successful, the cabins were rebuilt, and even the little garden produced before the snows set in to stay.

Everyone was aware of Jessica's and Cole's redeclared love. They were teased good naturedly when they went on long walks in the snow. When the weather permitted, they would take Aaron outside and build snowmen and always, to the little boy's delight, Jessica would fall backward in the snow, fan her arms and make a beautiful snow angel.

Their nights were filled with peaceful calmness. Cole had salvaged an old beat up guitar and fiddle. He and Virgil would sometimes play Irish melodies into the wee hours of the morning. Sometimes, their nights were filled with marathon chess games. At first, they reminded Jessica so much of William, it was difficult for her to sit and play, but even that gradually became easier to cope with.

It seemed as though everything worked in a perfect union that winter. The weather was comparatively mild considering some of the winters the men had spent there. However, the women couldn't help but wonder if the weather was warmer, or if the winter seemed mild because of the fact that the men were not lonely anymore.

Blizzards would rage for days on end. One could not venture outside without taking several precautions in order to make it back to the safety of the cabins. Paul came up with the idea to string ropes between the cabins. Even during the most severe storms, they could go from one house to the other if the need arose.

The weather broke several times, never enough for

the snow to melt and it was always cold. During one of the so called warm spells, the men ventured out and inspected the mines. Their worst fears were confirmed when they found huge boulders in the working areas and the shoring timbers cracked and split. Just the men's presence in one caused a cave-in. They barely escaped with their lives. It was quickly decided they would seal the mine's entrances with dynamite in the springtime when all chances of an avalanche were over. It was feared that the blast would bring a mountain of snow down on the valley.

Time passed by. Before they knew it, Christmas was upon them. Days before, the tiny village became a beehive of secrecy as each one of the inhabitants prepared gifts for their friends. Helen and Jessica dipped into their ration of sugar and honey and baked tea cakes for the other couples as gifts. Together, they gave the other women yarn, ribbons, and Jessica generously gave each one of the women a piece of yardgoods to make a new dress. She simply could not bring herself to use any of the material for herself. She was just now beginning to get over William's death and the entire circumstances surrounding it. Her gift to the men were woolen scarfs, and to Aaron, she gave a pair of mittens plus a scarf. But to Cole, she gave a special gift. During one of the times he had been outside doing chores, she had painstakingly measured his clothes, traced out a pattern, and had sat in her room with a blanket wrapped around her shoulders while she sewed him an entire outfit to wear, tan trousers, a white shirt with long flowing sleeves, and a beautiful green velvet vest. He had mentioned several times how he wished for one to help keep off the chill, especially when a coat was too heavy.

Cole surprised Jessica with a strand of beautiful pearls. When she asked how he came by them, he merely shrugged his shoulders. He was too embarrassed to admit he had had one of the men who had gone into San Francisco after supplies buy them for him right after he had won a week of her services during that poker game. Luckily, he had stashed them in a safe place.

Helen and Ed gave Jessica a shimmering piece of violet colored material that Helen had been saving for herself. For a moment, Jessica was almost afraid to hold it up to her. She had always been afraid to wear striking colors because of the vibrant color of her hair. To her surprise, the color of the material couldn't have matched her better.

Their Christmas feast was bountiful. They had saved one of the wild turkeys especially for this occasion. All of the people congregated at the large house for the opening of presents and the huge meal all of the women helped to prepare. The table actually groaned and creaked under the burden of all the food; cornbread dressing, fat sweet potatoes, roasted in their own skins, giblet gravy, dried pearl onions simmered in a creamy white sauce, apples cooked with a tiny hint of cinnamon, sour dough bread, smeared with fresh butter, mince and pumpkin pies, topped off with their homemade version of eggnog. One would never known only a couple of months earlier, they had been worried about having enough food to last the winter.

After the Christmas feast, they all retired to the parlor where they roasted acorns over the open fire. To Jessica's surprise, the nuts had a sweet, crunchy flavor to them. They were delicious!

She and Cole sat by the fire while the others told of

past experiences. Some even told tales of their ancestors and how they first came to the new land of freedom. Jessica snuggled close to Cole. She was content in the knowledge that this was but one Christmas, with many more to come.

After the holidays passed, everything settled back into the normal routines. Whenever weather permitted, the men hunted in order to help replenish their dwindling larder. By being frugal, they would have enough food to last until spring and until a garden could be planted. Money wasn't necessarily the problem. All of them had money except for Cole. As soon as the weather permitted, they would go to San Francisco and restock their flour, sugar, coffee and tea, the basic items that could not be grown.

As spring approached, Jessica began to grow impatient. She had known all along Cole was the man for her. Now, there was not a doubt in her mind. Their relationship had grown and blossomed until she could hardly wait until spring and the time he could take her in his arms and satisfy the passion that continued to grow deep within their souls. The winter had proved to be a time for healing. William had been truly forgiven and they were even able to fully accept the reason why he had betrayed them.

The cold gray days gradually grew longer. One day Jessica was in the kitchen and Aaron ran inside with a tiny bouquet of wild daisies. Jessica ran outside. Shielding her eyes against the glare of melting snow, she looked at the upper meadows and saw tiny flowers showing their faces to the sun. They were even nestled in sprigs of green grass.

Spring had come to Utopia.

Chapter Thirty-three

Nothing was more beautiful than the Sierras in the spring. All traces of snow disappeared except for what remained on the tall mountains. It seemingly happened overnight. The meadows became a rhapsody of color, looking as though a rainbow had exploded and rained colored dust upon the land. The trees; cottonwoods, elms, poplars, and oaks seemed to stand taller, stretching their eager branches toward the sun filled sky. The pale greens of virgin leaves blended with the stark vividness of the jade, emerald, moss, and malachite greens that enhanced the tall pine trees. And the sky was magnificant! Big, fleecy white clouds dotted the cerulean blue heaven. It was like a wonderful paradise, created exclusively for them.

Jessica was beginning to wonder when Cole would approach her with another proposal. She wasn't worried. She knew he loved her as much as she loved him. She was now very anxious to become his wife. She knew if some of the people did start to come back from San Francisco, they would demand much of their precious time. She didn't feel a bit selfish for wanting Cole all to herself for a while.

One evening, after finishing the chores, Jessica walked out on the front porch and sat down on the steps. Cole had gone hunting that day, and he had not returned yet. She anxiously cast her eyes in the direction in which he had gone. To her relief she saw him riding in. She walked out to the stables while he was tending to his horse.

"Hello, I was starting to worry about you," she said as she closed the latch gate behind her.

"Oh, we're gonna feast tonight!" he exclaimed happily, holding up an entire covey of quail. "The hunting was good!"

"Er, Cole, we have already eaten. It is late," she added.

Bewildered, Cole walked to the edge of the stable and glanced out at the darkening sky. He turned around to Jessica, his face bathed in surprise. "I had no idea it was this late. I was up in the higher meadows, and I guess I got carried away and forgot about the time. I wondered why you said you were worrying, now I can see why."

"Come on," she took his hand. "I saved you some supper."

"Just a minute," Cole chuckled as he pulled her into his arms. "I don't think the conquering hunter has been properly welcomed back home."

Jessica eagerly parted her lips for him, feeling the tip of his tongue shoot deeply inside her mouth, and she answered his passionate kiss with a response all her own. "Oh, Cole, I love you so much," she whispered softly when they broke apart and gasped for breath.

"And I love you too." He looked down at her and

smiled. "If memory serves me correctly, it seems there's something I've been forgetting to do." He closed one eye and squinted the other in the direction of the rafters, as he acted as though he was trying to recall something.

Jessica put her fingers against her mouth and a frown creased her forehead as she mused aloud. "Now that you mention it, it does seem like we're forgetting something." She patted her foot impatiently, "Now, I wonder what it could be?"

"Jessica," Cole breathed huskily, "There's something I have to ask you . . . but I don't want to do it here." A grin pulled at his lips, "I can think of a million more places that are more romantic."

Jessica glanced down at the soiled hay on the floor and giggled, "Yes, I can too." Although she was teasing with Cole, she was singing inside. He was going to ask her to marry him! This was the moment she had been waiting for.

Cole removed his hat and swooped down low, bowing like a knight of the olden days, "Madam, may I have the pleasure of your company on a picnic tomorrow. We shall dine on roasted pheasant," he held up the quail, "And brandied wine."

Jessica presented her hand to him and curtsied. "T'would be my pleasure, m'Lord." She posed a frown, "But tell me kind sir, who will prepare our feast?"

Cole stepped back in mock surprise. "Why, tis your chore, m' Lady. Would be unwise indeed to not to honor the brave young knight who puts such a wealth of food on the table.",

Jessica pressed her hand against her breast. "Oh, m' Lord, perhaps this fair maiden received the wrong idea. I thought we were going to repast at a picnic. I had no idea you would drag a table along!"

"Come here, you little vixen!" Cole laughed, pulling her back into his arms. "You know you drive me mad, don't you?"

Jessica chuckled. "Yes, and you know what you do to me."

"I do?" he mocked, his lips a mere inch from hers.

"Yes!" she stated boldly.

A firey light flashed in Cole's eyes momentarily, then he sighed. "We had better go inside. If we stay here a moment longer, I can't be held responsible for my actions."

"Yes," Jessica sighed heavily. "We do need to go in." For a minute, she was almost sorry Cole had stopped the events that were about to happen. She wanted him very badly. However, she realized they had waited so long, a few more days shouldn't be too difficult.

The following morning, Jessica woke up bright and early. She was anxious to prepare their lunch in order to be able to leave as soon as possible. She packed the roasted quail, a loaf of fresh bread, a slab of white cheese, and a bottle of brandied wine into a reed basket. After she had finished, she went back to her room to dress for the special outing.

Jessica had already planned what she would wear. She laid her favorite dress across the bed. She had made it with the material Helen and Ed gave to her for Christmas. With the water she had heated while cooking their lunch, Jessica prepared her bath water, pouring a dollop of lilac water in it for an overall fragrance.

Gingerly testing the water with her toe, Jessica stepped into the small wooden tub and gratefully sank into the steaming warmth. She did not want to tarry long, she wanted to take extra pains with her hair. In a few moments, she climbed from the tub and draped a Turkish towel around her slim but curvacious body. Padding over to the mirror, Jessica let the towel slide down to the floor, all the while examining her reflection in the mirror. She looked at her breasts, and finally decided they were not as attractive as she wished. At least they are firm and don't sag, she thought with a shrug.

The clock outside chimed the hour. Jessica gasped in surprise. It was getting late! She would have to hurry. Jessica retrieved the towel from the floor and hurriedly dried her body. She quickly slipped on her undergarments after making sure the personal items had been sprinkled with lilac water, then gently lowered the dress over her head. She turned and stared at herself in the mirror. The dress was beautiful! And, she even had to admit how nice she looked in it. She recalled the fun she and Helen had when they made it. The skirt was full and flowing while the waistline fit snugly, revealing how tiny it actually was. The bodice was daring and showing more bosom than Jessica would have normally worn. They had sewn battenburg lace around the entire neckline, and had layered the flowing sleeves with the lace also. After she had donned the dress, Jessica stared once more at her reflection. Her cheeks were pink and glowed enchantingly. Whether this was due from the heat of the bath, or the excitement of meeting Cole, she did not know, although she had a very good idea where the culprit lay. Her lips were a natural color that blended so well with her dress. Her eyes were smoldering with excitement and desire. She fastened the strand of pearls around her neck, then picked up the brush and began grooming her vibrantly shiny hair. She brushed it back away from her face, then pinned a pretty wild flower behind her ear. She took one last breathless glance in the mirror and decided, quite modestly, she was pretty.

When Jessica entered the parlor, Ed was sitting on the sofa while Cole stood in front of the fireplace. Cole broke off what he had been saying to Ed when she entered the room. He gave a long, low whistle.

"My God, Jessica, you're beautiful!" his voice came raspy.

"You look very nice yourself," she said, appraising him quickly. She was very pleased he had decided to wear her Christmas gift to him.

Cole happened to glance over at Ed. It would have been hard to not notice him, because a silly grin had spread completely across his broad face. "What are you grinning about?" Cole chuckled.

Ed placed one of his hands behind an ear and cupped it. He batted his eyes and rolled them upward. "What's that I hear? Wedding bells?"

"That's none of your business," Cole bantered. "That is between me and the lady. Which," he glanced down at Jessica who was staring intently up at him, "If we don't get going, we'll get there in time for supper instead of lunch."

"Oh? And where exactly are we going?" she asked.

"A secret place I discovered while out hunting one day." He shot a look at Ed. "There's no need for you to try and find us. I know you and some of the wild pranks you pull. You'll never find this place, not in a million years."

Ed jokingly remarked, "Heck, Cole, I wouldn't even be able to look for it if it took that long. I'm sure I would have a good case of rheumatism by then!"

Jessica folded her hands over her mouth and giggled. She was so fond of the ornery Irishman. He was like the big brother she never had. "Come on, Cole. Let's go. We could stand here and joke all day long. In fact, I'm almost afraid the quail I cooked this morning will have grown tough with age."

Cole quickly stepped across the room, picked up the picnic basket then extended his arm to Jessica. "Your wish is my command. The horses are saddled and raring to go."

"Where are you going?" a small voice came from the doorway.

"We're going on a picnic, Aaron," Jessica answered.

"Oh, goody!" He jumped up and down clapping his hands. "Can I go too?"

Cole ruffled his hair, "I'm afraid not today, son. This is a special picnic, just for grown-ups. Maybe some other time."

"Oh," his face crumpled in disappointment, then it suddenly brightened. "Oh! I know what you're gonna do! You're gonna get married, 'cause my mama said so!"

Cole's eyes crinkled merrily as he glanced at Jessica, who was also laughing.

"Aaron!" Ed said scoldingly, although desperately trying to hide the laughter in his voice. "I thought you were supposed to be chopping kindling for the kitchen stove?"

"Yes sir, I think I am," he answered politely. But when the little boy turned and walked out the door, his bottom lip was stuck out, and he was muttering, "Aw, heck, I never get to have any fun!"

Cole glanced at Jessica. "Now that that crisis is over, we had better go before Ed decides he wants to come along too."

"Go on you two!" Ed shooed them out. "Get out of here. Have fun," he shouted as he closed the front door behind them. Cole helped Jessica on her mount, then he climbed up on his horse and they were off. They rode side by side at a leisurely pace. He kept stealing little glances in Jessica's direction, marveling over the way the sun shimmered and danced on her flaming hair.

"Where are we going, Cole?" Jessica had been afraid for a brief moment that Cole had stumbled on to the place where she and William used to go. She was greatly relieved when Cole turned his horse in the opposite direction.

"It's just a little meadow I found. And I found it by sheer accident," he added. "Just be patient, we'll be there soon."

They rode up into the upper meadow until they reached the double pine with the golden cross, then veered sharply to their left. Both of them had to ride low, ducking underneath heavy pine branches as they made their way to the secret hide-a-way. The horses made their way over heavy boulders, and through deep stands of wild grass. Finally, they burst into the clearing. It was exactly as Cole had said. It was beautiful!

A tiny mountain brook ran alongside the edge of the meadow, bubbling and sparkling its way over the rocks and the water made its way down into the valley. The meadow was a profusion of wild splashes of color.

"Oh, look!" she cried, pointing to a huge but gnarled pine tree. Lavender flowers grew in mass confusion around the trunk of the tree. "There! We will have our picnic there!"

Cole helped Jessica from her horse, then removed the basket and other supplies they had brought along.

Then, he led the horses close to the stream and staked them out. He came back toward Jessica with a huge smile on his handsome face.

"I told you it was nice, didn't I?" he boasted proudly.

"Oh, it is, Cole. It is exactly like you promised." Jessica answered as she wound her arms around his neck and shamelessly sought his lips.

"Oh, my God, Jessica!" Cole breathed when he broke away gasping for air. "I love you so much!"

"And I love you too!" she panted.

Cole pulled abruptly away. It was clear something was troubling him.

"What's the matter?" she wanted to know. Surely she had done nothing to anger him. When she caught a glimpse of his face, she knew it was not anger that bothered him. "Tell me Cole," she repeated, "What's the matter?"

He shook his head. "No, I'll talk to you in a moment . . . after we have eaten." He flashed a brilliant smile. "I'm starving!" he growled.

Jessica turned to the basket. Food was the farthest thing from her mind. She spread a red and white checkered cloth on the ground, and placed the meat, cheese, bread and wine, on it. Then after fishing in the basket, she pulled out two sparkling crystal glasses.

Cole's brow shot up. "Ooh, how nice!"

"I wanted everything to be perfect for this special day," she whispered softly.

Cole looked down at the ground and frowned. "Speaking of being perfect," he spoke hesitantly. "There is something I have to tell you. And please, let me say it without any interruptions." He took a deep breath, "It was my intention to bring you up here and propose.

However, I can't do it."

Sudden pain flashed across Jessica's face. She couldn't believe what she was hearing.

Cole rushed blindly on. "As you know, the mines back at Utopia are worthless. You are also aware of the fact that all of the money I had in the world was stolen. Don't you see Jessica, I have nothing to offer you! Right now, I couldn't even buy you food."

"Cole," she whispered, "I don't care about that! I don't care what you have or don't have. *I love you!* Besides that, as William's widow, I'm sure I will inherit his money. See, we do have plenty!" she said eagerly.

Cole shook his head firmly. "No, Jessica. It wouldn't be the same. I couldn't take his money." He gazed intently into her eyes. "Just think about it for a moment and you'll see that I'm right about that."

Her head bobbed numbly, "I suppose you're right. Then an idea came to her. "Cole," she said slowly. "What about the land in Texas? When everything happened, the deal had already been made about that land. And besides," she cried, "You know William would have wanted us to have it!"

"Perhaps you're right about that," he agreed slowly.

"And as for the rest of the money, I don't need it, we don't need it, and Cole, I don't even particularly want it. It really wouldn't seem right." She thought for a moment, then spoke slowly, "I have an idea if you are agreeable to it?"

He shrugged sadly. "All right. I guess we've nothing to lose."

"Let's take the land in Texas, and give the rest of the money to our friends in Utopia. Why, this spring and summer, we could do some prospecting, and I know we could have enough money to buy a few cattle with, and to live on until the ranch started paying off. But Cole, please let's get married now. I want to be your wife . . . I want to be your wife now! I don't want to wait. Please!" she begged.

Cole looked at her strangely. An odd gleam came into his eyes. "You know, it just might work," he uttered slowly. He gazed directly at her. "Jessica, I wouldn't feel bad about taking the ranch. But I would about the rest. That's a brilliant idea! Jessica, you've solved the problem! Not only are you beautiful, you're smart!"

"Did you think I wasn't?" she laughed.

Cole rose to his knees and pulled Jessica into his arms. "My darling," he whispered tenderly, "Will you be my wife? Will you marry me and live with me for all the days of our lives?"

"Oh, yes, my darling!" she cried flinging herself closer to him. "I would mary you this minute if a preacher was here!"

"My God, Jessica!" Cole rasped hoarsely, "I can't wait. So help me, I can't wait."

"Oh, my darling," she whispered, "we don't have to wait. Why," she gave a sweep with her arm, "We have the grandest minister right here in God's wonderland. We are like Adam and Eve and this is our Eden. We can stand before God and pledge our vows!"

Cole raised and lifted Jessica to her feet. "Yes," he whispered urgently. That's exactly what we can do!"

They walked out into the center of the meadow. Cole stopped and picked her a bouquet of wildflowers, handed them to her, then slipped his arm around her waist. He took a deep breath, smiled at Jessica, and began, his voice ringing strong and clear.

"I, Cole Robertson, take this woman, Jessica Tate Stockard, for my lawfully wedded wife. To have and to hold, in richness and in health, for richer or for poorer, until death us do part. I also promise before God, to love her, to keep her from harm, and to cherish her with all my heart and soul."

"I, Jessica Tate Stockard, do take this man, Cole Robertson, to be my lawfully wedded husband. To cherish, love, honor, and obey, to give my all to him. To have his babies, to cleave only unto him, to share his life, and to love him with all of my heart and soul. These vows, I willingly pledge."

With their hands entwined, Cole and Jessica bowed their heads and uttered a silent prayer.

When Jessica raised her lips to accept Cole, a tiny droplet of a tear slid down her cheek. It was not a tear of sadness. It was a tear of extreme happiness.

Cole took her gently into his arms. "My wife," he whispered.

"My husband," she breathed breathlessly. "Now, make me your wife completely."

Cole looked at her hungrily. He gently began to unfasten the back of her dress, then tenderly tugged the bodice down past her waist. It was only a few moments later that she was standing before him, completely nude, and completely unashamed.

Then Jessica painstakingly started to unbutton his shirt. She slipped the vest from his shoulders, then slipped the shirt from his arms. Her hands were trembling by the time she unhooked his belt, and by the time he was standing nude in front of her, she was a shaking mass of trembles. Not from being afraid, but from wanting and desire.

In one fluid motion, Cole swept her into his arms and carried her back to the tree and placed her gently on the thick carpet of grass.

Jessica's mind broke into a sharp awareness as Cole guided her hand down to caress his desire. His lips rained kisses over her entire body, as his hands stroked and coddled the soft flesh of his willing wife.

His caresses continued, following the curving arch of her hip. A throaty moan of passion escaped her lips and his hands sought the delicate chamber between her thighs. He was so gentle, so infinitely gentle. His hand continued to wander over every detail of her body, as though he was memorizing it in his mind, as if he was branding it as *his*, with every caress.

A small cry broke from Jessica's lips as his mouth found the golden tips of her breasts. "Tell me that you love me, Cole, it's like music to my ears."

"Oh, my darling, I love you, I love you, I love you," he repeated endlessly.

Jessica's body was trembling with passion. Her breath was rapid and uneven. Cole's loving and caressing was building, constantly bringing her closer to the plateau of supreme bliss.

Cole's hand wandered with deliberate slowness over every detail of her, as if he was savoring all of the delights he found. His mouth went back to hers, tasting the sweet nectar as his tongue plunged deep inside.

"My husband," Jessica whispered breathlessly, "I need you now. Make me your wife, now! Please!" she moaned.

Cole voiced a throaty growl as he pressed her against the tall carpet of grass.

Jessica parted her thighs as she eagerly anticipated

the marriage of their bodies, the complete union, the ultimate joy of man meeting woman.

Jessica gasped with pleasure as his fiery shaft penetrated into the very essence of her being. She panted, gasping for breath as her nails tightened on his back. He urged her on, cupping his hands beneath her body, pulling her even closer to him and he thrust deeply into her.

Jessica took him completely, giving all of her love, all of her soul to the man she could now call husband.

The ultimate moment of supreme satisfaction came. The birds, the trees, and flowers, and yes, even God witnessed the perfect union of Cole and Jessica Robertson.

Much, much later, when everything drifted back into place, Jessica lay with her head across Cole's lap.

"My husband . . ." she whispered in awe. "God, how wonderful that word sounds!"

"I know, it sounds almost as perfect as the word, wife." Cole trained a delicate flower along her cheek. The food had long since been forgotten, but the wine had been drunk as they toasted the start of their new lives.

Finally, Cole sighed, "Jessica . . . even though I hate to, we're going to have to get back. If I know Ed, and if we're not back by dark, he'll be out looking for us. You know what a worry wart he is."

"Yes," she giggled, playing with the matted curls on Cole's chest. "I can even imagine how much we would shock them if someone happened by right now."

"Why? Simply because we are here in the wide open spaces, completely naked? Do you honestly think that would shock them?"

Jessica giggled. The brandied wine had nothing to do with her giddiness. She had never known such happiness was possible.

"Come on, lazy bones," Cole urged. "We have to leave now."

"Wait a minute, Cole. What about tonight? What will we tell Ed and Helen? I can't bear the thought of being parted from you."

"We'll simply tell them the truth. They'll understand," he reassured her.

"You're right. They will know we couldn't wait a moment longer."

"We do have to go now, my love," he whispered tenderly.

"I know. I guess I'm trying to avoid facing reality right now. I want to savor this moment forever."

"This moment *will* last forever," he vowed adamantly.

After they had dressed and gathered up the things they brought, Jessica looked at Cole and smiled, "You know, I think it will be kind of exciting."

"What?"

"Both of us prospecting for gold. It will be fun. Just think of all the possibilities we'll have for a honeymoon."

Cole took her into his arms. "I know, but," he frowned slightly, "I wish our start in life could have been a little different. I would have liked to bathe you in precious jewels, and laid the world at your feet."

"I don't need any of those things, Cole. All I will ever need is you and your love." She kissed him. "In fact, I think it will be exciting. Just think, one of these days when we're old and gray, we can sit in our rocking chairs and tell our children's children how we started with nothing except the clothes on our back."

Cole stood thoughtfully for a moment, then he said, "That sounds good. Although, it's hard for me to imagine that mass of fiery hair being gray."

She laughed, the sound of it tinkling and young, as Cole swept her into his arms and twirled her around and around. Then he stopped and put her down. Her eyes fell on a lovely sight. "Oh, look, Cole!" she pointed toward the edge of the meadow at a group of wildflowers. "What kind are they? They're lovely," she gushed.

"I don't know," he admitted. "They are pretty though, would you like a bouquet?" he asked thoughtfully.

"Oh, yes, I would!" she squealed excitedly.

Cole gave her a loving smile as he walked over to the edge of the meadow. He knelt down and was gathering the flowers when suddenly, he caught a gleam out of the corner of his eye. He turned slowly, then just as slowly a wide smile broke across his face. "Jessica! Jessica!" he shouted excitedly, "Come here, look what I've found."

Jessica ran as fast as she could. When she reached Cole, she was out of breath. "What is it?" she asked gaspingly.

"Look! Would you look at that! Would you have ever believed it!" he shouted incredulously.

"Oh, Cole! It's an answer to our prayers!" she squealed.

Cole swept her up into his arms. He gave her a long, loving kiss. At that moment, they knew their happiness was secure. For, on a long flat stone, gleamed the thirteenth cross. The cross that signified a vast treasure of wealth. Whether they would remain in the foothills of the high Sierras or whether they would trek across the burning sands to the rolling plains of Texas, they knew they were secure in their new lives. They knew they would find the supreme happiness they sought. Standing side by side, the sun began to slowly make its way over the high treetops. As in the master scheme of things, the sun would let the land sleep, rest, and replenish itself. The slumber would be that of peace, and the beginning of a bright new tomorrow.